The Milky Way

{Bel Tra Chart Pack XVII}

Drenard

☆ ?

Lok

Palan

Glemot ☆ ? Dakura

Darrin

Canopus Menkar
Sol

20K LY

100,000 Light Years

molly fyde

Fyde

and the land of light

THE

BERN SAGA:

BOOK 2

by hugh howey

Molly Fyde
and the Land of Light

Copyright © 2013 by hugh howey

ISBN: 1481222929
ISBN-13: 9781481222921

www.hughhowey.com

Give feedback on the book at:
hughhowey@hotmail.com
Second Edition

Cover art by Jasper Schreurs

Printed in the U.S.A.

~*The First Verse*~
"Out of lock, a key will come,
Drenard and Human, arrive as one.
As killing floods find long sought release,
brave swords, unseen, will fight for peace.

$$\bigcirc$$

And while a thousand eras come undone,
the canyon queen shall bare her sun.
Thus the burning war, partly won,
ushers the chaotic calms...
just now begun."

~*The Bern Seer*~

PROLOGUE

THE COMMONS

"In the commons, a singular event occurred . . . "

~The Bern Seer~

A cold wind twisted through the woods, wove between the trunks of alien trees, and then rushed out across the prairies of Lok. The frigid air joined other breezes, and together they wrapped around the remote outpost on the old frontier planet. Residents called it a town, but it was nothing more than a rectangle of shacks huddled together under another freezing, moonless night.

Through loose clapboard siding, miniature zephyrs of forest wind invaded the homes, chilling inhabitants curled under sparse blankets in tight fetal balls. The town had not yet been named, its identity as vague and hidden as most of its residents. It existed on no book

1

of official record—a condition many of its inhabitants might find enviable. Almost everything and everyone in the collection of huts was wanted for something, but not in a good way.

And the least lawful among them, as was such a group's wont, continued to stir at that late hour. They gathered around the hearth of a dying fire, rubbed their calloused hands over the fading warmth, and openly dreaded the morrow's toil.

Their whispers traveled up a chimney, shrouded in smoke. In this meager trail, the wisps of conversation and soot drifted out over the sagging huts, carried along by the wind from the woods. And if the smoke and whispers peered down—if either could do such a thing—they would have seen two figures, foolish and desperate, staggering through that frost-dusted commons.

Clinging to each other, laboring across that patch of open ground, they seemed eager to reach that fire. From their mouths, streams of breath-smoke trailed out in plumes of precious warmth. And from the woman, something else leaked out: a path of wetness leading back through the trampled grass, her bodily fluids sparkling on the dark green blades, freezing alongside the next day's dew.

The woman clutched at the pain in her stomach, doubled-over, her feet sliding like broken skates.

The other figure pulled her along, urging her with desperate whispers.

The woman's mouth parted; she fired a wail of agony over the sleeping village, a warning shot for what was to come. The insects across the prairie and deep into the wood stopped their nighttime twittering and seemed to wait. Expectantly.

The woman's legs went numb.

She collapsed in the cold grass while the man grasped at the air for her, mouthing his own misery. The frosty atmosphere captured it all in smoke signals of suffering, puffing out in visible screams that rang through the loose caulking of the surrounding huts.

The citizens of the village were used to such sounds. The fetal balls kicked in protest and turned, but they did not stir. There was more concern for the warm air seeping out than for the chilling cries worming in. They pulled their rough blankets high and continued to yearn for sleep.

Out in the commons, Mortimor bent over his new wife, Parsona. "Get up," he pleaded. "We're almost there."

Parsona cried out again. Her body folded in half, her thighs up against her swollen belly. She shook her head at the request, and loose strands of sweat-soaked hair matted to her face, wisps of steam forming on her fevered scalp. The steam was rising, along with her fever—but she wouldn't be.

Mortimor looked across the commons at the row of huts, at the one with a window flickering with the promise of a fire. Less than a hundred meters away. So close.

He worked an arm under his wife's back to lift her, to carry her the rest of the way, but the spasms of her tortured moans sparked through her and into his own body.

The child would come there or not at all.

"I'll be right back," he assured her. He flexed his legs to rise—to run for assistance—but Parsona's hand, squeezing with the last of her fading might, clutched him in fear.

Mortimor froze, unable to seek or provide help. And so he yelled for it. He begged the heavens for it. He blasted his pleas in several directions—but no human stirred.

Parsona's shivering grew worse. Mortimor's coat was a paltry barrier between her and the frozen ground. Her teeth chattered in response to the cold, pausing only to grind together in paroxysms of pain. Mortimor tore off his thin shirt and draped it over her chest. He fell into a rhythm of crying for help, sucking in deep breaths of his own, comforting his wife, and cursing.

When grunts and pants of labored exertion mixed their way into Parsona's wails, Mortimor's own body began vibrating with fear. The only two things he truly loved in the galaxy were being taken from him. Slowly, horribly, before his very eyes and on a miserable, cursed planet.

A flash of movement caught his eye.

He glanced up to find a tall, thin figure sliding through a crack in the darkness. It was a man, his skin so pale it reflected the starlight. He came to the couple with long strides, bony joints poking through his clothes. His head was bald and uncovered, but his face showed no sign of discomfort. He held a large wad of cloth against his narrow chest—a bedsheet.

The strange man folded himself down to the grass at Parsona's feet. "It'll be OK," he said, his voice fuller than his frame.

Mortimor was too transfixed to thank him, or even nod. He was stricken by the man's gaunt face and skeletal features. The stranger turned to him slowly. Bright blue eyes pierced Mortimor, chilling him more than the removal of his shirt had.

"Everything's going to be fine," the man assured him. He spread the thin sheet by his knees and arranged Parsona's legs, one at a time, sliding the dry cloth between her and the ground. Both hands coordinated every movement with calculated efficiency and gentleness, his long, reedy fingers wrapping around each calf and moving them into place. He told both of them what to do, the confidence in his voice removing the fear and panic from Parsona's screams—leaving just the pain.

"Push when I say push," he said. His narrow hands went under her dress, resting on her belly while eyes the color of ice squinted into the black beneath her hem. The slits widened into blue orbs, as if seeing something for the first time.

"Push," he commanded, a hint of excitement in his calm voice.

Parsona grunted with effort, her head rising off the grass as she contracted muscles in a stomach formerly lean and hard. Her eyes narrowed with the strain, her ears closed off to all noise but her own pounding pulse.

Mortimor brushed the hair off her face with his palm. He cradled her neck as it rose from the effort, and with his other hand he tucked the edge of the sheet close to her body.

"Breathe."

The voice was so compelling, they both heeded it without realizing they'd heard it. Mortimor kept an arm under his wife's head; he leaned down to press his lips to her cheek, to whisper his love into her ear. Her eyes rolled back in exhaustion as she fought for long pulls on the night air.

"Push."

The stranger asked the impossible, but his tone demanded satisfaction. Parsona tried to tighten her abdomen again, wrestling against the stabbing pain that threatened to overwhelm her senses. She felt trapped in a nightmare that promised no end.

"Breathe."

Something happened. Something *different*. A release. Parsona felt a path reveal itself, an opening that would lead her away from the pain. She forced her energy toward it.

"That's it. *Push*."

She no longer needed to be told.

Mortimor looked across his wife's body at the stranger; he could tell something had changed. Hope swelled in him as he held his wife, urging her and the child along. He felt otherwise powerless. Guilty. He wanted to absorb her torture, to wick it away like moisture from her brow. The forest wind dove down from the rooftops, peeling away layers of heat from his bare back as he leaned over his wife, professing his love.

Parsona heard Mortimor above the roar of pain— and the words gave her strength. She fought for all three of them. Gnashing her teeth, her eyes flowing with tears of exertion, she pushed so hard the world went silent. All that remained was the distant thunder of discomfort and the weak thrumming of her pulse.

And something marvelous happened. A reward for the agony. A living thing, long sustained by a cord and dwelling in darkness, moved into the universe.

Under a canopy of stars, a baby girl was born.

The stranger cradled her like a precious gift, her small limbs waving in protest of the cold, of the pain that came with breathing.

Parsona reached for the baby. Unable to sit up, she extended her arms, her fingers writhing in a primal display of a mother's want.

The stranger moved the child to one arm, freeing his other hand. Steel glinted in starlight as a knife materialized from the folds of his shirt.

A cord was severed, the child placed in her mother's arms. And thus a single life became two, each heading in opposite directions. Both were destined for much suffering and heartache, one over a long and tragic life—the other during a slow and drawn-out death.

But that was all to come. For one moment, during their brief crossroad of post-birth euphoria and perfect naiveté, they simply held each other. And over the soft cries from the newly born, a word was whispered. Parsona's breath became visible in the cold night, ice crystals from her quiet exhalation swirling and coalescing like a nebula in the vacuum. They gathered, like a star at the center, to form a single name:

Mollie.

PART VI
THE TURING TEST

"We tend to discover only those things we seek."

~The Bern Seer~

NEED YOU TO HELP ME RESCUE YOUR FATHER_

The words stood out in green phosphor on the nav screen. They would burn there if left too long, becoming seared as they were in Molly's retinas. Still, she couldn't tear her eyes from them. She looked across the simple sentence, left to right and back again, waiting for it to morph into something she could grasp and understand.

Her parents were dead. Her mother passed away during childbirth; her father had left her on Earth six years later and disappeared forever. And yet this *thing*—this *computer*—now claimed to be her mother. Worse yet: it insinuated that her father might still be alive.

Sitting in *Parsona's* cockpit—the ship her father had named after her mom—Molly felt as if someone had keyed open the airlock and sucked every cubic meter of atmosphere right out.

She scanned the sentence once more, waiting for it to change, to grow handles. In her peripheral, she could see Cole, her boyfriend and navigator, glancing from her to the screen. He started to say something and then stopped. He leaned forward and directed a single word toward the dash:

"Hello?"

He said it cautiously, as if it might set off a bomb. It pulled Molly's attention away from the incredible sentence.

"Hello?" he asked again.

"You have to *type* something." She gestured toward his keyboard, as if the proper method for communicating with the deceased through one's nav computer should be obvious to him by now.

"How do we know it can't hear us?"

"Because ships don't have ears—" Molly stopped. She looked at the radio mic on the dash and then glanced over at the intercom system. She turned to Cole; they studied each other. A new message crawled across their nav screens:

HELLO? MOLLIE?_

"What do I say?" she asked.

Cole reached toward his own keyboard, stopped, and shrugged. He raised his hands up to his shoulders in quiet defeat.

Molly let out her held breath. She needed more help than that. And she needed more time. There were so many questions — it was impossible to know where to begin. She pulled the keyboard closer and typed:

I'M HERE. CAN YOU GIVE ME ONE SECOND? THIS IS A LOT TO TAKE IN_

I UNDERSTAND. BUT PLEASE KEEP IN MIND THAT MY PROCESSING SPEED IS A BIT SWIFTER THAN YOURS. IT FEELS LIKE HOURS ARE PASSING BETWEEN SENTENCES. I WILL COUNT TO A QUADRILLION. YOU TAKE YOUR TIME_

Molly didn't even know how to incorporate this dollop of new information. She turned to Cole for better advice than a shrug, only to find him rising out of his chair.

"Where are you going?" she asked, a note of panic in her voice.

"I have a hunch this is just Walter messing with us. I'm gonna go make sure." He bent down and kissed Molly on the top of her head, smoothing her hair with his hand. "If you see the airlock light flash on and off, that means the problem's been taken care of."

She started to complain, then found herself alone with the computer claiming to be her long-lost mother.

What to ask? Where to start? Should she voice her doubts? The computer knew the original spelling of her name. Was that enough to believe it might be her mother? Why else would she be hidden in her father's ship? What about the clues from her childhood that had led to its discovery, the question about the unnamed village in which she'd been born?

Once again, the atmosphere in the ship felt thin, the gravity weak. She bent her fingers over the keys and managed the two most pressing questions, the ones still visible through her confused haze: WHERE ARE YOU? WHERE'S DAD?_

The words flitted across the screen as she typed them and bounced up as new text flowed across from the left:

I'M IN THE SHIP. THE NAV COMPUTER, TO BE PRECISE. MY PERSONALITY AND MEMORIES WERE STORED HERE LONG AGO. YOUR FATHER_ The cursor blinked twice. I'M SORRY SWEETHEART, I CAN'T TELL YOU WHERE HE IS. YOU MIGHT DO SOMETHING RASH TO GET THERE QUICKLY, AND THERE'S MUCH TO BE DONE BEFORE WE GO_

Molly closed her eyes; she could feel her questions multiply faster than they could be answered. *What was there to do? Go where? What would be rash about rushing off to save Dad?* She added these to her growing list, took a deep breath, then turned and looked over her shoulder

14

down the length of the ship. She could see Cole beyond the cargo bay, standing at Walter's door. He was right to be wary, and she knew she should be cautious as well.

But she couldn't.

Too many childhood dreams, impossible fantasies, beckoned at her fingertips. Molly turned and rested her hands on the keys. She cursed herself for being naïve, for setting herself up for another crushing disappointment. She imagined—if any narcotic could be as exhilarating and soul-splintering as simple hope—that drug addicts might feel the same way. Knowing better, she typed:

MOM, WHAT DO I NEED TO DO? I'LL HELP YOU ANY WAY I CAN_

I KNEW YOU WOULD. FIRST, WE NEED TO GET TO DAKURA. I HAVE MEMORIES THERE THAT NEED TO BE_ TAKEN CARE OF. THEN WE MUST TRAVEL TO LOK, BACK TO WHERE THIS ALL BEGAN. FROM THERE, WE CAN RESCUE YOUR FATHER_

The mention of Lok reminded Molly of something her godfather Lucin once said. She wasn't sure how to break the news of his betrayal and subsequent death to her mom—if indeed, this *was* her mom—but Molly needed to know what he had meant. Before he died, he had said something about Lok, about how her parents' work there might end the Drenard War.

WHAT EXACTLY HAPPENED ON LOK? She typed. LUCIN SAID MY BIRTH CAUSED ... PROBLEMS_

There was no answer at first. It felt as if hours went by for Molly; there was no telling what it felt like for her mother.

Eventually, the text moved, haltingly:

BAD THINGS HAPPENED ON LOK_ BUT IT WASN'T YOU, SWEETHEART. YOU WERE THE ONLY GOOD THING THAT EVER CAME OFF THAT DAMNED PLANET_

Molly read the sentence twice. Then once more. Certain parts made her feel better, soothing away worries she'd been harboring since that fateful conversation with Lucin. Other parts caused tinges of doubt to creep up inside. She'd never heard her father curse, even lightly. And though she knew almost nothing of her mom, this language felt out of character. It didn't feel right to her at all.

Which meant she was being duped. Either that, or something truly awful had taken place on Lok, something that had to do with her parents.

Either way, she could feel the buzz of her favorite drug wearing off. Hope began dissolving into dread.

oooo

As much as Cole wanted to feel excited for Molly, as happy as he would be if her parents *were* alive, his

16

logical mind had settled on a simpler answer: Walter, their devious junior-pirate-in-training from Palan, was up to something. He'd recently used his computer skills to frame Cole, nearly getting them all killed for a stupid reward. Impersonating Molly's mom would be a step down for him—both in skill and moral depravity.

He reminded himself of this as he strode through the cargo bay. Part of him—the part that wanted revenge for Walter's betrayal—hoped he'd open the door and find the runt typing away on his little computer, an evil sneer on his metallic-colored face. If the sleeves on his flightsuit had been a bit looser, Cole would've been rolling them up as he marched aft.

He keyed open the door. It was pitch black inside. He could hear the hissing sound of Palanesque breathing leaking out of the boy's bunk. Cole flicked on the room's light and watched Walter pull his head under the sheets in protest.

"Walter. Wake up."

"Hnnn?"

Cole couldn't tell what he was saying. Right then, it was because of the barrier of blankets, but usually it was due to the dreadful lisping problem Palans have with English.

"Wake up!" he said again.

Walter flapped his covers back, clearly annoyed. His eyes squinted against the light, two dark slits in a plate of dull steel.

Cole pointed a finger at him. "If you're the one doing this, I swear on my life—you'll be airlocked."

Walter cocked his head, opening his mouth to ask something, but Cole flicked the light off, allowing his threat to linger in the darkness. He stood in the doorway for a few moments, trying to make his silhouette as large and menacing as possible, and then stepped back in the hall and shut the door.

o o o o

Walter found himself alone. In the dark, and in more ways than one.

Whatever they suspected him of, it was *bad*.

And the annoying injustice was that he was *innocent!* For once.

o o o o

Cole hesitated outside of Walter's door. If the kid was responsible for the nav computer, it was a pretty clever trick. He looked up the long central shaft toward the cockpit, where he could see Molly's elbow jutting out over the flight controls, her fingers obviously still pecking away at the keyboard.

If it wasn't Walter, Cole wondered who—or *what*—she was talking to.

What if that really was her mom? It wouldn't be much crazier than some of the other things they'd seen in the last month. He glanced toward the rear of the ship. One of those crazier things could be heard snoring just down the hall, his low, rumbling growl rolling out of the aft crew quarters. Cole took a few steps toward the open door and checked in on the most unlikely of couples.

He could see them both in the soft light left on for Anlyn's benefit. The sight of her filled Cole with mixed emotions. As a Drenard, Anlyn represented everything he'd been programmed by the Navy to hate. Here was the enemy of the rest of the galaxy, a member of the race of aliens humans warred with all along one of the Milky Way's spiral arms. Moments ago—before the nav computer interrupted—he and Molly had been arguing over whether Anlyn could be trusted, not to mention the insanity of their current plan to take her home, far behind enemy lines.

As much as he wanted to doubt Anlyn, however, there was something endearing about the poor creature. Maybe it was the manner in which they'd discovered her: shackled and starving, a slave in chains. She still looked so thin and frail, her blue translucent skin catching the soft light, making her look innocent, pure, and harmless.

But Navy training videos had shown Cole what the Drenard people could do—at the helm of their fighter crafts and with their deadly lances. He had no diffi-culty seeing past her fragility to the horrors her people had wrought. This mix of emotions made him as wary around the young girl as he was around Walter. Wary of Anlyn because of her fierce potential, Walter due to his past treachery.

Ironically, Anlyn's sleeping companion was a per-fect mix of these two horrible traits, and yet, Cole trusted him completely. It didn't matter that Edison had lied to them a few weeks ago, engineering one of the worst tragedies in the history of the Milky Way. It didn't mat-ter that the pup's ferocious bulk and fierce claws could rend Cole in two. They had fought alongside each other, forging that bond of war that overrode all else.

Leaning against their doorjamb, the rumbling snores of the Glemot washing over him, Cole considered this bit of personal hypocrisy. He feared an innocent-look-ing creature that had saved his life a week ago, but he completely trusted a bearlike alien that had commit-ted genocide against his own race. He had to shake his head at how effective the Navy programming was and at how eager he must be to rank personal expe-rience above tragedies too vast in scope to properly comprehend.

He just hoped he could learn to judge Anlyn the same way: by her actions and not by the biases he'd formed over years of schooled hatred.

Cole pulled himself away from the slumbering couple and headed back to the cockpit, eager to see what the nav computer had to say. As he wandered through the cargo bay, he felt a stab of jealousy at having seen Anlyn and Edison snuggled together. Ever since Lucin's death, he and Molly had been working through some problems. Even so, he'd considered broaching the subject of sharing a room, but he didn't know how to bring it up.

Or perhaps he was just scared of what Molly would say if he did.

She was still clattering away at her keyboard as he squeezed back into his chair. "If Walter's screwing with us, he's doin' it in his sleep," he told her.

Molly stopped typing and looked over at him. "Hey," she said. "Be honest with me. Am I crazy to think this might be my mom? Because this is something I really, really *want* to believe, and I'm sick and tired of being lied to and disappointed."

Cole rubbed his face. He'd been on shift for a long time and really should've been getting some sleep. But there was no way he could rest while Molly dealt with something as surreal as this. "I don't know what to tell you," he said. "You sure nobody else could know how to spell your old name?"

"I can't think of anyone. Not besides a bunch of backwoods frontier people on Lok, and they shouldn't be involved in any of this."

"What about the titles of those old books?"

Molly shook her head. "Nobody besides me and my dad, I'm pretty sure."

"I just don't know." Cole scanned the screen, taking in the snippets of conversation above the flashing cursor. "I don't wanna get your hopes up, but we've seen some crazy stuff in the past month. The technology they had in the Darrin system blew my mind—"

"Have you ever heard of the Dakura system?" Molly asked.

Cole thought for a second. "No. But the name seems familiar. Why?"

"That's where my mom says she was integrated into the ship, and where we need to go. Watch."

Molly typed another question: COLE AND I WANT TO KNOW HOW WE CAN BELIEVE THAT IT'S REALLY YOU_

I CAN PROVE IT TO YOU AT DAKURA_

"See?" Molly asked. She turned to Cole. "Pull it up on one of our newer charts. How far we are from this place?"

Cole leaned forward and switched the nav computer from the bizarre conversation to the duller use for which it was intended. Pulling up the Bel Tra charts—the most accurate depiction of the Milky Way they owned—something horrific occurred to him. He slapped his forehead and shouted, "Flank me!"

Molly startled like the hull had been breached. "Gods, Cole! What?"

"When we were on Darrin, installing these new charts, do you remember how close I came to wiping out the old ones?"

She turned white. "Oh, my gods. I'd forgotten all about that. Do you think it would have—*erased* her?" She nodded toward her nav screen, having very nearly said "killed" instead of "erased."

"I don't know. We need to find out how fragile she is, or if we need to make a backup or something."

"Good idea. I'll add it to my to-do list." She gave Cole a wry smile. "Now, if you're done giving me heart problems over stuff that nearly happened weeks ago, you can get back to navigating."

Cole grinned and gave Molly a crisp Navy salute. "Aye, aye, Captain," he said.

She rolled her eyes and returned to her keyboard.

○ ○ ○ ○

MOM, WE'RE AT 24% ON THE HYPERDRIVE. COLE IS CHECKING DAKURA AND OUR CURRENT LOCATION_

She hit enter and then thought of something else.

CAN YOU SEE ANYTHING? ACCESS THE SHIP'S COMPUTERS OR CAMERAS?_

NO, MOLLIE, BUT I WOULD LIKE THAT. I WOULD LOVE TO SEE WHAT YOU LOOK LIKE, AND MAYBE ONCE WE GET TO DAKURA OR LOK, WE CAN WORK ON SOMETHING_

There was a pause. And then her mother fired off a question of her own:

WHO IS COLE? IS HE A BOY? HOW OLD IS HE?_

Molly smiled, and some of the doubts rising up inside began to settle back down. The questions comforted with their normalcy. She glanced over at Cole to make sure he was busy with his calculations, then she leaned over her keyboard to shield the screen from his eyes and launched into a conversation she had long dreamed of having with her mother—but never thought possible. *And not just because her mother had never been around*, she thought, glancing over at her navigator.

A few minutes later, Cole sighed and flopped back in his chair.

"Not good," he groaned. He leaned forward again to switch back to the conversation with the ship, and Molly started tapping the enter key furiously, filling the screen with blank lines to push what was being said off the top of the display.

Molly stole a glance at Cole and saw him surveying the blank screen of empty prompts, his head tilted as he tried to puzzle it out. She could feel sweat popping out of the pores on her scalp and became consumed with the impulse to scratch her head.

Her mother lobbed a bomb into the stillness.

AS LONG AS YOU TWO ARE JUST KISSING, MOLLIE, THAT IS WONDERFUL NEWS. HE SOUNDS LOVELY_

A contest began: seeing who could turn the brighter shade of pink. Cole tried to look distracted, fiddling with the flight controls, but *Parsona* had been floating in empty space for hours.

"Uh . . . nowhere near enough juice to get us to Dakura," he said. "We can't even make it back to Lok, which we passed two jumps ago. Our course from Earth to Drenard took us near both, but now we're too close to our destination to do anything but forge ahead. Unless, of course, you want to get arrested while we ask the Navy for some fusion fuel."

Molly began communicating the bad news to her mom, eager to change the conversation away from romantic advice:

NOT ENOUGH FUSION FUEL FOR DAKURA. AND WE'RE IN A BIT OF A SPOT WITH THE LAW—CAN'T TOP UP AT ANY ORBITAL STATIONS. WE'VE BEEN HEADING TOWARD DRENARD FOR SEVERAL DAYS NOW_

DRENARD? WHY ARE YOU GOING TO DRENARD? IS THE WAR OVER?_

This woke Molly up to how long her mother must have been shut away in a computer. It felt nice to not be the only one with gaps in her knowledge. Even better was the feeling of having answers to someone *else's* questions.

WE HAVE A DRENARD ON THE SHIP WITH US. HER NAME'S ANLYN, BUT DON'T WORRY, SHE'S A FRIEND. SHE SAVED MY LIFE. SHE SAYS WE'LL BE SAFE ON DRENARD AND THAT THEY'LL STOCK US UP WITH FOOD AND FUEL_

The screen stayed blank, the cursor flashing. Her mom seemed to need some time to digest the news. Molly really wanted to jab the enter key a dozen more times and get the "kissing" sentence off the screen. She felt as if Cole could see the sweat beneath her hair and then worried her mom was gonna be angry at them for having an enemy alien on the ship.

Her stomach knotted up with worry, impatient for a response.

When her mother finally typed out her reply, Molly realized she hadn't been queasy enough.

I NEED TO SPEAK WITH THE DRENARD. ALONE. AS SOON AS POSSIBLE_

2

"Should I go wake her?" Cole leaned forward, his hands on the armrests of his seat. Molly couldn't tell if he was eager to help or just feeling the urge to get away from the nav computer before it said something even more peculiar.

She looked from the screen to Cole, and then back again. Shrugging, unable to make sense of anything herself, she whispered, "I guess so." Her voice sounded weak and feeble, as if she'd been temporarily stunned.

Cole crawled out of his chair and padded away, leaving Molly alone with the computer once again. She reached for her keyboard, partly obliged to keep her mother occupied—not sure what the passage of a few minutes might feel like to a consciousness that could compute billions of operations a second—but also in an attempt to alleviate some of her confusion.

MOM_

She wasn't sure how to phrase what she felt, so she finally settled on being completely honest:

YOU'RE SCARING ME_

I'M SORRY. IT ISN'T LIKE THIS IS EASY FOR ME. I_ THERE IS SO MUCH I WANT TO TELL YOU, TO CATCH UP ON. THE LAST TIME I SAW YOU, WE WEREN'T EVEN SURE IF YOU WOULD LIVE A YEAR. AND I WAS VERY SICK. EVERYTHING I KNOW ABOUT YOU ARE JUST FACTS GIVEN TO ME LATER. I'M SORRY, IS THE DRENARD THERE YET?_

NO, COLE IS WAKING HER UP. WE'RE ON A NIGHT SHIFT. AND HER NAME IS ANLYN _

VERY WELL. PLEASE INTERRUPT ME AS SOON AS ANLYN IS THERE. WHAT I WANTED TO EXPLAIN EARLIER IS THAT MY WORLD FEELS VERY STRANGE RIGHT NOW. STRANGER, PERHAPS, THAN YOU CAN IMAGINE. I HAVE MY THOUGHTS, AND THEY SEEM LIKE A WAKING DREAM. LIKE I'M IN A DARK ROOM WITH MY EYES CLOSED, ALONE WITH MY MEMORIES_

Molly heard someone stomping through the cargo bay. She peered around her seat and saw Cole heading her way, Anlyn in tow. The young blue alien was wearing one of Cole's oversized shirts as a nightgown and was wiping sleep from her eyes. Her tail drifted lazily behind her.

Holding up a hand, Molly urged Cole to stay back for a moment. She felt guilty for delaying her mom's conversation with Anlyn, but she needed to hear more:

MY MEMORIES COME SO FAST, MOLLIE, EVER SINCE YOU WOKE ME. I HAVE TO TRY AND OCCUPY PROCESSING CYCLES BY DOING OTHER THINGS IN THE BACKGROUND. ALL I HAVE FROM THE OUTSIDE WORLD IS THE TEXT YOU INPUT. JUST WORDS IN A VACUUM. I'M JUST AS SCARED AS YOU ARE, SWEETHEART, AND SOME OF THE THINGS I KNOW ARE TRULY AWFUL. NOT ANYTHING I WANT TO BURDEN YOU WITH RIGHT NOW. IS ANLYN THERE?_

SHE JUST WALKED UP_

Molly turned to Anlyn, only to find her friend standing just beyond the boundary of the cockpit, her face rigid and expressionless.

"I'm so sorry!" she said, scrambling out of her seat and sickened by her thoughtlessness. Anlyn hadn't been in a cockpit since she escaped the Darrin system, where she'd been chained to a flightseat and forced to pilot a ship as a slave. In all the excitement over her mom, her friend's fears had slipped her mind. She pushed past Cole to turn Anlyn away, but before she could get to her, the young Drenard stepped over the boundary, crossing that threshold.

"It's fine," Anlyn said softly. She held both hands out in front of her as she crept forward, almost as if probing for obstructions. "As long as the engines are off."

"Are you sure?"

Anlyn nodded, her face aglow in the cockpit's constellation of lights and readouts. Peering about, her eyes eventually settling on the radio set into the dash. "Cole said you need me to talk to someone?"

Molly was unsure what to reveal. She hated lying, but the truth would take hours to relate. She decided to leave it up to her mom to explain it however she liked.

"That's right. You'll have to communicate with—" Molly paused, realizing how little she knew of *Parsona's* young crew members, even after two weeks of living together. "You'll have to talk using the keyboard. Can you read and type? In English?"

Disappointment flashed across Anlyn's face. "Not much," she admitted. "Enough to fly, mostly indicators and alarms."

Of course, Molly thought. *Why teach a slave pilot to read anything else?* She turned back to the nav computer, a surge of guilty relief washing over her. There had been enough secrets lately. Translating the conversation between her mom and Anlyn would mean Molly might learn what was going on. It would certainly keep her from assuming the worst.

She leaned over her seat and typed:

ANLYN SPEAKS ENGLISH, BUT SHE CAN'T TYPE OR READ MUCH OF IT. I'M GOING TO HAVE TO INTERPRET_

There was almost no pause before the reply came:

SHE DOESN'T NEED TO RESPOND, SHE JUST NEEDS TO READ ALONG. TELL HER TO PRESS A KEY ONCE THE TWO OF US ARE ALONE. AND PLEASE GIVE US PLENTY OF TIME_

Molly took a deep breath before typing her response: MOM, ANLYN CAN'T READ ENGLISH_

THAT'S OK, DEAR. I SPEAK DRENARD_

○ ○ ○ ○

Cole and Molly retired to the lazarette, the rearmost compartment in the ship, so Anlyn could have some privacy. Cole had wanted to hang out in her room, but Molly was too anxious to sit still. She had grabbed some tools and crawled into the thruster room to work out her nerves. The center reactor was still having intermittent issues ever since they backed into that asteroid in the Darrin system, and she insisted on crawling beneath the floorboards in the laz to check it out.

Cole found he didn't have much room to argue since *he'd* been the one flying at the time. Holding a medium spanner out, he waited for Molly to reach up and grab it. "Can our nav screen even *display* Drenard?" he wondered aloud. "I don't even know what Drenard looks like, do you?"

"Not a clue," Molly said. Her voice leaked out from below the center thruster's reactor, tinny and muffled. A hand came up holding a power screwdriver; Cole took it and slapped the electric spanner in its place. "I don't see why it couldn't display it, though," Molly said. "That screen can show star charts. Any language has to be just a bunch of pixels."

"I guess you're right." Cole put the screwdriver back in the tool pouch. Below, he could hear Molly wrestling with an overly tightened bolt. "Hey, maybe we should let Edison have another go at this instead."

"I like knowing my own ship, smarty pants. Besides, Edison would have to pull the floor beams out just to get down here. Probably why it's still acting up." Molly pushed her upper body out of the hole and looked back at Cole. "The question we should be asking ourselves is why we had to leave the cockpit if Mom is typing in Drenard. It's not like either of us could follow what she's saying. And how does she know Drenard in the first place? I always heard the language was a complete mystery, even to the Navy."

She left her doubts in the air and went back to work, her head disappearing below the decking.

Cole felt relieved to hear some of his skepticism rubbing off on Molly. Prior to recent and unfortunate events, she used to think him pessimistic and paranoid. Conspiratorial, even. He moved closer to the access hatch. "Have you ever heard of the Turing Test?" he asked.

"I've heard of the Turing star system," Molly said after a pause.

"Yeah, same guy. It was named after him. He was an old twenty-first century math dude—or maybe it was the twentieth. I get those periods confused—"

"What in the world does this have to do with anything?"

"I'll get to that if you stop interrupting. You see, Turing was one of the first guys to start thinking about artificial intelligence—"

"Is that what you think my mom is?"

"Gods, Molly, gimme a chance. And I can barely make out what you're saying, anyway. Where was I? Oh, Turing devised what he called the Turing Test as a check for artificial intelligence. What you do is put your program in a room and talk to it through a door, or some other way. The important bit is this—if you can't tell whether the thing on the other side is human or machine, it passes the test."

Cole inched deeper into the mechanical space to make sure his voice was dropping down the hole in the floor. "Did you hear me?"

"I'm not interrupting you."

"Well, that was it. That's the story."

Molly pulled her head out of the hole again. "What's the *point*?"

"The point is, whatever we're talking with up there passes the Turing Test, but that doesn't tell us if it's human or not. In fact, there's this other guy—Surrel, I think his name was—who came up with another scenario called the Chinese Room."

Cole paused.

"You know, your mom speaking Drenard must've made me remember Turing. Anyway, Surrel said you could have something stupid in a room, a simple program or a book that would look intelligent from the outside, but it wouldn't be. It goes something like this: you have a man in another room who doesn't speak Drenard. But he has a book of rules. Someone slides a piece of paper under the door with some Drenard on it. The guy looks in the book, follows the rules, and writes out a reply.

"The person on the *other* side will think they're communicating with a real Drenard. The Turing Test will be passed. But the guy *inside* the room, or the program, is just following simple rules. And that's all a computer does, really. Follow rules. It can *look* smart without *being* smart."

Molly shook her head. "I can't believe I'm listening to this instead of fixing the pressure problem with the thruster."

"Hey, this stuff's important. You need to keep it in mind when you're talking to your . . . whatever it is."

Molly grabbed a clump of hair off her cheek and tucked it behind her ear. She rolled her eyes at Cole. "That Surrel guy was an idiot, just so you know."

"I think I have his name wrong," Cole said. "But trust me: the guy was a genius."

"Well, I must be a Glemot, then. The *guy* following the rules might be dumb, but the *woman* who wrote the rules for him to follow speaks Drenard fluently and is quite intelligent. Which means there *is* a smart person in the room who's passing the Turing Test, not just some algorithm. It doesn't matter if *she* wrote *her* smartness down or was sitting beside the guy whispering the answers. If the result's the same, the delivery method shouldn't matter."

Molly bit her lower lip and glanced past Cole. "Whether it's a brain or a computer holding her memories—either way—I think that's my mom in there, talking to me."

She ducked down below the decking and then popped back up. "And this is what I hate about these philosophy debates you drag me into. The questions are only baffling if you have the IQ of a Venusian sea slug—"

"Wait," Cole interrupted, lifting a hand. "Did you hear that?"

They both fell silent. "That's the SADAR alarm," Molly said.

Cole scrambled backward, out of the cramped space. Molly followed, her hands leaving greasy prints on the decking. They both rose and sprinted toward the cockpit, forty meters away, the pounding of their feet on the metal decking waking the rest of the crew.

o o o o

"Contacts! At least two dozen ships!" Cole looked from the SADAR screen to the porthole on his side of the ship. A small fleet had appeared off their starboard side. Anlyn backed out of the cockpit, her eyes still on the nav screen, which remained full of bizarre symbols.

"Everyone in flight suits!" Molly called out, which broke Anlyn's spell and sent her scurrying toward the crew quarters.

"That includes you," said Cole.

Molly looked down at her dirty work shirt and greasy hands as if confirming his suggestion. "OK," she said. "Turn on the radio and find out who they are.

And tell Mom what's going on. I'll be right back." She left him alone in the cockpit and raced to her room.

Cole plugged his own suit into the console between the seats. He put the radio on channel 2812, the galaxy-wide standard for hailing and ship-to-ship communications.

Someone was already transmitting.

"—yourself. Repeat. This is Naval Task Force Delta KPR76 calling the vessel point two AUs off our bow, velocity zero knots absolute, identify yourself."

Cole's nav screen was covered in gibberish. He typed in a quick line to whoever was on the other side of Turing's door.

TROUBLE. GOTTA RUN_

He hit the enter key and switched over to the Bel Tra nav charts. Comparing *Parsona's* location to the position of the Navy fleet made his stomach drop. He heard someone run up behind him.

"Troublesss?"

Walter. His hissing voice scraped across Cole's nerves even more than usual. "Go strap in," he told him, "and stay out of the way." He didn't look back to see the expression on the boy's face, which was just as well.

The next set of approaching feet left no doubt as to their owner. The vibrations came up through Cole's nav chair as Edison stomped his way to the crew seats.

Cole flipped on the cargo bay cam and made sure everyone had their helmets on and their harnesses secure. This would be the first time Anlyn wore one of Walter's spare flight suits; he hoped his alterations would keep her smaller frame protected.

The radio demanded identification again just as Molly arrived at a dead run. She vaulted into her chair, landed on her feet in a crouch, and let them shoot out from under her into the pocket below the dash. She fastened her harness and plugged in her flightsuit, all with the coordinated swiftness of an emergency drill.

"Navy?" she asked.

"Yeah, and we're in a spot here." Cole pointed to the SADAR. "My anniversary gift is the hard place and that fleet is the rock."

o o o o

Molly looked out her porthole. The "gift" Cole referred to loomed off the port side of the ship. It was a binary pair—a black hole and a large star locked in each other's orbits. A wide trail of plasma leaked off the star and swirled into the black hole, the rotation of the system creating a pinwheel of light millions of kilometers across.

The display had been Cole's one-month anniversary gift. Beautiful and touching ten minutes ago, now it created a gigantic wall of gravitational mass that prevented their escape into hyperspace.

"This is Naval Task Force Delta KPR76 to the stationary vessel off our bow, please identify yourself." The voice had become more insistent, and the SADAR unit flashed a warning that they were being scanned. Molly admired the way the fleet was spreading out before closing in. Without a zero-gravity chunk of the cosmos to jump from, *Parsona* was trapped.

She grabbed the flight stick and pushed *Parsona's* nose toward the nearby star. With one of her three thrusters on the mend, she was able to give the ship full throttle without worrying about the forces on her and the crew; the anti-grav fluid in their flightsuits could handle anything *Parsona* might dish out in a straight line. Which was unfortunate, really. She would need more if they were gonna outrun these guys.

"GN-290 ship identification *Parsona*, do not flee. Cease thruster burn immediately. We will fire. I repeat, this is Naval Task Force Delta KPR76, and we will fire to kill. You are in a hostile no-fly zone. Cease thruster burn immediately. Over."

Cole tagged each Navy ship with hostile indicators. *Parsona* had received a few upgrades over the past two weeks: two laser cannons recessed in the leading wings, a missile pod hidden in one of the large rear wings, and some basic defenses to boot. It wasn't enough to take on a few Firehawks, much less an entire fleet, but the routine tasks seemed to give him something to do from the nav seat.

"What'd you tell my mom?" Molly asked.

"Are you serious? I told her we'd get back to her. Now what's your plan, 'cause I don't see any way out besides a brig and a court-martial."

"I'm thinking—"

The radio cut her off. "GN-290 *Parsona*, this is Naval Task Force Delta KPR76. There's a seizure notice out on your ship. You will be considered hostile. Cease thruster burn, or we will begin firing missiles. Over."

"Think faster, babe. We've got two chaff pods, and I'm just guessing here, but they probably have more than two missiles."

"The first thing we're gonna do is not call me 'babe.' Ever." Molly shot Cole a menacing look and leaned forward to study the nav charts and SADAR display. She had the ship in a straight-line burn away from the fleet and toward the black hole and star. She did some quick-and-dirty math in her head. Even if the Navy fleet came after them at full speed, *Parsona* would still get to the two-body system first.

"OK, I've got an idea. I need you to use that charming mouth of yours and talk the Navy out of firing their missiles. I'm gonna make a full burn right at the star and get there before they do."

Cole reached to the controls that patched his helmet mic through to the radio. "I'd like to veto hiding inside the star. Can you give me a few other options to choose from?"

"I'm not going to hide in the star, wise guy. I'm gonna use it to catapult us into clear space on the other side, just like we slingshot cargo from one orbit to another back home."

"Not bad," Cole said. "I'll buy you some time." He keyed the radio mic. "Naval Task Force Delta KPR76, this is *Parsona* KML32. We're having a thruster malfunction. Requesting assistance. Over."

Molly shot Cole a look of disappointment.

He shrugged. "What?"

The nearest Firehawk spat out a missile in reply.

3

"Gods, Cole, I wanted you to *buy* us some time, not *instigate* them."

"It was the first thing I thought of," Cole said. "I figured the grain of truth would help. Can't they see we're running with a limp?" He keyed the radio again. "KPR76, *Parsona* here. We're having thruster problems, I repeat, we are having thruster problems. Cease fire. Over."

Molly watched the SADAR to see if another missile would punctuate Cole's lie. This was the first time she'd seen his charms fail so spectacularly. She'd always thought it'd be an enjoyable experience if it ever happened—but she was wrong. Without doing the math, she could see the missile would reach them well before they got a boost from the star's gravity.

"Less comms, more chaff," she said.

Cole keyed up their new chaff modules. "You want me to release early so we have time to arm the second pod?"

It was a good question. If they waited too long, they were giving themselves only one chance to fool the missile. On the other hand, if they showed their cards too soon, the Navy would see they were dealing with an armed vessel and ramp up the attack.

As a team, Molly and Cole had hundreds of hours in Navy simulators together, facing these exact tactical quandaries. Only this time, they wouldn't get yelled at if they made the wrong decision; that red dot on the SADAR was not part of a game or training exercise—it represented their deaths.

Molly marveled at how calm she felt. Her brain seemed clearer than it had ever been in the simulator. Despite the reversal of roles—her piloting from the left while Cole asked *her* advice—she felt as if *this* was what they had trained for. And it was more than just the thousands of hours in the simulator. In many ways, the fear of dying could not match the anxiety of humiliation. Not for her, at least. She considered the approaching missile and the timing on the chaff pods and performed some quick-and-dirty math.

"Wait for it," she told Cole. She keyed the short-wave radio and tried a bit of old-fashioned honesty.

"This is KML32 *Parsona*, Captain Molly Fyde speaking. I'm a former Naval cadet. There are children aboard this ship. I repeat, there's a crew of five youth aboard this ship. Cease firing. Over."

A second missile spat out of a neighboring Firehawk.

Cole fired a curse at his SADAR screen. Molly started to protest, but the radio chimed in before she could. "*Parsona*, Naval Task Force Delta. If you cease thruster burn, we will de-arm both missiles prior to impact. This is your final warning. Cease thruster burn and prepare to be boarded. The missiles will be de-armed. Over."

Molly pulled her hand away from the mic and rested it on the accelerator controls, contemplating pulling back. "What are our chances here?" she asked.

Cole surveyed the situation on SADAR, watching the second missile speed after its companion. "If both chaff pods work, we could stop these two and probably get to your slingshot gambit in time. But only if they don't fire again in the next few minutes." He looked over at Molly and raised his visor; she could see the worry on his face, clear as carboglass. "I don't think it'll go well for you and me if they pick us up, but we gotta consider the rest of the crew."

"Trust me, I *am* thinking about them. They're the reason I haven't pulled back on the throttle yet."

"I don't follow. And we have about two minutes before we need to decide."

"You think they're gonna to be harsh on you and me for Lucin's death? And Palan? Think about Walter being sent back to his uncle after breaking us out and stealing *Parsona* from them. Think about what they'll do to Anlyn, Cole. Or how kindly the Navy will take to Edison after they were run out of the Glemot system. I would poll our crew if we had the time, but I have a feeling they'd rather take their chances with the missiles."

"We need to decide," Cole said.

Molly tried. If it were just her and Cole, she probably would've taken their chances in a Navy courtroom, explaining what had led them to their current predicament, trusting their status as minors, *anything* to guarantee Cole would live another day. But they all were running from something. Each of the crewmembers was placing his or her trust in Molly and Cole. They had to do everything they could to escape.

The radio crackled: "*Parsona*, Naval Task Force Delta. Advise, you have one minute before impact. Cease thruster burn immediately. Over."

Molly turned to look at Cole. They were pushing over sixteen Gs, and she could really feel it through her flightsuit and in her neck. Cole's visor remained up, those hazel eyes of his wide with trust, awaiting an answer.

"Release chaff pod number one," she commanded.

o o o o

Cole thumbed the defense controls, and the new and untested chaff module in the rear of their ship popped open and ejected the decoy. It showed up on SADAR as a second ship with the same signature and mass as *Parsona*. Molly altered course slightly to see if the missile would follow.

It stayed on its original vector, homing in on the chaff pod.

"How long before the second impact?" Molly asked.

Cole was already working on it. "Under two minutes—damn! Contact. Three more missiles incoming."

Molly saw them on her SADAR screen. Things were getting ugly.

"They're gonna reach us after we slingshot," Cole said, confirming her mental calculations. "If they vector around the star after us, they're gonna get the same boost we will. They'll track us down before we get to clear space for a jump."

Molly looked up from the nav screen and had to lower her visor. Her new course had them heading right for the star. The automatic filters in the carboglass handled most of the direct light and all the harmful radiation while the visor in her helmet took care of the

47

rest, allowing her to gaze upon its surface. For a brief moment, she became lost in the sight of the fiery orb, transfixed by the hundreds of black spots on its surface, the "cooler" areas where magnetic disturbances prevented the plasma from mixing properly.

She surveyed the wide trail of fire that streamed out from the star toward the black hole. They were approaching from above, but getting so close that the overall shape and beauty of the spiral had become lost. Now it was just the massive, deadly, intoxicating details.

"Release chaff pod number two," she said.

Cole thumbed the controls while she altered course, heading toward one edge of the star. The missile behind them jogged slightly, following *Parsona* rather than the pod.

"We've got a problem," Cole said.

"I see it." That was their last chaff pod, and the missile wasn't fooled. Molly started composing their surrender in her head, losing herself in the beauty of the star and the long, curving river of plasma coursing off its surface. A solar flare had erupted recently, its smaller stream of hot matter jetting out tens of thousands of kilometers, curving close to their current heading.

Very close to their current heading.

Cole's gift had become a threat, but Molly saw that it could also be their savior.

"Hold on," she said, altering course slightly toward the thick column of plasma that made up the solar flare. Even the gradual change in direction could be felt at their high rate of acceleration. Molly glanced at the three crew members strapped in on the cargo cam. They were awfully still; she hoped that meant they were doing OK.

After a moment, Cole seemed to get the plan. "How close are you going to try and get to that mess?"

"Not too close. Shouldn't have to. The heat radiating out from the plasma will detonate the warhead from a distance. Those things can't carry the shielding we do and still be that fast."

Cole worked some numbers through the nav computer, his glove fixed to the panel by his side. Molly watched the results crawl across her own screen.

"I hope you're right," he said, "because that missile is gonna get to us before we get to that flare."

She glanced at his calculations and started to agree. His results had them a thousand kilometers short of the solar flare when the missile struck, farther away than she had hoped. Then she saw he hadn't factored in the difference in mass between *Parsona* and the missile. They were going to get more suction from the combined gravity of the star and the black hole than their little friend was.

"It's going to be close," she admitted.

"We've still got three more missiles behind this guy, and the fleet is closing in pretty fast. What happened to surrendering?"

It was a lot to think about at once. Even if the plume of plasma set off the first missile, they were going too fast to come to a complete stop and let the heat take out the other three. Besides, any decrease in speed would just bring them in range of the fleet's lasers. Molly felt completely cornered, as powerless as the coil of fire being sucked off of the star's surface, rolling across space into the black hole.

The black hole.

"The what?" Cole asked.

Molly must've said it out loud.

"Do I get two vetoes per day?" Cole asked. "Because I'm against hiding in the black hole as well."

She didn't have time to explain herself. The missile was half a minute from impact, and the wide column of fire streaking off the star and joining the spiraling river was close enough to see its features. Smaller arcs of plasma leaped up and crashed back into the main body like fiery fish breaking the surface of a lava lake and diving back in.

Cole updated the situation: "Fifteen seconds to impact."

Molly couldn't just hold her breath and see if the gambit with the missile would work; she needed to calculate her next dumb idea. She keyed the ridiculously large numbers into the nav calculator with one hand while she gradually altered course with the flight controls. The key was to keep assuming everything would work, like during the Tchung simulation when she'd moved from one audacious move to the next. Only this time, with very real consequences.

She moved *Parsona* gradually closer to a new heading, using a rough guess while the nav computer struggled with an enormous Lagrange calculation. She wondered if Cole could feel the slight change in their heading and the forces acting on their bodies.

He counted down the second missile's impact over their private channel:

"Six . . ."

Molly concentrated on the nav computer, waiting on it to spit out an answer.

"Five . . ."

She remembered, all of a sudden, that her mother was in there somewhere.

"Four . . ."

Hopefully the grueling load on the CPU eased her boredom, slowing down her sense of time—

"Three . . ."

Molly shook the thought out of her head, amazed her brain would even go there.

"Two . . ."

The calculation finally popped up. Molly was impressed to see how close the answer was to her rough estimate.

"Detonation!"

○ ○ ○ ○

The missile behind them expanded into a miniature version of the nearby star. Cole felt a change in his flightsuit as the explosion slewed the back of the ship slightly. He tried to pump his fist in celebration, but they were moving at a blistering pace. The suit could keep his flesh from being crushed—and the gravity panels in the dash could make it easier for his hands to work the controls—but nothing could help him wave his limbs in jubilation.

Then he realized there wasn't anything to celebrate. Molly had altered their heading, giving up on the slingshot maneuver. Even if the other three missiles exploded from the heat, the fleet was going to catch up to them, engaging them while they were trapped in this crazy system. A red warning indicator flashed on the SADAR screen. It finally struck Cole that Molly's new vector had problems. Whatever celebratory mood he had felt quickly drained away.

"Why are we heading toward the black hole, Molly?"

He wasn't sure he wanted to know.

"We aren't. We're heading for the L1 in this system."

"This system doesn't have an L1, it's—" Cole realized he was wrong just as he voiced his complaint. It was easy to see the star orbiting the black hole as an anomaly, as if there was only one "body," the black hole an exotic companion. But they were both just points of gravity to the computer. *Lots* of gravity in the case of the black hole. Between the two masses, there had to be a Lagrange point, an L1 where the force of gravity from both objects cancelled out. And *Parsona* should be close to the L1 —it would be much nearer the less-massive star.

Cole looked at his nav screen and saw Molly had already calculated the spot. When had she done *that*?

"Uh . . . we might be going too fast for a safe jump to hyperspace," he told her. "We aren't gonna to be in the L1 for a full second at this speed."

"I know. So you'd better time it just right."

"Me?"

Cole looked over the numbers, trying to remember the recommended limitations for their hyperdrive. It wasn't a question of whether they were exceeding them—he just couldn't tell if they were tripling or quadrupling the max speed on the warranty card.

"Yeah, you, *navigator*. And try to anticipate the flinch that'll probably come just as you thumb the drive."

Cole checked the hyperdrive. It was still spooled up from his last shift. A glance at the three missiles on SADAR told him they'd be a nonissue—the jump would come before the explosion. Still, the warheads trailing behind were like snarling dogs chasing him toward a high fence, helping to steel his resolve.

Most likely, they wouldn't come into play at all. Because *he* was probably going to get them all killed first.

○ ○ ○ ○

Molly smiled to herself, resigned. Just as with the last missile gambit, the die had already been cast. Now she could enjoy the wait while Fate read the pips.

The radio hissed to life, interference from the solar flares garbling the transmission and drowning out every other word in a chorus of pops and hisses. It sounded as if the Navy was warning them of the impending danger.

Someone in the command ship must've plotted their new course and realized what they were up to. *Probably someone right out of the Academy*, Molly thought. *Someone whose creativity hadn't been beaten out of him.* She pictured a young navigator, someone a class or two ahead of her, possibly even someone who'd picked on her. She could imagine the young officer going to the fleet commander with a sense of excitement, his voice trembling as he explained her wild plan.

The radio crackled loudly, ending the garbled warning message.

"So says the assholes trying to blow us up," Cole remarked.

His voice, and the laughter that followed, sounded good in Molly's helmet. She checked her nav screen and made sure they were on a perfect line for the L1. It was a shame she had to approach it from this direction—skimming past the star and heading straight for the black hole. It made their window narrower than if they'd come in perpendicular to the system.

She imagined the Lagrange point as a runway in space, stretched out in a wide plane of safe jump points between the star and the singularity of the black hole. Anywhere along that plane, the gravities pretty much cancelled out. But the way they were moving, that plane was more like a sheet of tissue they would tear right through rather than a long safe zone they could run down for a length of time. Their jump needed to occur the exact moment they bisected it.

They had another problem. A big one, even if it was created by something very small. The actual black hole was probably no larger than a fist but its effects, its incredible density, spread out before them like a mitt poised to catch a hurtling ball.

"Cole, if that hyperdrive doesn't fire," Molly took a deep breath, her chest heavy as the grav suit could no longer remove all the force of acceleration, "I can't clear the event horizon."

She could see the invisible border clearly. It formed the edge of a black circle ringed with a halo of light. No stars could be seen through the circle, and any photons that fell into that disc were consumed completely. However, a lot of the stars on the other side *could* be seen along the rim. Their light bent around the black hole, coming to Molly's eyes from the edge of the event horizon.

If the hyperdrive didn't fire, *Parsona* would be another dollop of mass added to the crushing center. The Gs required to pull up wouldn't matter; they'd already be in the object's massive grip.

"I already thought about that," Cole said, a tenor of calm resignation leaking through the physical strain in his voice.

The radio hissed again. Molly snapped it off with the switch in her glove. She sank back in her chair, allowing the Gs the flightsuit couldn't handle to wash over her. It felt comforting, like a heavy blanket on a crisp night. She'd done all she could, and now it was up to Cole. She could spend the next minute just admiring the rare sight in front of her, the black emptiness that could crush entire worlds.

Beside her, meanwhile, a river of orange and white plasma flowed in a column, arcs of flame licking out as the torrent fell parallel to them, toward the dark beast ahead.

She took it all in as if the sight would be her last. The void ahead loomed larger and larger, a blackness so rich there needed to be another name for it. A new color. A *primary* color. It was the shade of absence. A nothingness so real it had an edge.

Molly imagined them falling into a pit in space—a gaping well with no bottom. Then the bubble of black seemed to expand rapidly, like the ground rush she'd felt the first time she'd trained with a parachute. There'd been a moment when it seemed as if she'd waited too late to pull the ripcord—that the plummet would be to her death.

Just like that first fall toward Earth, the visual spectacle overwhelmed her other senses, the sight of approaching doom drowning out all else.

She didn't even hear Cole cursing into his mic, yelling with fear as he jammed the hyperdrive switch.

4

The bubble of absolute darkness popped, the disk filling with stars that hadn't been there a moment before. The color of the cosmos—the usual hue of space that lies between the stars like black velvet—suddenly seemed gray compared to the oily substance that had just been there. Molly's brain churned through it all, still in an observational, not a thinking state.

In the background, she could hear Cole yelling. It wasn't coming through her speakers—he must have keyed the mic off in his glove—the sound came to her through both of their helmets, arriving muffled, like the dull roar of a beach a block away.

Molly pulled her gaze from the stars to look at him; her head snapped to the side, pressed painfully into the back of her seat. She looked down and saw the throttle still pressed all the way forward, *Parsona* continuing to accelerate as fast as it could.

Straining against the Gs—and assisted by the grav panels in the dash—Molly reached forward and got a hand on the throttle. All she had to do was relax her muscles and let the rearward pull bring the stick to neutral. The thrusters shut down completely. Molly eyed the temperature gauges warily.

As soon as they stopped accelerating, Cole's arms joined his mouth's jubilation. He waved them, clapped them together, slapped Molly's back. She tried to process what he was so happy about, the memory of the extreme L1 gradually returning as he tore off his helmet and threw it over the back of the seat. His dark complexion made the wide, white smile of his seem blinding. Molly stared at him, still a little dazed, her hand on the throttle, her helmet resting on the back of her chair.

Cole leaned over and kissed her visor, leaving a comically perfect moist imprint of his lips on the plastic shell.

"CAN YOU BELIEVE THAT?" he yelled through her helmet, shaking it with both hands. He smiled wide and planted another kiss on her visor.

Molly reached up to snap her own helmet off. She had a sudden impulse to check the SADAR for missiles, and then she realized the threat no longer existed. The image of the black hole, with its mesmerizing event horizon, returned. Molly tried to focus, but her ability to think straight had been sucked down that well, pulled in and destroyed by the attraction of something too beautiful to remember.

Cole held her head just as he had the helmet and pecked her face with loud kisses. He broke away and attempted a frown, which came out more as a subdued grin. "Don't you put me in a situation like that ever—"

A strange roar interrupted him—an anguished howl rumbling up from the cargo bay. It dissipated the fog in Molly's head and brought an end to Cole's celebrations. They both tried to scramble over the flight controls at the same time, jostling with each other in panic.

Molly shoved Cole back into his seat.

"We're going too fast," she told him. "Spin us around and decelerate, but no more than the gravity plates can compensate for."

He nodded gravely and reached for the forward thruster controls; the couple had spent too many hours in simulated warfare to unlearn that ability: snapping to an important task, distractions set aside for later.

Molly jumped down from her chair and nearly passed out. She caught herself on the cockpit wall and waited for the dizziness to pass, for the blood in the rest of her body to redistribute itself after all those Gs and the effects of so much anti-grav fluid racing through her flightsuit.

"MOLLY!" Edison yelled her name in that deep, guttural voice of his, the solitary word thundering up the passageway like an enraged animal. She staggered forward, fighting off another dizzy spell, worried about her large friend.

As soon as she rounded the corner, she saw the problem lay with Anlyn, not Edison. Walter, strapped to the neighboring seat, leaned as far as he could away from her. Edison knelt before Anlyn, his normally dexterous paws fumbling at the flight harness.

Anlyn's face looked awful. Blotchy and bruised. The sight should have exacerbated Molly's dizziness, but she was in charge.

Responsible. Adrenaline surged through her body, working miracles. She unbuckled Walter first.

"Give us room," she told him, which he did eagerly.

Next, she tried to push Edison back, but his bulk was a steel wall draped in fur. "Edison, I need you to get back."

Edison shook his head but did as she asked. He cradled Anlyn's helmet in both paws, rubbing it.

Molly knelt down in front of the young Drenard. The girl's skin, normally a translucent, light shade of blue, had turned a splotchy purple. Individual capillaries and veins streaked across her bald head in a tangled web. Two rivulets of blood snaked out of the hearing holes behind her jaw and tracked forward to the center of her face, pulled there by the force of acceleration.

Her chin rested on her chest as if she were merely sleeping, but the back of her head was ashen. She was clearly suffering from SLAS. Molly tried to remember how many Gs they'd been pushing before the jump and whether any of Cole's alterations to her suit had required retooling the anti-grav pockets.

She reached into the collar of Anlyn's flightsuit and encircled the Drenard's thin neck with both hands, the universal method used to locate an alien's pulse. It occurred to her as she waited for a sign of life just how unprepared she was for commanding her own ship and its crew. The Navy had taught her how to shoot down aliens from a distance but not how to manage *living* with nonhumans while caring for their well-being.

Looking over her shoulder, she asked Edison, "Do you know where her heart is?"

The pup shook his head. Molly could see the skin around his nose where the fur was thin. Normally it was pink and healthy—now it was as pale as the back of Anlyn's head.

"Take her to your bunk and get her flightsuit off," she told him. Molly reached to unplug the suit from the anti-gravity and life-support module but noticed some-one had already done so. She ran back for the first aid kit above the galley sink.

As she unstrapped the kit, she watched Edison scoop up his small friend with a paradoxical mix of strength and gentleness and then surge past her with long, even strides, back toward his crew quarters.

○ ○ ○ ○

Walter watched the ordeal from across the cargo bay and then slid across the wake of all the frenzied activity. He settled into his chair, his elbow stretching out into the seat beside him. Anlyn's seat. But he could remember back when this whole side of the crew lounge had been *his*.

Even though he said the word silently, to himself, he did so in English.

Within his Palan brain, it came out as a *hiss*.

○ ○ ○ ○

By the time Molly made it back to Anlyn with the first aid kit, Edison already had her flightsuit off. He stood there, the empty suit draped over one massive forearm as he looked to Molly for more instructions. She could tell he needed to be told what to do next.

64

Something. *Anything*. The color seemed to be draining from his very fur.

Molly knew the two aliens had gotten close during their brief time together, especially over the week they spent alone repairing *Parsona*. She also recognized Anlyn had taken to clinging to Edison for security. But she had no idea they might be in love.

She did now. The same emotion bursting within her own heart for Cole seemed to visibly pour out of Edison. She recognized it in his worry, in his fear. As Molly knelt to attend to Anlyn, she also realized she had *two* patients in the room.

"Go get some clean rags and water," she told him. "I want you to clean up her face and keep her head cool."

That was the prescription for Edison's heart. Now she needed to locate Anlyn's.

There had been no pulse in her neck, and unless she was like the Bel Tra—with their arteries hidden within their very spines—that wasn't an encouraging sign.

At least the girl was on her back, the blood able to drain down toward the gravity plates in the hull's decking. Now Molly just needed to get those fluids circulating again. Every known sentient being relied on the potent chemical energy locked up in ATP and fueled by oxygen. Without a constant supply, the girl would die.

Molly unzipped a side compartment on the aid kit, pulled out two plastic tubes, and slid them into the small breathing holes above Anlyn's mouth. There was no way to know how far to do this, so she pushed until there was some resistance before backing the tubes out a little. With the press of a button, a small compression fan on the side of the aid box whirred to life.

Reaching into another pouch, Molly pulled out the small medical reader and searched "Drenard," even though she was almost certain she wouldn't find anything. The race wasn't in any of the Navy's aid manuals, either from absence of knowledge or lack of caring. Why she thought there'd be anything in her parents' old civilian gear was beyond—

Her parents.

Molly turned and bolted out the door, nearly breaking her nose as she crashed into Edison. "I'll be right back," she shouted over her shoulder. She dashed through the cargo bay, leaving Edison behind, the poor pup not knowing what to do.

Tears streaming down his fur.

o o o o

Molly bolted into the cockpit, not bothering to crawl into her seat. She leaned across the flight controls and switched the nav screen over to *Parsona's* old charts.

"Everything OK?" Cole asked.

Molly ignored him. A chart of astral information went off the screen, replaced with line after line of text—her mother wanting to know what was going on.

NO TIME. I NEED TO KNOW WHERE THE DRENARD HEART IS_

THE DRENARD HEART?_

LITERALLY. MEDICALLY. ANLYN DOESN'T HAVE A PULSE. DO YOU KNOW WHERE HER HEART IS?_

OH, DEAR. I USED TO. IN THE UPPER THORAX, ANTERIOR, I BELIEVE. MOLLIE, WHAT'S GOING ON? THE COMPUTER WAS WORKING ON A CALCULATION THAT DOESN'T MAKE ANY SENSE_

Molly pushed off Cole's chair, ignoring another question from him and several more from her mom. She darted back across the cargo bay, past Walter playing his video game, back to Edison's room.

"A little space, buddy." Molly pushed Edison gently on the shoulder, and the pup moved aside. It was stuffy with the three of them in the small cabin, but Molly didn't have the heart to ask him to leave, and the circulation pump should be pushing plenty of oxygen into Anlyn's lungs.

The girl had suffered a severe case of SLAS—her skin two-toned as all of her blood pooled up in the front half of her body. Molly wouldn't be able tell if anything was ruptured or what kind of hope they had for saving the girl until she could help the heart distribute the fluids evenly. Rolling Anlyn onto her stomach was going to make things worse, but Molly *had* to get to her circulation organ, and according to her mom, it was high up and in her back.

Anlyn felt incredibly frail as Molly rolled her over. "Keep those tubes from kinking," she told Edison. He reached out, eager to assist, and managed the air supply. Molly grabbed the pillow Anlyn's head had been on and placed it under the girl's chest. It went right below what must be her race's taboo area, encircled as it was with a white undergarment.

Edison's fur waved with nervous energy. Molly considered her other patient before she began. "I need you to keep her head to one side, OK? Make sure she's getting air."

He nodded vigorously and moved to cradle Anlyn's head. Molly straddled the girl's back as if she were about to give the Drenard a massage. She placed her left palm high on the girl's thorax and wrapped her right hand around it. Locking her elbows, Molly leaned forward to apply some force straight down. She used her first tentative thrust to gauge the effort that was going to be required; she didn't want to accidentally hurt her friend while attempting to save her. Resistance was surprisingly stiff; Anlyn's bones were unusually rigid to be so light.

Lifting her knees off the bunk, Molly shifted the full heft of her torso onto her arms, hoping the recent break in her right one could handle the thrusts. She pressed down with a fast and hard shove.

A loud crack shot out into the room. Molly felt a stabbing pain in her wrist, buckling her and sending her forward. Edison's head snapped up in concern as Molly gasped in anticipation of severe pain.

But the snapping sound hadn't come from her arm. It had come from Anlyn's back!

Molly's right arm felt tender, but not broken. She probed below Anlyn's nape with her left hand and could feel the difference beneath her palm, as if some wall of subcutaneous cartilage had broken free.

A new pocket of softness lay there. Molly had no idea if her efforts were helping or hurting, but she knew what would happen if she did nothing—Anlyn would die. She gritted her teeth against the pain in her wrist and started performing a series of steady thrusts.

Waves of purple spread out from beneath her hands with each push. Something definitely moved beneath Anlyn's skin—fluids, perhaps, spreading out through her back. Molly counted twenty pushes while she watched for an evening of the color, and then she rested and reached for the alien's neck again. She encircled it completely with both hands, careful to not let her thumbs press too hard and fool her with her own pulse.

Nothing.

She rubbed her right wrist before putting her hands back in place and watched a bead of sweat drip off her nose and splash on Anlyn's bare back. Molly had a sudden impulse to tear her own flightsuit off; the damn thing was cooking her without the life-support system plugged in.

She felt Edison looking at her and met his eyes, saw the question on his face.

She shook her head.

Edison grimaced as she began another round of thrusts. A dozen more. She began to wonder if the purple waves of fluid beneath Anlyn's skin were signs of forced circulation or just subcutaneous flow from the pressure.

Once again, she searched for a pulse, her wrist throbbing. She visually scanned the rest of the alien's body for any sign of internal life, anything moving. Something twitched near the first knuckle of her left hand. Maybe. She slid the pads of two fingers there, holding her breath. Molly could hear her own pulse in her ears, confounding her. Was the skin on the back of Anlyn's arm turning a pale shade of blue? Molly tried to guard against wishful thinking. Focus on—

But, there! A pulse. Molly searched the opposite side of her neck and found a weak sign of life there as well.

She smiled at Edison. "Help me roll her over."

Edison tried to say something to her but couldn't. Molly noticed for the first time that he'd been crying, that her normally verbose friend had not said a single thing since wailing her name. She wanted to ask him to say something, anything, to get the horrible echo of his groans out of her head.

But Edison seemed lost in space. He cradled his friend in his large arms, rocking her slightly. Molly watched him reach down to adjust one of the oxygen tubes coming out of her nose. She noted the delicate precision of his movements—one of his race's defining characteristics—but saw something tender in the way he did it as well.

Molly touched both of her friends softly and hurried out of the room.

They needed to get help. Anlyn wasn't out of the asteroid field yet.

○ ○ ○ ○

"What's going on?" Cole asked. "Is Edison OK?" He leaned around his seat, looking back through the cargo bay.

Molly worked her way into the pilot's seat as she tried to work out Cole's question. "It's Anlyn," she said. "Edison was just yelling for help. She has a bad case of SLAS. Really bad. Two-tone. It's hard to really gauge because she's so translucent."

Cole looked as if he'd been punched in the gut. "Was it my alterations? Gods, I *knew* we should have tested them harder. It was only a matter of time before something like this—"

"Don't jump to conclusions and don't beat yourself up. We just need to get her to Drenard, and fast." Molly checked their velocity. They were back to a sane rate of speed, but it was still higher than she'd like for another jump.

"We can probably make it in three more jumps. I'm guessing we've run the blockade by shaking the Navy back there."

"Too much time cycling the hyperdrive. We need to try it in two. Pull up the Bel Tra charts and see if there's a shortcut you feel comfortable risking. Maybe an L4 or an L5 we haven't considered. And jump us as soon as our speed gets out of the red." Molly pulled her nav keyboard out of the dash and rested it on her thighs.

"What're you gonna do?"

"I need to have a chat with my mom. Find out what's going on here."

Cole looked over from the star charts. "Yeah, that'd be great."

Molly skipped past the new questions on her nav screen. She felt bad about her mother being trapped in absolute darkness, calling out with no response for what probably felt like ages. This guilt, however, was offset by the way *she* was being kept in the dark. She just wanted to know where her father was, and what she needed to do to rescue him.

MOM?_

SWEETHEART, WHAT IN THE GALAXY IS GOING ON?_

ANLYN HAS A BAD CASE OF SLAS. WE'RE GONNA TRY AND GET HER TO DRENARD. I WANT TO KNOW WHAT YOU TOLD HER. HOW YOU SPEAK A LANGUAGE NOBODY IS SUPPOSED TO KNOW_

"Got it in two jumps," Cole interrupted. Molly gave him a thumbs-up but concentrated on what her mother was typing.

I CAN'T TELL YOU YET. I'M SORRY. YOU NEED TO TRUST ME. I PROMISE, I WOULDN'T KEEP ANYTHING FROM YOU THAT YOU NEEDED TO HEAR. TRY AND UNDERSTAND, YOUR FATHER AND I TRUST YOU WITHOUT EVEN REALLY KNOWING WHO YOU ARE. IT'S BEEN A LONG TIME_

There was a lull in the flow of words. Molly jumped in with another question: IF YOU TRUST ME, THEN JUST TELL ME WHAT'S GOING ON. THE NAVY WAS WILLING TO KILL ME TO GET THEIR HANDS ON THIS SHIP. LUCIN TRIED TO KILL ME, MOM_

She hated revealing this while she was angry. It was something she planned on getting to gradually. She felt bad as soon as she hit "enter," wishing there was some way to delete it from her mother's memory.

NO. NOT LUCIN_

The flat denial dissolved Molly's will to remove the words. Now she wanted to pound them home.

YES, LUCIN. HE HAD A GUN ON ME. HE WANTED THIS SHIP BADLY ENOUGH TO KILL ME FOR IT. I WANT TO KNOW WHAT'S GOING ON. I'M NOT A KID ANYMORE. I'M 16 AND I'VE BEEN CLEAR ACROSS THE GALAXY ON MY OWN, I'VE BEEN THROUGH SOME CRAZY STUFF IN THE PAST MONTH – I THINK I CAN HANDLE WHATEVER IT IS_

Molly watched as Cole finished an emergency spin-up of the hyperdrive, preparing for the first jump. She trusted his calculations and didn't bother double-check-ing them. Instead, she concentrated on the nav screen while her stomach tightened up, maybe in prepara-tion for the jump, possibly because of what her mother might tell her.

MAYBE YOU COULD HANDLE IT. THE NAVY COULDN'T, BUT MAYBE YOU COULD. WE'LL SEE. JUST KEEP IN MIND THAT WHATEVER SORT OF FAITH YOU'RE USING TO TRUST THAT THIS IS ME, I'M HAVING TO DO THE SAME THING TO TRUST THAT YOU ARE YOU. IT'S A DARK PLACE HERE. I'M JUST

AS SCARED AS YOU ARE. MAYBE MORE, KNOWING WHAT I KNOW. WE'LL SORT THIS OUT ON THE WAY TO DAKURA OR LOK_

Molly tried to digest the idea that her mother couldn't know who *she* was talking to. That she was just as much a stranger to her own mother as her mother was to her. It seemed to plug missing pieces into her view of the world. And no matter how many times this happened—that Molly learned things weren't always what they seemed—she couldn't yet seem to generalize the idea. She constantly felt wiser, yet she kept getting fooled. Or hurt. She leaned over the keyboard.

WE'RE GOING TO DRENARD FIRST. AFTER THAT, AND ONCE MY FRIEND IS OK, WE'LL GO TO DAKURA. I PROMISE_

OK, the screen read, BUT PLEASE, TALK TO ME. IT'S THE ONLY THING I'VE HAD SINCE YOU UNLOCKED ME_

Molly thought about that, her fingers resting on the keyboard. She understood completely. Suffering a childhood alone, lying in her bunk at night in the Academy, surrounded by darkness and the whispering of strangers . . . she understood. She used to lie in that state and dream of the comforting presence her missing parents could bring her.

She never imagined it could be the other way around. Or reciprocal.

Molly considered the things she'd like to have heard from her parents when she was alone and confused. She wondered what her mother would enjoy knowing. Once again, the realized dream of having a conversation with her mom paralyzed her. She didn't know where to begin. As she peered out through the carboglass, gazing at the stars, her fingers hovered over the keys while her mind raced.

Maybe just tidbits to start with. Random likes and dislikes. She started to type the first thing that came to mind while Cole thumbed the hyperdrive.

Outside, the constellations shifted.

Ever so slightly.

5

"**S** sandwich?"

Molly turned from her typing to find Walter holding out some sort of food concoction, layers of leftovers neatly arranged between chunks of bread like geological strata.

"Mmm. No, but thank you," she said politely.

Cole reached for the refused victuals. "Thanks, buddy."

Walter snapped it back. "It'ss for Molly," he hissed, his eyes narrow slits.

"I appreciate it," Molly told him, "but my stomach isn't feeling great. Cole can have it if he wants." She looked over from her typing. "And why don't you check in on Edison, see if he needs anything. And find out if Anlyn's improved any."

Cole took the reluctantly offered sandwich. "Thanks, man."

"Don't mention it," Walter spat as he slunk out of the cockpit.

"That boy adores you," Cole said around his first bite of sandwich.

Molly nodded. "I know. I wish he didn't. Not so much." She checked over her shoulder and then leaned toward Cole. "He creeps me out sometimes," she whispered. "Then I feel like I'm just being xenophobic." She straightened back up and pulled the keyboard close. She considered telling her mom more about Walter, but she wasn't sure she could stick to saying nice things.

"He makes a mean sandwich, though. Oh—" Cole swallowed and then continued, "The Bel Tra have a general layout of Drenard, but they don't have an orbital schedule. We were kinda expecting Anlyn to guide us in. Do we wait for her to come to, or do we just cross our fingers and hope we don't jump into a small moon or a satellite?"

Molly typed: ONE SEC_ to her mom and switched over to the chart.

"Hmmm." She studied the Drenard system. It was one of those charts every Naval cadet recognized in an instant. Students pored over them while dreaming of a final assault, making plans for a massive invasion that would end the war.

Drenard was a binary star system, which created some strange orbital permutations. Strange for systems with sentient life, at least. Even though binaries are an extremely common astral configuration, they lead to orbits nonconducive to the evolution of large and complex life forms.

Without an orbital schedule, Molly could only see where the planets and stars had been when the Bel Tra scouted the system, but not the dynamics of the Lagrange points in motion. Using estimates of mass and distance gave them rough guesses, which wasn't good enough for the exactitude that safe jumping required.

"Why don't we come in the same way we escaped from the Navy?" she suggested. "We shoot for the L1 between the two stars, a point we know doesn't move, and someplace too unstable for debris to be hanging out."

"Good idea," said Cole, "but it'll be a long burn to Drenard from there. For Anlyn, I mean."

"Any other choice gambles with *all* our lives. And we could risk another short jump once we're in system and have a visual."

"Good point. OK, the hyperdrive should be spooled up in a few minutes. And just so you know, we'll be down to less than two percent on fusion fuel when we arrive. These quick cycles are murdering our fusion supply."

"We'll worry about that after we get Anlyn some help. Go ahead and jump as soon as you can." Molly switched back to her mom and scanned the screen to see where she'd left off.

"What're you ladies gabbing about over there?" Cole asked.

"Glemot," she said.

Cole looked over, his eyebrows raised. "Really? Huh. I'm surprised."

"Yeah, well, I'm telling her about the planet we found, not the mess we left behind."

Cole turned back to the nav computer; he seemed to want to say something but restrained himself.

A sad silence fell over the cockpit before Molly's loud and rapid typing broke the spell. She concentrated on the good, withholding the bad.

A style of communication her mother knew quite well.

○ ○ ○ ○

The strangest thing about the jump into Drenard—the home system of Molly and Cole's sworn enemy—was the naive nonchalance with which they did it. Piloting with the hubris of their youth, rather than the caution of their training, they had jumped across the front lines of a major war along unproven routes and arrival points. Desperation, and the pursuit of their own Navy, had pushed them far. Concern for their sick friend took them, unthinking, the rest of the way.

The only thing on Molly's mind—beyond having rescued Anlyn from slavery and reuniting her with her people—was getting a friend some medical assistance. For Cole, trust had become a relative term, a commodity with fluctuating prices. Running from their own Navy for a month had him not just reconsidering allegiances, but forgetting where they once lay.

Still, there was no rational justification for what they'd just done: jumped into a hostile system with the sole local among their crew unconscious and unable to communicate. Of course, Drenard's Orbital Defense Patrol saw their unexpected arrival much more clearly. It was a dire threat. A suicidal attack. A GN ship come to rain bombs on their home planet.

Such was their fear as the DODP jumped out to the unidentified contact on their SADAR units, weapons arming . . .

○ ○ ○ ○

"Whoa. Lots of contacts." Cole zoomed his SADAR unit out. "Hostile formation," he added.

Molly saw it. And the representation of *Parsona* on the SADAR unit surrounded by a Drenard fleet shook her to her senses. She saw at once how this must look to them: a human ship popping out of hyperspace between their tightly orbiting twin stars. It'd be exactly where Molly would try to sneak into the system, even if she were dumb enough to try such a stunt on a race this technologically advanced.

Gods, I am *that dumb*, she realized. She looked over at Cole; neither of them had their helmets on. Anlyn was in her bunk, suffering from SLAS, and not even in her flightsuit. They'd be dead before the hyperdrive wound down and could be cycled back up.

"We're so *stupid*," she said.

None of the Drenard ships had fired yet, but they were closing in with a staggered formation—making it impossible to jump out even if the hyperdrive were ready. What did she expect? Without Anlyn to translate, was she really thinking she'd just fly in and land on the enemy's home planet?

Molly flipped the radio on and grabbed her helmet. It was probably useless—Drenards weren't known to communicate with Navy ships before destroying them—but she had to try.

"This is the starship *Parsona* to the Drenard fleet. Do not shoot. We come in peace. We have a sick Drenard youth onboard." To Cole, she said: "Start flashing *Parsona's* exterior lights in the GN distress patt—"

Parsona.

For the second time that day, Molly remembered she had someone else onboard who spoke Drenard. She reached to the keyboard and hurriedly typed to her mom:

QUICK, I NEED TO KNOW HOW TO SAY "WE COME IN PEACE" IN DRENARD_

A bizarre pair of symbols appeared on the screen in front of her—composed of straight lines, they looked as if someone had dropped two bundles of sticks into separate piles.

PHONETICALLY_ she hurriedly typed, and glanced up at the SADAR screen. The rough encirclement was complete; a staggered line of Drenard fighters probed forward. In the back of her mind, she wondered if she'd spelled "phonetically" right.

SHEESTI LOOO. LONG E. AND THE LOOO SHOULD BE DRAWN OUT FOR AT LEAST TWO COUNTS_

Molly shook her head as she read the instructions. Her mom spoke Drenard, but no one else in the Navy did? It was too much—almost as crazy as having an *actual* Drenard as a friend. A shiver ran up her spine as she considered what the Navy would have done with Anlyn if they'd been captured. She activated the mic in her helmet.

"Sheesti Loooo. Sheesti Loooo. Sheesti Loooo," she intoned, using the triplets common to Naval comms. She figured the repetition couldn't hurt, even if Drenards did it differently. She looked over at Cole and nearly burst into laughter at the expression on his face. He was looking at her as if she were crazy, both of his brows down low, casting a shadow over his narrowed eyes.

"Mom's giving me Drenard lessons," she explained, pointing to her nav screen.

The formation around them tightened, but no weapons were fired. Cole turned back to his displays. "I guess I don't have room to talk, considering how fast I drew fire from the Navy."

The radio squawked to life. Over the static created by the nearby stars, a strange yet pleasant cooing could be heard. Molly felt her eyelids growing heavy with the calm sounds.

"Any way for your mom to translate that?"

She turned to Cole. "Could you sound out what they just said?"

He shook his head.

"Well, we just about killed ourselves running from our own Navy," Molly said. "What say we open the outer airlock and invite our enemy aboard?"

Cole flashed her the same look from a moment ago, his eyes retreating warily into dark caves. He reached for the airlock controls but kept his gaze on her. "I do this under protest, Captain."

"Duly noted," Molly said. She unclipped her harness and watched through the carboglass as the flashing distress lights scattered across the nose of her ship.

She hoped the Drenards saw it as the white flag of assistance—not surrender.

o o o o

Back when Molly and Cole first saw Anlyn in the Darrin System, they'd been shocked by how small and frail she seemed. The few front-line training videos they'd been shown at the Academy featured large and muscular aliens with dark blue flesh not nearly as translucent as hers.

After spending a few weeks with the young female Drenard, their reintroduction to the males brought another shock.

The first one came through the inner airlock stooped over. Even in the cargo bay, he couldn't stand fully erect, which put him a bit under three meters tall.

He had a gold-colored helmet over his head and a thick neck, bunched with muscles, that led down into a decorative tunic. Powerful arms came out of a standard torso and clutched a metal lance of menacing proportions.

He kept his weapon down, pointed at the deck of the ship. Molly took it as a sign of respect, but the size and shape of the thing, combined with the fierce appearance of the large creature holding it, made her wonder if their ship itself was being threatened.

Two more Drenards squeezed through the airlock. The second was identical to the first; the third a bit smaller and weaponless. Rather than a single tunic, the last of the trio wore dozens of layers of them, each richly decorated. The innermost tunic was so long, he had to clutch the extra fabric near his stomach, which he did ceremoniously. He turned in place, surveying the crew and the ship, then launched into a soft and pleasant speech.

None of which made any sense to Molly, Cole, or Walter.

"Sheesti Loooo," Molly repeated, showing her palms.

The unarmed Drenard, already bent over slightly, bowed even further as he pulled the longest tunic up to his chin. The xenothropologist in Molly stirred at the gesture, but she didn't have time to marvel at the cultural exchanges and the rarity of the encounter. Sworn enemy or not, all she wanted was to have them tend to Anlyn's health without anyone else getting hurt in the process. She held up both hands to her chin, bowed as the Drenard had, and then slowly stepped toward the three fearsome figures. Somehow, she needed to squeeze past them to Edison's room without increasing the tension in the ship.

The warriors didn't seem to take her approach as hostile—or perhaps they couldn't see Molly as a threat. They simply rotated their bodies to follow her movement, stepping aside slightly to allow her to pass. The ranking officer cocked his head in what Molly anthropomorphized as curiosity, but it could have been disapproval for all she knew.

She had to turn sideways to move through them, their bulk towering to either side like slabs of curtained blue steel. They loomed so close she could smell them, a scent like warm stone.

Molly glanced down at one of the soldier's massive hands, curled around his lance. She passed mere centimeters from him, her head not much higher than his waist. She imagined trying to fight one of these monsters and flashed back to the fight in that Glemot bunker.

"Sheesti Looooo," she repeated in a breathless whisper, more to herself than anyone else.

Getting past the barrier of raw muscle and into the after hallway gave her shivers of relief. If there'd been enough room, she probably would've taken off in a run, brushing at her arms to get rid of the willies from being so close to actual Drenard warriors. She held it together, though, and turned to the aliens as she backed away, waving with her hands for them to follow.

The officer complied. One of the warriors turned to size up Cole, his relaxed attitude suggesting no threat to be found. Molly watched this exchange as she backed into Edison's room, where her Glemot friend sat on his bunk, his long legs stretched out, Anlyn's head on his lap.

The Drenard officer ducked through the door. When he raised his head, the two large aliens locked eyes, and Molly could feel the tension sparking across the room. The Drenard said something over his shoulder to his two companions. One of the warriors appeared at the door, his lance at a higher angle than before.

"This situation is nonoptimal," Edison said. "And the spatial requirements of our combined forms are not adequately met by the dimensional constraints of my room."

Molly waved him silent. His English might be hard to understand, but the deep growling tenor of his voice might be something that cut across alien divides.

Using slow motions with her arms, Molly directed their guests' attention toward the prone figure in Edison's lap. Anlyn looked to be stable, but the front of her body remained heavily bruised from her bout of SLAS. She hadn't moved, nor shown any signs of awareness, since they had escaped from the human Navy. For all Molly knew, they were returning to the Drenard system with a brain-dead husk.

As soon as the officer saw the female Drenard, something changed. The muscles in both arms flinched, and he nearly dropped his tunics. He threw the lengths of fabric over his shoulder to get them out of the way and crossed the crowded room with one large step. He leaned over Anlyn, reached into her armpit gingerly, his other hand resting on Edison's chest. *Not* so gingerly.

"Don't move," Molly told the cub.

Edison's face twitched with the effort, the fur on his face and shoulders bristling. Molly pleaded with wide eyes for inaction. Her friend begged her in return with narrow slits—for something else.

The Drenard touched Anlyn in a few places and then felt her cheeks with both palms, his massive hands engulfing her small head. He turned to the warrior and said something short and soft.

Molly looked back and forth between them, trying in vain to read their body language, to get some sense of whether or not her friend would be OK.

When the officer scooped up Anlyn with one arm, Edison raised his hands in protest. Molly started to say something to calm him down, expecting the massive Drenard to shove at him with the large hand on his chest, but the officer pulled away.

Wrapping Anlyn in both arms, the officer leaned away from Edison, distancing himself.

Finally, a gesture Molly recognized. And not a good one.

"Wait—" she squeaked.

Edison rose as the crackle of electricity filled the room. A dazzling light whizzed past Molly's head and struck him in the chest, sending him into a few brief spasms of vibrating limbs before his head crashed back against the bulkhead.

Molly spun to protest—to say the only two words of Drenard she knew—and saw the lance. Horizontal. Level with the deck. Her brain processed the meaning of this as the crackle of ionized atmosphere reached her ears.

The blast hit her square in the chest, sending her flying toward the bunk.

She dearly wanted to arrest her fall before she passed out, but every muscle betrayed her—all of them contracting at once—vibrating with their refusal to cooperate.

PART VII
THE THIN LINE

*"Symmetry, by surrounding us,
makes itself invisible."*

~The Bern Seer~

6

Cole woke up sore. Full-body sore. It felt like he'd just played two games of galaxy ball with no pads on.

He tried to sit up, but the muscles in his stomach spasmed—cramping up and sending him crashing back down on the bed.

The very *soft* bed.

Sitting up hadn't worked, so he rolled onto one side and surveyed his surroundings from there. He recognized the place. Or a place like it.

Lisbon.

He and some friends had broken into a five-star hotel, posing as busboys. The lobby, the hallways, everything had looked just like this. He must be in one of those rooms, or in a place just like it.

He rolled onto his back, soaking up the luxuriousness of the sheets and the perfect mattress; he closed his eyes and felt some of his stiffness slide away. When he opened them and looked down at his toes, he noticed the chandelier hanging from the vaulted ceiling. Thousands of crystals were arranged around hundreds of tiny lights, all twinkling like stars through carboglass.

Cole followed the light to the walls, which appeared to be made of a mottled-yellow marble. A darker material, some species of wood, cut up the expansive slabs with windowsills and support beams. Above the sills, large panes of glass allowed natural light to pour in, bathing the room in a warm glow.

Slowly, Cole pulled his legs out from the thick covers and worked them to the edge of the bed. It took some effort and a few grunts to get his body to comply. What it really wanted to do was stay there for a week, recuperating.

He swung his feet over the edge—they dangled a meter from the ground. The soreness in his calves and quads warned him not to do it, that they couldn't promise to catch him if he jumped from such a height. Heeding the warning, Cole rolled onto his stomach and pushed himself backward, sliding toward the ground. The silk sheets slid together like layers of grease.

Yelping, Cole clutched at the heavier blankets, falling to the ground and pulling them after. They barely slowed his crash before smothering him. He swam through the fabric, emerging in a heap of finery that spilled across a landscape of lush carpet, the material piled so high it looked as if it need to be mowed.

Cole fought another round of temptation, his body urging him to lie flat on the soft surface, tangled up in silk. Grudgingly, though, he pushed himself up on sore muscles and stood, swaying slightly. Now that he was out of bed and upright, his nakedness felt awkward. He reached down, slowly, as an old man might, and fumbled for one of the sheets.

He attempted to knot the fabric around his waist the way the Glemots had taught him, but the fabric was so slick, it was impossible to tie. It wouldn't even stay draped over his shoulders, slipping off like beads of water on fur. After some experimentation, he finally settled on a few wraps around his waist, holding the material together with one hand.

Eager to know where he was, Cole approached the window to peer outside. Even from a meter away, however, he couldn't see through the harsh light lancing into the room. It was just a plane of bright whiteness, nothing beyond. He leaned close and reveled in the heat radiating through; it reminded him instantly of the hot Mediterranean days of his childhood. He closed his eyes and let the heat loosen his muscles. It felt like *two* suns pouring their energy into him.

Two suns. *Drenard*. That's where he was. The L1 between the twin stars. What had happened?

Cole leaned forward and covered his face with one hand, straining for the images. A fleet closed in on SADAR; there was a thud as two hulls locked together; Molly saying something funny. Soldiers.

The last images he had were like scenes from an action holovid: the Drenard guarding him and Walter had raised his menacing lance. The other soldier in the hallway fired off an energy beam into Edison's room. Then another. Cole couldn't see the effects of those blasts, but he clearly saw the one that caught him in the chest.

He remembered going down. His body vibrating. The sound of his skull cracking on the decking. He slid one hand around the back of his head and felt the lump; just the slight brush against it sent another thunderbolt through his head.

Where was everyone else?

Cole turned from the window—he couldn't make out anything through it anyway—and looked to the doors arranged around the enormous room. He went to the nearest one and found a closet. There were hooks and arms up high and cubbies with baskets in them below. Cole pulled a few out, but they were all empty. He took a moment to snug the silk sheet tighter around his waist and went to the next door.

That one opened into a bathroom twice the size of his quarters on *Parsona*. He stepped inside. The floor looked like wood but felt like stone. There were knots and wavy lines in the material, yet it felt cool under his feet. Cole spun back around and looked at the door. It looked like a loose-grain wood, but touching it gave him the same crisp jolt that only marble invokes. He pressed on the door with one finger, and it moved silently and effortlessly.

Cole left this curiosity for later and turned to the high counter with the mirror above it, hoping to find some water to drink. The surface was made of the same strange material and came almost to his chest. He gave himself a comical appraisal in the mirror, hitched his sheet tight with one hand, and leaned over to survey the deep bowl cut out of the stone.

The only feature beyond the basin was a neat vertical row of three cylinders. Cole twisted the one on the left, and it spun freely but did nothing. He pressed down on it and then tried pulling it up. The plug slid out of the hole easily, and water began flowing through the channel and splashing into the basin. Steam rose from the fluid; he didn't need to touch it to verify the danger.

He replaced the cylinder and pulled the one on the far right. There was a gurgle, and he was rewarded with bone-chillingly cold water. He forced his sore calves to lift him to the stream, wiggling his stomach up on the edge of the counter so he could reach a sample. It tasted excellent; he drank it in large sideways gulps as it dripped from his cheek and ran back toward his ear.

Raising his head, Cole wiped the moisture from his chin, cupped one hand, and gathered enough to splash on his face and push through his hair. There weren't any towels nearby, so he made do, wiping himself dry with the edge of his sheet.

Cole picked up the plug from the counter and dropped it back into place, stopping the flow of water. The workmanship was remarkable, to create stone that could prevent seeps while sliding so smoothly. He ran his hands along the counter as he turned toward the exit, and then he walked back to the bedroom and gave the door a slight push, watching it intently as it swung shut with a satisfying click.

This place was outrageous. Cole felt as if he could soak it in without an ounce of stress. Surely his friends were being treated just as well.

Was this their thanks for rescuing Anlyn? Or were the Drenards trying to make up for the spot of miscommunication from earlier?

He double-checked his silky coverings and went to the next door. It stood alone on the adjoining wall, right across from the foot of the bed. It was larger than the other two, and Cole's innate sense of layout and aesthetics suggested this one would open into a marble hallway. He could imagine the plush runner that would lie beyond, Molly padding down the middle of it, a silk robe fluttering behind. She was probably coming right then to pull him by the hand so the two of them could rush off to see marvelous, alien, things.

I'm back on Glemot, Cole thought to himself, more of the dull aches in his muscles and joints slipping away. He reached for the gold-colored doorknob on the massive slab of rock, and it clicked open with a twist. Making sure he had his silk sheet tightly clutched, Cole pulled the door toward him and began to step around it—into the exact hallway from his imagination.

But the gold bars that ran vertically through the doorway were too close together to squeeze through. Cole looked them up and down, confused. One hand reached out to touch the cold metal barrier in his way. He lingered on the poor design of the passageway before it finally hit him:

This wasn't Glemot.

It was *Palan*.

7

Cole shouted down the hallway. He tried Molly's name first and then ran down the list of crew and friends, thinking of each. Hopefully they were rolling around in their beds, enjoying their captivity with all the bliss ignorance could provide.

But now that he knew, what was *he* supposed to do? Lie in bed and wait on his captors? Or was he even being held here? This seemed like an unlikely prison. Perhaps the bars were for his safety? To keep something from getting to *him*!

The thought put a shiver up Cole's spine. It seemed the only way to solve the paradox presented by the room. It was too lush for ill intent, but obviously he wasn't meant to go anywhere else. Until he found out for sure, Cole decided to choose the option that made the lump on the back of his head cease its pounding. *He was here as a guest*, he decided. Protected in a room he'd never be able to afford for the rest of his life.

He was going to enjoy it.

He returned to the bathroom to investigate the larger basin sunk into the floor. Dropping the silk sheet, he knelt and inspected the three stone stoppers along the wall. Going with his hunch, he pulled the center one out, and warm water began flowing into the large rectangular pit. He let it fill a meter up, adding quite a bit of the pure hot water as well. When it was deep enough to cover him, Cole replaced the stoppers and lowered himself into the steaming pool.

"If this is prison," he said to himself, "I'll join Walter in a life of crime."

Almost instantly, the soreness from his capture began melting away. He let out a long groan of pleasure and forced his legs straight, elongating every muscle and tendon to allow the heat in. He lay like that for over an hour, hovering on the border between sleeping and waking, his brain not able to dream or think. Just *be*.

It wasn't until his hands felt callous from the pruning that he decided he'd had enough. He rubbed them up across his face and through his hair, pushing tepid water across his skin. With a series of protesting grunts, he pulled himself out of the tub and removed the stopper by his feet.

The liquid relief swirled away with happy gurgles; he moved in front of the mirror and began stretching, both arms raised high as his muscles cooled. Looking at his reflection again, Cole noticed he'd lost a bit of muscle over the last month. He was too lean. Being on the run didn't seem conducive to good health, and eating out of pouches had taken its toll.

But his face . . . it looked *right*. He looked as he ought to look. Happy. Relaxed. He wished Molly could be there to feel it with him, to see him in such good spirits.

Then he remembered he was completely nude.

He grabbed the silk sheet and tried to wipe away most of the water before wrapping it around him. After attempting a few more configurations, he gave up again. The "garment" was destined to be a precarious wrap on his slender hips, one hand formed into a fisted buckle.

Back in the bedroom, he checked the bars again and found everything as impenetrable as before. He looked around for anything meant to entertain and found nothing. Going back to the large window, Cole pressed both hands to the glass and cupped his face. He still couldn't see anything through the blinding glare.

The silk sheet hit the floor.

He bent to pick it up, wondering if he should just poke two holes in the fabric, drape the damn thing over his head, and walk around like a ghost.

Surveying the room one more time, Cole figured this was one of the most perplexing jams he'd ever been in. He was being forced to luxuriate in conditions beyond his upbringing. Nobody seemed to be expecting anything of him right now. He could crawl back in bed and sleep for days or take another bath until he was one giant wrinkle.

But those bars made it hard to relax. Especially since he didn't know what they were for.

As tempting as it was to laze around until the answers came, Cole decided to prepare for the worst. He went back to the bathroom and drank as much water as he could, then splashed some on his face to jolt his senses. Setting his bedsheet aside, he launched into a standard-grav exercise routine: stretching, push-ups, sit-ups, and an hour of tai chi.

Cole switched from his tai chi routine to shadow-boxing. He threw out his fists in snappy jabs, the head in the mirror ducking and weaving to avoid each blow. Combining uppercuts, elbow strikes, and body blows, he imagined a roomful of foes coming at him one at a time. With each punch, he blew out his breath, tightening his stomach muscles to absorb every possible counter from his opponent.

It wasn't until he heard someone speak that Cole realized he had visitors—and that he was dancing around with no clothes on. He whirled around, his hands still up in a defensive posture.

The Drenard in the doorway cooed pleasantly, but the sight of his lance sent a zap of fear through Cole's spine. Around this guard stepped one of the ornate Drenards dressed in layers, but this time with an additional cloak that covered his arms, a gold braid tied around his waist to link the open sides together. His longer tunics were pulled up through this belt and folded over, freeing his hands.

It could have been the same male from the ship; Cole couldn't be sure. The red band around his blue head was different, but the face looked similar, as alien races tend to do until one gets to know them. The large alien approached on bare feet and held out a small bundle. He continued to make the pleasant sounds that had disturbed Cole's exercises.

Cole accepted the proffered gift; it was a colorful tunic, similar to one the guard was wearing. He draped it over his head, and the hem went almost to the floor. He looked back to the Drenard, whose identical tunic barely fell to his knees.

Turning to glance at himself in the mirror, Cole saw a little boy playing dress-up—a pauper pretending to be a prince. He decided it was more humiliating than being stark naked.

The Drenard waved at him, breaking his spell and gesturing toward the door.

"Fine," Cole said. "Lead the way." He waved a hand toward the door and followed the large alien into the bedroom. The obligatory escort of double guards, each with a ferocious lance, formed up on either side. Cole cast a wary glance at them, happy to see the infernal devices aimed at the ground. He was also ecstatic to see the bars in the doorway were up.

The cloaked alien led the two guards into the hall and then turned and looked back at Cole. Cole shrugged, mostly to himself, and strolled out to join them. Judging from the odd mix of treatment thus far, he figured they were either going to lead him to a sumptuous feast or a torturous interrogation.

But certainly not both.

8

The Drenards led Cole down the ornate hallway, past a series of marble doors with lowered gold bars, until they came to a doorway that stood open. They waved him inside, where he found a table hewn out of the now-familiar grainy rock. It was covered with plates and bowls of foodstuffs, but only a single chair sat before it. The Drenards moved Cole to the chair and gestured to the victuals, almost as if to say "whatever you subsist on can be found here" rather than "look at all the yummy stuff we made for you."

Cole sampled a few things and didn't find any of it too unpleasant.

"Thank you very much," he offered.

None of the Drenards budged. Cole could sense they were waiting for him to get his fill before whatever came next. He felt tempted to draw the meal out, to stall for time, but the cold politeness was unbearable, and his curiosity growled louder than his stomach. He really wanted to know whether they considered him a prisoner or a cherished guest, so he ate just enough to energize him for the day before pushing the bowls away, making several hand gestures he hoped would suggest "no more."

The leader nodded and said something to the other two in that gentle voice of his. The guards strapped their lances across their backs and began clearing the table; another Drenard entered with a second chair and topped Cole's water up.

Having the large creatures swirl around him in furious activity completed the young prince illusion from the bathroom mirror, making him feel extra ridiculous. Even more so when he was "crowned" a few moments later by yet another Drenard male, who came in and showed him a red headband just like the one his escort wore. The alien held the thing reverently for Cole to see, and then he reached up and placed it around Cole's forehead—arranging it just so.

The rough material itched his scalp; Cole reached up to scratch it, but the Drenard pushed his hand down gently. He decided it was best to quietly bear the discomfort.

While the new Drenard tended to him, the others finished cleaning up, their movements uncannily orchestrated. Every action was performed with a precision that reminded Cole of his own military training. When the maneuvers finally completed, he found himself left in the room with just the presumed officer seated across the table. A glass of water stood before the Drenard, full and sweating slightly.

"*My name is Dani Rooo,*" Cole thought.

But why did he think that?

His right hand came up to touch the red band, as if it knew the answer.

"*No it's not. My name is Cole,*" he thought to himself.

"*Hello, Cole.*" The Drenard across from him opened his mouth and made a funny shape with it. The voice in Cole's head was his own, but they weren't his words.

"*You have to think on the surface, or speak aloud. I cannot hear you unless you're forming the words in your head.*"

An image flashed in Cole's head. A woman. Aunt Carol? Crazy Aunt Carol who heard voices. Gods, he hadn't thought about her since he left Portugal. What in the world made *her* come to mind?

"*Let's start with where you found Anlyn Hooo, Cole.*"

Now he understood how Aunt Carol felt. His own voice was in his head, and it was telling him to do things. He had a powerful urge to grab the red band and throw it across the room.

But something told him that wouldn't be a wise move.

"*Can you hear me?*" Cole thought it out loud in his head.

"*Very good. Now, where did you find Lady Hooo?*"

"*How does this work?*" Cole asked, unable to concentrate on the alien's question with so many of his own, both sets of thoughts jumbled up in the same head. "*Do you speak English?*" he added, tossing another on the pile.

Dani Rooo leaned back in his chair. There was silence in Cole's head for a moment.

"*Do you know why life forms are so similar, Cole?*"

It seemed a bit off-topic, but he was interested in playing along. Not so much by the question—a classic in xenophilosophy—but by the tone of his own voice. It was as if the alien across from him *knew* the answer and was just testing him.

"*Because they're the simplest solutions to common problems? Problems of survival?*"

Dani made the shape with his mouth from earlier. Cole labeled the expression a "smile," and then realized he no longer had to guess.

"*Do you find my answer funny?*"

"*No. But it does make me happy. Women and youth are not very good at keeping secrets. The combination almost guarantees a spill of information. With Lady Hooo unconscious, there's no way of knowing what you know or don't know.*"

"Trust me," Cole thought to Dani, "I know less than nothing. Why don't you fill me in—how's Anlyn? Am I a prisoner here? Where are my friends? And how are you talking in my head?"

Dani leaned forward and placed both hands, wide apart, on the table. "Whose soldiers are outside the door, boy?"

They stared at one another for a while. Both thinking—but deeply. Silently. Dani leaned back again, folding his hands in his lap. "Forgive my outburst. I am worried for Lady Hooo as well; as such, I am not myself. Lady Fyde—"

"Molly? Where is she—?" But Cole couldn't force his thoughts to rise above the alien's.

"—insists that you rescued Anlyn from captivity, and if this is true, you deserve an answer. So. I will give you **one** before we begin our session. One answer, an honest one, to any question you like. And **then** you will begin responding to my questions."

Cole considered the offer. In his heart, he wanted to know where Molly was and whether she and the rest of the crew were safe. His natural curiosity, however, wanted to riddle the inner workings of the red bands. Meanwhile, the philosopher in him shouted down the rest, wanting to know the root of common forms, the riddle that taunts every theory in the field of biology and serves as the foundation for all major religions.

These questions and more rattled around in Cole's head. He saw the muscles in Dani's vast neck twitch under his blue skin and could sense—could almost *know*—that he was becoming impatient. It just made it harder for Cole to think. To choose.

Panic spilled over his litany of queries, drowning them, making it impossible to pick the best response. The pressure to get it right dried his mouth out. He felt as if something important was taking place—and he was about to blow it. He reached for his sweating glass of water.

Dani leaned forward, mirroring his movement, his mouth contorting into a new expression. *"Well?"* The strong and confident version of Cole's voice sliced through his worrisome thoughts.

Then, in a flash, Cole's very confusion provided the answer he was looking for. It dawned on him that he was being offered a single answer from Dani, but that didn't mean it would be the last question he ever asked *anyone*. Many of the trivial ones would be answered in time, if he was patient. In fact, the *reason* he had an impossible time choosing was because he didn't know the trivial from the profound. And *that* was the question.

Cole's hand, still frozen in the shape of a cylinder, stopped short of the dripping glass of water. He brought his other hand up and clasped the two of them together.

Leaning toward Dani, he forced a calm thought to the surface:

"My question is this —" Cole took a deep breath. *"Which question **should** I have asked?"*

Dani froze for a moment, then his mouth changed into something new. A shape with *teeth*. One of his large, powerful hands shot up into the air between him and Cole and came crashing down with lightning speed. When his flat palm hit the stone table, it rang out like a cracked whip, an impossibly high note ringing in the air for too brief a time to have been so loud. The glass of water leaped up, throwing a small wave over the lip to join the puddle of condensation below.

Dani's entire body shook, his cooing transforming into a growl as throaty pockets of air moved back and forth through his vibrating cheeks. The Drenard raised his hand from the table, pointed at Cole, and made a fist. He shook his head, which roared with the vibrato of a small engine. He waved his fist in the air and hit the table with it again.

Cole leaned back in his chair, distancing himself from the display. When Dani shot out of the seat across from him, he wondered if he'd been wrong—if he really *did* have only one question left in him. But Dani didn't rush around the table in attack; he strode out of the room and into the hallway, fighting to form words through the amplified and gruff cooing sound.

Swiveling in his chair to watch the alien go, Cole felt his body surge with adrenaline, preparing for danger and defense. He heard Dani struggling to give commands to someone outside, the sound of coarse hacks mixing with the forced purring of their language.

Less than a minute later, his interrogator returned and stood in the doorway, a beverage of some sort in his hand. The Drenard took long swigs from it, his physical attack subsiding.

"Dani?" Cole squeezed the mental word through a crack in his confusion.

His interrogator raised one hand and continued to drink. *"I am fine. I just haven't laughed that hard since I was your size. It felt . . . **amazing**."*

Dani lowered the glass and tilted his blue head slightly to one side, took a deep breath, then let it out. *"There are two ways I could answer your question. If I answer it honestly, I will cheat you, for the truth is: that **was** the question you should have asked. I only realized this as soon as you thought it to me.*

*"I could satisfy my end of the bargain by admitting this, couldn't I? I could point out that you **did** ask me the right question, and you would get nothing. But your choice suggests something interesting: that you are looking for the **beginning** of a path rather than a method of skipping to the end. And even though you will never walk down the trail you seek—not now that you are here with us on Drenard—I*

would like to reward you with more answers than I initially promised."

Dani took another long pull from his stone cup, studying Cole over the lip. When he was done, he made a popping noise with his mouth, jerked his head to the side, and formed in Cole's head what he assumed were the same words:

"Come with me," Dani thought.

Cole stood, the surge of fear draining away, and followed Dani into the hallway. Two armed guards framed the door, but Dani acted as if they weren't there. He turned left, away from Cole's room and farther down the long passage. Cole hurried to keep up, having to nearly jog in order to match the alien's long strides.

As they hurried past room after room, Cole noticed more than half had gold bars lowered in front of the door. He read them as "occupied" signs, wondering which one Molly was being kept behind.

He wondered it too loudly.

"She's not on this hall," said the voice in his head. "Males only. Women have an extremely important status in our culture, unlike your own. Ah, so many answers that I feel like giving you now. Even if Anlyn pulls through and confirms our worst suspicions about you, I will always respect you for that single insight." Dani looked down at the carpet. "And the laughter," he added.

Cole glanced up at his walking companion, his head just above the Drenard's elbow. It felt strange to be having a conversation without eye contact and in the near-silence of their bare feet shuffling through the lush pile of the runner.

"You have yet to answer the question," Cole reminded his unusual captor, *"nor have you asked me what you want from us. We just came to drop off a friend and get some supplies—"*

"We will sort that out when and if Anlyn recovers—and all of my hopes are that she will—but you will not be leaving Drenard anytime soon. We cannot allow that. Anlyn should know this, which is why we find the story you and your friends are giving us a bit hard to believe. Especially since there are . . . inconsistencies."

Cole wondered what this meant as they reached the end of the hallway. Dani paused in front of a massive door that spanned the width of the passage; he turned and addressed the consternation on Cole's face and in his thoughts. *"Forget these things for now."* The alien waved one hand and reached for the door with the other. *"You will have many years to dwell on them here. But first, let me show you where **here** is,"* he thought.

With that, Dani pushed the large door open and entered the next room. Cole followed—and stepped into a prism, a carpeted cube of dancing lights. The wall across from them was identical to the one they had just passed through, yellowish marble bisected by a closed door. Cole scanned for the source of the spectacle. It was the wall to his left, revealed as Dani allowed the door to swing shut. The entire face was transparent glass, or crystal even. His human brain had a difficult time absorbing the view beyond.

It was a sunrise—or sunset—that defied his own understanding of what potential beauty that meteorological event could possess. The colors banded gradually through every hue imaginable. Between neighboring buildings, he spotted a horizon gilded with gold; it turned through the oranges and reds, but there were colors between that Cole's boy-brain simply had no vocabulary for.

His feet took him closer to the sight, as if of their own accord. He craned his neck up as he neared the glass, watching the last of the deep violets as they were absorbed into the black of space. What made the sight truly unique was the way the colors *moved*. It was a sunrise or sunset in *action*. Waves rippled up now and then to make the rainbow shimmer, like the Northern Lights of Earth, but brighter and with more color, all of it squeezing between towering buildings to all sides.

"Wow."

It was all he could think. He wondered how it translated in Dani's head, if it came across as a soothing coo or a baby's babble.

"The view is better from the roof," Dani thought.

Cole didn't believe him. He wouldn't until he saw it for himself.

Dani strode across to the wall opposite the glass and called for a lift. Cole followed. He walked backward, still riveted by the sight. The elevator arrived just as he did, and Dani guided him in, thinking bemused thoughts at the mesmerizing effect his planet had on another human.

Cole grunted as the elevator doors squeezed the colors away. The lift moved—and fast. He could feel it in his legs, still weary from the exercise. Despite the obvious speed with which they were traveling, the ride was a long one, and both men rode in silence, mental and otherwise.

When Cole felt himself lighten several kilos, he knew the ride was almost over. The doors opened, and he followed Dani into the morning, or twilight, air. Not knowing which time of day it was irked Cole; he needed a label for what he was seeing, as if the word might bottle some of the splendor. As they walked toward the side of the building facing the glorious sight, Cole asked Dani in his head: *"What time of day is it?"*

"There are no days here," Dani replied.

Cole barely heard his own voice give him the answer. It *was* more beautiful on the roof.

All around them stood a transparent barrier shielding out what sounded like a powerful wind. Cole could hear it race through holes in the enclosure above, a crisp zephyr descending to swirl around them. The walls held back the air, but there was nothing obstructing the view all the way to the horizon; he saw none of the other buildings that had been crowding the view from the room below. Here, Cole could gaze from one edge of the horizon to the other, and in no two places could he find the visual feast repeated.

He pressed his head to the glass and peered down, spotting the rooftops below. Observation platforms dotted most of the structures, which got progressively shorter as they went toward the horizon, stepping down so each building behind had a view. The city didn't go very far into the distance, he saw. No more than a dozen kilometers, possibly less—the height made it impossible to gauge.

He turned to his interrogator-turned-tour guide.

"No days?" he asked.

"It's hard to turn away from this sight at first. I know. It takes many years to become used to it, to take it for granted, even. However, to understand, you need to walk with me and look at the other two views."

Staggering backward again, with his eyes locked on the dancing lights, Cole slowly moved with Dani—reluctant yet curious.

"Drenard is like the moon of your Earth. One face is gravitationally locked with our two stars, just as only one side of your moon ever looks down on your planet."

They stood in front of the glass that ran down one of the building's sides. Dani fell silent for a moment and looked down at his feet. *"You are the second human I've had this conversation with. On this very rooftop."* He looked at Cole and continued to think aloud. *"It was an accident then. My being up here nothing more than mere chance. And now—"* He stopped and made the coughing sound from his fit of laughter. *"I am considered a human expert, sent to deal with you and the girl."*

"Molly—?"

Dani raised his hand, his thoughts overpowering Cole's. It wasn't pleasant to be shouted down with one's own voice, Cole decided.

"I'm sorry to drift off like that. The similarities to that old conversation took me back to better times. My people are extremely sensitive to symmetry. Look at why."

He pointed at the line of buildings stretching off in the distance, converging like the train tracks in Portugal that Cole had grown up near. Both men thought back to ten years ago, but their memories were a galaxy apart.

"Drenards live on a line. A border between light and dark. That way," he pointed back to the colors, *"is a boiling land where even shadows can turn to ash. And over there,"* he nodded to the darkness opposite, *"you have a frigid wasteland*

where your breath will freeze in your lungs." He paused and looked back over the city stretched out toward forever. *"Most of our people choose to live on better planets now, but* **this** *is where we evolved. Along a thin halo—a temperate respite—crushed between two extremes.*

"There's another significance inherent in the shape of our habitat. It isn't just a line, it's a circle. It's the root of our fondness for symmetry. For things that repeat themselves." He turned and faced Cole. *"The universe is like this. Our lives are like this. I've been here before, just like this. And if you look hard, you will see the same story playing out in* **your** *life. Things beginning and ending the same way. The same conflicts with the same resolutions. It keeps going, but not on its own. Each cycle requires work."*

"I don't understand," Cole responded. *"Why are you showing me this? What's the question I should've asked?"*

Dani turned away from him and peered through the glass. *"You remind me of him,"* he thought. *"The only other human I have spoken with like this. He brought so much hope. But that's not why I think of him. It's that neither of you seem anything like the . . .* **humans** *our war department deals with every day."*

Cole tried to force another question through, but the Drenard's thoughts were too powerful.

"I cannot speak of the war, so do not ask. Come and look at what I love about the rooftops."

Dani led them to the next side of the building, the one opposite the shimmering rainbow. Some of the colors bled around the elevator structure, stray bands of subdued prettiness that rode the glass overhead. But once they reached the far side, the spectacular view was just a throbbing memory. Now they were overlooking the dark side of Drenard, the sky bursting with stars and fuzzy galaxies.

A thick swath of unbelievable density let Cole know they were looking toward the center of the Milky Way, right along the width of the galaxy. Billions of pricks of light stood out; he could even see the glow of a pink nebula, the color of planets forming. The sight made him feel a long way from home and choked him up inside. One hand went to the cool glass while his thoughts warped back to Earth.

The two men fell quiet again, Dani giving Cole a minute to absorb it all—or perhaps the Drenard was taking a moment for himself.

It was the human who broke the mental silence:

"*Beautiful,*" he thought, unable to know the soothing purr this word translated to in Dani's head.

"*Beautiful, yes. And even more dangerous, my friend. Nothing lives on the surface. Well, almost nothing. The fire on the other side fuels the life of our planet and drives many of our customs with its ancient and inhospitable landscape. Over here, we find the absence of everything. Just powerful winds that are nothing more than the air being sucked from the cool low pressure to rush toward the rising heat.*

"I brought you up here so you could look at yourself, Cole. And to give you an honest answer to your sage question. Up here, my boss will not hear, and there is no guard to trust with a secret." He turned to face Cole. *"You are very much like a Drenard,"* he thought. *"You have a hot side and a cold side, and you use them to balance each other. I feel your anger, mostly when you dwell on the well-being of your friends. And I also feel your patience, which you use to temper yourself. I believe you are one of the few of your kind who is trying to live on a line, just as a Drenard must."*

Dani turned from Cole to gaze at the stars, and then his eyes drifted down to the planet's surface. Cole looked as well, out over the shadowed land as black as ruined Glemot. His own voice was clear in his head as Dani thought: *"The question you should have asked, Cole, and that I would not have been allowed to answer, is this: what is fusion fuel **made** of?"*

Cole rolled this around in his mind for a moment. *"You've gotta be kidding,"* he thought to Dani.

The alien nodded slowly. *"It's the start of a path, young friend, and one that leads far over the horizon. You can't see the end from here because of the long walk. Now let's get below before my superiors become suspicious."*

He turned and walked back across the roof, leaving behind a confused and disappointed human.

And not for the first time in his life, nor in that same spot, Dani thought.

Quietly.

9

On the long ride back down, Dani explained the circumstance of their captivity. They would not be allowed to leave Drenard. *Ever*. But their stay would be made as pleasant as possible until they died of old age. If Anlyn woke and verified their story—or other evidence came to light that absolved *Parsona's* crew of her disappearance from Drenard and the condition in which she returned—the friends would be allowed to visit with one another. Until then, they were to be kept apart to prevent collusion of any sort.

Cole took this as well as he could. The idea of not leaving Drenard didn't sting as much as it might have. It would be disastrous for Molly, who was now on a quest to find her father and do her ship's bidding, but all Cole wanted was for his friends to be safe, to find a place where they could stop running long enough to catch their breath. Perhaps they had found just such a spot there on Drenard, the home of their enemy.

He knew this feeling would waver over the years to come. It would not be easy to persuade Molly to stay put and remain safe, rather than rush off and get killed in another wild adventure, searching for her lost past. In a way, the Drenards would be doing him a favor by forcing her to remain there. It would probably take an entire race of powerful beings to buttress Cole's will if she asked him to leave, to break out of another prison and go on the run once again.

Cole glanced over at Dani and hoped he wasn't thinking too loud.

They stepped out of the lift and turned to the long, carpeted hallway. Cole forced safer thoughts to the surface: *"I have to ask about the red band,"* he thought to Dani.

"I'm afraid I won't be able to assist you in their duplication. There are few secrets my people guard more closely than their operation. And that's saying a lot."

"Of course," Cole conceded, *"I'm actually more interested in the philosophical underpinnings. Theories of universal language acquisition were long ago crushed on Earth. Linguists found—"*

"Your linguists know less than nothing," Dani interrupted. *"Besides, the answer you are looking for has more to do with biology—with the reason all forms in this galaxy are almost identical."*

Cole saw an opening for more answers and pressed the point. *"You said something about this before—"*

Dani made a gruff coughing sound. *"Excellent attempt, but I was merely deducing what you **didn't** know."*

They arrived at Cole's room; the bars were still up. Dani opened the door and held out his hand, his eyes focused on Cole's forehead.

He didn't want to give it up—the band or the line of questioning. *"Why are we so similar?"* Cole thought.

He watched the fingers in the outstretched hand curl into a blue fist. Dani fell silent for a moment, looked up and down the hall, and relayed a cryptic answer: *"I have become an expert, as much as a Drenard can, on your planet Earth. What fascinated me the most was the way its plates move, how they shift continents over time. Where once they were bunched up, now they are far apart."* Dani paused and scanned the hallway. *"Our galaxy—even our **universe**—is like this. It wasn't long ago that things were much closer—in a strange sense of the word.*

"Information used to flow back and forth between worlds, even between galaxies. Sometimes it still does. Take the pouched mammals on your southern continent: they are

unique but similar to the other fur-covered animals elsewhere. Information was shared, but eventually those plates grew apart. For the same reasons, our galaxy is dominated by common forms."

Cole looked at Dani's fist, then met his gaze. *"You're talking about homology. Divergent evolution. But how is that possible? How, over such vast distances—?"*

Dani peered down the hall and thought to Cole without looking at him. The words came soft, like a mental whisper: *"Are you familiar with extremophiles?"*

"Yeah," Cole answered, *"small organisms that live in acid, or deep in the crust, or around thermal vents."*

*"Keep your thoughts soft. Yes, but you have it backward, friend. **We** are the extremophiles. We live between the cold and hot, up in the wild weather and under an assault of radiation. A thermal vent is safe by comparison, a stagnant niche. Our planet, like your own, is dominated by invisible creatures, smaller than one of our own cells. **They** rule the universe, much as your genes rule your own behavior."*

The fist blossomed into a palm, insisting. *"There, I've thought too much."*

Cole reached up, but before he could peel the red band from his head, he heard one last compliment.

"You've taken the next step down that path," Dani thought.

○○○○

128

The "days" that followed were marked by the window in his room. The pane would glow to full strength and then fade to black in what Cole quickly recognized as artificial aesthetics. They fed him twice a day on an exacting schedule; Dani joined him for every morning meal. During one of these sessions, he asked Cole if the twenty-four hour cycle pleased him. Cole had to explain to his friend and captor how very little sunlight he and most humans got back home, which turned into an interesting conversation about the universality of youth.

Amazing topics such as these were welcome. It dawned on Cole one day that he was furthering Dani's research, and he wondered what his instructors at the Academy would say about his inability to withstand such a pleasant interrogation. They would likely point out what a dupe he'd been to fall for the comfortable bed, the lavish meals, the blatant good cop/bad cop routine.

The prison bars, gilded with gold, would undoubtedly become official Navy policy for softening up detainees. Cole had no doubt they would've mocked him for his performance, right before they airlocked him for committing treason.

He had little doubt this was taking place, that his friendship with Dani—formed out of mutual respect and a fondness for philosophical musings—was nothing but a ploy. He even wondered, with every topic they covered, if the data gathered would one day be used to invade Earth, kill and maim his fellow humans, or just turn the tide of a major battle.

If such were the case, he would be devastated, but he would be surprised. Something about the red bands, the ability to share thoughts directly, overcame all else. There was a level of trust, of *connecting*, that Cole would never have imagined he'd enjoy so much. One night, alone in bed, he imagined sharing the experience with Molly, of hearing her thoughts over the red bands.

But then, knowing what *she* might hear in return, it gave him pause . . .

Four days went by. The exercise and the conversations with Dani were the only variables. Everything else remained the same.

Until Anlyn woke up.

The first sign was a slap on the stone door during Cole's morning bath. The break in the routine startled him; he reached for a towel and dried himself hurriedly, expecting guards to barge right in.

Instead, there was another bout of insistent slapping. He fought the urge to yell, "Coming!" in English and hurried to the door, twisting the edges of his towel together to hold it in place.

The first thing he noticed as he pulled the door slowly toward him was the gold bars. They were still in place.

Then he saw his next surprise:

Molly.

The bars didn't stop them; the cold metal just became a part of their embrace. For days, Cole had kept his emotions damned up, knowing that worry would not do her any good even as it eroded his own strength. He could feel that all break, spilling through the gaps in the barrier.

Molly started crying, her head resting on his arm. He reached through the bars, embraced her, rubbed her back, and pressed a corner of his forehead against hers. Tears of joy streaked down his cheeks.

When she said his name, it sounded like honey tastes. And it was great to hear English spoken in someone else's voice. Especially hers. She started rambling, and Cole let the sound of it wash over him.

"Anlyn's gonna be OK," she said. "She woke up yesterday, verified our story. They told me last night and said I could be the one to tell you. Oh, gods, how I've missed you—" She sniffled and tried to calm herself down. Cole glanced down the hall at her silent Drenard escorts, lances in hand.

Molly broke off and snuck one hand back to wipe at her face. She smiled up at Cole, flush with embarrassment. "I'm a mess," she said.

"You look great," he assured her.

She laughed once and looked away. "I have to go," she said sadly. "They want to talk with each of us over one more meal. I'll see you tonight, OK?"

Cole could just grin and nod. He watched her pad away, her shapeless Drenard tunic somehow riveting— her long limbs moving with ease and the whites of her bare feet winking back at him as they flew up from the carpet. He could have bent the solid bars and walked right through, he was sure of it. He could feel it welling up in his chest, his arms, his cheeks.

He finally shut his door, went back to the bathroom and finished drying off. Then he got dressed and sat on his bed, staring at the soft artificial light glowing through the window, waiting for it to get brighter, willing the false day along as fast as it could go.

○ ○ ○ ○

When the Drenards came for him that evening, Dani was not among them. Two guards led Cole down to the interrogation room and waved him through the door. He was the last to arrive.

Molly jumped out of her chair and wrapped him up in a tight squeeze. Edison sauntered over and slapped at his shoulder hard enough to knock Molly out of the embrace. Walter, of course, stayed in his chair, his mouth already full of food. His only greeting was to wave a large piece of meat back and forth.

"Where's Anlyn?" Cole asked.

"Alert, but unwell," Edison grumbled. "A personal visit is currently under some degree of consideration."

Cole rested his hand on his friend's back. "It might've been my fault," he said. "The alterations to Walter's old suit and all. I'm really sorry. I'm just . . . I'm glad she's OK."

Edison swiped at his cheeks, too choked up to say anything.

Molly waved Cole into the empty seat on her side of the table; she kept one hand on his arm as they ate, as if terrified of losing contact with him. They dug into the usual fare, but Cole couldn't believe how much better it all tasted with his friends around. They traded snippets and stories. Edison had some singed fur on his chest that everyone had to see, and they all agreed with Walter that the beds slept extraordinarily well. Molly went on for a solid ten minutes on the bathtubs, how ingenious the plumbing system was, how hot she could stand the water, and the fact that she'd practically been living in the thing.

Nobody mentioned the rooftop and its perpetual sunrise, so Cole didn't either. Still, each of them seemed to know much that the others didn't. Their individual personalities had steered the sessions along unique paths. Walter could tell them more about the gold bars, the doorknobs, and marble than the rest of them combined. Through large and rapid bites of food, he told his friends about how the planet used to spin and be full of trees and life, but that over billions of years it had wound down like a clock due to the pull of the two stars, and how all the trees were petrified and that massive machines quarried them out of the dark side of Drenard.

"It'ss jusst rock," he said, "yet it'ss *pricselesss*!" He hissed this last word through his teeth, one of the few English words with such a construction that Palans repeated it with relish.

As Walter tore into another plate of food, Cole noticed Edison picking at his plate, his eyes level but focused on something in the distance.

"Cuisine not up to your standards?" Cole asked. "Miss the dehydrated stuff from the ship already?"

Edison shook his head quickly and returned to eating.

Molly set down her fork. "What's up?" she asked him. "Is it Anlyn?"

He nodded.

"She's gonna be OK, right? Isn't that what you heard?"

Edison shrugged his massive shoulders, his reluctance to speak uncharacteristic and troubling. Molly wiped her mouth with her napkin and reached a hand across the table. "Is it something else? Do you want to talk about it?"

The Glemot remained still a moment, looked up at her, then to Cole. "Unsound reasoning to transport Anlyn to this destination," he finally said.

"Why?" Cole asked. "Isn't this where she wanted to come?"

Edison remained silent.

"I wouldn't have if I were her," Molly said, picking up her fork. "Not after learning about Drenard culture from Dani."

"What are you talking about?" Cole asked. "They practically *worship* women here. They put them on pedestals, for Pete's sake."

"They aren't raised up on platforms, darling, they're hoisted in cages. Gods, no wonder I feel so connected to her, she's dealt with the same stuff I have. Except, here, the males are even more disproportionately large, so the women aren't allowed to do *anything* for themselves—"

"Good idea," Walter said.

"It sounds like hell to me," Molly countered.

"Too much like the Academy?" Cole asked.

She turned back to him. "It was more than the Academy." She looked away, the mood of the feast shattered. "You wouldn't know what it feels like," she muttered.

"What *what* feels like? Being small? Defenseless? Scared?" Cole pushed his plate away from him and lowered his voice. "The next time you ask me about my childhood, I promise I won't dodge it, OK?"

Molly nodded as the table fell silent, save for Walter's smacking sounds as he inhaled another plate of food.

"Sso, you guyss hear about the Wadiss?" he asked between shovelfuls.

Cole looked across the table and noticed Edison's strong reaction to the word, his fur bristling.

"Highly adapted to the calefactōrius hemisphere," the Glemot said excitedly. "And symbolic trinkets of entry to Drenardian racehood. Female Wadis—"

Edison went on, his voice droning like the roar of distant thunder, coming in never-ending rolls. Cole picked at his food and zoned out as Edison and Walter compared notes on the little critters, which he best understood to be some sort of desert lizard.

He daydreamed while the others gabbed about the creatures. After Walter finally had his fill of food, Drenard guards entered to clear the plates. Dani arrived soon after, accompanied by another large Drenard wearing one red band and holding another. The Drenard with the band crossed to Edison, who bristled with recognition and leaned forward to have the device put into place. It was the first time Cole had seen one of the silent conversations from the outside, and it was a bit eerie: two beings looking at each other in silence, nodding, moving their arms, making faces.

Whatever they were thinking, it didn't take long. The band was removed from Edison's head, and he rose from his chair, turning to his friends: "The large delta of positional coordinates X and Y; X being Anlyn and Y being—"

"Whoa, buddy. Deep breath," Cole said.

The poor cub tried again, concentrating, "The distance separating Anlyn and me is to be decreased immediately."

"That's wonderful!" Molly squealed, jumping up to embrace him.

Cole rose as well and touched paws with his friend. Walter pressed his finger into a smear on the table and then placed it in his mouth, sucking at it idly and staring at the far wall.

After Edison followed the Drenards out the door, the three original *Parsona* crew members were left alone as the last of the dishes were removed.

"The bedss are nicse here," Walter said. Again.

Molly nodded. "Yeah, so what's our plan, guys?"

"Plan?" Cole asked. "Our plan was to find someplace safe where people would stop shooting at us—"

"*They* shot us," she reminded him, pointing at the open door.

"OK, but it must've looked pretty bad, the way we barged in. Besides—" Cole eyed her suspiciously. "Wait a minute—are you planning another jailbreak?"

Walter nearly stood up in his chair. "No jailbreak," he said, waving his arms level with the ground. "No way." He pointed straight down at the table. "Walter stayss *here*. Forever. Eatss and ssleepss."

Molly held out a hand to calm him down. "I agree with you. Both of you. It *is* nice and safe here. And comfortable." She turned to Cole and narrowed her eyes. "But there are certain things I need to do. *Important* things."

Her father, Cole thought. And Lucin's hints of a war-stopping secret. She would never be happy here, he realized. Pampered and comfortable weren't viable options for her. He could see it on her face: dire things screamed at her from within, things that needed *doing*.

He felt sick to his stomach thinking about his plan to keep her here. To protect her. He'd planned on putting up a fight when this conversation came up. To employ the same paranoia that had saved them several times since they'd left Earth. Now he felt miserable for even considering it. He should've been thinking about what Molly *wants*, not focusing on his own selfish desire to keep her safe. His mistake, it dawned on him in that moment, was in assuming Molly shared his primary concern: *her safety*. But she was just like him, thinking about other people's well-being more than her own.

He reached under the table and found her hand. Gave it a gentle squeeze. He felt more connected to her right then than he ever had in their hundreds of hours in the simulator.

"I'm sorry," he whispered. "Of course. You're right. But no more mention of it until I bring it up, OK?" He glanced up at the chandelier dangling over the table.

Molly nodded as if she understood. Walter hissed, confused. It reminded Cole that the last time they'd escaped a prison, it had been with help.

Only, he wasn't sure they had that luxury this time.

He gave Molly's hand one last squeeze and rose from the table; he strolled out to the guards in the hallway, insisting he think with Dani.

○ ○ ○ ○

The view from the roof was just as amazing the second time, if not quite as startling. Cole looked out at the colors with a twinge of sadness. Maybe Dani was right. After many years, the alien sight might become familiar, then normal. Perhaps it could eventually become banal.

Cole concentrated on the view and on the sensations it stirred. He noted how the waving colors made him feel *right then*. He tried to store the memory away, preserving it against the erosion of time.

While he corralled the experience, Dani considered his plea.

"I cannot help you," the Drenard finally thought back. *"However, I do understand that you would not be perfectly happy here. Most Drenards choose contented lives elsewhere and come here only on vacation or for official matters. I am one of the few natives that never considers leaving. And non-Drenards? They're not **allowed** to leave. Ever."*

"What about the other human, the one you brought up here. Did he die on Drenard?"

Dani hesitated. *"I'm not allowed to say."*

"Is he still here? Still alive?"

"I cannot say. I'm sorry."

Cole turned toward the hot side of Drenard, squinting his eyes into the bright display, working to temper himself—to remain cool. He took a deep breath from the moving air wafting in from above and felt his tensions melt away.

Dani reached out and placed his hand on Cole's shoulder in a rare moment of contact. *"**Non**-Drenards are never allowed to leave,"* he repeated.

It was fortuitous Cole had steadied his nerves.

Otherwise, he would never have noticed the subtle inflection of "non" in his own voice.

140

"I know how to get out of here, but it won't be easy," Cole said.

Molly leaned back on a wall of pillows while he sat cross-legged on the foot of her bed, his hands in his lap. The gold bars were in place and her door had been shut, but Cole knew his words were probably traveling out to someone, somewhere. The good thing about his planned escape was that technically—it was legal.

"How?" Molly asked.

"We have to become Drenards."

Molly grabbed one of the pillows beside her and swung it at Cole, nearly knocking him off the bed.

"Don't mess with me like that," she said.

He righted himself, not laughing at all. Molly's indignation turned to shock mixed with something else. "Gods! You're serious, aren't you?"

"Yeah, I'm serious," Cole said. "And if you'd stop assaulting me and listen, I'll explain."

"All right," Molly said, placing her stuffed weapon in her lap and resting her elbows on it. "Tell me."

"I know it sounds crazy, but I don't think we would be the first to do it. I'm pretty sure other species have. Maybe even another human. And get this: every kid born here isn't really considered a Drenard until they capture a Wadi Thooo—"

"A whati who?"

"The lizards Edison and Walter were going on and on about."

"I'm sorry, I didn't understand half of what Edison was saying, only that he was excited. Did you follow any of it?"

"Not an ounce, but I got a little information from . . . someone else. And I think I know why Edison is fascinated with them."

"Why?" Molly asked, leaning forward.

"I think he already had plans on becoming a Drenard. Maybe for Anlyn."

Molly fell silent, looking down at the comforter as if reading the words there, trying to make sense of them.

Cole held up his arm in case it was a feint on her part, setting up another blow from the pillow.

"For Anlyn?" She looked up at Cole. "Why? Does he love her? Does *she* love him?"

"How would I know? I hate that kinda talk, don't you?"

"Yeah," Molly agreed. "It's silly, especially after such a short period of time. *Right?*"

Cole nodded slowly. "I guess. Still, I've seen them together and I know there's *something* there, something that formed between them while we were on Earth. It's the only reason I can think of for why he'd be so interested in the creatures."

"Maybe he's just looking for a way out of here."

"Then why not tell us? No, I think it's something else. I think he's trying to impress a girl. And either way, even if I'm wrong, we need to do this if we want to get out of here. The Drenards were never gonna tell us about the rite. I'm sure they'd feed us twice a day and give us all the bubble baths we want, but that would be the rest of our lives."

"So how do we become Drenards?"

Molly smirked as she said it, either not convinced or still finding the concept amusing.

"It's pretty simple, actually. Each of us goes beyond the terminator—the line between sunlight and darkness—"

"I know what a terminator is," Molly interrupted. "I was in the same class."

"Oh, yeah, sorry. So you travel beyond the terminator and through the canyons on the light side, you catch one of these Wadis—which is some sort of lizard— and you bring it back here. A council or something will judge the size and quality of the thing and determine what sort of Drenard you'll be. It's just a ritual, really."

Molly frowned. "I guess that means the females here aren't ever considered Drenards, because Dani's told me enough about their society to know there's no way they would let their precious little girls go out and risk their lives to hunt whati whatevers."

"Well, you might not like this, but it's actually really good news for us. A loophole, if you will."

"Oh, gods. What is it?" Molly droned.

"Wadi Thooo eggs. They count. And the eggs are laid close to the terminator, where the rock is coolest. It is a technicality, but if we go to the canyons, grab an egg each, and bring them back here—we're free to go. They know from Anlyn that we haven't done anything wrong, and Dani will vouch for us. I think he has a soft spot for humans."

"Some of us," she corrected. "I suppose the boys go in farther and capture a live lizard?"

"I don't know if they capture them alive or not; I'm not concerned with that stuff. Edison might know."

"How're we gonna do this if we aren't allowed out of our rooms except to visit one another?"

"All we have to do is initiate the rite. They *have* to allow us. They look at us as children, anyway, so we'll fit right in. And hey, just because they're bound to let us try, I don't think they'll appreciate us asking. A lot of Drenards are gonna be upset if we pull this off."

"*When* we pull it off," she corrected him.

○ ○ ○ ○

Edison wasn't back from visiting Anlyn by the time they gathered for their next meal. Cole went over the plan with Walter, who seemed excited—not about leaving the planet, but about pulling a "Jog and Flog."

"What's a Jog and Flog?" Cole asked him.

"A kinda heisst," he hissed. "Big on Palan. And call them 'Wadi Thooo,' not lizsardss, bad on my earss."

"Fine," Cole said. "If we're all in agreement, I say we get it over with. Once we get this out of the way, we'll find Edison and Anlyn and see about getting out of here."

Nobody had any objections.

They ate in silence, with their own thoughts. After the meal, Cole went to the guards in the hallway and requested Dani's presence by repeating his name aloud. When the old interrogator joined them, he had a set of red bands in hand.

"We would like to quest for Wadi Thooo, to prove our worth as Drenards," Cole thought to Dani.

The interrogator played the shocked and confused part well, demanding to know where Cole had heard of their tradition, how much the humans knew of it. Cole lied and said he had learned of it from a Bel Tra and that he would say no more.

Neither of them knew how successful their ruse would be, or if anyone was even "listening." It may all have been for Dani's benefit—to clear his conscience by accepting an alternate version of reality.

After pretending to demur, Dani said he would pass the request on and let them know the following morning. As he said this, and just before Dani held out his hand for the red band, Cole saw something flash across the interrogator's face. Or maybe he heard it in Dani's thoughts, down deep where only a quiet mind could hear.

Cole handed the band over, searching his friend's face, sensing there was more he wanted to say. A warning, perhaps.

The bad feeling lingered as he returned to his friends.

Once again, Dani was not with the group that arrived the next morning. Instead, there were four guards with lances and two other Drenards wearing the layered tunics with ornate cloaks on top, the outermost tunic pulled up and tucked over the belt. Both of the latter also had red bands around their heads; one of them reverently held out another to Cole.

He had never put one on himself, but he knew the seam went in back. He adjusted it until it felt as if it lay in its habitual place, and his own voice soon filled his head with thoughts.

"Human boy, do you really wish to initiate the Wadi Thooo Drenard rite of passage?"

"Yes." He tried to think it with a powerful calmness, but it sounded meek—even in his own head.

"Very well. Follow us."

The two officials spun, their cloaks spreading out and rustling into one another. They marched toward the end of the hall, and Cole hurried after. In the room with the lift shaft, Walter stood waiting with two more guards; the boy fidgeted with his tunic and kept adjusting the red band on his head.

The two officials instructed them to wait and then disappeared through the hallway leading to Molly's room.

"Hello?" someone thought in Cole's head.

"Is that you, Walter?"

"Haha." The boy laughed, but with Cole's voice. "Your esses sound funny, too!"

Cole looked at Walter's metallic face and found it difficult to reconcile his own voice with the Palan's thoughts. He didn't seem near as annoying without the hiss and the creepy way his mouth moved. Cole knew there was no way they'd be allowed to take the bands with them, but he couldn't help but think how nice they'd be for alien relations. Or just for *intercrew* relations, for that matter.

When Molly came out with the officials and her own red band on, Cole fought to control his thoughts, to keep them deep. Especially seeing how the loose tunic moved around Molly's body, exposing parts of her side through the wide opening below her arms—

He tore his eyes away, focusing on Walter's face. He could hear the boy starting to greet Molly, but the officials were able to dominate all their thoughts.

Fortunately, for Cole.

"*Follow us,*" one of the Drenards said; it was impossible to know which one.

o o o o

They were told it would take half of one of their solar days to travel to the staging area. After a long descent in the lift, they exited into an extremely busy lobby. Drenards, all males and all wearing variations of the colorful tunics, walked purposefully from one place to another. Almost all of them took a keen interest in the alien procession but were polite enough to not gawk. Much.

Cole looked around for Dani, or a sign of Edison, but found none of the latter and wasn't sure he'd recognize the former in a crowd. The blue planes that made up the Drenard face had distinguishing details too fine for their unpracticed human brains.

"*Where's Edison?*" Cole heard one of his friends ask the guards.

There was no reply.

149

The guards maintained a protective ring around them as they were escorted across the shiny floor of petrified wood. Cole tried to get a glimpse of the planet through the lobby glass, but all he could see was crowds of people and maybe another building beyond. They were led down a flight of moving stairs to a platform crowded with Drenards. Cole spotted two small females among them. He also noted that both had several large males encircling them. Protectively.

Behind the crowd, a transparent tube ran the length of the platform, instantly recognizable to Cole as some sort of transportation. Their group waited in a tense hush, Cole wondering if the silence was due to *their* presence.

After a few minutes, their ride appeared—a long metallic lozenge that slid to a noiseless halt. The glass tube parted in several places with the pop of a pure vacuum taking a whiff of air, and the transport's inner doors opened and disgorged an array of colorfully garbed Drenards.

Their escorts kept them pressed to one side as the two crowds fought to switch places.

Cole watched these new arrivals startle at the sight of them, their glances pulling away quickly and then transforming into sideways stares. A shiver ran up Cole's spine; the raw number of deadly Drenards crowded around him felt nothing like the few he'd gotten used to in the rooms above.

Then it occurred to Cole that *they* were this planet's enemy as well. He imagined what sort of stir it would cause to lead two Drenard captives through Grand Central Station in New York. He remembered what he'd felt when he first saw Anlyn in the Darrin system, and it made him feel ashamed. He glanced at Molly, whose eyebrows were down, her forehead wrinkled in thought.

Once inside the transport, they were given plenty of room. After pulling away from the platform, the vehicle slid to a stop at one station after another, repeating the process of unload, load, gape. Cole felt like a specimen on display. Some sort of alien protozoa in a glass test tube.

After a half dozen or so stations, however, he went from feeling like a scientific curiosity to something more like a zoo animal. The clusters of adult professionals gradually morphed into large groups of Drenard youth, as if thousands of field trips were converging on the same locale.

Even at their age, Cole noticed the boys were significantly larger than the females, but not quite as big as the officials and guards serving as their escorts. The young females were just a bit smaller than Anlyn, which shocked Cole. It occurred to him that he didn't even know how old Anlyn was, nor if she was even officially a Drenard yet.

Molly turned to one of the guards and raised her hand. *"Will we be performing the ritual in a group?"* she asked, breaking a long mental silence.

"No more questions," was the response. Cole could see Molly's shoulders sag as she bit her bottom lip and looked up at him.

He shrugged and widened his eyes. Already, this was not feeling like the best idea.

They stopped at a few more stations, Cole's ears popping at each one as the vacuum in the tube section filled, squeezing extra air between the door's seals. When they arrived at the next one, and every passenger on the transport started crowding toward the door, he figured it for the end of the line.

The guards confirmed this, leading them onto the platform. They held Cole's group up as the last of the children trotted up the steps. By the time they went into the lobby above, most of the young Drenards had already exited the building. Cole could see them through the wide expanse of glass along one wall as they were herded into lines and loaded into land vehicles similar to buses but with aerodynamic domed hulls that stretched nearly to the ground. The metallic panels covering the things gleamed in the colorful sunrise raging beyond them.

Cole watched Molly and Walter gape at the display, enjoying their reaction even though he was nowhere close to immune himself.

The guards waved them toward the door. To either side, small packets of Drenard youth stood marveling at the colors beyond, too excited to even notice the humans. Several of them cooed excitedly, and one of the larger children held up a recording device of some kind. Cole assumed these kids hailed from other Drenard planets. *This is the biggest day of their lives,* he thought.

Then he wondered if everyone else had heard him.

Outside, the segregation continued as their small group found themselves waved into a large shuttle alone. As soon as they'd seated themselves along the uncomfortable benches lining the walls, the vehicle lurched into motion, heading off in a different direction from the other shuttles.

"I'm feeling unwanted," Cole muttered to Molly. "Are you feeling unwan—?"

"*Silence!*" the voice rang harsh in Cole's head, and he noticed Molly flinch as well. Hearing himself like that made Cole think back, wondering if he'd ever raised his voice with Molly before—maybe in the simulator, once? He resolved to never do it again. It sounded awful. *Alien.*

More silence ensued, and the bands, with all their latent potential, made it unbearable. Any time surface thoughts bubbled up, one of the Drenards would force them back down. *Not* thinking, Cole found, required immense concentration, or the sort of daydreaming that came only when it wanted to, not when forced. He gazed through the glass of the domed vehicle as they drove out toward the hot side of the planet, trying to lose himself in deeper, more silent thoughts.

○ ○ ○ ○

The temperature in the shuttle rose noticeably as they drove across the desert. They followed a mostly flat road cut through the small rises, old metal bridges taking them over the shallow gullies. The gullies seemed to grow deeper and wider as they snaked toward the twin suns. In the other direction, they petered out to almost nothing as they twisted toward the city.

After a good number of kilometers, the shuttle turned parallel with the terminator, ushering them far away from the crowds of other hopeful Drenards.

Cole and Molly sat with their shoulders pressed together, each trying not to think too loudly. Heavy gusts of wind would occasionally rock the massive vehicle, causing the occupants to sway as if choreographed. Through the window, Cole followed wisps of fine dust as it hurried after the violent winds. The pent-up power outside the shuttle grew ferocious as they inched closer to the dual suns.

It wasn't long before Cole felt naked with just a tunic on. Defenseless. Another gust slammed the shuttle, and everyone swayed in time, bare shoulders rubbing against each other. The gaiety from the station and the excitement of the Drenard youth had disappeared — moving in the opposite direction. Left alone was a single transport pushing sideways through the wind and filling with a sense of dread.

Losing himself in his new assessment of the inhospitable land, Cole didn't see the squat building until they were nearly upon it. The driver parked on the sunward side, out of the wind. Even so, an angry breeze whistled into the shuttle as the doors cracked open. As he stepped out into the cool air, Cole could hear it battering the rear of the small building, tearing around the corners before whipping through his hair. Everyone's tunics flapped noisily in the persistent blow as they hurried inside, and above all these sounds, Cole could hear an eerie moaning working its way upwind, coming from the canyons beyond.

The two guards took up positions by the entrance, on either side of an old, large stain that spread out from the door and across the carpet. The two officials waved the group farther inside.

"This shelter is for alien use only," one of them thought. *"It has been closed for many of your years; it was reopened for your companion one of your solar days ago. You will rest for one of your nights and then gear up and depart on the Rite."*

Heads nodded to affirm that they heard and understood. The thinking continued: *"The rules are few and simple. Do not follow one another. Do not assist one another. Choose your own path and capture your own Wadi Thooo. If, in the extremely unlikely event you come across one of our youth that has wandered over this far, please do not interfere with his or her quest. The only advice you will get from us is to stick to the shadows, capture your Wadi Thooo, and try to return safely."*

Cole seriously doubted the sincerity of the last bit of advice, even hearing it in his own voice.

Molly raised her hand up to her shoulder. *"What do you mean by 'your companion'?"* she thought.

One of the two officials looked at her, his face expressionless and a chilly blue. *"The one you call Edison. He requested the rite after meeting with Lady Hooo. You will no doubt be sad to hear that he entered the canyons almost one of your days ago and has not been seen since."*

The thinker turned away from them to begin the tour of the facilities. The other official looked at Molly gravely.

"Only Drenards can become Drenards," he thought to all of them.

○ ○ ○ ○

After a brief tour, the red bands were taken back, and all three initiates were locked in separate quarters.

Even with Anlyn's testimony absolving them of any crime, they were still non-Drenards on the race's home planet. Certain rights were not yet theirs to enjoy.

Cole slept fitfully on one of the two small blue cots in his room. When he felt it should be morning, he got up, splashed some water on his face in the adjoining bathroom, and started his stretching routine.

His internal clock must have been off by several hours; it was that long before his hosts stirred and unlocked the doors. Molly was already up, but they had to go into Walter's room to wake him.

A simple meal awaited them, along with some water. Around bites, Cole explained to Walter the reason for the heavy winds, how the heat from one side of Drenard rose, leaving a vacuum, into which the air from the cold side rushed.

Although the boy had asked, he began nodding at the answer as if he already knew it all—a habit of the boy's that drove Cole crazy.

After the meal, the initiates were led to the gear room and assigned new suits and booths in which to change. First, a cloth underlayer went on, followed by the outer lining. These were silver, like foil, and extremely light. The shoulders were a tad low to suit the Drenard frame, which left a pooch of material bunched up on either side. Otherwise, the fit seemed to satisfy the officials.

Next came the boots, and there was a massive assortment of them. Walter had a great time digging through them, hunting for the newest-looking pair. Cole and Molly found some that fit and laced them up over the bottom of the suits. As they moved around and busied themselves with these tasks, the shiny material rubbed on itself and made a racket of sharp hissing. It sounded like three or four Palans on a looting spree.

Once they were suited up, they surveyed one another and took turns giggling. But back in the commons, all levity soon drained away. The Drenard guards stood at attention, the officials rigid and stoic. Cole, Molly, and Walter remembered why they were here—the seriousness of the ritual—and adopted a demeanor to match.

With much ceremony, each of them was given a small version of the guard lance. They lacked a trigger, Cole noted—just solid metal with a point on one end and a hook on the other. Next, each received a cloth map more than half a meter to a side depicting the canyons beyond. To Cole, the layout of the ditches resembled a vascular system or an upside-down tree. Thin and narrow lines, thousands of them, grew larger and fewer in the direction of the suns. A dot of blue ink represented their location in the shelter.

Red bands were passed around for final instructions, their voices filling their heads: *"We will wait for two* of your days. Not even Drenards can survive in the canyons for much longer than that. Since none of you are expected to enter our caste system or work in Drenard society, do not take unnecessary risks."

Molly raised her hand. "Have you heard from our friend? Is he OK?"

"The Judges he came with were resting when we arrived yesterday. Now they have gone."

"Gone where? To help him?"

"They gave him two of your days," was the response.

"So he's still out there?" Molly glanced at Cole. He could tell she cared less and less about this ritual, more concerned with Edison. He could practically *hear* her feelings through the band.

"I'm sorry to say that he would be dead by now," an official said.

"Concern yourself with not joining him," came another thought. The two officials stepped to the side and gestured toward the door.

The sky beyond bled rainbows through the glass. The trio shuffled toward the haunting, gorgeous sight, passing over the large stain in the carpet. One of the guards opened the door, and the other held out his hands. "Return the bands," he thought.

They did, and the three friends exited into a strange world full of howling winds and a chorus of moans from the distant canyons. With the bands gone, they found themselves feeling more alone than ever before, the flapping of their suits loud in their ears, no thoughts in their heads but their own.

The Rite of Wadi Thooo had officially begun.

12

The three of them split up outside the building, Molly walking straight ahead while Cole angled right, the direction from which their shuttle had come. Walter went to the left.

Once they were beyond the break provided by the shelter, the wind began pushing against their backs, propelling them forward. Cole tried to keep the direction of the breeze in mind as he found his pace; the hike back was going to be much more difficult than the walk in.

"Good luck and be safe," he thought to Molly, and then he remembered she couldn't hear; the habit of the red bands not yet worn off.

As he marched along, the loose folds in Cole's suit seemed to flap louder and louder. The noise rose from rustle, through various states of annoyance, and on up to sonically painful. He chose a small gully to follow and looked forward to descending into a canyon to see if the breeze would be reduced. As strong as the wind felt, the gale on the prison rooftop had sounded much stiffer. Whether that was due to altitude or the city serving as some sort of buffer, he couldn't tell.

Less than a kilometer into the hike, he could hear the moaning from the canyons again over the loud flapping from his suit. It sounded as if the entire land was clutching its belly, doubled over and dying. Then the wind freshened, and his suit drowned out the haunting sound once more.

Cole held out his arms, gathering the wind at his back, allowing it to push him along. It felt as if he were sliding down a rock incline, shuffling his feet to keep from falling. He was almost going too fast when he came to the terminator, the line separating night from day.

Pulling his arms in quickly, he leaned backward into the gusts to keep from being thrown forward into the light. Kneeling, Cole marveled at how defined the shadow was, even though it must be cast by a ridge some dozens of kilometers distant. He leaned down to get a closer look. Ahead of him, waves of heat rose off the rock like smoke, the lit areas of stone baking in the sun. Cole thought about how long the rock had endured that state, no respite from the glancing rays, no time to cool off for hundreds, thousands, perhaps millions of years.

He waved his hand through the sunlight and felt just a slight difference in heat. The air remained cooled by the wind from the dark hemisphere. He set his lance down and pulled one hand inside his metallic sleeve for protection. Reaching out, he pressed a finger to the sunlit rock.

A crackle and a hiss made him snap his arm back. He looked at his sleeve and gaped at the melted spot of fabric and then waved his finger in the air to cool the burning. There was no *way* he could step out in that.

He left the disappointing gully, which he could see deepen well into the sunlit side of the planet, and walked along the edge of the terminator. The landscape rose and fell, casting the border between night and day into a jagged and dangerous line. He kept his distance, wary of the steaming stone, until he came to one of the canyons.

Worn by the eternal flow of wind, it was deep enough, and angled just right, to provide a thin path of shade along one wall. Cole leaned over the edge and peered into the steep-walled ditch. Off toward the city, it grew shallow, becoming a rut. In the opposite direction, it deepened into an impressive-looking canyon, one edge lined with shade.

He dropped his lance, making sure it landed flat, and then lowered himself over the edge. Careful not to rip his suit, he pushed off with his toes to clear the rock face and dropped the last few meters into a crouch. The rising walls on either side gave immediate comfort. He hadn't realized how much that wide expanse of land had him on edge until he descended out of it.

Pulling out his cloth map, he determined, with a modicum of confidence, which line he had entered. He tightened his grip on the lance and started walking into the daylight side of Drenard, following the thin trail of shadow that clung to the base of the low cliff.

○ ○ ○ ○

Molly was half a kilometer down her own canyon before she noticed the holes. Several centimeters in diameter and scattered along the cliff wall, they seemed to be the source of the persistent whistling and moaning that filled the land. Molly peered into one of them, but it was too dark to see inside. She pulled her hood back and lowered her ear to one of the larger ones, pressing her head against the rock. A scratching noise seemed to emanate from inside, but over the wind, the flapping of her suit, and the agonized cry of the canyons, it was hard to tell.

Thus far, she had seen no signs of life in the canyons. The thick waves of heat rising up from the stone floor and the occasional dust-filled gusts were the only things moving besides her and her racing thoughts—most of which orbited Edison. Which gully had he gone down? Was his furry hide suited for this atmosphere? She kept an eye peeled for one of these ceremonial lizards, but she was far more interested in finding her friend.

The canyon Molly had chosen to explore stretched ahead in a roughly straight line. At a slight angle to the eternally setting sun, it cast a shady path on one side over a meter wide. It wasn't until the canyon turned in the other direction that she realized how tricky navigating this labyrinth would be. Her dark trail of coolness petered out ahead of her just as an impossible-looking shadow led across the lit canyon to the other side.

Molly stared at the black strip in the middle of the scorching rock. It had no apparent cause. She leaned away from the wall and looked up the canyon, toward the shimmering waves of light. In the distance, something glinted in the sunlight. Something metallic. It was far away, but she could see it spanning the canyon, high up the cliff faces, from one side to the other. It blocked the sunlight, casting a solid pathway down to her location.

It was a bridge made of shade!

Somehow, the Drenards had installed a metal column farther down the canyon, in just the right spot to provide a path to the other side. Molly stepped out onto the dark strip and felt an immediate difference in the heat moving down the center of the canyon, the air warmed by the blistering rock. Her mouth, already parched, felt full of sand. She licked her lips, but the moisture just burned in the dry cracks that had already formed, stinging like venom. She took a few more steps toward the center—

A gust hit her suit suddenly, nearly blowing her into the boiling stone to the side. She dropped her lance and fell into a crouch, fighting to regain her balance. Both hands went out to the shaded bridge to steady herself, the fabric of her suit flapping and trying to carry her away. Molly made herself as compact as possible, inhaling a deep, dry breath as she waited for the wind to subside.

As it did, she looked to her lance, which thankfully landed mostly in the shade. She pulled it back in and reached out, mostly out of curiosity, to prod the other end with a finger. It wasn't just hot, it would have burned her had she continued to touch it. In only a few seconds of exposure.

Swallowing a dry breath, Molly looked up at the ten meters of bridge remaining. She decided to stay on all fours, pushing the lance ahead of her, using a wide base to compensate for the changes in the wind's intensity. The air in the center stifled, even with the movement and the cooler temperatures from the night side blowing through. Sweat dripped from her face, precious fluids splattering down in front of her. Now and then, small beads were carried deeper into the canyon by the wind—out into the harsh sunlight. Molly watched them evaporate before they even reached the ground.

When she got to the other side, she collapsed against the rock wall and glared across the innocent-seeming line of shadow. The seriousness of her task struck her for the first time. Wadi Thooo was not a simple symbolic ritual—it was a *true* rite of passage. A test of will. A stroll through a foreign landscape suddenly had become a fight for survival. By crossing that narrow bridge, Molly had removed the easy, uninterrupted path of shade that led back to safety.

She no longer had room to run.

Glancing along the strip of shade ahead of her Molly saw not a path, but a *ledge*. A fall from it would be no less dangerous than from a great height.

The thought made her dizzy as she rose. She kept one hand on the cliff wall, grasping at the holes in the stone for balance. Gathering her wits, she made sure her map was tucked snugly in her sleeve and pushed forward, keeping the lance to the sunlit side where it was ready to brace her if another gust attacked.

The problem was, she had become so concerned with the danger on *that* side of her that Molly didn't notice something else: the holes in the canyon wall were getting bigger.

○ ○ ○ ○

Walter stood in front of the first hole he could fit his hand inside. He was hot, tired, and annoyed by the wind. He had already walked almost half a kilometer, including several hundred meters down a partly shaded canyon. The Rite wasn't as exciting as he had thought it would be, and he wasn't even sure he wanted to leave the planet, anyway. He'd mostly come along to keep an eye on Molly and make sure Cole wasn't bothering her with all his *boyfriend* nonsense.

He grumbled to himself about this when something in the hole pricked the end of his finger. His annoyance instantly flared up into fear, and then fury. He balled up his hand into a protective fist, but this just expanded his thumb, making it impossible to jerk his arm free.

Walter went kinetic; he created an even tighter fist and yanked furiously on his captured arm. He dropped his spear and flattened his other hand on the rock, pushing and pulling at once, his torso twisting in desperation.

Whatever it was, it got him again on one of his knuckles. He tried to shout above the wind, but his throat was too dry. He whimpered and pleaded and pulled, begging the cliff to release his hand, when suddenly it popped free.

Walter staggered backward and fell, the top of his head landing out in the direct sunlight, a sizzling sound coming from the back of his hood where it touched the rock. He screamed and rolled to the side, his scalp seared with pain, a brief glimpse of Drenard's twin suns burned into his vision.

The frightened portion of him longed to huddle in the shade, to cower and shield himself. But a different part, something from his father, rose up inside. It was angry at being hurt. It was the boiling rage his uncle had been known to stoke up, use for nefarious means, and beat back down after it bubbled over.

He looked at his fingers—two of them were streaked with blood. Walter felt an overwhelming urge to inflict damage in return. To lash out.

Grabbing his lance off the rock, he stood up and shoved it deep inside the offending hole. Rattling it in all directions, he pushed in and out and found enough mad wetness in his throat to toss threats in after whatever had done this to him.

Something within shrieked back. A wail—pitched high and piercing—shot out of the hole like a bullet.

The noise put a shiver up Walter's spine, but he shoved the lance in farther, feeling something softer than rock under one of his stabs.

The blare from within the hole went up even higher and louder—then fell silent.

Walter leaned on the rock, panting furiously. He could feel the wind fluttering his hood, the material pulling on his scalp where the two had melted together. His head pounded with the heat and the danger, and his hand tingled from what must be a toxin of some sort. He wanted to cry or scream but had the moisture for neither.

He looked at the hole, the lance still sticking out of it. Grabbing the lance, he lifted it up to the center of the tunnel and pushed it in as far as he could. When he brought it down, he could feel it rest on something soft. He pulled the lance back, scraping the thing across the bottom of the hole and out where he could reach it.

He grabbed the Wadi Thooo and brought it into the shade. The thing was still alive. Four legs, terminating in sharp claws, twitched slightly. A long, scaly tail with a sharp tip spun in a feeble circle every now and then. Its tapered head lolled to one side, two tongues hanging out past rows of overlapping teeth. The thing's back was covered with iridescent hues that shimmered like the Drenard sunset, especially across two bony stumps that rose from its shoulder blades.

Walter could feel a pulse of life in the creature, its round and white belly expanding and contracting in his hand. The thing was no more than eight inches long from tip to tail. He felt sorry for the Wadi as it seemed to weaken in his hand, its pale life barely distinguishable within.

Then he saw the blood trickling from his fingers and across the lizard's belly. His knees felt weak from the strain of his battle. Looking at the Wadi's rows of teeth, seeing his own blood on them, drained whatever empathy Walter had for the damn thing.

He made a fist, tightening his fingers around the soft underbelly, and squeezed the life out of the small beast. A raspy croak came out of the creature's mouth, fading into a sigh.

The small noise was carried off in the wind, drowned out by the howling of the canyons.

Satisfied—gloriously so—Walter turned to the narrow path and began retracing his shadowy steps. He marched toward the night side of the planet, back in the direction of the shelter, his head held high.

He was a *Drenard* now.

○ ○ ○ ○

Cole crossed over the third bridge slowly; he'd had quite a scare on the last one after the first bridge lulled him into a false sense of windless security. He quickly learned to drag the hooked end of his lance across the ground, helping him brace for the gusts.

As he approached the other side of the canyon, he noticed the strange holes in the side of the cliff had grown to nearly the size of his head. He still couldn't see inside of them or puzzle out their geological origin; he figured he'd keep going until the holes were big enough to explore, if they even increased to such a size. Surely the lizards they were looking for would choose to live in these natural caves rather than scurry across the baking stone.

Tracing the cliff wall with one hand, Cole stumbled upon a remarkable sight: the remains of a tree frozen in the face of the canyon. Split open and petrified, its pulpy interior had long ago been replaced with solid rock. He rubbed the grainy surface, the texture reminding him of his sink counter and the frigid, refreshing water that flowed from it. He wondered how long it had been since the planet was in motion and covered with life.

He was so focused on the beautiful patterns in the shaded rock, he didn't see the glistening eyes that appeared in the hole above him. They sparkled in the ambient light reflecting off his suit. Wrapping two sets of claws over the lip of the hole, the creature tensed itself up, prepared to defend its lair.

But Cole turned and surveyed the heated rock to his left. He looked at his map again and saw how a few other canyons would merge with his own a few kilometers ahead. He gripped his lance and set off deeper into the lighted land, desperate to find a Wadi Thooo.

o o o o

Molly knelt down in front of one of the holes and peered inside. She leaned close, but the light on the shaded side of the canyon only filtered in a few decimeters. Beyond that, it was just mysterious blackness emitting a weak moan. She considered reaching in to her shoulder and groping past the darkness for an egg-filled nest, but the thought of sticking her hand that deep sent a shiver up her spine.

The wind abated for a moment, pitching the moaning even lower. The sound made the deeper parts of the canyon creepier, the small caves more ominous. Molly felt a twinge of fear before kicking herself for being such a wimp. She felt positive Cole and Walter weren't having any problems with their hunt, so she needed to soldier up. If Drenard youth could do this, so could she. In fact, she didn't want to come out of this with any old Wadi—she needed to make sure hers was bigger than Cole's. She'd never hear the end of it otherwise.

She moved on, keeping an eye out for any movement up and down the canyon. At the next bridge, she sat down in the shade to adjust her boots, a loose lace nearly tripping her up during her last crossing.

She pulled her hood back a little and secured a double knot in the laces, and then she noticed her reflection in the side of her boot, her face smudged with sweat and dust, the skin beneath pink and sunburned, even though she hadn't left the shade. She checked her reflection, turning her head side to side—and then got an idea.

She pulled off her boot, rested her lance in her lap, and began weaving the laces around the hooked end. She tied them off around the shaft and cinched them tight, adjusting the angle a little.

Molly stood and walked back the way she'd come, to a hole about the height of her eyes and a little larger than the others. She peered into the darkness, her nose almost inside the lip.

"Hello?" she called into it, her voice ringing metallic as it reverberated in the cylinder of stone.

She heard no response over the wind and the groaning canyon.

Stepping back, she wiggled the boot on the lance one more time to make sure it was secure and then extended it into the sunlight.

The flash nearly blinded her. She'd naturally been looking right at the boot as she reached it beyond the shade, and the thing just happened to be angled right at her face. She turned her head away from the blinding light and nearly dropped the lance, cursing herself for not moving it out at a safer angle. Gradually reopening her eyes, Molly saw an image of the boot everywhere she looked—a white shape dancing in the center of her vision.

She tried to blink it away as she dragged the lance back into the shade. Leaning against the rock wall, she rubbed her eyes with her thumb and forefinger, the sound of her lids against her dry eyes like the click of claw on stone. She squinted across the canyon and waited for her vision to return to normal.

Pulling the cloth map from her sleeve, Molly traced her finger across the branching lines. She had no idea where she was now—the canyon had split and joined too many times to keep up. Getting out of here, however, should be as simple as leaning into the wind.

Since the map was now worthless as a guide, she wiped it across her face to soak up the sweat. She peeled her hood off the rest of the way and swiped the cloth down her throat, absorbing the moisture that had gathered in the depression at the top of her sternum. After wicking up as much as she could, she folded the damp cloth several times and placed it on the nape of her neck, the evaporating sweat cooling the blood that flowed up to her head, the pointed ends of the makeshift handkerchief hanging around in front, dripping precious wetness down her suit. Molly tucked the tips inside her collar, letting the water run down her belly and chest, pulling away even more heat.

With her vision returning and the wind cooling her exposed head, Molly rose to give her improvised flashlight another try. She moved the boot out into the sunlight again, this time looking toward the rock wall while she adjusted the angle. A bright spot of white sunlight splayed out near her knee. She experimented with different ways of maneuvering the lance until she felt some degree of control over the beam.

Moving the light up the wall, she brought her head level with the large hole and directed the beam until it shone straight down it, illuminating an interior acclimated to eternal shade.

She looked in.

Something else was looking out.

13

After another kilometer of arduous hiking, Cole finally found a hole big enough to crawl inside. He felt utterly convinced a family of these lizards would make their home in a nice, cool cave like this. If not, he wasn't sure he could wander much farther into the daylight. He'd been marching for dozens of kilometers, certainly farther than Drenard children could be expected to go.

He had explored a few holes with his lance along the way, scraping nothing but rock. If he couldn't find anything in the cave, he'd start heading back, searching the ground he'd already covered.

Crawling inside, he felt immediately refreshed in the cooler air. The sweat chilled his skin, giving him a renewed vitality; he berated himself for having just considered giving up. He paused in the entrance and enjoyed the echo of the canyon's moans as they filtered through the rock around him.

The air felt less dry in there as well, as if moisture was somehow stored up in the stone.

Looking deeper into the hole, Cole wished he had some way of making a fire or shining a light; he didn't want to step on these little critters if he could avoid it. At this point, he would happily take the easy way out and bring back a Wadi Thooo egg rather than a juvenile or an adult.

Once he felt somewhat rested, Cole pushed his lance ahead of him and began crawling into the darkness. After a few meters, he looked back, comforted by the circle of light behind him. He was accustomed to the blackness of space, but the absence of illumination ahead was different. It pressed in on him from all sides, and with the weight of solid stone behind it, rather than the vacuum of the cosmos.

Cole froze, imagining the rock giving way and collapsing on his back. He would be trapped there, unable to breathe. He could feel his stomach crawl up his neck in panic; he took a deep breath and hurried the wild thought out of his mind.

He concentrated instead on his environment. The details. Under his hand, he could feel the walls weren't perfectly smooth—they had even indentions running along their length. It didn't feel like erosion or anything geological. A deep part of his brain worked on this problem as he scrambled deeper inside.

A noise.

Cole whipped the hood off to free his ears. *What was that sound?*

Something poked him right between the shoulder blades, making him spin around in fear. He tried to get his lance out from underneath him, and he could feel a draft of air descending from the ceiling.

Another tap on the chest. The sound of his metallic suit crinkling as something struck. Cole reached down with one hand and felt something wet.

He brought his hand up to his face. It didn't smell. He touched his finger to his tongue, but couldn't taste anything. Another drop hit him.

Cole reached up into the darkness, searching the ceiling for the source, but his hand kept going up, farther than the tunnel was wide. He tried to sit up—and banged his head on the rock, falling back down.

"Damn!"

He rubbed his forehead, and another drop impacted his suit.

Reaching up again, Cole found the large hole his hand had entered. He could feel a ledge encircling the lip and a thin stream of fluid gathered on it. He probed just over his head and noted the hole didn't extend quite that far; he could feel where he had bumped it.

He tested the fluid again and felt certain it must be water. Fresh water. Just a trickle, like condensation collecting from somewhere. Perhaps the difference in temperature between the cave and the canyon? Could moisture gather on the cool rock and run together through these strange holes?

Cole reached for his map and soaked up as much of the fluid as he could. He squeezed the cloth over his tongue, letting some of the juice run into his mouth.

It felt great.

Refreshing.

He wiped the cloth over the rim, looking for some more moisture; he gathered it up, unappreciative of how natural and universal that tendency would be in *other* living things . . .

o o o o

When Molly saw the two eyes, farther apart and larger than she thought they'd be, she jerked her head back in fear.

The eyes launched out after her.

She tried to bring her lance around, but the boot tied to one end made the weapon unwieldy. The creature was on her head before she could even react.

180

She dropped the lance and brought both hands up, clawing back at the thing clawing her. It was in her hair, then back around her head and inside her hood, and everywhere at once. She could feel slices of agony across her face as claws opened her flesh to the dry, dusty air. As soon as she got one hand on it, she felt a sharp pain as teeth sank down to bone, gnawing on her wrist. She screamed and pushed away from the wall, falling to the ground in a heap. The vicious thing thrust off her, scampered up the wall, and wiggled into its hole.

Molly looked at her hand—it was dripping blood and burning as if on fire. She touched her face and felt the scratches, the pads of her fingers coming away slick with more blood. The sight of so much of it made her feel faint. Reaching behind her neck, she groped for her map, a perfect bandage—but it wasn't there. She rolled over on all fours and looked around on the shady path.

The handkerchief was gone.

That damn thing had stolen her map.

No, she realized, *it stole my sweat!*

These things go after *wetness.* And they're much bigger than she had thought they'd be. Meaner, too.

Molly peered up the wall at the dozens of holes gaping back at her. She glanced left and right and saw hundreds, thousands more of them ranging up and down the canyon. Looking over her shoulder, across the river of sunlight and at the other wall, she realized she was surrounded.

The holes weren't a geological feature—they'd been chewed out of solid rock!

And they got bigger the farther in the canyons they went.

The Rite of passage, the way Drenards might use this as the basis of a hierarchical society—it all made perfect sense. For all Molly knew, she'd stumbled into the realm of upper-middle management, or higher. And they'd sent her there with no instructions, completely ignorant. They probably didn't expect any of them to return. She thought of Edison again and wondered what had happened to her big Glemot friend.

Meanwhile, the eyes came back to the edge of the hole, looking for more water.

Molly picked up her lance and ran, one foot bare, past hundreds of holes—and into the wind.

oooo

Cole held the moisture in his mouth and just let his body absorb it. He lay on his back, his head pointing into the unknown. Beyond his feet, he could see the small disk of sunlight that marked his way in.

He reached up to gather some more water when a shape moved across the circle of light.

Or was that his foot? No. There it was again.

It was either really big or really close. Or both.

But that didn't make any sense. He had come in that way without passing anything.

Cole held his breath, one hand still up in the lip of the hole above him, when he realized what had happened: there was no telling how many shafts he'd passed before he stumbled on that one.

He shoved his map into the neck of his suit and reached for the lance. He held it out in front of him, pulling his feet in to scoot backward, deeper into the hole.

The thing moved across the entrance of the tunnel once more; he could see its outline. These were not the little lizards that Dani had described. Cole wasn't sure if he should crawl toward it with his lance and attack—or retreat into the darkness. He decided to move back and see if it would scamper up the dripping shaft; maybe it'd stop for a drink and become an easy kill.

Shuffling backward, Cole felt empty space below his hand and nearly fell down the hole cut out of the floor behind him.

"Damnit!" he uttered. One hand went into the shaft, and his other arm collapsed with the unexpected shift in weight. Cole fell back on his shoulder blade, his arm wrenched at an odd angle.

He lost his grip on the lance, and it became pinned beneath him.

The silhouette froze.

That noise just came from its favorite drinking spot.

The large Wadi Thooo rushed forward to defend its territory—its precious resources.

o o o o

Molly ran, leaning into the wind, until she came to the first bridge of shade. She had a full-blown fear reaction raging through her body—every hole seemed poised to spit out a legion of attackers. She could feel hundreds of invisible beasts stalking her heels, ready to run up her back and claw her to death at any time.

The sight of the bridge crushed this imaginary fright with an immediate one. She came to a panting halt, fell to her knees, fought to regain her breath. Facing the wind, she allowed it to push air deep into her lungs, but it was dry and chalky, offering little relief. She glanced over at the holes in the wall beside her, then back to the narrow path of cool rock.

She needed to get ahold of herself.

She needed to get her boot back on.

Fumbling with the knots, she tried to work the thing free from the lance. She constantly shifted her eyes up to the holes, not comforted in the least by the many kilometers of them she'd walked by without incident. They were *all* a threat after that last encounter.

By the time she worked the laces free and forced her foot back into the boot, her heart had calmed down somewhat, her adrenaline subsiding. She inspected her wounded hand and touched the gashes in her face— she needed to concentrate.

It's just an alien landscape and some pesky critters, she told herself. *I came out here to get one of them, and that's what I plan on doing.*

She nodded, sealing the resolution as she peeled the protective suit down to her waist, working her arms free. The outfit was designed to retain moisture, to protect her from direct sunlight, but she didn't plan on falling out of the shade. She worked the suit all the way down over her boots, leaving her in just the white jumpsuit liner underneath.

Using the sharp end of the lance, she cut the material at her waist, ripping it all the way around herself before pulling the fabric over her head. She still had her legs and hips protected and her boots on, but was otherwise naked. The wind on her sweaty body felt good, cooling her off a little, even though it was mostly a hot, dry breeze.

She cut one of the sleeves off and dabbed her face with it. The material stuck to her flesh, jerking on her clotting wound as she pulled it back. She winced as a jolt of pain shot down her spine, making her dizzy. The sleeve came away spotted with blood. She decided to leave her face alone and tied the fabric around the wound in her hand instead. Dried tracks of red already ran in jagged trails from wrist to elbow, but the bandage would prevent any more from leaking out.

Just that little bit of first aid made her feel better. Stronger. More in control.

Holding up the metallic fabric, Molly looked at a distorted reflection of her gashed face. The blood streaked back to her ear on one side, but didn't seem to be flowing anymore. She thought about the thing that had done this to her. All for a few drops of salted water. She wondered if it had meant to harm her this much, or if it had meant to harm her *more*. Was the violence indiscriminate? The thoughtless scampering of a thirsty creature?

She wanted to catch one and find out.

Molly used the torn top of the jumpsuit to soak up the sweat running in rivulets down her bare chest. She approached one of the holes cautiously. It was roughly the same size as the last one she'd messed with, perhaps a little smaller. She placed most of the moist material on the lip of the hole and kept a grip on the sleeve. With the metallic suit wrapped around her other hand, like a gauntlet, she propped her lance against the cliff within easy reach. Just in case it came to that.

The trap was set. She didn't know how long it would take, so she concentrated on the most minor of sensations: the sweat evaporating from her body in the wind, the constantly shifting dying sounds that groaned through the canyons, the stinging of the wounds on her face.

She fell into a trance of patience and control—of hypervigilance.

And waited.

○ ○ ○ ○

The silhouette reached Cole as he tried to free himself from the hole behind him. It came up his legs with the heft of a small gator, not like a lizard at all. Cole wrenched his hand from the hole and reached up with both arms to fend the thing off.

Loud, snapping jaws fought through his hands. He clutched at the thing's neck and tried to keep the gnashing, clacking teeth away from his face. Sharp claws raked his chest, ripping the fabric of his suit open and stinging his skin underneath.

The beast clambered forward, its legs scraping the sides of the tight tunnel, forcing Cole back toward the hole. Not knowing how far down it went, he strained back against the creature, pushing himself closer to the dangerous maw and furious, lashing arms.

The thing's hind legs tore into Cole's thighs, finding better purchase in suit and flesh than they did with hard rock. Cole couldn't believe the thing's strength; it was half his size but felt twice as powerful. His arms vibrated with the effort of holding back the attack. When he felt as if they were about to give out, he let them. Using the last bit of energy they possessed, he directed the monster up toward the ceiling and allowed his head to fall back in the hole behind him. He felt the momentum of the animal's anger propel it over his head.

The beast landed with a shriek on the other side of the shaft; he could hear it scratch madly to right itself—to rejoin the battle. Cole felt for the hole above him, stood up inside of it, and stepped onto the wet lip, balancing the weight of his body on the edge of his boots. He tried to shake some feeling back into his tired arms as a shape moved along below him, back in the direction *he* needed to go.

He took some deep breaths, leaning into the damp wall. He tried reaching up, but the shaft went beyond his hands. He needed to go down for his lance, anyway.

The question was, did he go after the Wadi? Or take his chances going deeper into the cave? Would the tunnel taper to an end, or would it open out into the neighboring canyon? The only way he could fight one of those things was outside these blasted tubes of rock.

188

They had the advantage of leverage here, and his only weapon was useless if he couldn't swing it around.

Cole didn't want to wait for the thing to figure out he'd ascended the shaft. He wasn't sure how long he would last without tending to his wounds anyway, so he lowered himself back down as quietly as he could. Glancing to the exit, he saw the dark shape slinking back and forth across the distant light. Looking the other way, he couldn't make out an end to the tunnel. He decided he would explore a little, let the thing hunt for him in the wrong direction while his strength returned.

Grabbing his lance off the tunnel floor, Cole stretched across the hole he had nearly fallen through and moved silently into the blackness.

Behind him, he left a trail of moisture.

Thick, and slowly clotting.

oooo

It seemed as if an hour passed before Molly's shirt twitched.

She jumped in front of the hole and lunged in with her protected hand, but there was nothing there. It must have been the wind.

She rubbed fresh sweat off her body and put the lure back in position.

More time went by. She felt completely alone and removed from the rest of the universe. Even the agonized moans that called out around her did nothing to provide any sense of company. Her only companions were the twin stars and the fixed shadows they cast, their unmoving nature turning every second into a trapped eternity.

Focusing on the shirt, Molly tried to make it the sole entity in her awareness, but the sight of her own valuable fluids dripping down the rock wall distracted her. Tormented her. The precious trickle evaporated long before it reached the ground, a miniature waterfall that led nowhere—just faded out of existence.

Her shirt moved again. The twitch coincided with a slight gust of wind, so she assumed it was another false alarm, but then the entire lure disappeared into the hole as if sucked inside a vacuum.

The sleeve made a loud, ripping noise.

"No!" she muttered, lunging for the hole. She pulled gently with the sleeve as her other arm dove in after the disappearing shirt.

As soon as she touched the creature tugging on the lure, she felt it focus its energy on her. It felt smaller than the last one she'd fought, wrapping itself around her hand and trying to tear through the fabric. Molly pulled it out of the hole, and the thing shrieked at her. It was as long as her forearm and twice as thick. She fell to the ground and pinned it on its back, its teeth fighting through the layers of her makeshift glove.

Molly gripped the sleeve of the wet lure and flung it in circles around her other hand, protecting it. She used it to hold the creature's jaw, trying to figure out if there was a safe place to hold a Wadi so it couldn't bite her.

She briefly considered putting a knee on its belly and forcing the life out of the thing, but it was smaller than the last one, and this wasn't the same monster that had gashed her face and hand. In fact, both of them were just looking for water, a craving Molly could easily understand.

She castigated herself for being weak, but a silly urge overcame her: she had to get this creature back to the shelter, alive, and only *then* release it back into the shade. The challenge fixed itself in her mind as a way to beat this inhospitable land. A way to prevent it from beating her.

Using some of the suit material hanging off her right hand, she started wrapping the Wadi's mouth, sealing it tight. The poor thing began panting out of its long nose, its soft, white belly rising and falling with quick breaths. But at least it stopped fighting as madly; its legs just pawed at the air, looking for something to push against.

Molly clenched her left fist and squeezed some of her sweat out, allowing it to run into the Wadi's mouth as it strained against the binding. This made it twitch a little more at first, and it clawed for the fabric with its front paws before it finally settled back down.

She took her first good look at the specimen, the iridescent scales along its back and arms glowing, even in the shade. Two bones protruded from the back of the thing's shoulders, stumps with no discernible purpose, like vestigial limbs. She worked quickly, trying to not get distracted by the beauty of the thing; she wrapped her flapping suit around the creature's entire body, tight enough to hold it still, but hopefully not so tight it couldn't breathe. She pressed the bundle to her bare chest.

The Wadi kicked a few more times, struggling against the metallic material, but Molly had it under control now. She could cradle it with one arm and pin it to her body as she soaked up more sweat. She dripped the fluids into the small crack along its mouth and felt the creature go limp with every drink.

Molly had no idea how long the thing—or she—would survive without proper water. Salt-free water. She double-checked the bundle to make sure the Wadi was secure before giving her lance a long look. She couldn't carry both, which meant risking her life in an attempt to preserve the strange animal's.

Turning around, she surveyed the first of many shady bridges that awaited, strong gusts tearing across it and down the blistering canyon. Molly crouched low and set off across the narrow path.

She left behind her only means of defense, propped up against the pockmarked stone. Both her arms tended to the prize against her chest as a harsh, hot wind ripped across her bare back.

○ ○ ○ ○

Cole worked his way across the next hole he discovered in the tunnel's floor. Looking over his shoulder, he could no longer see the light from the entrance. It had been lost around a bend, or perhaps something blotted it out. His hand slipped in a puddle of water, and another series of drips pelted his back. He didn't linger to refresh himself.

He crawled forward, the tunnel not getting any bigger or smaller. Cole hoped that meant it bored clear through to the next canyon. He stopped scrambling along and patted for his map, reassuring himself he still had it. As soon as he did so, he heard it: something moving behind him.

He took off as fast as he could crawl, the stupid lance slowing him down and forcing him to move with his knuckles on bare rock. When something bumped into the bottom of his boot, he kicked back at it, making solid contact and setting the tunnel on fire with screeches of animalistic rage.

Cole concentrated on moving away from the sounds, groping ahead for more holes in the floor, hoping the ceiling wouldn't start constricting down around him. Once again, he felt the amount of solid stone on all sides, the fact that dozens of these things could be coming—homing in on the racket he was making.

His vision spotted with fear.

No. He wasn't seeing stars. That was light!

Two spots, both perfect circles, as if the tunnel forked ahead. Cole hugged the right side and ignored the pain in his knees and shins, scrambling along as fast as he could. Behind, the angry, high-pitched sounds grew into peals of fury. There was no way he would get to the exit before it clawed up his back.

Cole dropped to his belly and spun over, bringing his knees up to his chin.

When he saw the blackness shift in front of him, he shot himself straight, kicking into the center of the rock tube.

It was poorly timed. Instead of landing a full blow, the thing slammed into the bottom of his extended feet. The creature made a vicious noise; Cole tried stabbing his lance toward the sound. It made a hit, but unfortunately it was the dull, hooked end. He had brought the spear into the tunnel expecting to defend *ahead* of himself—and the length of the weapon made it impossible to spin it around.

The impact must have stunned the thing, as the noise stopped and nothing clawed at him. Cole lurched back toward the dual lights, his body on fire from the constant impact of rock on bone.

Weary arms propelled him forward as the light ahead gradually grew brighter and bigger. Then, more scraping sounds came from behind—approaching fast.

The last ten meters were as psychologically painful as they were physically demanding. Cole began to lunge, rather than crawl, throwing the spear ahead of him and launching himself with his legs. On the third push, his arms failed to support him, and his chin scraped the floor of the tunnel. He could hear the large animal clawing up behind.

Leaving his useless spear where it lay, he pushed himself toward the light.

The *very* bright light.

When Cole saw the thin wedge of sunlight shining into the lip of his exit, he realized what a huge mistake he'd made. He'd assumed the tunnel would come out on a shaded path, but it didn't. It faced the eternal day.

There is no solace out that hole, he realized. And the lizard was almost on him.

He didn't have his spear anymore. Cole tried to kick the thing again, but it had learned: he heard it scampering along the ceiling above him. He moved forward, closer to the steam wafting into the hole, and rolled onto his back just as the creature dropped down. It landed on his thighs and came straight for his throat.

Cole pushed on the squirming beast, which just forced him closer to the deadly light. He could feel the heat from the twin suns where they baked a thin slice of the tunnel's interior. The giant lizard strained for his neck, pawing at the sides of the tunnel to push forward.

It drove Cole's head into the sun.

It felt as if his hair were on fire. His hood was still bunched around his neck, leaving his ears open for danger but his scalp exposed. Cole tried to retract his head down into his shoulders, but this just let the lizard's snapping jaws get closer to their prize.

He had to save his scalp, no matter the cost. He stopped pushing on the lizard and threw his forearm across his neck, just as he pulled his head out of the light. The lizard bit down on it immediately, locking its jaw above his wrist—teeth grinding against bone.

Cole let out a feeble scream. He grabbed one of the beast's arms, and with both hands, he lifted it over his head and out of the hole. The pain on his exposed flesh was intense, like some sort of toxin coursing through his arm, but the lizard had it worse. The thing hissed as it cooked, the white underbelly frying in the direct light. It tried to twist its back toward the rays, but Cole had its arm gripped tight; he moved the tender spot around even more.

The jaw finally loosened, its teeth sucking noisily out of Cole's arm. He attempted to pull the wounded animal in by its leg, but the weight was too much, his own arm at too unusual an angle.

His prize slipped out of his grasp and fell down—into the direct sunlight.

14

Molly continued to forge her way through the dry wind. She was pretty sure the shade bridge she'd just crossed was the last one, and the air seemed to be a bit cooler as well. As she trudged forward, her shoulder bumping along the side of the canyon, she dreamed of the shelter beyond the terminator.

She dreamed of glass after glass of water, even of hearing how much smarter Cole and Walter had gone about their rites.

The bundled Wadi squirmed against her chest; Molly squeezed a little more moisture in its mouth. The thing had been acting more and more content for the past few kilometers. That, or it was slowly dying.

Her thoughts drifted to Edison, any hope of rescuing him evaporating with the last of her body's water. She imagined being ten times the size of a Glemot, able to scoop him up and cradle him in her arms. She thought of the way he'd done this for Anlyn, the way she was trying to do this for the Wadi. She felt large and small at the same time, able to do so much for one, and almost nothing for the other.

When the leading edge of the terminator came into view, Molly confused it for another bridge at first. It filled her with a moment of panic, and then she saw that the blackness went on and on.

She sobbed with relief.

Raw exhilaration overcame her as she crossed the line from day to night. She was tired, wounded and dehydrated. She was several kilometers from the shelter. But she felt free. She could walk in any direction she wanted. She could lie down on the cool stone in the center of the cursed canyon, the walls of which grew shorter and shorter toward the horizon.

Molly picked up her pace. The squat building she needed to reach—where Cole could nurse her back to health—should be just a few more kilometers straight ahead. Clutching the Wadi against the chill, she lowered her head into the steady gusts and marched toward the glow of lights from the city beyond the horizon.

Behind her, the canyons wailed, almost as if mourning her departure.

O O O O

Cole finished bandaging his arm with a torn piece of shirt. He couldn't decide what to do next. It was a long crawl back to the safe side of the tunnel, but at least there were watering spots along the way where he could clean his stinging wounds and quench his thirst.

The problem was: he was in no shape to fight another of those things. If he encountered one during the long march upwind, he'd be mauled for sure. Beyond surviving and escaping the canyons with his wounds, there was still the matter of having a Wadi to complete the rite.

One had just died within a few meters of him, close enough for him to hear its shrieks, but there was no way to claim his prize.

Or was there? Cole grunted and rolled to his knees. It was slow going with only one arm, but he made his way back to the discarded lance. Tossing it ahead of him, he moved to the edge of the light leaking into the mouth of the hole.

He took his time replacing the metallic hood and adjusting it. He also pulled his left hand down into his sleeve, gripping the lance through the material. Moving the weapon out into the direct sunlight, he let the rays hit his hand. It was just like his experiments back at the terminator—the suit protected him from the light, at least temporarily. He just had to be sure not to touch the heated rock.

Cole inched forward and rested on his damaged arm as close to the steaming marble as he could. Once again, the lance was turned the wrong way. This time, he needed the hooked end, and it faced away from the mouth of the tunnel. He extended the long weapon all the way out the hole in order to spin it in his hand.

With the awkward fabric spoiling his grip, he almost dropped the thing as he rolled it around in midair. As it bobbled out of his grip, he lunged and seized it at the last minute, grunting from the effort.

He shook his head with relief and angled his face away from the sun before sticking it out to look down for the Wadi. As his exposed face passed by the lip of lit rock, the heat radiating up reminded him to be careful.

The moaning outside the hole went up an octave as a gust of wind coursed through the canyon. Cole peered down the wall and spotted the Wadi, charred black in places, its skin melting off where it touched bare rock. He lowered the lance, the hook sinking into the soft and bloated belly with a sharp, puncturing sound. He pulled himself back inside the hole and used his injured arm to help hoist the lifeless beast up, dragging it into the protective shade.

He let out his held breath, then pulled in a new, hot, dry one. He had his Wadi Thooo.

But he was a long way from becoming a Drenard.

○ ○ ○ ○

The lights in the shelter were on, making it easy to spot even against the glow of the city beyond. Several shapes moved inside. Molly hoped one of them was Cole.

When she was a hundred meters from the structure, the door burst open and Walter ran out, his tunic flapping in the wind. As he rushed to join her, Molly noticed the bandage around his head.

"What happened?" she asked, her voice a hoarse whisper in a windstorm.

Walter didn't seem to hear.

"I'm not allowed to help you!" he shouted, falling in beside her and matching her weary pace. "I'm a Drenard!" he added.

Molly could feel Walter leering at her bare arms and back; she had no cover other than the bundled Wadi across her chest, but she was too exhausted to care.

"Where's Cole?" Molly shouted, but her words were dry paper tossed into a blaze.

They marched the last dozen meters in silence. The Wadi had stopped moving nearly an hour earlier.

Molly felt sad for the little creature. It was strange, but she felt as if she'd bonded with the poor thing during their long march to safety. Safety for her, at least.

The Drenard guards were kind enough to open the doors for her. Molly stumbled across the threshold and sank to the stained carpet, the sudden absence of wind leaving a dull roar in her sore ears. She bent all the way forward until her forehead touched the soft floor, her small, motionless companion nestled between her stomach and thighs.

Exhaustion overwhelmed her, the end of the ordeal bringing an emotional release. She sobbed with relief, but there wasn't enough water in her body to form the tears. Blue hands moved all around her, joined by a chorus of cooing. Someone draped a blanket over her back and grasped her shoulders—someone else took her bundle away. A glass of water came to her lips, the wetness burning her cracked skin.

The Drenards surrounded her—tending to wounds and helping her to another room. In her haze she saw flashes of Walter scurrying in and out of the way, but no sign of Cole.

She kept asking everyone where he was, but without the bands, none of the words were relayed.

All she had was a head full of her own, terrible, thoughts.

PART VIII
THE CANYON QUEEN

"To prophesize, simply speak on those things that have already occurred."

~The Bern Seer~

15

Molly awoke in an unfamiliar room. Her entire body was sore, her stomach hollow. She reached up to her head and felt a tugging at her arm, looked down at the IV taped to her vein, confused.

The ordeal of the previous day came back like a foggy dream. She sat up, and a Drenard guard stiffened in the chair by the door. Their eyes met and his head bowed slightly, his chin dipping down toward his tunic. Molly looked at his lance, its point touching the floor.

She had a strange first thought: *I lost my lance.*

She swung her legs over the side of her bed, and her eyes followed the tube leading out of her arm up to the canister of fluids attached to the wall. As she slid her weight down onto wobbly legs, the guard came over to assist her. He popped the canister off its mount, held it aloft, and stood back a few paces. Molly thought about reaching for the blasted thing and doing it on her own, but both of her arms felt too heavy to raise, much less support something else.

She checked the coverage of her tunic and saw that it was a new one. Longer and more colorful, a straight-fitting dress laced up both sides with ribbon.

In the bottom of her vision, she could see something white on her face. Molly reached up and felt the bandage on her left cheek, saw the wrapping on her wounded hand. She shot the guard a look and shuffled toward the door.

As soon as she emerged, one of the officials rose and strode over to help support her. The two Drenards guided her to a soft chair in the lobby, and Molly saw they had the area to themselves. She settled into the upholstery and looked down at the bandage on her wounded hand. It no longer stung from the toxins.

An official approached her with a red band, the sight of it filling her with joy. It was as if she were a mute watching someone return with her voice.

"Hello?" she thought, testing to see if it was in place.

"Hello, Lady Fyde. Congratulations on completing the Drenard Rite of Wadi Thooo."

"It certainly wasn't what I was expecting," she thought, injecting as much venom in the tone as she could. *"How are my friends? Is everyone back? Has Edison—has he shown up?"* She had so much to ask, and not all of it kind. She rested her head back against the chair and reveled in the ability to think her mind, rather than speak it. Her mouth still felt full of sand, and every muscle in her body ached.

"The little one returned very quickly with his Wadi Thooo. Not much of a specimen, though. The other human has not returned. Your large companion has been gone too long, I'm afraid. This last will likely sadden Lady Hooo greatly; she—"

"Anlyn?"

"Informally, yes. I believe she had feelings for the hairy one." The cadence and vocabulary were strange, different from Dani's, but were still in her own voice.

*"I have feelings for them **both**,"* Molly thought. *"We need to go look for them."* She tried to think it forcefully. She leaned forward as if to rise, but her body refused to cooperate. It was weaker than her will.

The Drenard official raised a hand, and the guard paused halfway between helping her and halting her.

"You are not in any shape to go back out there, Lady Fyde. And even if you were, the Light Side is no place for a female Drenard. I would not allow you to risk yourself."

"Those are my friends!" Molly pointed toward the window, her hand heavy as a brick.

"And they assumed the risks that go with the Rite—"

"That's **crap***! You told us* **nothing***! You sent us out to* **die***!"* Molly found it easy to scream in her thoughts. Her throat even formed the words—she could hear them in her jaw. Her fist felt lighter as she shook it at both male Drenards, aliens more than twice her size.

The guard looked away, out the window and toward the bright canvas of colors. The official hung his head low, showing a humility Molly had not seen out of any of these people. Not even Dani.

"We apologize, Lady Fyde. We have been discussing this since you returned from your Rite. We were told lies about you. I think we even lied to **ourselves** *about you."*

Molly had no idea what he was thinking about. She tried to force up one of the questions roiling below her surface thoughts, but they were tangled with one another.

The official supplied one of his own before she could unknot them: *"Do you know why Lady Hooo ran away from Drenard?"*

Molly shook her head. *"I didn't know she did. I always assumed she was captured, a prisoner from the war—"*

The official bristled at this, his shoulders coming up to his ears; his eyes were wide, his mouth frozen in a lopsided grimace. *"Our women do not go to war.* **Ever!***"* He shook his head and ran his long blue fingers down the front of his tunic, calming himself. His chest rose and fell with deep breaths before he continued: *"Lady Hooo ran away from Drenard. She has been forgiven, but it was a great sin. It was a very bad thing she did."*

"Why did she run away?" Molly asked, but she already suspected the answer. She'd practically guessed it during that reunion dinner in the Drenard prison.

The guard turned to the official, and the official nodded. Molly realized, all of a sudden, that she had no idea which one she was communicating with. Both, perhaps?

"Lady Hooo is a very important person," one of them thought. *"Any son of hers will be fourth in line to the Drenard throne. She was to marry Bodi Yooo two years ago—"*

"Who's Bodi Yooo?" Molly forced in.

The two Drenards exchanged another glance, then her own voice continued in her head:

"Bodi is a very important member of the Circle, our governing body. He is the official who OKed your Rite of passage. He is also one of the two men who brought your large friend here and oversaw his Rite."

"What?"

"We are sorry, Lady Fyde. We were instructed to give you no guidance for the Rite. We were told to give you a lance and our oldest maps. No water. No food. And—"

There was a moment of silence in Molly's head. It brought the sound of wind wrapping around the shelter into focus.

"—and we were told that none of you would ever become Drenards. That all of you are as weak as our women but without the grace that makes them so wonderful and so important to protect."

"You brought us here to die."

Nobody answered. She had said it out loud. To herself.

"You brought us here to die," she repeated. In her thoughts and for everyone to hear.

"And you have proven us wrong. You brought back a female Wadi Thooo—alive! It is an incredible sign for—"

"My friends are going to die because of jealousy? Because we're aliens? We brought Anlyn here because she's our **friend**. To **help** her. And her fiancée is going to kill us rather than **thank** us?"

Everyone's thoughts fell silent. Molly looked through the glass at the alluring bands of colors waving in the desert heat. Reaching up, she touched the bandages adhered to her face. She would absorb as much fluid as she could and then set off in search of Cole.

"We are sorry—"

Molly grabbed her red band and tossed it off in disgust. She seized her IV canister and rose to fix a glass of water and search for solid food.

The two Drenards stared at each other as she rummaged through the pantry. She didn't care what they were thinking. She grabbed some protein bars and juice pouches, both wrapped up in reflective foil and likely meant for initiates to take out on their rite. She slammed them on the counter in disgust. She felt on the verge of covering her face and crying—or throwing something. Yesterday's ordeal, combined with this rage and sadness, filled her with one brand of energy while it drained away another.

She left the rations on the counter and turned toward the preparation room to gather a new set of gear. Before she went, she spun on the Drenards, wanting them to see the anger on her face . . .

But it evaporated like sweat on boiling stone.

She could see a shape beyond the glass, framed against the shivering colors in the sky.

Hunched over and shuffling, it stumbled forward, but Molly would have recognized him even as a dot on the horizon.

Cole.

She dropped the IV canister, ripped the needle out of her arm, and moved as fast as she could around the counter and toward the door. The Drenard guard hurried over to stop her, but the official shot up and grabbed his arm, pulling him back.

Molly exploded out of the shelter.

The two Drenards turned their backs, not wanting to know if any rules were violated and willing to swear before the Circle if they had known: that none were.

oooo

It was the longest fifty meters of her life. The breeze slid through her tunic and the cold stone shocked her feet, but she didn't care. In the soft glow of light radiating out of the shelter lobby, she could see Cole—and a mixture of heartbreak and joy overwhelmed her senses. She couldn't even hear the winds or the distant groans from the sun-baked canyons.

Cole dropped something from his shoulders as she approached, and then he practically fell into her arms. She didn't know where she got the strength to catch him—but she did.

He smelled like burned meat, hot skin, and sweat. Molly was just glad to feel his warmth. She cried and rubbed his back and said something over and over again. It was the third or fourth utterance before she even heard it, before she recognized her own voice, if not the words:

"I love you. I love you. I love you."

He pressed his cracked and dry lips to her neck, resting them there, unable to purse them or even create enough moisture for a kiss. Molly could hear him trying to talk. To whisper something in response. But his voice was not strong enough, his mouth too dry.

Molly didn't care. She knew what he was saying.

She wrapped him up even tighter, squeezing him with a new strength, a power she didn't know she had.

○ ○ ○ ○

When she realized how stupid she'd been to not bring a juice pouch to him, and that the embrace was keeping him away from the medical care he needed, Molly broke free and reached for the thing he'd dropped.

Cole stopped her. Gave her a look.

She understood.

He grabbed one end of the object, and Molly recognized it as a larger version of her Wadi. *Much* larger. She felt a wave of panic and fear at the sight of the beast, at the sudden knowledge that Cole had fought with it. The emotions were too late to do any good, but they tortured her anyway, useless fear chemicals pumping through her bloodstream. She could taste them like metal on the back of her tongue.

She turned to the shelter and led the way, breaking the wind in two for him. Through the glass, she could see the Drenards with their backs to the windows, ignoring her and Cole. Molly forced aside a new wave of anger and jerked open the door, holding it as Cole staggered across the threshold and fell forward into the lobby, crashing against the carpet.

Molly hurried inside to help him, but he was already on his back, pulling his vanquished foe up his body, its tail crossing the doorway just as the glass barrier slammed shut.

Immediately, the two Drenards went into action, calling out with loud, soothing sounds.

Another guard came out of the sleeping quarters, and several pairs of hands—human and alien—lifted Cole. As a group, they took him to the first-aid room and placed him on the same table Molly had recently vacated. They cut off what was left of his heatsuit and underbarrier and swabbed his arm clean for a needle. Molly held his other hand and brushed his brown hair back from his handsome face. Grime and scrapes made one side look as if it had been dragged across rough stone.

His lips parted; his tongue moved across them, running over the open splits. He looked up at Molly and smiled, which made the cracks look even worse. She hushed him, cooing like a Drenard as several blue hands tended to his wounds.

It took almost an hour to clean and dress his myriad scrapes. Several ointments had to be added to each wound, and a few of the larger gashes in his thighs and across his chest needed stitching. The damage to his forearm required special attention. Molly had to look away as they opened it up and flushed it with water. Normally, she had no problem with the sight of damaged flesh, but there was something about knowing that this flesh was *his*.

By the time they were done, Cole was fast asleep— whether due to the drugs in the IV, the pain, or the exhaustion—Molly couldn't tell. She pulled a chair close to the bed and held his hand, stroking the back of it as fluids dripped into his system. One guard acted as if he would stay, but a look from Molly cut across their language barrier, articulate in a thousand tongues.

The couple was left alone while Cole slept and Molly thought. Thought about what they had gotten themselves into on their enemy's home world. Thought about how much Dani had known of the politics involved. About whether Edison could be alive out there and how they could find him. She imagined flying *Parsona* into the desert, landing on the buttes, and using the loudhailer to call for him. She had no doubt the taboo against such actions was strong, but she didn't care.

Cole slept a long time, and Molly's mind zoomed out, focusing on an even larger picture. Her supposed mother was still trapped in a computer, her father in need of rescue. And a pointless war needed to end. Less serious but still troubling: her old nightmares had returned ever since arriving on Drenard, and they would likely plague her until she returned to the ship or found her family.

Then there was her own Navy, who made their every move constricted and dangerous; by now they must be doggedly searching everywhere for *Parsona*.

It seemed no place in the galaxy was safe.

In a very short period of time, she had visited places that few would ever see, and they all looked the same in that regard. Everyone seemed to be out for themselves, and she and her friends were just in the way.

Molly found herself growing sleepy; she began dwelling on how nice it must be to not care. How much easier if only she didn't feel the impulse to do what was right by others. It would be such a simple life.

Simple and lonely . . .

16

M olly awoke in the first aid room, curled up in the large chair, alone. Both medical beds stood empty. At first she thought Cole's return had been a dream, and then she noticed the remnants of his clothes balled up in the trashcan and signs of heavy bandaging strewn across one of the tables.

She stood up from the chair, stiff and sore as she had been the day before—but a new pain gnawed at her. A healthy one. Hunger. A renewed appetite.

She left the first aid room and checked the initiate quarters Cole had used their first night there.

Empty.

She went out to the lobby and found Walter digging into a steaming plate of food.

"Man, that smells wonderful," she said, her voice sounding somewhat close to normal.

Walter snapped his head up to look at her. "It'ss your Wadi," he hissed.

She froze, her face flushed with heat.

"Jusst kidding," Walter stammered, seeming to get that the joke hadn't gone over well. He crammed another bite into his sneer. "You want me to make you ssome?"

"I'll do it," Molly murmured. She grabbed one of the packages from the pantry and looked at the symbols on the silver wrapper. It was more of the Drenard writing her mother had shown her: piles of sticks that she couldn't believe anyone could discern at a glance.

She looked at Walter and his sneering broadened, his eyes wide as if waiting on something.

"Show me," she sighed.

The small Palan dropped his utensil and scurried over to her side. He busied himself with buttons on the electric oven and placed the packet inside, arranging it carefully. He constantly glanced at Molly to make sure she was watching appreciatively.

"Where is everybody?" she asked.

"I don't know. Time iss funny here. I can't tell if we sshould be awake or assleep." The machine beeped, and Walter moved the package to a plate, opening it up carefully and spilling the food out. "Ssome Drenardss left sseveral hourss ago. They took much sstuff with them." He rummaged for utensils in a drawer and presented them to Molly.

"Thanks," she said, more out of habit than feeling. She plopped down to eat while Walter beamed at her. She could see over the counter and through the glass that the shuttle was still parked up front, out of the wind. "Have you seen Cole?"

Walter frowned. He pointed straight up. "Outsside," he hissed.

Molly dropped her fork, grabbed a juice pouch and ration bar from the cabinet, and went out to find him and drag his butt back to bed. She pulled the glass door open and squinted into the dancing colors. There was no sign of him.

"Up here." The words drifted down on the wind, barely audible.

Molly turned around and looked up; Cole sat at the edge of the flat roof, a blanket wrapped around his shoulders.

"There's a ladder on that side," he said. The blanket shifted, a hand gesturing vaguely from within.

You idiot, Molly thought as she ran around the side of the shelter. She climbed up the ladder and walked across the flat roof to Cole, kneeling down beside him.

"What are you doing up here? You should be in bed." She adjusted the blanket around his shoulders.

"I should be out *there*," he croaked, the blanket slipping down again as he pointed toward the horizon.

"And you'd be dead in a minute. Flank, Cole, you're probably gonna die up *here*. You do know this canister isn't doing anything if you don't hold it up, right?" Molly grabbed the IV container and rested it by her shoulder.

"They're going for Edison," he said. "I should be helping them."

"He's alive?" Molly sat down next to Cole and put her head close, obviating the need for him to strain his voice.

Cole nodded. He looked over at Molly, managed a weak smile, and then tried to open the blanket to allow her inside. She put her free hand on him, keeping him wrapped tight.

"How do they know?" she asked.

"They have a tracker of some sort, or a sensor. I stumbled out last night, or whenever, and found a bunch of them arguing over it. I grabbed a band and asked them what they were doing."

"I think they were planning on all of us dying out there," Molly said.

Cole nodded again. "I tried to go with them, but they were insistent. Told me to stay with you." Cole looked over at Molly. "The way they were talking about you . . . what did you *do*?"

"I didn't do anything. I just about died out there. I came back with one of the Wadis and asked about you. I got pissed and tore the band off my head."

"You did *something*." He looked to the horizon again. "They're acting different."

"I know. I don't like it."

"*I* do. They've been acting like robots up 'til now. Not like Dani. What I saw this morning, it was like they *cared* about something." There was a pause while Cole licked his lips and took a deep breath. "I just wish I was out there."

"I know you do. Stop talking. Here, I brought you some juice." Molly set the IV down long enough to rip the juice packet open; she pushed it into one of his hands as it snaked out of the blanket. "I don't suppose I can talk you into coming inside, can I?"

He shook his head slowly, moving the packet of fluids back and forth so he could keep sipping.

"Well, can I rethink the blanket offer, then?"

Cole peeled it open, and Molly sat beside him. She moved the IV canister to her other hand and draped her arm around his back. He wrapped the blanket around her, and they wiggled to get it closed.

They both looked to the horizon. The sky would have looked so beautiful if it were over any other landscape.

A landscape more alien to them. Molly tilted her head to the side and rested it on Cole's shoulder.

"I meant what I said last night," she said. "Or whenever it was."

Cole stopped sipping from the pouch. "Me, too," he said.

"Yeah, but I couldn't hear you over the wind."

"That's OK," Cole mumbled. "I still said it. And I meant it."

She lifted her head. "Say it again."

Cole leaned away to look at her. When their eyes met, she saw he was going to protest, or make an excuse—

"I love you, Molly Fyde."

She pulled his shoulder back under her cheek and closed her eyes, allowing the strange and alien words to wash over her again and again.

They were alien, but in some ways . . . it sounded to her like something he'd said a million times before.

○ ○ ○ ○

Cole shook her awake. The blanket was falling off them, and the bandage on her face had stuck to his tunic. He said something, but it floated away on the wind. He pointed after the words, as if she could still catch them on the breeze.

She followed his finger and saw what he was gesturing toward: a group of figures marching back toward the shelter. They moved along in a wide pattern, walking very slowly. It was hard to make out any detail, but there was something about their pace or posture that didn't resonate as a successful rescue operation.

This was the sad plodding of a hearse, not the eager anxiety of an ambulance.

Molly felt Cole trying to get up, to race after them, but he could hardly speak, much less run. She knew he was in no condition to help. Besides, there were plenty of idle bodies already out there. She pulled him tight and gave him a stern look, but he looked rapt, leaning forward, trying to pick out a familiar shape.

At this distance, they were all dark blobs silhouetted on the dimly lit rock. As they got closer, however, Molly could see a figure in the center.

It was laboring.

Molly felt a jolt of hope. It could be Edison, tired and hurt, but it could also be a Drenard. The figure pulled something along. A large shape—at least as big as a Glemot.

And it wasn't moving.

Cole saw it too and twisted feebly away from Molly. She threw the blanket off and handed the IV canister to Cole, hoping it would slow him down. She beat him to the ladder and clambered down, racing off toward the group.

Molly concentrated on the central figure as she ran, but when she got close, one of the guards on the perimeter caught her and held her back. She slapped at him, her tunic flapping in the breeze, mimicking the swinging of her wild arms, but the large male effortlessly pushed her toward the shelter, cooing sharply into the wind.

Molly couldn't see around his wide body, and she *had* to know what that was being dragged across the ground. Forced backward, nearly tripping over her heels, she turned to see Cole stumbling and falling on the rock halfway between her and the shelter.

In her head, she screamed. But nobody could hear.

The large Drenard caught her and lifted her into strong, blue arms. She welcomed it, clawing up and peering over the guard's shoulder to see if her friend was there.

She looked to the ground, expecting to see Edison's dead body, but it was bigger than her friend. It was the size of an adult Glemot, a Wadi Thooo that must've been four meters long.

No—*Longer*.

The thing's tail was off the ground, leading up into the air, over the shoulder and clutched in both hands of . . .

Edison.

Molly gasped and pawed at the air for him, but his eyes were down, his entire body sagging with fatigue. She could see large patches of blood matted across his fur. Every step appeared to be pure torture, like a mountaineering video she'd seen once with men who had to test every foothold before leaning forward into the next.

Why wasn't anyone helping him?

She beat at the chest of the Drenard carrying her, but was too tired and weak to make the gesture anything more than symbolic. Strong arms pulled her tight and carried her along.

When the group reached Cole, she saw someone scoop him up as if he were a child. Molly brought her hands up to her face and screamed into them, wailing with the sound of a heavy wind, passing over holes in stone.

17

The next day, a second shuttle arrived. It rocked in the wind before pulling into the lee of the shelter. Molly and Walter and a few of the Drenards stopped eating their meal to watch. Cole was in the first aid room taking a turn with Edison, whose strength was gradually returning.

The two officials put their utensils down and walked out to greet the new arrivals. Molly recognized Dani through the glass; he and another official stepped through the door and out of the wind.

"Is that your interrogator?" Molly asked Walter, nodding at the Drenard with Dani.

"Yesss."

Molly fought the urge to go and greet them. The last twenty hours had been tense. Her crew was still healing, still determining whom they could trust. The Drenards had been extremely kind and deferential, but their miracle ointments worked only on the physical wounds. None of her crew particularly cared to don a band and listen to the Drenards explain themselves. Instead, they huddled together around Edison's bed and strengthened their bonds with one another, swapping Wadi stories and marveling at one another's trials. When Walter showed the mild burn on the back of his head, Cole and Edison had acted suitably impressed; Molly pretended to be horrified. He had beamed with the pride of a true warrior.

Which was why, hours later, as Dani entered and crossed the lobby toward Molly, she rose and went to the first aid room instead. She still didn't know if she could trust anyone beyond her friends.

She heard Cole and Edison in an animated discussion before she pushed through the door. The conversation pinched off into silence at the sight of her.

"Done eating already?" Cole asked.

"Lost my appetite. Dani just pulled up with some other officials. I was scared of what I'd say to them."

"So you came to get *me*?" Cole lifted his eyebrows and tilted his head. "I sure hope you don't think I'm gonna be Mr. Polite."

"No, I just didn't wanna be out there." She walked over and squeezed one of Edison's hands.

The back of his bed was raised; he smiled at her. "My performance in such a conversation would exceed system resources," he said.

Molly patted his arm and beamed at her friend. "I have no idea what you just said."

"They have him on some pretty strong drugs," Cole explained.

"Surpassing pharmaceuticals," Edison said.

Molly laughed. "You said it, buddy—"

The door opened, slicing another conversation in half. Although Dani walked in alone, Molly saw several other brightly garbed males in the hallway. He held a red band out to her, but Molly shook her head and turned back to Edison. The pup's eyes were wide, his brow furrowed into ridges. The look said so much—so clearly. She glanced to Cole, whose lips were pursed tight. He raised his eyebrows, leaving it up to her.

"I don't want to find out it was him," she told them both.

○ ○ ○ ○

Cole nodded and reached across Edison to accept the ribbon. He checked inside to find the seam and lined it up with the back of his head.

"Hello, Dani," he thought.

"I was told on the way over, Cole. I am so sorry—"

"You're the one that hinted at this as a way out of here—"

Dani lifted both hands, showing Cole his palms as he shot a glance toward the door. *"Careful,"* he thought to Cole. He gestured toward Edison. *"Your friend already knew about the rite from Anlyn. Before your ship arrived in the system. I talked to his Questioner on the way here. Edison asked about nothing else for two days."*

Cole interrupted him. *"What does that have to do with—"*

"Cole, listen. I had no idea it would be like this. If I had known they were bringing you to this shelter, I would have—"

*"Why? What is it about **this** shelter?"* Cole felt impatient and was surprised to find he could force his thoughts on top of Dani's. He watched Molly idly scratch Edison's arm, her eyes narrowed.

"This area isn't used for alien initiations," Dani thought. *"It's . . . **special**. There aren't any eggs here; it's not a well-populated area; there's not much water—it doesn't matter, it's just that I would have known something was wrong if they told me where you were being taken. I should have been checking anyway. I am sorry."*

"He's sorry," he told Molly aloud.

"Yeah. Me, too," she spat back.

Dani kept his thoughts to himself. Cole sighed, mulling over what Molly had said about her last conversation with the officials, the part that had upset her.

"Was this all about Edison and Anlyn?" he asked Dani. The Drenard Questioner nodded.

In the human fashion, Cole noted, so many of their quirks rubbing off on him.

"I spoke to Lady Hooo yesterday," Dani thought. *"After we were summoned and while the party formed to look for your friend."* He indicated Edison again.

"His name's Edison," Cole offered.

"Actually, that is in question right now, I am happy to report. And it goes to the heart of the matter. His name might be Lord Campton, according to his Questioner and a member of the Circle. Records are being—"

"Lord Campton?" Cole looked at Edison. "What have you done?" he asked.

"Who, Edison?" Molly asked.

"Dani's referring to him as Lord Campton."

Edison spoke through the drugs and his overly verbose brain: "The specimens have already been cross-referenced and compare favorably for my betrothment?"

"Your *what?"* Molly and Cole said together.

Dani started to think something, but Cole raised his hand.

"Anlyn and I are to be legally unioned if the specimen acquired point two radians ago surpasses that of Bodi's from eighteen radians ago."

Cole looked to Molly for help, but she appeared just as confused as he.

Then he thought of something. *"Can I borrow your band?"* he asked Dani.

The Drenard hesitated, giving Cole a serious appraisal. Then he gingerly removed the band and handed it over as if it were encrusted with precious jewels.

Cole helped Edison put it on.

"Can you hear me, buddy?" he thought.

"Clearly."

"Say something else."

"What do you want me to say?"

Cole gave Molly a thumbs-up and a big smile.

"What is this about you marrying Anlyn? Who's Bodi?"

"Bodi is Anlyn's fiancé. But she doesn't want to marry him. She wants to marry **me.***"*

"And you want to marry her?" Cole had no idea their relationship was that serious. He glanced at Molly and thought about how many years they'd known each other, the hundreds of hours in the simulator and the crazy few weeks they'd just had together. Despite all that, he'd only told her how he felt after being frightened that he'd never again get the chance.

"Yes. She and I understand each other."

Cole laughed. He found that hard to believe.

Edison went on: *"The only way I could do this was to outrank her fiancé, who had laid claim to her."*

"So you went and tried to get yourself killed?"

Cole glanced over to Molly, her forehead lined with creases. "He almost killed himself over a girl," he told her.

"My auditory functions are still operational," Edison said, smiling.

"And who are you to judge?" Molly asked Cole.

"That's not the same thing. You keep saving my butt, so I—"

"It's OK. Just let me know when you boys get to something important. Like whether or not it's safe for me to have my back to the door."

Cole shook his head and focused his thoughts for Edison: *"Pretend we're talking about something else—I just . . . I need to know why you felt like you had to do this. Why you didn't come to me for help."*

"I'm sorry. I never thought you'd end up out here. And I didn't know it'd be this dangerous, either. Somehow, Bodi found out what we were up to . . . maybe Anlyn and I shouldn't have been talking aloud about this when we thought we were alone. I didn't even know that was Bodi with us until Molly told me."

Edison scratched at the bandage on his forearm.

"The problem was, nobody knew precisely how big Bodi's Wadi measured. Those things aren't public record. But knowing the position he was given, Anlyn told me it'd be about my size. So I needed one bigger."

"Why? What does that change?"

Edison broke into a huge smile, flashing his large, square teeth at Cole. *"If I outrank him, I can claim Anlyn for my wife."*

"And you really think you love her?"

"I don't know. It's hard to say. But she wouldn't come back to Drenard unless we tried. It was the only way she would return. And we needed a safe place to go—"

"You did this for us, as well?"

"No. No. I do like Anlyn. I think I'm in love with her." His smile faded, his brow drooping. *"And it's not like I'm gonna meet any nice female Glemots, is it?"*

The reference to his race's genocide, an occurrence in which Cole and Molly had unwittingly played a huge part, stung. But so did the idea that Edison would take this risk to help them without consulting them first.

Dani waved to get Cole's attention; he rocked nervously from one foot to the other.

Cole patted Edison's shoulder. "Thanks, pal," he said out loud.

○ ○ ○ ○

Dani took his band back eagerly and affixed it to his head.

"Everything OK?" he asked.

"I think Anlyn's jealous boyfriend nearly got us all killed."

236

"That's what I've been trying to explain. When I found out what was going on, I enlisted the help of three Circle members and the other Questioners and brought them straight here. Two of them are Anlyn's uncles. We can trust them. When we left, we didn't even know if your friend would be found at the time, but we wanted to look at the Wadis and settle these issues immediately."

"Issues? What's there to figure out besides weighing the damn things, or measuring them, and telling Bodi to back off?"

Dani shifted his weight around. His eyes darted to Molly for a second. *"There is also her Wadi to consider."*

Cole looked at Molly. *"Hers?"*

"Yes. The Wadi she brought back is alive, docile, and . . . Well, we believe she is a juvenile that has never taken a mate, never reproduced. This, and the fact that she's much older than a baby, but not quite an adult, The Circle will take as a great sign. A momentous occasion. Especially since the discoverer is human." He looked at Molly again, his eyes flashing. *"And now a Drenard."*

Cole turned to stare at her as well. Perplexed. He furrowed his brow . . . *hard.* One of the bandages on his head tore free.

"What?" Molly asked.

"Your Wadi is alive," he said, pressing the tape back in place. "I think that means something to them."

"Alive? But I thought—" her voice trailed off into thought. Cole wished he could listen in.

He turned back to Dani. *"This is a good thing, though, right?"*

"Possibly. In some ways. All of you are going to be considered Drenards, and what happened here will become a legend one day, I am certain of that. But . . . I can't imagine they will let her off the planet now. She will mean too much to too many people."

"Are you kidding?" It was a deep but powerful thought. Cole groaned aloud.

"What is it?" Molly asked.

"We might be stuck here, even after all that work."

18

The Drenard officials cobbled together an impromptu ceremony in the rarely used shelter. Normally, such an occasion called for banners, custom tunics, and symbolic lances too long for practical use, but Dani had agreed to force the issue and try to get them off planet before Molly became a cause célèbre.

They gave the four friends fresh tunics to wear, signifying their status as Drenards and their place within the culture. Each was unique, thrown together from borrowed layers of material from the officials.

Naturally, they had to take turns agreeing with Walter that his was by far the most important-looking in order to settle him down.

"Befitting a supply officer," Molly managed to tell him with a straight face.

The four friends knelt in a line while lances were passed around and alien words were spoken. Not a moment of the ordeal made sense to Molly, but she didn't mind. Her focus was on getting off that planet, and she wasn't yet sure she should feel proud to be a Drenard.

After a round of deep bows from the officials, directed at the young foursome, a second ceremony began. They ushered Molly forward as a large red box was produced and placed on the carpet with great care. Pushed toward the box, blue hands on her back, Molly wondered what was expected of her. Dani held his palms together, then pantomimed a lid being opened, his hands hinging apart.

Molly knelt in front of the box, imagining a special tunic of some sort. Despite her anxiety to leave as quickly as possible, she found herself tingling in anticipation as she fumbled with the box's small, unintuitive clasp.

Someone behind her shuffled nervously. The entire lobby had fallen deathly silent.

Finally, the clasp came free. Molly cracked the top — and then the lid exploded open. She stumbled back, yelping, as the Wadi inside leaped out and attached itself to her chest, its claws pricking her through the layers of tunics.

Walter hissed furiously from behind her. Edison roared.

Molly turned and raised a hand to calm them down. All eyes were on the creature scrambling up her torso. She could feel her cheeks cramping from smiling so hard, her body flushed with excitement.

She tried to wrap her arms around the thing, but the Wadi wiggled out and scampered up to her neck, its tail swishing contentedly. She patted its head while a tongue darted out, as if tasting the air.

She turned to face Dani, her vision blurred with tears of joy. "Can I keep her?" she asked.

Even without the bands, she felt that Dani understood. And the answer was even clearer as the officials removed the Wadi from her tunic, peeling away each claw as the thing clutched desperately to her.

"Why?" she asked, as they returned the Wadi to the box. The poor creature writhed in protest, its limbs pushing at the edge, its head twisting back to look at Molly.

They shoved it inside and the lid slammed shut just as a desperate, croaking sound emanated from within.

The display horrified Molly, but the members of the Circle seemed extremely satisfied. They conferred in the gentle bubbling of their language while Dani presented a red band to Molly, both ceremonies clearly at an end.

"We need to go, Madam Fyde," he thought, once she had it in place.

"It's over? Can I—?"

"It is over. And no, you cannot keep the Wadi. It will go to the Royal Zoo and be kept on display. But let's hurry—Bodi and his allies on the Circle are heading this way from the train depot. We need to avoid them if at all possible."

Molly gave the red box another glance as it was shuffled out the door. Soft thumping noises resonated from within. She felt sick with the poor Wadi locked away like that, even sicker that it would be put on display rather than set free.

The look on Dani's face told her it was no use arguing. She turned to her friends.

"We need to go," she told them.

oooo

The four of them boarded one of the shuttles. Dani and Walter's Questioner joined them, as well as the three Circle members, one of whom cradled the red box in his lap. A guard settled into the driver's seat and began fiddling with the controls. The large half-circle of a vehicle rocked slightly as everyone settled among the rows of benches.

Molly got comfortable and peered through her window, watching the guards load into the other shuttle. They looked like a small Marine contingent gearing up for war. Their shuttle would set off toward the train station to intercept Bodi's group, which reportedly had refueled and turned around after hearing of Molly's and Edison's completion of the rite.

The shuttle with Molly and her friends, meanwhile, would head directly for the city and meet another shuttle to transfer some fuel before proceeding on to a defense spaceport. The Circle members, two of which were related to Anlyn, would log the new Drenards into the planetary system—and they supposedly would be cleared to leave.

Molly wondered how and where they would meet up with Anlyn and whether she was being protected from Bodi's scheming. She also was having trouble believing they really would be allowed to fly away with so many people after them. Her trust of the Drenard people was on the wane.

The driver snapped the door shut, locking out the wind, and took them around the shelter. He headed straight for the glowing city over the horizon.

Molly had so many more questions for Dani, but the red bands had been taken, and along with them with her ability to communicate. The frustration of not being able to speak, of having relied solely on human tongues and their wide adoption, fixed her resolve: she was *going* to learn some other languages. Maybe get her mother to teach her Drenard.

She wondered if her mom had had a similar experience years ago and if that was why *she* had taken up the alien language.

The shuttle lurched side to side in the oncoming breeze, the occupants swaying together. The sound of gusts roaring against the metal hull became deafening at times. Molly sat with Cole, their hands interlocked, her eyes fixed on the red box in the Circle member's lap.

Cole asked Edison how he was feeling, and Molly heard something about "meeting expectations" and "being up to spec." She smiled at Walter, who was bugging his Questioner for a red band and pantomiming a complaint. One of the first bumps had spilled red juice down his new tunic, and he kept inquiring about a fresh one.

After what felt like several hours, the tall buildings in the distance seemed no nearer than they had been. New, smaller buildings had come into view—so Molly knew they were approaching the horizon—it was just a testament to how far away the city lay. And how tall those buildings must be, stretching up since they couldn't build out. The only structures out this far were tall towers with five blades—an ancient windmill farm. The rusting hulks hung against the black sky, monuments to an age before fusion power and fuel cells.

"Seems like a lot of prime real estate," Molly mused aloud, her forehead pressed to the glass.

"They can't build out here," Cole told her.

"Why not? Seems shady enough."

"You and Dani didn't spend much time on planetary astronomy, did you?"

"Ha. No. I spent our time together trying to convince him the Drenard treatment of women belittled them rather than honored them."

"Gods. I'm glad I wasn't there for that one."

"Why? You just would've seen us staring at each other in silence. Well, with my arms waving now and then."

"You know what I mean."

"Yeah, you would've been miserable. But you would've been taking my side, right?"

Cole sighed for effect. "I would've been saying whatever you wanted me to say, *Madame Fyde*."

Molly slapped at Cole's shoulder playfully. "See? You sound just like them!"

"See why you never learned about this planet? You can't stay focused. Typical—"

"You say anything gender-related, and my jabs are gonna turn into haymakers, buddy."

Cole held up his hands in mock surrender. "Can I tell you why they can't build out here?"

"I guess," she said, her arms crossing in mock anger.

"It's because there are *two* Drenard stars. They have overlapping cones of light the planet swings through."

"So they have seasons?"

Cole laughed at this. "Yeah, I guess. Summer and Sum*mest*."

Molly rolled her eyes.

"It isn't really seasons, not like we have. Dozens of our years go by before the two stars orbit each other and the planet lines up just right for the terminator to move. Then it'll stay like that for dozens more years. There are probably Wadi shelters on the other side of the planet that you can't get to right now 'cause they're baking in the heat for another cycle."

"Wow." Molly turned and gazed through the window, thinking on these cycles. "How much you wanna bet," she asked Cole, "that all the old species on this planet were migratory at some point?"

"I wouldn't doubt it."

"Any ideas about where that water came from in those caves you were in?"

"I haven't had a chance to ask Dani about that. Probably condensation. If some of those tunnels go all the way to the cool side, you might get a convection current—"

"Look!" Molly interrupted.

It was the other shuttle, parked on a small rise and facing them, waiting. There was an armed Drenard male standing by the large vehicle, his tunics flapping in the breeze. He waved at their driver, who raised a hand in response. Their shuttle slowly pulled past the parked one and swerved to line up on the other side.

Molly watched the Circle members lean together and converse in low tones. Edison had his head against his window, softly snoring, while Walter ran down the aisle toward the rear glass so he could get a better view of the recharging process. The guard outside waved their driver back until the flattened sterns of both vehicles were just a meter apart, lined up for the energy transfer.

"Should we step out and stretch our legs, see if we can help?" Cole asked.

"I'd rather stay inside," Molly said. She watched Walter press his metallic face to the rear of the shuttle, peering down. Beyond him, through both sets of glass, she could see several shapes moving in the other vehicle.

"Besides," she said, "something doesn't feel—"

She was about to say *right*, just as things started to go very wrong.

Armed Drenard guards spilled out of the other shuttle and marched around toward theirs. One of the Circle members that had ridden with Molly's bunch stood outside the door of their shuttle; he urged the soldiers forward, waving his blue arm frantically.

"Cole—"

"I see it."

"Edison, wake up!"

Molly moved into the aisle and turned to the one armed guard they had on their side.

The guard raised his lance.

But not in the direction she'd hoped.

And Molly finally saw just how wrong things were about to get.

19

The world slowed down, coming to a halt like a Drenard day. Molly saw Dani yelling at the official with the red box in his lap. The third Circle member stood in the aisle, facing Molly's group with his hands wide, palms out. Their driver watched from the front of the shuttle, his lance parallel to the floor and pointed back their way.

Without bands, there was no way to ask anyone what was going on. Dani seemed furious about something. The other Questioner approached the front of the vehicle and the driver. Out of the corner of her eye, Molly could see the line of guards advancing up the side of their shuttle.

What a perfect plan, she thought. The Circle members had sent Dani's contingent of guards in one direction while they led them, defenseless, into a trap in the middle of nowhere. Before she could fully admire the scheming involved, the world around her burst back into motion. A cacophony of soothing sounds—Drenards arguing in their cooing tongue—rang out. Behind her, Molly could hear a fierce and throaty roar.

"Easy, Edison," she heard Cole say.

Spinning in the aisle, she saw Cole, bent over the back of his seat, trying to keep Edison restrained. Walter remained by the back glass, but he was looking forward, trying to hiss something.

He pointed, his arm quivering, at Molly.

Or past her.

She whirled around just as the driver's lance arced out, cutting Walter's Questioner in two. The upper half of the Drenard's body kept going forward, arms flailing, while the lower half kicked back between the rows of seats. Both halves trailed ropes of gore, glistening wet with blood.

Molly's eyes burned from the bright flash. She felt someone grabbing her around her neck and looked down to see a blue arm across her chest.

Through the haze, she watched Cole leap forward, wide-eyed and wild looking. Molly tried to tell him not to try anything, but in slow motion he and Edison started moving over the seats toward the front of the bus. The Circle member who had Molly pinned began dragging her to the front, cooing something in her ear.

Her back was toward the danger: the guard in the front of the bus. She tried to wiggle around to see what he was doing, but the best she could manage was to look sideways. Her captor dragged her past Dani, who remained frozen in his seat, his arms up in the universal stance of submission. His eyes locked with Molly's as she was pulled by. Then she saw him glance down at something—something ahead of him. It came into view as she was pulled closer to the front of the shuttle.

The red box.

The third Circle member clutched it with one hand; his other one held a small device leveled at Dani, a gun of some sort.

Molly reached up and grabbed the arms holding her across her chest. She gripped them as she tightened her stomach muscles, pulling her knees to her chin, her feet high off the ground. The Circle member started pulling her forward faster.

Almost out of range now, she lashed out with both feet, aiming for that frustrating clasp. The kick drove the red box into the abdomen of the Circle member.

The air rushed out of the elder Drenard.

And something else rushed out of the box.

o o o o

The Wadi Thooo was free!

She shot from her prison and under a ledge of some sort, looking for a dark place. The air was full of scents. Many of them. More than she had ever smelled in close proximity. Some were tendrils of fear, leading back to their source as vividly as colored columns of smoke. Other smells were bright arms of rage and deceit, smells the female Wadi knew well. *Male* smells. Powerful odors from *big* Wadi. But she'd fought plenty of large Wadi in her day. The males of her kind might grow large with age, but the females grew *wise*.

And she was older than she looked in those ways.

She kept her moisture tongue tucked in its pouch and flicked her scent tongue in wide patterns through the air. There was another smell here, fainter than the others, and new. Not as primal and dominant as those she'd known for so many cycles of the two lights.

It was the *good* smell. A trace of kindness floating in the air, thin as a single ray of light and surrounded by all that reeking blackness given off by fear and rage.

The Wadi stuck her head out from under the ledge and sniffed it all in, her tongue sampling the many wisps of mingling emotions, all wrapped around one another. There was much going on—much feeling—but she could see exactly where they all led. Could tease them apart like bright plumes of smoke emanating from holes in the rock.

○ ○ ○ ○

Another bright flash erupted by Molly as the driver's deadly lance lashed out again. The bolt split between Cole and Edison and shattered the transparent shield out of the rear of the shuttle.

Walter fell to the ground, showered with chunks of glass. Edison roared and grabbed his arm, smoke rising from his fur, but he and Cole renewed their push forward. Molly yelled for them to stop as Dani continued to struggle with the stunned Circle member, trying to wrestle his small weapon away—

Something rushed at Molly's head, something small and fast. It pushed off her shoulder and went right by her ear. The blue arms clutching her chest flew away, pawing the air above her.

Molly threw a high elbow back into the stomach of her captor. Then she spun around the Circle member, took three large steps, vaulted over the remains of the Questioner in the aisle, and threw herself at the driver.

He brought the lance around from Cole and Edison to fend off the new threat.

Molly crashed into the large blue arm holding the lance; it was like trying to tackle a marble column. The guard's other hand came around and grabbed at her tunic. She found herself climbing a rock face, looking for purchase, kicking off a large blue knee and scampering toward the head high above.

The guard seized one of her arms and wrenched it, filling her entire body with pain. Molly cried out, then looked up to see the Drenard sneering back down at her. Both combatants had open mouths—one in the effort of causing pain—the other in the resulting agony.

Molly felt herself slipping, forced down by the strength in that one arm. The other brought the lance up to lash out at her two friends. Molly saw the handhold she needed but wasn't sure if she could reach it. She lunged against gravity and the powerful blue grasp and stretched her body out, one arm extended as far as possible.

Three fingers went into the Drenard's mouth; she pulled his jaw down with all her weight and felt sharp teeth sinking down to the bones in her fingers, but they just improved her grip, her flesh hanging on a line of razors.

The chin snapped down, and another flash from the lance went wide, exploding through the side of the shuttle. Molly pulled herself up as the grip on her arm loosened, a confused shock rippling through her towering blue enemy. She pulled her other arm free and made a fist, her thumb out and stiffened. She drove it as hard as she could into the Drenard's large eye, the only visible weakness on the alien's massive frame.

Warm fluid splashed back onto her hand and coursed down her arm. She pulled back to strike again when someone grabbed her from behind.

"Watch out!"

Cole pressed her flat as another shot flashed through the air, right where she'd been. She found herself sandwiched between the fallen Drenard and Cole, her cheeks crushed from both sides. Her eyes faced the shuttle steps, where several guards held lances, trying to work their way aboard single file.

Molly felt Cole roll off her and pull her away from the driver. Edison took their place on the prone guard and began doing something brutal with his claws.

"Let me go!" Molly yelled, trying to fight off Cole, but her shoulder hurt too much.

Another light flashed at the front of the shuttle. Molly spun, expecting to see Edison cut in half, but he was holding the driver's lance, had it leveled at the open door. Smoke and screaming billowed in from outside.

Cole stumbled backward; Molly pushed off him and ran forward.

"Help Dani!" she shouted over her shoulder. She didn't look back to see how that was going—she had to get up front. The guards outside still had them trapped, and in a vehicle that didn't have enough fuel for an escape!

Edison knelt on top of the dead driver, his lance pointed at the smoke by the door. Molly squeezed around him and threw herself in the driver's seat. There were dozens of buttons and indicators on the dash; she knew Walter or Edison would be able to tell at a glance how to operate this thing—

Then she saw something familiar. A single black handle rising out on the left side that looked like a stand-ard flight control. Hoping logic guided Drenard design aesthetics, Molly grabbed the joystick. Movement to her right distracted her—another guard charging the shuttle, his lance raised and ready to lash out. He was almost in the door when Molly jerked back on the control stick.

The shuttle lurched in reverse, driving the jamb of the door into the guard, sending him spinning.

No sooner had the shuttle shot into motion, it slammed violently against the rear of the shuttle behind them.

Edison fell backward into the aisle, and Molly was nearly thrown to the ground. She spun out of the seat, dazed, and grabbed handfuls of Edison's fur, helping him up.

"The glass!" she shouted, pointing at the lance.

"Acknowledged." He lumbered back down the aisle, stepping over several dead Drenard. The sight of so much violence and blood stunned Molly, but the sounds of guards rallying outside forced her back into action. She took a step toward the rear—

And something flew up from one of the dead Drenards and latched onto her tunic. Molly nearly fell back in panic before she realized what it was: the Wadi. The creature pulled herself up Molly's tunic and curled around her neck.

Behind them, feet stomped into the shuttle. Molly saw Cole helping Dani, whose arm was bleeding but otherwise seemed OK. She ran to them, urging them both toward the rear, where another burst of light flashed, followed by an explosion of glass. Molly looked up to see Edison tossing Walter from one shuttle to the other. The Glemot turned to beckon them forward, looking incredibly fearsome in his tunic, waving the long metal lance about.

Molly and Cole pulled Dani with them as they struggled toward the rear. Molly heard a lance crackle—a now familiar and sickening sound. A bench to her side exploded in a cloud of fabric and stuffing, the hair on the back of her neck standing at attention from the static discharge. Ahead of her, Edison made to retaliate, but there wasn't a clear shot. He waited until Molly, Cole, and Dani reached him and then fired an electrical blast forward, providing some cover.

Dani went through the abutting windows first, stepping over the matching, crushed jambs. Cole helped

Molly through next, yelling at Edison to get a move on. Molly didn't waste any time. The guards outside could see what they were doing through the glass. She saw two of them race along the outside of the fuel shuttle, trying to get to the open front door.

Weary, Molly sprinted in a footrace with the figures outside—one unarmed human female rushing toward the same finish line as two armed Drenard males. The Wadi wrapped its tail tightly around her neck, holding on but also making it difficult to breathe, its little claws digging in and burning.

She didn't have time to see if Cole and Edison were through the improvised escape hatch. They were or they weren't—they would *all* be dead if she faltered. Passing the last bench, she threw herself around the side of the driver's seat and slammed the control handle forward as hard and fast as she could. Outside, the first guard came into view, lance raised. She felt the hair on her arms tickle as the thing charged, the point aimed inside the doorway.

And then he was gone. Electric motors flew into gear, propelling the shuttle forward, knocking the lance to the side and sending the blast out over the empty wasteland. Molly held the lever forward, hurtling them, unguided, away from the fracas. She peered back down the aisle toward the rear.

Cole and Edison were there, holding themselves against the jamb of the glass, the lurch forward having nearly sent them out through the opening.

She sighed as they clutched each other, regaining their balance.

Safe.

20

Molly rested in the bench behind the driver's seat. The hand she'd injured in the guard's mouth was wrapped in strips of torn tunic; her good one was intertwined with Cole's. Ahead of her, Dani drove with one hand, his right arm black and singed from a glancing shot. Without the bands, they couldn't tell how bad his injuries were, or if it was the gun or lance that had caused them. Molly had tried to tend to the wound while he steered, but he had waved her away.

The other shuttle had given chase for a few kilometers before its fuel cells ran completely dry. Molly and Cole had debated on whether it was even safe to be heading for the city and whom they could trust. Dani, they were sure of. Both Questioners had risked their lives for them—one paying the ultimate price.

In the end, they decided to leave their escape up to Dani, who had to be as paranoid as they after that last trap. Part of Molly was too exhausted to care, eager to have someone else decide. She looked down in her lap where the Wadi lay, curled up and content. Walter had found some food supplies and juice pouches scattered from the crash; the lizard had sucked one of them dry and then fallen asleep.

Every now and then, Dani craned his neck around to gaze at the thing, his eyes wide in wonder.

Leaning forward, Molly looked across the aisle to check on Edison. He'd been tinkering with his lance for the past hour, using his adaptable, prehensile claws to inspect its innards. Molly cautioned him twice to watch where he pointed the thing—she could only guess at what sort of modifications he was making. As if the things needed to be more deadly. She tried to shake the image of Walter's Questioner out of her mind—his body cut in half, guts spilling everywhere, the putrid odor—but couldn't quite do it.

As soon as they pulled onto a paved road along the city's outskirts, the ride improved immensely, and the shuttle became less noisy. A breeze continued to waft in from the broken window in the back, cooling the sweat on Molly's neck. She squeezed Cole's hand as they passed a glass dome with trees and plants inside.

"I see it," he said.

The strange sights outside had Molly longing to ask Dani more about his home planet. But even if she had the means to communicate with him, he seemed too lost in his own thoughts to have hers intrude. Then again, if his morose and contemplative demeanor had anything to do with having been betrayed, she could certainly give him some advice on that. Even if it was just to warn him that it never got easier to take.

For a few kilometers, they continued to approach the distant band of skyscrapers. Then, Dani turned to the right and merged onto a busy road dozens of lanes across. Molly watched the lights illuminating the highway fly by and then followed the vertical poles ahead as they converged on the horizon. She pictured the wide swath of pavement and steel stretching all the way around the planet, like a wedding ring around a finger. She imagined one could drive in a straight line, forever, ending up right where they started. Circumnavigating Drenard would be one endless trip through an unchanging, dawn-soaked city. As boring as that seemed, she felt a strange compulsion to do it, driving all the way around, just to say she had.

Compared to Earth freeways, the traffic was heavy yet swift. Molly watched Cole's head spin to follow the odd vehicles that went past, sorting out shapes and models and doing boy-brain things. She was far more interested in spotting the people *inside* the shapes.

She could see smaller females that made her think of Anlyn riding in the back. Children often had their faces pressed to the glass, watching the large shuttle rumble past. Every now and then, blue eyes would widen and flash as they spotted Molly—a human! Disbelieving shock would register on their pale faces and then be lost, replaced with the see-through reflection of Molly's own image in the glass.

She could see Cole's reflection in the window as well, looking past her. When their eyes met, they smiled at each other's reflections. An old habit from the simulator.

They spent almost an hour on the road, moving at a blistering rate of speed. Molly felt tiredness creeping into her head, tugging at her eyelids, but her heart was still racing, her body too keyed up, her accelerator pinned. She wouldn't be able to sleep until they were safe, even though such states usually ended up being illusory.

"Whatcha thinking about?" Cole asked.

"Hmm? Oh, nothing. Just tired. I feel like we haven't stopped running in over a month."

"Yeah. Except for whenever we're in prison."

Molly laughed. "I guess we should start appreciating that time a little more."

"No thanks," Cole said. "At least when we're running, we're together."

Molly faced him and batted her eyes sarcastically. "Awww. Aren't you romantic?"

"I'm serious. In fact, that's what I've been thinking about for most of the ride. Along with why this planet doesn't seem to have any billboards."

Molly looked out her window to confirm his observation.

"If I hadn't gone on that trip to Palan with you, what would the rest of my life have been like?"

"Peaceful?" Molly offered.

"Boring, more like. Or empty. I don't know. Forty years of crunching jump numbers, if I was lucky and didn't get blasted out of the sky."

"Why are you thinking about stuff like that?"

"Because I've nearly died a few times in the past two days." He released her hand and rubbed the back of the Wadi as if to remind her of one of those times. "And I'm not freaked out by it. Not like I should be."

Molly watched his hand slide across the colorful scales between the two protruding stumps on the Wadi's back. "Do you feel numb or something?"

Cole looked over at her. "No. The opposite. I feel really *alive*. There's something about being around you, but I . . ." He paused.

"But you what?"

"I've always felt it a little bit. Even back at the Academy. I always felt like you were special. *Different.* And back then I thought it was because—"

"Because I'm a girl?" she offered.

"Yeah. But not . . . *that.* Not the way I feel about you now. Not at first."

He stopped petting the Wadi and rubbed his face with both hands. "Man, it's so hard to explain. And not because I can't say it—it's like I just don't understand it. All I'm saying is that I feel like I've lived a good life just by being around you. As friends, and now . . . whatever else we are."

Molly reached over and cupped his far cheek, pulling his head around to face her.

"Just tell me you *love me.* That's what you're feeling. That's what the words are for."

"I love you," he said. "I do. But it's more than that. I promise. When I figure it out for myself, I'll explain it to you."

"You do that, handsome." And she leaned over to give him a kiss.

The Wadi in her lap stirred, sniffing the air. Now *that* was an emotion she hadn't sensed in several shifts of the two lights.

○ ○ ○ ○

The defense spaceport came into view well before they got there. Tall, streamlined shapes stood vertical against the waving tapestry of colorful, sun-setting lights. The shiny hulls scattered the hues in all directions, mixing the beauty of natural wonders with well-planned, artificial forms. The accidental and the engineered played off each other to the betterment of both.

They had to pull through a guard station to enter the facilities. As they queued up in a line of boxier vehicles, Dani turned around and showed them his palms, cooing calmly. Molly hoped he was right if he was trying to convince them that everything was OK.

They filed up to the gate, and a long conversation with the guard ensued. To Molly, the Drenard looked no different from the men they'd battled with several hours earlier. She looked over at Edison and saw the fur dancing in waves across his arms, one of which draped over his seat where she knew his lance lay hidden.

But the gate opened without a fight, the guard waving them through and directing them off to the side.

When they rounded a row of hangars and Molly saw *Parsona* sitting gracefully on the tarmac, she nearly burst into tears. The ship had gone from representing a lost past and deceased parents to standing for a hopeful future—one that contained the possibility of reuniting with them.

In some ways, the ship was *becoming* her mother. Text on a nav screen already felt like the closest thing to a female role model she'd ever had. And although it had been annoying at first, she had sorely missed the motherly doting over the past few days. Molly found it heart-wrenchingly tragic that the only kids who truly appreciated their parents seemed to be the ones who had already lost them.

"Thank gods," Cole muttered at the sight. Behind them, Walter hissed with delight and scooted up the aisle to get a closer look.

All their excitement paled in comparison to Edison's reaction as Anlyn descended *Parsona's* loading ramp. He growled with delight and nearly crushed Walter in his rush to the door. The shuttle was still moving, but Edison turned and roared at Dani, who was compelled to thumb the door open.

Edison bounded out, almost falling as he fought to match his inertia, his legs pumping him toward Anlyn, who raced out to greet him.

Molly's eyes filled with water as she watched the two friends swallow each other up. Edison pulled Anlyn off the ground and swung her side to side, feet and tunics waving with delight. Molly squeezed Cole's hand, recalling the way it had felt to be reunited with him after the Wadi Thooo rite.

Walter stood by the door, hissing at having been stampeded. As soon as the shuttle lurched to a stop, he filed out and hurried toward the ship, waving at Anlyn before disappearing inside. Molly and Cole exited ahead of Dani and waited their turn to greet their friend.

Edison finally set her down, and she turned to face them. She looked . . . *different*. All Molly had seen her in was the rags of a slave, Cole's T-shirts, or one of Walter's modified flight suits. Here she was, decked out in colorful regalia, her posture erect and proud. She stood beside Edison and commanded attention, despite the difference in size.

Cole stepped forward and gave her a big hug, but Molly saw her looking past him, concentrating on the creature perched on her shoulder.

"So it is true!" Anlyn whispered. She smiled at Cole as she pulled away from him, walking over to Molly with her hand out and shaking. She cooed to the Wadi in her native tongue.

"Hello, Anlyn," Molly said.

Anlyn broke her pale blue eyes away from the Wadi to meet Molly's. "I'm so sorry you got mixed up in this," she said.

Molly put a hand on Anlyn's arm, squeezing it affectionately. "Don't be. I'm glad. I'm happy for you and Edison." She smiled up at him. "I just wish we'd *known,* so we could've helped you."

"I know," Anlyn said. "I didn't plan on . . . on arriving in a coma. I'm sorry. I don't know what happened.

I . . . I was fine one minute, and then I just blacked out. I woke up here and—"

"It's OK. Everything's going to be fine, now. Right?"

Anlyn frowned. "Eventually, perhaps, but not right now. I've already heard the reports about the Circle members and their ambush. The government is going into shock, and rumors are spreading about you and . . ." she glanced at the Wadi wrapped around Molly's neck. Its tongue flitted out into the air.

"I haven't named him, if that's what you're wondering."

"It's a *she*," Anlyn said. "If that were a male . . ." she chuckled in Dani's fashion, the first time Molly had ever seen her laugh. ". . . you'd be crushed!"

Dani joined in with her, panting as he came up behind Molly. The spot of levity slightly cracked the dour mood. Molly turned to him, remembered he couldn't speak English, and looked back to Anlyn. "Can we leave? Is there anything we need to do before we go?"

Anlyn and Dani spoke in Drenard, and the seriousness in her face returned. She turned to Molly. "You can go. Planetary Defense probably wouldn't attack you right now, even if the Circle demanded it."

"*You*? You mean *we*, right? You're coming with us. Dani, too."

Anlyn shook her head. She reached a hand out and grabbed a fold in Edison's tunic, as if anchoring him in place as well. "I can't, Molly. I need to stay here. Sorting out the Circle will take time, and I'll be needed."

"Oh, my gods, I completely forgot. You are like fourth in line for the throne or something, right?"

Anlyn formed a small circle with her mouth and clucked, shaking her head sadly. "Wrong on two counts, I'm afraid. If I were a male, perhaps. Or if I chose to produce a male—which I will not. And I'm *second* in line now. The stir we've caused is not just because of your Rite and the Wadi, but the news in the last hour that two of my uncles are dead."

Molly felt her stomach sink. "Uncles? Oh, gods, Anlyn. I'm so—"

Anlyn waved the thought away with her thin, blue arm. "Don't be," she said. "If you will not allow me to apologize for their attempt to kill you, I'll not hear you explain your self-defense. I heard the wireless report from the guards you stranded, and I know how to translate their lies. I've been around Circle members all of my youth, and I am fluent in *that* language."

Edison followed up Anlyn's crushing news with another emotional blow: "My proximity to Anlyn will remain decreased," he told Molly.

And she understood. All too clearly.

Stepping forward, she pressed herself into his tunic, her friend's paws wrapping around her back. Molly remembered the last time they'd held each other like that, just a few weeks ago. Edison had asked to join her crew aboard *Parsona*—and now he was leaving.

She felt the Wadi move from her shoulders and attach itself to Edison. Pulling away, she wiped her cheeks and laughed as the colorful creature scampered to the top of Edison's head. It swung its neck back and forth, as if taking in the commanding view.

"Ascertain its function," Edison pleaded, his hands comically frozen halfway to his head.

Cole laughed. "I think it just laid claim to you, pal." He reached up and coaxed the Wadi down to Edison's shoulder. "Now do me a favor and hold off on the wedding for a week or so. As soon as we figure out what's going on with Molly's parents, I'm coming back to be your best man."

Edison cocked his head at the expression. "Best by what metric?"

Anlyn patted him. "I'll explain later." She started to say something to Cole and then stopped. Instead, she embraced him, and Molly could hear her sweet whisper: "Take care of Molly."

"I will," said Cole. "And you take care of Edison."

The Wadi leaped back to Molly's shoulders, the movement hardly startling for once. Anlyn turned back to the creature, her eyes lit up. She seemed mesmerized by the sight of the living, docile Wadi.

"Be very careful with her," she advised.

The tone suggested a responsibility Molly wasn't sure she wanted to bear.

"Should I leave her with you?" she asked. "How will she survive if we pull Gs or lose cabin pressure? I should leave her here with you, shouldn't I?"

Anlyn shook her head. "I don't think you could if you wanted to. You're bonded, the two of you. Besides, the Gs shouldn't be a problem, but atmosphere might. She can crawl into my old suit if she just needs some air to breathe. Either way, trust me, she's less safe here right now."

Molly nodded. "I wish you didn't have to stay."

"I know. Me, too. But there's something bigger going on than any of us. Something that involves trillions of lives and thousands of galaxies. I thought I could run away from that, avoid duty and take care of myself, but I was wrong. In fact, I was wrong to *want* to."

"I don't understan—"

"It's OK. Your mother does. She's been through this before and can explain a lot. I've given her permission."

"My mother? What have you two been . . .?" She didn't know how to finish the question.

"She and I have spent most of the last two days together. Talking. I had some Defense Port engineers make a few changes that helped us out, and they should serve you as well. But I'll let her tell you about them."

Molly felt a tinge of jealousy, betrayal even, with the passing of secrets, the idea that someone else knew her mother more intimately than she. An alien, no less. She fought these negative emotions down, comforting herself with the knowledge that her mother had company the past few days and had stayed abreast of events.

Anlyn reached out and squeezed Molly's arm. "Thank you for setting me free," she said.

Molly felt the tears welling up in her eyes, her heart racing and empty. She leaned in to hug Anlyn.

"Thank you for saving *my* life," she told her friend.

o o o o

Molly and Cole watched the cargo door close on the three friends they were leaving behind. Walter stomped around behind them, opening cubbies and storing away the food and supplies that had been loaded into the ship. He had already changed into his flightsuit, and after the door sealed, Molly and Cole moved off to don theirs.

In her room, Molly shrugged off her filthy tunics and suited up, expecting the worst. The Wadi sat on her dresser and looked at the mirror, bobbing its head up and down while she changed. She laughed, wondering what the creature thought of its reflection.

Scooping the Wadi up, she left her room and heard Cole in the lazarette cycling up the thrusters. She made her way to the cockpit and performed a quick systems check. Everything looked good. She wondered about radioing for clearance but wasn't sure how to communicate with the tower. As soon as Cole returned and gave her a thumbs-up, she lifted off the tarmac and arced away from the band of buildings ringing the planet.

Parsona rose up through the atmosphere, out toward the colorful horizon. Before breaking the ionosphere, the twin Drenard suns popped into view, bathing the cockpit in a warmth that seemed gentle, innocuous even.

While they waited for the hyperdrive to spin up, Molly navigated through the outbound buoys, waiting for an attack that never came, flying past menacing ships that spun in place, not even radioing her, just *watching*.

She tried to concentrate on the gauges—and then saw the fusion fuel at one hundred percent, which gave her some tenuous sensation of freedom.

They were back on the run, but at least they had fresh legs.

She began visualizing the half-dozen jumps it would take to get to Dakura, but she did so in her head, leaving the nav screen free to check in with her mother. She pulled the keyboard out and typed:

MOM?_

"Mollie?"

The voice came out through the radio speakers, scaring the hyperspace out of her and Cole both. Cole reached for the mic as a reflex, obviously thinking they were being hailed. Molly jerked her hands away from the computer; the Wadi scurried to the back of her seat.

"Mollie?" the voice said again.

"Hello?" Cole asked.

"Is that Cole?"

Cole turned to Molly. "I *told* you she could hear us!'

"I can now," the ship said—her *mom* said. It was a pleasant voice, not chipped and halting the way her old reader used to spit out text. It sounded natural, as a computer might if it could generate sounds from scratch.

"Is this what Anlyn did?"

"Yes. And more. I can see now."

"What do you mean?" Molly asked.

"They tied me into the SADAR unit. And the cargo camera. Oh, Molly, it was all I could do not to say something when you guys boarded, but I knew it was best to explain on the way."

"You can see through the cargo bay cam?"

"Yes. And you are so beautiful, Molly. Just as I imagined you."

Molly reached forward to turn the volume down and power the cockpit door shut. She pulled up the cargo cam and saw Walter strapped to his seat, playing his videogame contentedly.

"Hey, Mom?"

"Yes, dear?"

"Can we keep these upgrades between the three of us for now?"

"Of course, sweetheart, but may I ask why?"

"You can. And I'll tell you later."

"Take your time. Speaking of time, having something to look at paces it for me, like a little clock. The agonizing wait between sentences is gone. And I can read the old ship's logs from the nav computer, the entries your father and I wrote—"

"That's great, Mom. After we jump out of here, I'm gonna need to ask you some questions."

"Of course. And I'll be happy to tell you what I can."

"*Can?*" Molly glanced at Cole. "Because of what you know or because of what you're allowed to say?"

"Some of both," her mother said, the worry in her voice not sounding artificial at all.

21

The stars shifted positions, and *Parsona* exited hyperspace.

Molly looked down at the Wadi in her lap, wondering if it was going to throw up on her flightsuit as it experienced its first bout of hyperspace. The curious creature just flicked its tongue and looked at the dash as if it were already bored of space travel.

"Ninety-four percent," Cole advised Molly.

"Plenty. Should be enough to get to Dakura and then back to Lok. We'll fill up in Bekkie."

Cole leaned forward and peered at the star charts. "Keep in mind that we aren't going in a straight shot, though. We can't risk leaving the Drenard arm of the

Milky Way anywhere along the center. The Navy'll be looking for us."

"It should still be enough. If we jump out to *here*, we can make a really long jump across the arm divide to here; there's not much mass out there to throw us off." Molly marked rough waypoints on her screen so Cole could see them on his.

The cockpit door slid open, and Walter stuck his head inside. "What are you guyss doing?" he asked.

Cole turned. "Just planning out our run to Dakura, buddy." He said it with sincerity, impressing Molly once more with how hard he kept trying to make friends with Walter.

His reward, she noted, was the boy's familiar sneer.

He turned to Molly. "Can I hold the Wadi?" he asked.

"Why don't you get a juice pouch and see if she's thirsty?"

He scampered back to the galley, and Cole and Molly exchanged a look. The Wadi flicked a tongue out at the dashboard.

"You really need to name her," Cole said, nodding at the Wadi.

"I know, but the pressure's killing me. Anlyn and Dani seem to think she's important somehow." Molly thought for a second. "Do I have to give her a last name with a bunch of o's? Just for tradition?"

"How about Collette?"

"How about not."

Walter ran back in with a juice pouch and peeled the suction tube straight. He leaned over the flight controls and waved it in front of the Wadi. The creature sniffed the air, crawled up Molly's flightsuit, and wrapped itself around her neck.

"I guesss sshe issn't thirssty," Walter hissed sullenly.

"It's OK," Molly told the Wadi, peeling its tail off and handing it to Walter. The boy took the thing at arm's length and hissed playfully at it.

"Be very gentle with her."

"I will," Walter promised. He walked out of the cockpit, the Wadi's arms pawing at the air.

Molly tapped Cole on the elbow. "Can you take the next shift?"

"Yeah, sure. You gonna get some sleep?"

"I wish." Molly grabbed her helmet off the rack above her head. "I need to have a talk with Mom. Keep an eye on the cargo cam, would you?"

"Sure thing. You OK?"

Molly leaned over Cole's chair and kissed his cheek. "I'm fine. I promise. I just have some questions I want answered."

"Take your time. I'll radio you before our next jump. I'm doing a slow spool—I'm worried we might've damaged the drive with so many emergency cycles earlier. So it'll be a few hours before we can jump again."

"Perfect. You get some rest up here. If you can." Molly entered the cargo bay and saw Walter holding a juice pouch over his head, the Wadi swinging its claws at it.

"Don't tease the Wadi, Walter."

"Yesss, Captain."

She glanced up at the camera in the corner of the cargo bay and gave Cole a stern look. Just in case he was watching.

o o o o

Molly plopped down on her bed and pulled her helmet down tight. She didn't bother locking the collar, and she left the visor open to breathe the ship's air. Crossing her legs, she keyed the radio mic, hoping this would work.

"Mom?"

"Yes, dear?"

The voice sounded just as pleasant through her helmet as it had in the cockpit.

"We need to talk."

"I have plenty of CPU cycles to devote to you—oh, we're on your private channel. Is this about Cole? Because I don't know that I'm ready for that talk—"

Molly brought her palms up to her helmet in disbelief and embarrassment. "Mooom! Ew, noooo. I do *not* want to talk about Cole. We barely kiss—"

282

"I just want you to be safe—"

"You want me to be safe? Good, because *that's* what I want to talk about. No more secrets, Mom. I mean it. If you knew what I've been through the last two days—"

"I do know."

"You know what? Just what Anlyn told you? Because I don't think even she—"

"Molly."

"What?"

"Your father went through the same ordeal."

Molly had a sudden impulse to plug in her suit and enrich the O_2. She gasped for a full breath, shaking her head. She tried to voice her disbelief, but all she could squeeze out was a small *"No."*

"I'm sure your experience differed from his somewhat, but I think I know what you've been through."

"Dad? He—A *Drenard*? And . . . and it was more than the rite, Mom. Politicians wanted us dead. I've had to help kill people with my bare hands!"

"As have I. It's what the Navy trained us for. It's why your father and I wanted you to stay with Lucin, to join the Academy."

"You *planned* that? I thought you were dead!"

"It's complicated."

"You keep saying that." Molly could feel her head sweating in her helmet; she reached across her bunk and lowered the air temperature. "Try and explain it to me. Tell me about Lok, about my birth, about where you've been. Tell me where Dad is and how I can help him. I'm sick of groping about like a blind person."

"Give me a minute," Parsona said.

Molly grabbed a pillow and put it behind her neck. Leaning back, she sandwiched it between the bulkhead and her helmet. "Take your time," she told her mom. "We aren't jumping into Dakura until I know what we're getting ourselves into."

"Sometimes it's better to not know what you're getting yourself into," Parsona said. "When I was stationed on Lok, I had no idea what lay ahead. I may not have gone if someone had told me. Even if they'd told me how important my work would be. Even if it meant not having you, I don't know if I would've been brave enough to go.

"I met your father on my second day there. But of course, I was having to act as if we'd been together for years—"

"Wait. You weren't there on your honeymoon? Did Dad lie to me about *everything*?"

"No, darling. Not everything. The honeymoon was the cover the Navy cooked up. They thought they had everything planned out, as usual, but then they couldn't even manage to get us on the same flight to Lok. The mission was a mess from the start.

"I thought I knew everything about your father. I spent months with a reader loaded up with his files and bio, memorizing every detail about him. He was doing the same for me, of course, like two illegals marrying for an Earth permit. That part of the mission scared me more than any other, I think. We were *both* scared, as I found out later. Scared we wouldn't like each other, that the ruse would be a strain.

"But nothing in those files prepared me for what I felt when I first met him."

"What do you mean?"

"Oh, it's hard to explain. Or maybe not. Maybe you felt the same way when you met Cole—"

Molly laughed. "I doubt it. I thought he was a jerk at first. That was my default expectation at the Academy. But we got paired up in the simulators . . . No, I don't think that's right, actually. I *do* remember feeling something when I met him. He was so handsome, but there was something else. A confidence, but one you could *believe* in. Like an assurance that had been paid for in full."

"That's it!" Parsona said. "That's what I felt with your father. Of course, he used to say he saw the same things in me—"

"What were you guys doing on Lok?"

"Please understand, there are some things I can't tell you. And it isn't because I don't trust you, I promise.

I've seen you; I know it's you, but there are other people I don't trust."

"Like who?"

"Almost everyone."

"Ha. I think I can appreciate that."

"Molly, what your father and I uncovered on Lok is bigger than any of us. We've both had to make some tough decisions, choices I wouldn't wish on anyone else—"

"Like what decisions? Like having me?" Molly felt ridiculous saying it, but the words hung in the air as if someone else had uttered them. She heard their echo and felt angry and sad.

"Yes. Choosing to have you was one of the hardest decisions we made. It nearly killed me. The decision, I mean . . . but I don't regret that choice. I never have. I—"

"Where *are* you, Mom? Are you still alive somewhere? I don't want to talk to a computer."

"Alive? Possibly. Or probably. My body is most likely still alive on the moon of Dakura."

Molly tried to reach into her helmet to wipe the tears out of her eyes, but the visor wasn't designed with that in mind. "You have to tell me what I'll find on Dakura, Mom. I'm not jumping in there if I don't know what to expect."

"Of course. I had planned on it. When I say Dakura, I actually mean the large moon that orbits the privately owned planet."

"Someone owns an entire planet?"

"Arthur Dakura does. Or did. It was sixteen years ago. I was very sick, and your father was willing to do anything to save me. You were a few months old when a man we hardly knew arranged to have me taken to Dakura."

"The doctors there were able to help you?"

"Yes. But they aren't the kind of doctors you're thinking of. Not all of them, anyway. The colony on the moon was founded by Arthur and funded with his vast fortune. He wanted to find a way to cheat death, so he concentrated on the human brain, decoding it, teasing apart the programming like a hacker might reverse engineer some software—"

"Why? How would that let him cheat death?"

"Because—and I can only explain it as it has been explained to me—all we are and all we feel is just filtered through the pathways of our brains. If you keep the brain healthy and ticking, feed it the right programming, you can make it feel alive forever."

Molly grabbed the pillow from behind her head; her helmet thunked back against the bulkhead. She pulled the pillow into her lap, grasping and releasing fistfuls of fabric anxiously.

"Are you like that, Mom? Am I gonna see your brain in a jar or something like that?"

"No, dear. Well, not exactly. I mean . . . I look at you and I see a brain in a very lovely jar, a beautiful shell designed to protect it, keep it nourished, move it out of danger. They left me in my own jar, if that makes any sense."

"I feel like I'm gonna be sick."

"What I'm about to tell you next will likely make you feel worse, I'm afraid."

"Oh, gods, Mom. What?"

"I haven't been completely honest with you about what needs doing on Dakura, sweetheart."

"You said we needed to go there because you're missing some of your memories."

"That's mostly right. But it's more like misplacing a set of keys. A copy of very important keys. And now we need to make sure nobody else finds them."

"What do you mean?"

"Sweetheart. When we get to Dakura, I need you to kill me."

22

Molly nearly ripped the pillow completely open. "Do *what?*" she asked, hoping she'd misheard.

"I need you to kill me. The *old* me."

"What in hyperspace for? I thought we were going to *rescue* you!"

"Sweetheart, you already *have* rescued me. The real me is the one in *here*, the one that spent the last few years with your father. The old shell we left behind—"

"Your body."

"OK, the body we left behind . . . it was dying. The man that helped us, he had Arthur's doctors hook me up to their computers to keep me alive. We thought it was a favor for us, but later, your father realized the man did it for himself. It was years before your father could find a way to steal a copy and install it in the ship."

"Who was this guy? Why would he do that? And why go back to kill your body? Why does it even matter?"

"We didn't think it would, your father and I. But years later, we found out who that man was. He isn't a very nice man. In fact, he isn't a man at all."

"Wait—what? Who—or *what* is he?"

"He's our real enemy, not the Drenard. That is . . . it's hard to explain. We have a complicated past with him, your father and I. You as well, for that matter."

"Me?"

"He's the reason you're here. He helped deliver you."

"Deliver me where?"

"*Deliver* you. As a baby. Your father never told you about your birth?"

"I was six! The only thing I ever asked him about was you, but it just made him quiet."

"Of course. Poor Mortimor, he always blamed himself . . . "

"So, who is this guy? Why was he there when I was born?"

"He was following us. Your father and I were tracking down some men for the Navy, and we led him right to them."

"And he's not human? What is he?"

"He's one of the—he's a burglar, that's what he is. A simple crook trying to break into our galaxy and open a back door so he can let in . . ." Her mom fell silent.

"Let in what?"

"I can't say. I'm sorry. And we're getting off topic, anyway."

"That's fine with me because I don't wanna talk about killing you. The old you, I mean."

"If I'm—if *she's* even still alive. And if we don't get there before this man does, it might not matter."

"If it's been sixteen years, how do you know he hasn't already?"

"Because he hasn't had sixteen years; he's had half a year. And he isn't the only person that would be interested. Besides, if he'd already accomplished what we aim to prevent, we would know."

"Gods, Mom. What in the galaxy could you know that's so important?" *Besides how to speak Drenard,* she thought.

"It's difficult to say how much my old self has put together in that brain of hers. It took years for your father and me to realize that all the pieces were there, and stewing. And for all that time, there was nothing we could do about it. You have to believe me, destroying that old body of mine is more important than rescuing your father. And it's best if you start thinking of that shell as a jar and me as your mother. Neither is easy, I know."

"I don't know what to believe," Molly said. "And I still don't understand what you could know that's so important."

"When your father and I were on Lok, there was a popular game show from Earth that was all the rage—"

"Pick That Door," Molly said.

"That's right! You've seen it?"

"Reruns on flat panels, not the holovids. And just once or twice—I really hated that show."

"Yes, well, so did everyone else, but we all watched it. Do you remember the gist of it?"

"Yeah. It was dumb. There were two doors. One had a vacation package to a distant planet, and the other had something dangerous from the same planet, like a wild animal or a noxious gas. They described each in detail, and the contestant chose to open a door or just go away with nothing."

"That's about right. And actually, you make it sound more interesting than it was."

"What's your point?"

"Well, dear, *that's* what I know. I know which door to open."

"For a *game show?*" Molly nearly tore her helmet off in disgust.

"No, sweetheart. Of course not. *For real.*"

"Real doors?"

"Oh, yes. And there are terrible things behind one of those doors. Things that other people, some of them in our own Navy, are dying to let out. I know where one of those doors is, and so does . . . my former self. She also might know what fusion fuel is made of, which could lead to problems."

"I can't believe either is more important to you than rescuing Dad."

"If we don't do this first," Parsona said, "the hell your father's living in will be the only safe place in the universe. Sweetheart, if we fail—there'll be nowhere to rescue him *to.*"

o o o o

Molly wasn't sure what to make of the plan. She half-expected to arrive at Dakura and discover she'd been played a fool the entire time. Cole's doubts about her mother's artificial existence gnawed at her. She tucked her helmet under her arm and went to speak with him, but as she entered the cargo bay, she saw Walter and the Wadi, and froze.

"What are you *doing*?" she cried, rushing toward them. Walter had a red band around his head, and he was attempting to fit another one around the Wadi's. "Where'd you get those?"

Walter looked up at her with an innocent expression. "I'm trying to talk to the Wadi," he explained.

"And where did you get those?" she asked again.

Walter looked at the ribbon in his hand, as if he needed to confirm what she was talking about. "During the fight in the sshuttle. Finderss keepersss." Walter touched the one around his head. "Thiss one iss *mine*."

Molly reached down to pick up the Wadi. It leaped to her arms before she got all the way there and wrapped itself around the back of her neck.

Its tongue flicked out twice. Once in Walter's direction and once to touch Molly's cheek.

Walter pouted at the loss.

"I'm going to need to keep those." Molly indicated the band in his hand and the one on his head.

"They're *mine*," he insisted. His metallic-colored face flushed with a dull glow.

"And they can stay yours, but I'm going to keep them in the cockpit, OK? They're too important to play with like toys."

Walter looked devastated. "I'm the *ssupply* officser," he said.

"And I'm the captain," she reminded him, her hand out.

Walter took the band off his head and placed them both in her palm. "It wassn't working, anyway," he said, consoling himself.

Molly wrapped her fingers around the bands and marched to the cockpit.

"Thanks for keeping an eye on the cargo cam for me," she said to Cole as soon as she entered.

"No problem . . ." Cole spun in his seat. "Wait. You're being sarcastic, aren't you? But he's been right there this whole time . . ." he stopped and stared at the red bands in her hand. "Where'd you get those?"

"Walter stole them. He was playing dress-up with the Wadi."

Cole gestured at the security screen on the dash. "Like I could tell that from *this*." His eyes narrowed. "Can your mom hear us fighting?"

"Probably not. Not with the mic turned off." Molly placed her helmet on its rack, and the Wadi moved to the back of her seat. She climbed over the control console and slumped into her chair. "Hyperspace on ice," she murmured, looking down at the bands.

"What's the big deal? He *is* a born pirate, you know."

"Yeah, no . . . gods, I don't know." Molly dropped the bands and rubbed her face. She tested her theory: "Mom?"

There was no response.

"Do you need to talk?" Cole asked.

Molly turned to him. His thick, perfectly shaped eyebrows formed twin arcs of concern over his green eyes. Molly reached over and squeezed his arm. "Mom told me why we have to go to Dakura."

"Something about her memories, right?"

"Yeah, but she doesn't want them back."

"What, then?"

"She wants them erased. Permanently."

Cole looked out the carboglass at the stars while Molly told him what she'd learned, what little of it made sense to her. The only thing she left out was her mom's mention of fusion fuel, and maybe knowing what it was made of.

It didn't seem important at the time.

PART IX

HEAVEN

"Happiness can come solely from within, but not for long."

~The Bern Seer~

23

The stars shifted as *Parsona* jumped into Dakura, and a dark, gray sphere popped into view amid the smattering of stars. Molly reached forward and flipped on the radio to let her mom know they'd arrived.

"That's Dakura?" Cole asked. "Not much to look at."

It was Parsona who answered. "It will be," she said. "Eventually. It used to be a frozen wasteland, much like Mars."

"Well, it still looks that way to me," Molly said, thrusting off toward the planet's largest moon.

"What color is it?" Parsona asked.

"A darkish gray. Why? What color should it be?"

"When your father and I were here sixteen years ago, it was a dull red—the color of rust."

"Looks like it's just getting worse, if you ask me," said Cole.

"It's a long process. That gray dusting will trap heat over a long period of time, thawing the crust and releasing the water inside. It will take thousands of years."

"Makes sense," Molly thought aloud, "for a guy dedicated to immortality to plan something like this. I bet he got a great deal on the planet."

"Someone *owns* that planet?" Cole asked.

Molly looked over. "I thought I mentioned that."

"Who are you guysss talking to?"

Molly and Cole spun in their seats to see Walter standing behind their chairs. The Wadi's tongue flicked out into the air.

"Flight control," Cole lied. "Getting permission to land, buddy."

"Starship *Parsona*, you're cleared for landing pad four," Parsona said through the radio speaker. Molly smiled at Cole, who bit his lip to keep from laughing.

Before Walter could respond, another voice—heavy with static—crackled through the same speaker. "GN-290, ship ID *Parsona*, this is Dakura flight control, come in."

"Who'ss *that*?" Walter asked, pointing to the dash.

"Uh, that's Customs. We'll have to clear in with them, now."

"Why did he call himsself 'Flight Control'?"

"Hey, Walter, I don't question the way you organize the cargo bays, do I?"

"No."

"OK, man, you just have to trust that Molly and I know what we're doing."

"Yeah, but you guyss keep getting uss in trouble," Walter said, pouting.

Molly laughed out loud at this and switched the radio over to her helmet. "Dakura Flight Control, *Parsona* here, looking for clearance. Over."

"Roger, *Parsona*, you're cleared for landing pad two. And welcome back."

Molly looked to Cole to see if he was listening in, but he and Walter were busy arguing about something.

"Strap in for the landing, boys."

Walter huffed and looked down at his flightsuit, brushing his hands across it as if to remove some dust. He marched back to his seat, gurgling in Palan.

○ ○ ○ ○

Only one other ship sat on the moon's landing pads as they descended to the surface. "Looks like we have the place to ourselves," Cole said.

Molly nodded and followed the beacon for Pad Two. Once she had a visual—the large number etched into the paved surface—she decreased the thrusters and brought her altimeter to zero. The shocks in the landing gear took out what little jarring there was, making the arrival so smooth, it felt as if they weren't there yet.

"Nice landing," Cole said. "We did land, didn't we?"

Molly beamed. "Yeah, and this moon is massive. A lot of gravity here, but no atmosphere, so keep your helmet on."

Molly reached to unbuckle her harness when the entire ship trembled slightly. She put both hands out in confusion, preparing to steady herself against more tremors.

"Nebular," Cole said, lifting his visor up and peering through the porthole on his side of the cockpit.

Molly looked out her side and saw the surface of the moon sliding up to block out the stars. "A lift?" she asked.

"Yeah, and we don't have this place to ourselves at all."

Below the artificial surface of the moon lay a lit parking facility. It stretched farther than they could see, filled to bursting with a wide variety of gleaming hulls, some of them being tended to with long, robotic arms.

"Whoa. That's a Viking 500 over there."

Molly unstrapped herself and leaned over Cole to see. Walter ran in to investigate the clamor, nearly climbing over their backs to get a better view.

"That's a pricey ship," Cole pointed out.

"I wanna sssee!"

Molly scooted over and patted her armrest. "Get up here," she said. He jumped up at once, and the Wadi leaped from the back of Molly's chair over to Cole's.

"There's no people," Molly said.

She longed to ask her mother some more questions, but not with Walter around. It was imperative they hide her mother's existence from the people on Dakura, and she trusted Walter with a secret as much as she trusted him with a computer. As Parsona had reiterated earlier: she was stolen contraband, an unauthorized copy snuck off the planet. If they found her, she'd be deleted, and they'd all be in a ton of trouble.

Molly didn't like the situation, but she felt relieved to have a warning. *At least I know what to avoid doing here,* she thought.

Meanwhile, Cole and Walter went nuts over space-ship designs. While they took turns pointing out which paint jobs were the flashiest, Molly imagined what *Parsona* must look like to all these other ships; her outdated hull was streaked with micro-burns from space debris; the paint job was original and boring, covered in drab, stenciled lettering. Reflexively, she reached out and rubbed her hand across the dash, as if her mother could feel the comforting touch.

As *Parsona* sank down to the level of the other ships, Molly braced for a jarring halt, but the lift continued to lower them through the floor of the parking garage. Beside her, the boys moaned over how quickly the show had come to a close. She actually felt relieved to have the gaudy things out of her sight. *Better to not compare*, she figured.

They descended into a hangar the same size as the landing pad. Molly looked up through the carboglass window in the top of the cockpit and watched the ceiling come together, sealing them inside.

"Stop squirming," she told Walter. He was practically bouncing around on her lap as he tried to take it all in.

"Ssitting in the cargo bay ssucksss," he spat. "It'ss nebular in the cockpit."

Molly saw him look down at Cole's seat, almost as if he longed to own it.

From above, a dull thud sounded out as the doors slammed shut. Atmosphere hissed into the sealed room from vents along the wall, the condensation billowing out like steam. The same male voice cracked through the radio and told them to wait five minutes for pressurization.

"Expensive setup they have here," Cole said, leaning forward and gazing up at the large chamber.

"I'm sure immortality doesn't come cheaply."

"Yeah. Hey, I thought you always said your parents were poor, from a frontier planet and all that."

"They were. Trust me, I'm as confused as you are." She shot the radio speaker a look, reveling in the situation her mother was in thanks to Walter's presence: forced to sit and listen and not say anything in return.

Her mom's instructions had been vague, mostly because even *she* didn't know what their options were. The first step would be to pay her other self a visit and see what she knew. They also needed to find out if anyone else had come to see Parsona in the last half year. And finally, if there was any legal way for a surviving family member to take her body off-line, they would do that. But the last was not something Molly wanted to consider. It would remain a nasty contingency in case all else failed.

"Let me out," Molly told Walter. "I'm gonna go get changed."

"Me, too!" he yelled, jumping off her lap and dashing back through the cargo bay.

"What in hyperspace are we gonna do with him?" Molly asked, watching him tear through the ship.

Cole shrugged. "My vote a long time ago was to airlock him. But more immediately, what are we gonna do with the lizard while we're here?"

"She'll stay in my room. And she's a *Wadi*, not a lizard." Molly looked down at her flightsuit. "And at least she doesn't leave footprints on me the way Walter does."

Cole laughed. "Yeah, she just tried to claw your face off."

Molly touched the small bandage on her cheek. "She did not! That was a different lizard."

"So that one was a *lizard*, eh?" Cole unstrapped himself and worked his way out of his seat, laughing.

"Yeah," Molly pouted. "The boys are *lizards*, the girls are Wadis."

Cole's laughter got louder as he disappeared into the cargo bay.

Molly and the Wadi stared at each other.

They understood the difference.

oooo

By the time Molly came out with a clean outfit on—a nice blouse and a pair of pants she'd picked up in Darrin—Cole was already waiting in the cargo bay. Walter stood nearby, playing his video game. Above them, both the atmosphere and pressure lights flashed green, signaling it was safe to lower the ramp.

"You wanna pop the hatch?" Molly asked Walter, trying to break his attention away from his computer.

"Pretty good wirelesss ssignal here," he murmured.

"Do *not* hack the network here, Walter," Cole said. "Now put the computer away."

Walter sighed but holstered the device. They waited on him to lower the ramp, a job he insisted belonged to the supply officer, since, as he put it: "That'ss where the cargo comess in."

He made a great show of lifting the protective glass shield over the release button before pressing it. Molly swore she heard him making missile-launching noises as he activated the door. It was all she could do to not crack a smile.

As the captain, she exited the ship first, her soft shoes giving her a bounce and gripping the loading ramp in a way her flight boots couldn't. It felt great to be arriving someplace where they were welcome, and at a stop they'd actually planned. The novelty of things going so well took her mind off the difficult task they were there to accomplish.

She stepped away from the ship and looked around at the hangar bay. It was basically a cube, about two hundred meters to a side. The floor had been painted a neutral shade of tan, a color that also went up the walls about to eye level before a light blue hue took over, which expanded upward to cover the ceiling. It seemed designed to make landlubbers feel at home.

On the far wall, two double doors stood, large enough to drive a loading truck through. Molly faced them, expecting the entry to pop open, when a smaller, almost invisible door set within them slid back instead.

An older man in a well-fitted suit strolled through the new opening. He had his hand out, a smile frozen on his face. Molly walked toward him and extended her arm in greeting. She was a dozen paces away before she realized he was an automaton, the sort of android that had been banned from most human planets.

"Greetings and welcome. I am Stanley, and I will be your host for the duration of your stay." The voice was the same one from the radio. It sounded perfectly natural, but the lips didn't move quite right. They flapped open and shut to mimic speech, but they clearly weren't forming the words. Near the corners of the mouth, the rubbery coating substituting for flesh folded unnaturally, distracting Molly.

She shook her head, trying to remember what the robot had just said. "Hello. Uh—I'm Molly Fyde, and, uh, this is my navigator, Cole Mendonça, and my supply officer, Walter Hommul." Cole came forward to shake hands as well. Walter waved from a distance, his video game already sneaking out of its holster.

"And this is *Parsona*?" the robot asked, gesturing toward the ship behind them.

"Uh. The ship? Yeah, I guess. Um, we just refer to it as a GN-290. None of us are into really thinking of ships as women, you know? Uh, my father named it after his—"

"His wife. And your mother. Yes, it's all on file. Welcome back."

"Uh, this is my first time, actually. But I guess the ship was here a long time ago?"

The robot tilted its head to the side; its eyes moved up and down, almost as if scanning her. Molly stood close enough to hear the small servos buzzing in its artificial skull.

"Yes," Stanley said, "I suppose you were much too young to remember. No matter, I recall you well. And I must say, sixteen years is not so long a time at all. Just a blink. Now, if you will follow me, your friends may rest in our hospitality suite while you visit with your mother. Family only, I'm afraid."

Molly held up her hand. "Actually, before I get straight to the visit, I was wondering if we could get a tour of the facilities? Maybe hear a little about how all this works. I still don't understand why my mom came here or even what it is that you guys do."

"Oh, but of course. I'm terribly sorry. Most people are in such a rush these days. It pleases me you are willing to take your time and do things in the proper order. Most excellent. Very well, then, if you will follow me, I will show you all that LIFE has to offer."

"Life?" Cole asked as they followed Stanley through the door.

The android spelled it out: "Ell eye eff eee. Longevity through Interactive Fantasy Environments. LIFE."

Walter straggled behind, coming through the door last; it swooshed closed behind him. The sounds of heavy machinery whirring into operation emanated from the hangar, and a light above the door winked from green to red.

"Uh, Stanley?" Molly said. "Is our ship gonna be OK?"

"What? Oh, of course. It will be valet parked until you are ready to leave. Must make room for our new arrivals! Busy, busy." As if to demonstrate, Stanley turned and started walking swiftly down the long, tiled hallway.

Molly pictured *Parsona* being parked in the vacuum of the hangar and thought about the poor Wadi in her crew quarters. She guessed there was several days of atmosphere locked up in the ship, and their visit shouldn't take nearly that long. She tried not to worry and hurried after Stanley, past doors labeled "Hangar Six" and "Hangar Four." Their guide kept up the pace as he launched into a history of the company.

"Founded in 2312, LIFE was designed to offer an alternative to the finality of death. The brainchild of Dr. Arthur Dakura, a wonderful philanthropist and brilliant psychologist, it fulfills the broken promise of so many ancient systems of belief—"

Stanley spun around on the group and threw his hands wide across the hall.

"—*Heaven,*" he gushed, saying it as if he were about to unveil a new private-class GN starship model. The maneuver was flamboyant enough to make Walter glance up from his computer.

Molly and Cole froze. She wondered if they were supposed to ask a question at this point, but then Stanley whirled back around and continued to walk and talk.

"What Dr. Dakura discovered in his mapping of the human brain was that it works just like a computer. Data flows in, the computer does some crunching, and data flows back out. Simple as that."

"If it's so simple," Cole asked, "what makes this Arthur guy so smart?"

"Excellent question. Step right through here, please." A door opposite Hangar Eight led the small group into a lobby of sorts. There were several other figures in suits milling about, all of them identical to Stanley in every way. One of them looked up from behind a large wooden desk and smiled. Another passed right by them, escorting an elderly lady. This Stanley reached into his suit and proffered a handkerchief, which the woman accepted and sniffled into.

Molly moved aside to let them pass, watching the duo head out toward the hangars.

Dozens of identical voices could be heard talking with prospective clients, family members, and one another. Molly nodded to another human whose eye she caught, the feeling of evolutionary kinship as powerful as it was absurd—a sense of tribalism thousands of years past its usefulness.

The place really *was* busy, she saw. And being run like clockwork. Several species Molly didn't recognize moved through the lobby, listening to a Stanley as he gave them a tour.

"Fyde, Parsona," their Stanley said to the Stanley behind the desk. Then he turned to Molly and explained, "Your mother will be told to expect you. How long will you be visiting?"

Molly hadn't thought about that. How long would she need? How different would this be from talking to the "mom" in her spaceship?

"A few hours?" she asked out loud.

"Put her down for three hours, Stanley."

"Very good, Stanley." The man behind the desk produced three visitor passes.

Their guide turned and handed them the passes, which they draped over their necks. Then he turned to Cole and pointed to a large portrait on the wall. "Your question, my good man, regarding Dr. Dakura's intellect is still awaiting its answer. Let's go down a few levels and see for ourselves, shall we?"

Molly nodded eagerly and followed along after their energetic guide. She put one hand on Walter's elbow and guided him through the lobby and down a short hallway, allowing him to play his game without crashing into anyone.

An elevator dinged ahead of them and disgorged an elderly human couple. Molly and Cole both nodded, reflexively, as their group entered the lift. Stanley pressed a button and typed some commands into a keyboard affixed to the wall.

The back of the elevator flickered for a moment and then displayed a video. The first scene showed an elevator descending toward the center of a circular, gray moon. Below this stood a side-on view of the human brain.

"We begin our tour at the center of Dakura's moon," Stanley began. "At the heart of LIFE. Of course, 'heart' is a poor metaphor, a holdover from the days of anatomical ignorance. We now know primal emotions lie *here*, at the core of our brains."

Stanley faced them but still managed to trace his fingers over appropriate portions of the image. It was an uncanny and jarring sight, similar to holovid weathermen back on Earth.

"Dr. Dakura's genius," he directed this to Cole, "was to understand the computer programs and previous attempts at AI were doomed due to their complexity.

For hundreds of years, computer scientists tried to recreate an object about which they knew nothing. It took a psychologist who understood that object, and dabbled in computer science, to make the breakthrough."

The video flashed to a shot of a scientist standing over a man as he slid into a scanning machine of some sort.

"Dr. Dakura knew two things about the brain these other researchers neglected to take into account. First, the illusion of a single program is just that: an illusion. Second, the brain is imperfect." Stanley's mechanical eyes peeled away from Cole and resumed their steady flicking over the trio. The video changed back to a graphical representation of their descent to the center of the moon with an overlay of the human brain on top.

"The human brain is composed of thousands of small programs, many of them working against one another. All of them are imperfect. They make mistakes. Dr. Dakura was the first researcher to introduce competition between his simulated brain modules and also program in a degree of randomness. Every now and then, his AI would 'see' or 'hear' things that weren't truly there. They would incorporate lies as truths. It was brilliant work for which he never sought recognition, neither through publication nor awards."

The elevator dinged. It must have been moving swiftly, but there had been no sense of it ever starting or stopping. Molly looked to her feet, wondering if there were gravity panels in the floor.

"Right this way," Stanley said.

They filed out while another group, a Stanley and two Callites, stood to the side. The Stanleys greeted each other politely. Molly smiled at the Callites, assuming they were a couple. She remembered the race from her childhood on Lok and was somewhat surprised the notoriously impoverished people could afford the services. The female Callite smiled back at her while the male struggled forward on two canes, barely able to walk. There was no need to guess which of the aliens was considering enrollment.

Molly stepped out of the elevator and made room for them to pass, pulling Walter along with her. Their group exited onto a long, wide balcony. Two other groups stood by the low wall lining the edge and listened intently to their own Stanleys. Beyond the railing loomed a massive chamber, carved out of raw moon, that stretched out for kilometers. Flat concrete walls rose up, covered with gigantic shelves on which stood colorful drums easily large enough to hold a human body.

"This is where it all happens," Stanley said, waving his arm across the vast expanse. "Almost forty-three thousand heavens."

"That's how many *clients* you have?" Molly asked.

"And counting. As you can see, we're signing people up every day. Not just humans, either, as Dakura's advances have translated well to other biological systems. And not all of our clients are sick or dying, I might add. Many of our clients are just bored with their normal lives and ready to plug into ours."

Molly walked to the balcony and looked at the canisters in the distance. She thought about the analogy her mom had made of people in jars. "Is my mom in one of those?" she whispered.

"Oh, my dear, no. Our clients are sleeping in another portion of the moon. These cylinders are packed with spools of fiber-optic cable. Each cylinder contains billions of terabytes of data, stored as little pulses of light that move in and out of a reading and writing device thousands of times a second. We love to point out that people who've had brushes with death always saw a light approaching. We offer that. Literally. An entire afterlife created by light waves, a land of li—"

"It'ss a hard drive," Walter said. Molly turned, shocked to see how rapt the boy had become. The computer had even been returned to its holster. His silvery hands grasped the railing as he leaned forward, peering across the expansive chamber.

"Why, yes, my boy. They are like old-fashioned hard drives. I'm impressed someone your age would even know such a thing."

"He's from Palan," Cole explained. "Lots of antique equipment there."

"What would heaven be like?" Molly asked, her thoughts far from the technical wizardry. "For my mom," she added.

"Excellent question, young lady. I was just getting to that." He addressed them all in hushed tones of wonder: "Heaven would be whatever you *wanted* it to be! Imagine that. A place where you can be forever happy, no matter what."

"Wouldn't that get boring?" asked Cole. "Or repetitive? And how can you know what makes each person happy? Or even leave it up to them to decide?"

"Quite right, and you are extremely sharp, young man. If Dr. Dakura were still around, the two of you would get along quite famously. And he encountered those very problems before he stumbled upon a simple solution."

Cole narrowed his eyes. "Which was?"

"Leave the brain in charge! Dr. Dakura's algorithm is tied to the pleasure module of his brain program. As soon as the client becomes less happy than it was earlier, the environment shifts. If the unhappiness continues to increase, it tries a new tactic. It keeps doing this until it maximizes data output from the pleasure center. It's the same way a robot—much simpler than myself, of course—learns its way around a darkened room by bumping off things and trying a new direction.

"And the best part is, every interaction is recorded to make the process go smoother and smoother. Since the problems Dr. Dakura ran into never surface until *after* an initial honeymoon phase, the algorithm has you figured out before you even begin to challenge it!"

Cole raised his eyebrows at this. Molly knew the look well: he wasn't impressed—he was skeptical.

She asked a question of her own: "When I visit my mom, will she be happy to come out of there?"

For the first time during their brief tour thus far, Stanley seemed at a loss for words. He pointed out to the barrels behind him, his head cocking to one side.

"My dear lady," he replied. "She will not be joining you out here. You will be joining her in *there*."

24

"'ll be going into one of those canisters?" Molly asked, pointing over the rail.

"I'm so sorry. You requested a tour of the facilities, but I can see now that I really should have broken you into two groups. Ms. Fyde, you need a *visitation* tour. This is more of a facilities tour for prospective clients. Let's go up to the guest suites and get you caught up and plugged in, shall we?"

"Before we do . . ." Molly hesitated. "Can I *see* her? Her body, that is."

"Oh, my dear, no. I'm afraid that's strictly forbidden. If you would like to continue the facilities tour, I can show you where the clients sleep and how that procedure works, but it is just a demonstration. Most of our customers pay dearly to be remembered in a state other than the one in which they arrived. It is a responsibility we take quite seriously here at LIFE."

"Yeah, I'd like to see that. Before my visit."

"Of course. Let's hail one of our elevators, shall we?"

There were at least a dozen shafts that opened onto the large balcony. Despite the congested feel of the place, they didn't have to wait long for one to arrive. Once inside, a video of a female in a patient's gown popped up on the rear wall. She conversed happily with Stanley-doctors in a silent promotional video.

"We provide the best medical care offered anywhere in the galaxy," their guide intoned. "Whether you are coming to us with an intractable disease or in top condition, our painless preservation procedure will maintain you and your brain for all of eternity. Neural growth is stimulated with the latest hormone therapy and stem-cell technology. Our own studies show conclusively that your brain will grow younger even as your body hardly ages at all."

The video switched to a shot similar to the person being scanned, but this time the client was slid into something resembling a morgue drawer. "Inside your personal rest compartment, you will find an eternity of peace and wish fulfillment. Family members can network with one another, and you may even reserve the rest compartments next to you so loved ones may be just as close in body as they are in spirit."

"How do you network the people?" Cole asked.

The interruption didn't faze Stanley at all; he smiled and seemed to launch down another branch of his tour logic-tree. "We let our guests know when family members have joined them at LIFE. How they incorporate one another once a link is made is entirely up to both members and their individual pleasure algorithms. We have had very few cases of family members rejecting one another or not wishing to combine their experiences into a shared environment."

"But you can't include people that aren't here, can you?" Molly asked.

"My goodness, no. How could we? They haven't been scanned. No, the people who inhabit their own heavens are personalities they make up. Just like when you dream."

The elevator dinged again; the video screen showed them three quarters of the way to the surface. Stanley waved Molly and Cole through the door and then looked back at Walter, who was reaching for the keyboard by the elevator terminal. "Let's not touch anything, OK?" he said cheerily. "Excellent. Follow me, please."

Molly shot Walter a stern glare and waited for him to exit the lift. She looked around at the large lobby they'd entered, the same bank of a dozen elevators lined up along one wall. The other three walls were broken up with hallways leading away in various directions, each cordoned off by a solid glass barrier. Stanley walked toward one of these and waved them along.

Through the glass, Molly could see the edges of the corridor, but not its end. The hallway stretched out so far in a straight line that the opposite wall became an illusion of converging planes. She watched Stanley reach into his coat and produce a card similar to their visitor passes; he swiped it through a reader, and the glass barrier slid silently into the jamb.

Walter hissed with delight and reached for his own pass.

"I'm sorry, my dear boy, but your pass will only open limited doors on the surface levels. Now, allow me to show you one of our unoccupied rest compartments."

They followed him down the hallway, which Molly now saw as just a long line of other hallways connecting at right angles. The layout created as much surface area as possible, just like the folds of a brain. Stanley turned down the first of these branches, and the rest of the group followed.

The sight humbled Molly.

Ahead of her, and stretching out for hundreds and hundreds of meters, lay a passage lined with square doors, each of them about a meter to a side. Stacked four high, the top row would have been difficult for even Edison to reach. Small LCD screens on every door flashed with a series of numbers along with the word "Unoccupied."

"Is my mom here somewhere?" Molly asked.

"Down a different main branch, yes. This is our phase four expansion. We use it for demonstrations and meetings with prospective clients." He swiped his card through a reader on the door nearest them, and the cover hinged open with a pop and a hiss.

"This rest compartment could be yours one day," he intoned. The door opened fully and a long metal tray slid out. "Imagine all the amazing dreams you could have here. An eternity of happiness. Is that something you're willing to wait for? Why not start creating your heaven today?"

"Not interested," Cole said, a tad rude for Molly's liking.

"Of course," said Stanley. "Just think about it. There's a lot to take in, and we urge you to return for another tour at any time." He turned to Molly. "Have you seen enough of the facilities? Would you care to visit your loved one now?"

Molly looked to her friends. Cole shrugged. Walter gazed longingly down the row of compartments; he looked ready to move in.

"I think we've seen enough," she told Stanley, pulling Walter away from whatever he was thinking.

Stanley swiped them through the glass barrier as yet another group filed out another elevator. It was one of the same clusters they'd seen on the balcony below. The other Stanley held the adjacent elevator door open for Molly's group.

"Thank you, Stanley."

"Of course, Stanley."

Molly waved to the touring family and then heard a commotion to her other side. She turned and saw that Walter had walked right into the other group's Stanley, dropping his video game and hissing with alarm.

"I'm so sorry," she apologized for her friend. "He doesn't watch where he's going."

"Not a problem," the Stanley assured her, straightening his jacket. Walter grabbed his game and hurried inside the elevator while Cole and Molly exchanged an embarrassed glance.

Their Stanley was all smiles, artificial yet sincere. He swiped his card to keep the tour moving, and the doors slid shut on the group outside.

The other Stanley stood at the glass barrier to expansion phase four, patting his jacket and apologizing profusely to his group.

○ ○ ○ ○

"The visitation and guest suites," Stanley announced. The elevator doors dinged open, and they stepped out into a grand, carpeted lobby. Plush furnishings and chandeliers dominated the space. Elegant columns pretended to do something structural with the ceiling. Paneled walls and detailed moldings adorned everything, signifying class and wealth.

It wasn't a Drenard prison cell by any stretch, but it was awfully nice.

A dozen Stanleys strolled purposefully in every direction, almost always accompanied by a guest or two. People and aliens lounged on the furniture with electronic readers, a reminder to Molly of the one she'd lost on Palan and still hadn't replaced. A Stanley behind the registration counter directed a group, pointing down a hall and giving directions through a broad smile.

Walter's eyes were as wide as Molly had ever seen them.

"Remind you of the Regal Hotel back home?" she asked him.

"Not even closse," he whispered.

Stanley led them to the registration desk. "Fyde, party of three," he said.

"Of course. Excellent," the seated Stanley said. "We have two guests on the West Wing, suite thirty-eight, and one visitor—a Molly Fyde?" he searched their faces until Molly nodded. "Of course," the Stanley said. "You will be in visitation room twelve." He smiled and held out his hand. "Passes, please."

They fumbled for their passes, and the Stanley swiped them through his computer. The two Stanleys smiled at each other before their Stanley waved them out of the crowded lobby and down a lushly carpeted hall.

"Hey, Stanley," Cole said, "I have a question."

"Absolutely, my dear man. Ask away."

"Why did Dr. Dakura decide to put people's personalities and memories in barrels of fiber-optic cable when he has such good android technology? I mean, no offense meant, but your model is really impressive, and you would think—"

Stanley turned on the group, cutting off Cole's question. "Suite thirty-eight," he said. "Let's go inside."

Walter insisted on using his card to open the door, his delighted hiss providing a fitting sound effect as the passage slid open. Molly giggled to herself.

Stanley waved them inside what appeared to be a lovely and large hotel room and turned to Cole. "Excellent question, my good boy, superb. It's no secret that our work here is being done alongside an even grander project below—"

"The canisters?"

"No, my boy. Below the moon. On Dakura. We have begun a very long and expensive project there—funded primarily by LIFE — to terraform the planet into a custom-made paradise." He grabbed a small device off the suite's kitchen counter and pointed it toward the wall opposite the beds. A video projection flashed up.

Stanley worked his way through a few menus while Walter threw himself onto one of the beds and made a pile out of the pillows. "Thiss iss like Drenard!" he told the room.

A video began playing; Stanley handed the remote to Cole.

"Watch this," he suggested. "It's all about the future of Dakura and our expansion plans to offer a different *kind* of afterlife." He addressed Molly. "Upgrades will be offered to our existing clients first, of course. And we are already scouting other planets that could be purchased cheaply and set aside for future phases.

"Now, while you catch up on that, I am going to get Ms. Fyde situated. Room service menus are on the table if you're hungry. Everything will be credited to your unlimited LIFE account."

Molly and Cole exchanged a look. She waved, nodded her head, and followed Stanley back to the lobby and down a different hallway.

"Will my mother know who I am?" she asked Stanley.

"Why, of course she will. She has already been notified of your visitation."

"Yeah, but—it's been a long time. I mean, I was only a few months old when she last saw me."

"Not quite three months," he said. "Don't worry. We have visitors all the time who have never met nor known their relatives." He lowered his voice to a whisper. "Usually here begging for money, if I can be so blunt."

Molly thought about what *she* was here to do.

It gave her a shiver.

"Visitation room twelve," Stanley said, waving her toward a door. Molly swiped her card, and the passage opened without any of Walter's sound effects.

They entered a room very similar to the one they had recently departed—same color scheme, same tasteful fabrics. However, unlike the suite where Cole and Walter were likely wrestling over the remote, this room was much smaller and had only a single cluster of furniture. It formed an arrangement in the center of the room: a lush chair, a matching ottoman, and a metal table. The last was covered with expensive-looking gadgets that gleamed in the light from the suspended chandelier.

Molly followed Stanley as he led her to the chair. As she got closer, she noticed the IV stand behind the chair, from which hung a full bag of fluids.

"Please sit," Stanley said, sweeping one arm through the air.

"What's with the IV?" she asked.

"Oh, you shouldn't be needing that. It's for our clients who wish to have an extended stay with their loved ones. Of course, if you change your mind, your unlimited account would allow us to move you into a long-stay visitation room. Entirely up to you, of course."

Molly shook her head. "Uh, no. Thanks. I probably won't even need the three hours, to be honest. I'm not even sure what to say to her."

"That's every visitor's biggest fear. Trust me, it goes smoothly. The time will whiz by faster than you will want it to."

"You're probably right. But no needles, OK?"

"Of course, of course. Now, please, do sit."

She settled into the chair, and Stanley scooted the ottoman toward her. Lifting her legs, she let them fall to the padded surface of the stool. The chair was extremely comfortable, but only physically. It reminded Molly of the yearly dental checks the Navy used to subject her to, the thought of which made her stomach feel hollow.

Stanley lifted an object from the tray and held it reverently, both palms up and perfectly flat. A thin wire spooled off the back of the device as he raised it to her head. Molly was reminded of the red Drenard bands as Stanley fit the hoop in place. He stepped back to survey his handiwork.

"Excellent," he said. "As soon as you are ready, I will begin the visitation. Your mother should be expecting you. If you decide to leave early, just exit by using the door you entered through. Also, some of our clients can be quite insistent that their visitors stay longer, so if your time runs out, we will simply bring you back ourselves."

He reached to the side of the chair and brought up a padded strap, placing it over Molly's wrist.

"Wait." Molly shifted her arm out of the way. "What's that?"

"Oh, this is for your safety. The visit will be indistinguishable from reality. When you move your arms and legs, they will often try to comply here. These are simply to make you as comfortable as you can be." Stanley smiled at her, the flesh-colored plastic folding unnaturally at the corners of his mouth.

Molly attempted to smile back, and likely did it just as convincingly. "I think I'd be more comfortable without them."

"Trust me, Ms. Fyde. You wouldn't be. They are very comfortable. Now, lay your head back and relax."

Molly shifted herself a little and pressed her head back into the chair. Stanley secured her wrists and ankles with the straps. His face hovered close to hers as he fastened a padded belt across her chest, the smooth skin on his face poreless and plasticy up close.

"Excellent," he said, stepping back. "Now, when you are ready—"

"I'm ready," she lied.

The frozen smile returned as Stanley reached for something on the small table beside her. He held it up and moved to press a button.

That image—a robot in a nice suit pressing a small device—burned itself into Molly's brain.

It was the last thing she would ever see of the room.

25

A wall of wood appeared directly in front of her, so close she could see the rise and fall between the grain. It swung away from her, and as soon as more light spilled across it, she recognized it for an old-fashioned door.

Molly squinted into the light that poured through.

Natural sunlight.

She reached out with one hand, guiding the door all the way open, and stepped through.

She stood on a porch. Below her bare feet, she felt the rough ridges of poorly milled planks. A flimsy-looking rail stood before her, beyond which lay a grassy lawn crowded with people.

Children. The ages varied, but they were all female. Light-colored dresses trailed behind several as they chased one another and squealed with delight. Another cluster sat on the grass, laughing. Ringing the large lawn was a collection of similar houses, their doors squeaking open and banging as children flew through them with more chirps of delight and laughter.

Molly scanned the crowd, looking for her mom. She moved to the railing and leaned out into the bright sun. It all looked and felt so *real*. She could smell the grass, could feel the cool wind on her cheeks. Something fluttered against her thighs; she looked down the front of a bright yellow dress, just like the others wore.

She'd entered a *dream*, only more vivid and solidly consistent.

A thrill grew in her with the weather and the sounds of so much joy. She felt her mission slipping away, replaced with an immediate fondness for this place. Nostalgia constricted her throat, choking her, but in a good way.

She *knew* this place. Memories, long forgotten, tried to make themselves known—

"Mollie?"

She turned, searching for the source of the voice. On the porch of the neighboring house stood a woman, cradling a cloth bundle. A baby. Molly ran down the steps of one porch, through the bright green grass, and vaulted over the steps leading up to her mother. She found herself giggling and smiling and leaving a wake of fluttering yellow, just like the other kids.

Rushing into her mother's embrace, careful of the baby, she cried out: "Mom!"

"Oh, sweetheart." Her mother held her with one arm, rubbing it up and down her back. It felt alien and normal at the same time.

"I'm so glad you've come to visit." Her mother pulled away and looked to the other porch with bright, brown eyes Molly recognized as her own. Her cheeks, sprinkled with a constellation of faded freckles, rose up in cheerful bunches atop a smile. Her mom looked so *young*—full, wavy hair hung down past her shoulders and wrapped around her thin, flawless neck.

"Is your father here?" her mother asked.

"No, Mom. Dad couldn't make it."

"Oh well, not surprising." Parsona took a step toward the edge of the porch and called, "Mollie!" into the crowd of girls. A single child turned her head before rushing over to her mother. She was one of the older children, ten or eleven years old.

"Yes, Mother?"

"Will you hold Mollie for me while I visit with my daughter?"

"I would *love* to!" she squealed, cradling the bundle carefully and skipping back down the steps.

Molly watched her go, then asked her mom: "Are they all named Mollie?"

"Every one. Your father and I just adore that name."

Molly turned and saw one of her mother's hands rubbing a swollen belly. She looked back to the lawn. "How many of them are there?"

"The next one will be number thirty-two. They come even faster now, which makes me happy." She gestured to a swing set tucked in one corner of the yard. "Would you like to swing?"

Molly laughed. "I'm a little big for that, Mom."

Parsona nodded. She turned toward the end of the porch, where a double swing hung on the end of two chains.

It hadn't been there before.

Molly took its appearance in stride and thought of Stanley's encouragement. This certainly was more natural than she'd hoped.

But then, she hadn't gotten to the hard part yet.

They crossed to the porch swing and sat together, their dresses folding over each other in the soft breeze. Parsona pushed them back and forth with her long legs, and a comfortable silence grew as they watched the children play in the grass. Molly recognized the scene; she felt as if she'd played there herself in the few good dreams she'd had.

"How's your father?" Parsona eventually asked.

"He's good," Molly lied, unsure of why she would. Maybe to not spoil the world her mom had created? Or perhaps because she sought to gather information, not leave it behind. She tried reminding herself that she sat beside a copy of her mother from sixteen years ago. Her *real* mother lived within the ship that bore her name.

But . . . Molly could reach out and *touch* this one, could smell spring in her hair. The other one was just a voice and some green phosphorous font on a nav screen.

Doubt crept up, followed by fondness and familiarity. Filial duty joined them. These internal saboteurs arranged themselves in a phalanx of worry, all armed to force Molly to waver.

She summoned her military training and shouted them down, calling them to attention. She realized she hadn't come adequately prepared for this. Especially not to handle it all by herself.

"Well, tell your father I'd love it if he stopped by," her mom said, interrupting her thoughts.

"I will," Molly promised, but from what Stanley had told her, the fact that her father didn't already exist in her mind meant her mom was the one lying this time. To *herself*, perhaps.

"I do enjoy getting visits," Parsona continued, "and catching up with news from the outside."

Molly froze.

Visits?

"Who's been by to visit, Mom?" She tried to ask the question calmly, but wasn't sure that she succeeded.

"Well, nobody lately. But an old friend used to drop by all the time. He stopped coming years ago—now, what was his name? Come now, you must know him. He and your father were such good friends."

"Are you talking about Lucin?"

"Wade Lucin? Of course not. How could I forget Wade's name? No, this was a new friend. We met him on Lok. On the very day you were born, in fact. It happened right out there."

Parsona pointed beyond the playing children. Molly looked across the commons and noticed the sunlight fade, as if a cloud passed overhead. But then a rainbow popped up in the distance. And out of nowhere, a flock of doves appeared, fluttering above the children who ran after them with little hands spread open, shrieking with delight.

"Now isn't *that* lovely," Parsona said.

Molly turned back to her mother.

"This is *Lok*?" she whispered, even though she knew it was. Part of her knew this old house, the very porch. But it had been so long ago, and she'd been so young.

Parsona's eyes didn't leave the rainbow and the dancing children. *Couldn't*, perhaps.

"Yes," she said, smiling.

"You and Dad were working on something here, weren't you? What was it? Anything important?"

"Now, sweetheart, why would you want to know about that?"

"It's important, Mom. To me."

"It's dreary stuff, that's what it is. And it's all my visitors ever want to talk about for some reason."

Molly looked at her arms and marveled at the simulated goose bumps. "I'm sorry, Mom. Honest. I wouldn't ask if it wasn't really important." She rubbed her arms.

"I suppose it can't hurt. I don't see how any of that can be considered top secret now, right?"

"Of course not. I just want to hear your side of it—to get to know you better."

The pace of the swing picked up; Molly couldn't tell if the motion was making her nauseous, or if it was something else.

Her mother spoke, her brown eyes focusing beyond the horizon. "Our investigation ended up leading us to this very house." She glanced at Molly before gazing back over the commons, toward the past. "Isn't that funny? Anyway, it was a routine assignment, my very first undercover operation. I was so excited to get the job. You just wouldn't *believe* what I put up with on my way to Special Assignments . . . "

Her voice trailed off—another cloud passed over.

"Anyway, your father and I posed as a couple—blending with the frontier life on Lok while we looked for an unauthorized source of fusion fuel—"

"Fusion fuel?" Molly asked, diverting the stream of consciousness.

"That's right." Parsona studied her intently. "You sound surprised. Anyway, we tracked the source all the way back to this very village. It took us almost a year to work our way into the group." Parsona frowned. "A bunch of anti-GN radicals and Drenard sympathizers, they were. And we were getting close to their source, the initial supply point, when—"

The porch shimmered, the wooden planks waving as if they were fluid. Parsona planted her feet, jarring the swing to a halt.

Two Mollies dashed up, their feet slapping solid wood. They had trays of goodies with them.

"Tea and cake, Mom? We made them ourselves!" They said it in unison. In *harmony*.

"Now, isn't that lovely of you girls. Go ahead, Mollie, take some." What Molly took in was the scene around her. All four of them in identical dresses. Everything so real and yet so *surreal*. When she'd first arrived, the girls had looked nothing like her, but now they bore an eerie resemblance.

She managed a meek "thanks" and accepted a cup of tea. She blew the steam into wisps but didn't take a sip. She wasn't even sure what it would mean if she *did*.

"Mom, I need to know if something important happened here. Something that might mean big trouble for the galaxy—or anything like that. Does 'two doors' mean anything to you?"

Parsona seemed to chew on this. She cupped her tea in both hands and nodded to the two Mollies. They ran back to the commons to join the others. "There was one thing," she said. "My other visitor always wanted to talk about it. I'm not sure why. While we were here, a bunch of settlers started going missing. We were looking into it on the side and reporting back to the Navy, but—"

"Mrs. Fyde?" Molly and her mother both turned; a Stanley walked across the lawn to greet them. He nodded at Molly, "I'm so sorry to interrupt your visit." Then he turned to Parsona. "You have another visitor, Mrs. Fyde. Normally I wouldn't intrude, but it's your account benefactor. He would love to see you at your earliest convenience."

Parsona smoothed her dress across her thighs with both hands, her cup of tea somehow gone. "Well, isn't this lovely," she said. "Two visitors on the same day! Is it my tall friend?"

"I believe so, Mrs. Fyde. It's the only other visitor you have ever had."

"Well, this is simply too delightful! Molly, would you like to meet him?" She turned to Stanley before Molly could respond, "Can we do that?"

Stanley smiled. Molly noticed his flesh looked flawless in this place—perfectly natural.

"I will inform Mr. Byrne that you are with your daughter and see what he says."

"Splendid," Parsona replied.

Stanley bowed, and Molly waved goodbye. Moments later, she felt a sharp prick on her arm—as if she'd been pinched. It hurt so bad, she nearly dropped her tea. Molly looked down at her skin, but it appeared normal. She glanced around the swing, but they were alone.

Probably nothing, she thought, blowing simulated steam from the surface of her tea.

o o o o

"Problemss."

Cole looked over at Walter. The boy had his computer out, probably playing that stupid video game of his.

"Did your guy die again?"

Walter clucked his tongue. "No. *Real* problemss. Molly'ss mom hass a vissitor."

Cole turned back to the video of a Stanley showing off a terraformed Dakura, all covered with beautiful androids living in harmony. "Yeah she does, it's your captain—" Cole sat up in the bed. "Wait. Are you hacking into their system? I told you not to—"

Walter hissed, cutting him off. "*Another* vissitor, dummy. And I think . . . I think they're moving Molly."

"What?" Cole got off his bed and walked around Walter to look over his shoulder. "What are you talking about?"

"Sshe wass in vissitation room twelve. Now sshe iss in ssomething called Long Sstay nine-two-one."

"What does that even mean?"

"They have a sschematic."

"Pull it up," Cole said, reminded again how wicked smart Walter was in some things to be so annoying and juvenile in others.

"Long Sstay nine-two-one," Walter said, pointing to a small square on a long hallway somewhere.

"Is that on this floor?"

Walter shook his head. "Not the hotel. Thiss iss where the bodiess go," he told Cole.

"Which bodies?"

Walter looked him in the eye. The boy's face was a dull sheen, like an old coin.

"The dreaming oness," he hissed.

o o o o

"How long has it been since you've seen this other friend of yours, Mom?"

"Oh, it's so hard to keep track of time here."

Parsona rubbed her belly as if calculating the time in trimesters. "Ten years?" she guessed.

Ten years, Molly thought. This was too much of a coincidence.

"What can you tell me about this friend of yours?"

"Oh, I would love for you to just meet him and see for yourself. I'll have the girls make some more tea and cake."

Molly sighed. "It would just be nice to know what sorts of things he enjoys talking about, so we can avoid any awkward moments."

"Aren't you thoughtful? Hmmm. I *do* recall him being into politics."

"Politics? What kind?"

"Navy stuff. The war with the Drenards. Hey, is that war still going on?"

"Yeah, Mom. It hasn't let up. Speaking of Drenards, did you and Dad ever go to their planet?"

Parsona gaped at her as if she'd lost her mind. "The *Drenard's* planet? Of course not, dear! They were my sworn enemy. Still are, I suppose."

"So you don't speak Drenard?"

"Where in the world . . . ?" Parsona paused. "Although if I did, the Navy would've taken me a bit more seriously, wouldn't they?" She studied her daughter closely. "Now, where are these questions coming from? What has your father been telling you?"

"Nothing, Mom. I just heard you guys were onto something really important on Lok and that maybe my being born messed some things up. I hoped—"

"You hoped you could make things better by picking up where we left off? Oh, sweetheart, that is such a wonderful gesture. It really is." She put her arms around Molly's shoulders and gave her a squeeze. "Thank you, but I don't have any regrets. I'm perfectly happy here, and I have so many wonderful girls to keep me company."

"Maybe I need to do this for *me*, Mom. To make *myself* happy."

Parsona's eyes twinkled, as if something registered. "You know, you mentioned two doors. Well—and it's probably nothing—but after you were born, I was in pretty bad shape for a while. Your father would hardly leave my side. We were here, inside this very house. Wait, that's *right!* The group we were investigating, *they* took us in that night. Kept us warm. Mr. Byrne didn't come with us for some reason, just led us to the porch. Carried me, in fact, while I carried you. We didn't see him again until I got really sick. But I—the last thing I remember is those people we were cracking down on—they tried to do everything they could to help me."

"What about the doors, Mom?"

Parsona looked at Molly and brushed some of her brown hair off her head. She gazed out over the commons, where dark clouds and rainbows battled for supremacy.

"Oh, they took great care of you," she said. "And your father—he was a wreck. When my fever wasn't too bad, I can remember them talking. About the Drenards. About a race from another galaxy. No, maybe that was something I dreamed at the time. We haven't made contact outside of our own galaxy, have we? So hard to remember."

Parsona shook her head.

"I do recall one of the fellows, an older gentleman with a thick white beard—clever fellow. He went on and on about hyperspace. Very agitated man. I'm sorry, dear, I'm afraid I forgot what I was thinking . . . wait! I do remember. Oh, no. That must've been a symptom of my fever."

"What was it?"

"Oh, nothing. Just a dream I must've had. I'm just awful at remembering."

"Even if it's weird, Mom, I'd love to hear it."

"Promise not to laugh? Because this is not the sort of dream I usually have, but I wasn't in the best of shape at the time."

"I promise, Mom."

"One night—like I say, it must've been a dream, but vivid as this one that I live in now—the wall of the living room opened up. They had you and me set up on a cot out there, keeping us warm by the fire. I remember— what a crazy dream—that the wall just opened right up, like it'd been zipped open. And—don't laugh— but people came out of it. Well, not people, *aliens!* All kinds. Thousands of them."

"Thousands?"

"You promised not to laugh."

"I'm not laughing, Mom, I'm flabbergasted. This house doesn't look big enough for twenty people, much less a hundred."

"It was a dream. It had to be. But they weren't all in there at once. They passed from one wall to the other, appeared and disappeared. They marched right through the living room for hours."

"Sounds like a great dream."

"It wasn't. I remember being terrified and power- less to do anything. You were bundled up next to me; I thought they might take you or do something awful. It must've been the fever. And every last one of them wore armor and carried foul weapons of all sorts. Probably a metaphor for my body trying to fight off whatever took me. Or nearly took me. It was one of the last things I remember before we came here. That, and the fight in the commons."

"What was that about? The fight in the—"

Parsona stopped the swing, cutting off Molly's question. She rose, gazing out at the grassy square.

"Look, Molly. We have a visitor."

Molly turned to follow her mother's gaze. Over the sea of children, she could see a tall, pale man strolling their way like a mast pushing through the mist. His white linen shirt and matching pants sagged on his skeletal frame like becalmed sails. He seemed familiar to Molly, in the ephemeral way this setting did. He was a walking déjà vu and heading right for her, a wide smile on his face.

And something altogether different in his eyes . . .

26

Walter strolled through the lobby and ignored Cole, who was trailing along behind him. The human kept hissing at him, trying to persuade him to go back to the room without being overheard. It sounded as if he was making fun of how Walter talked.

"We don't even know that she *needs* saving," Cole whispered.

The lobby buzzed with activity. Several Stanleys turned to watch the two boys as they weaved through the organized chaos. Walter felt exposed—conspicuously unattended, as all the other guests had escorts— he hurried toward the elevators. The situation reminded him of many a clumsy heist he'd attempted in the past that he shouldn't have. Well, he should've planned them better, at least.

"I know sshe iss in trouble," he hissed over his shoulder. "You can sstay here if you like."

A tour group popped out of one of the elevators—Walter veered toward it, dodging around a Stanley that seemed to be heading for the same elevator. He beat the robot to the lift and pressed the button to close the door. The Stanley stopped and stared at him, confused. Cole, unfortunately, managed to shoulder the android aside and squeeze through the shutting doors.

The human seemed angry.

"Listen, Walter—hey, where'd you get that card?"

Walter looked at the pass he'd swiped through the elevator reader; it differed in color from the ones around their necks. The human might not be quite as dumb as he looked.

"I borrowed it," he said. He typed away at the keyboard by the elevator and turned to look at the back wall. The tour schematic of the complex came up. It showed their elevator descending the shaft.

"How do you know how to do that?" Cole asked.

Walter sneered. "Englissh makess me ssound sstupid becausse of *Englissh*, not becausse of me." He looked to his handheld computer. "They usse the ssame passssword for everything here," he said, shaking his silvery head.

○ ○ ○ ○

Mr. Byrne stomped up the porch, the steps creaking with a heft his frame kept hidden. Parsona rose to give him a hug—Molly remained seated. As the two adults embraced, Byrne peered down at Molly over Parsona's shoulder.

"Mollie Fyde?"

"Isn't she lovely?" Parsona asked, breaking off the hug and gazing adoringly at Molly.

"Mr. Byrne," the man said, holding out a thin hand, pale as a corpse's.

Molly warily accepted the outstretched hand and shivered as her small grasp wrapped all the way around his fingers.

Parsona clapped her hands together. "Let's go inside where there's plenty of seating, shall we?"

Mr. Byrne held Molly's hand and stared at her long enough to make her uncomfortable. "That sounds splendid," he said.

A roaring fire greeted them inside, despite the pleasant weather. Three comfortable chairs faced the hearth, a low table before them. Quaint pictures of frontier life adorned the clapboard walls, and folded quilts were draped over anything that would hold them. An especially ornate one stretched out across one wall like the skin of a cottage drying for the tanner. Random pops sounded from the fire, and worn wood creaked under their feet.

Even the imperfections are perfect, Molly noted.

"I'll sit in the middle, if you two don't mind," Parsona said. "I just can't believe my luck to have you both visiting." She lowered herself gracefully to the center chair and turned to Mr. Byrne. He eased himself down into the floral upholstery as well. "This is Mollie's first visit with me, and I haven't seen you in almost, what, ten years? Quite the coincidence, don't you think?"

"Quite," agreed Mr. Byrne. He smiled warmly, looking past Parsona and eying Molly.

"After we catch up, perhaps we could go for a horseback ride or head into town for a play. They always have the best shows at the opera house."

"That would be lovely," said Mr. Byrne. Molly saw him glance to the coffee table and then back to Parsona. "Perhaps the girls could make us some cake or tea?" he asked.

Parsona slapped her thighs. "Why, of course! I say, what manners!" She looked at Molly apologetically. "You can tell I'm out of practice. You two get to know each other while I go see how the girls are coming along."

The floor squeaked with her passage. As the door flew open, the sounds of laughter and play flooded through like a joyous outburst and then fell silent as it closed.

Molly narrowed her eyes at the man. "Who are you?" she asked.

Byrne folded his fingers together and rested his elbows on the cushioned armrest, leaning toward Molly. "Why, I'm your godfather, Mollie."

"I don't think so."

"Oh, but I am. Your father and I were the closest of friends."

"Then how come I've never heard of you before?" Molly asked.

Byrne looked to the fire; embers spat out on a rug that seemed incapable of burning. "There are many things your father never told you."

"Yeah? Maybe that's because I was six years old and I didn't need to know them yet."

Byrne shook his head and clucked his tongue. "No, no, no, Mollie. Things he *couldn't* tell you."

Molly thought about the elusiveness of her mom—the one trapped in *Parsona's* nav computer—but she refused to let this creep trip her up or cast doubts. This had to be the man her mother wanted her memories kept from.

"You don't scare me, and I don't believe your lies," she said.

He spread his arms; the skin above his eyes rose in surprise, or amusement—it was difficult to tell without hair on his brow.

"Scared? I'm not trying to scare you—"

"Whatever. Just so you know, my last godfather tried to mess with me, and I *killed* him."

"Ah, yes. Lucin. I heard about that." He shook his head again. "Shame, really. I should have gotten to the old bastard first."

"Yeah?" Molly challenged. "Why? What did you want with him? What do you want from my mother? Why are you even here?"

He leaned closer, his voice lowered to the level of the crackling flames. "Why, Mollie, I'm simply here to collect what's mine."

"Which is?" She tried to conceal the very real sense of dread creeping up her spine. The door burst back open and Parsona entered, joined by a cough of laughter from outside. The sound of joy just augmented the creepiness of the situation. Molly stared at Mr. Byrne, her question hanging in the air.

He lifted a hand, unraveled a long bony finger, and stretched it out in Molly's direction. He didn't say it, just mouthed the single word with thin lips that gaped open and formed a small circle.

"You," he mouthed.

○ ○ ○ ○

Cole still didn't believe Molly was in any danger, and he was normally the paranoid one. Recently, he'd been right more often than not, so he decided to trust his gut and assume Molly was fine. He just needed to concentrate on keeping Walter from causing any trouble.

"Are you sure Molly was moved?" he asked.

"Possitive," Walter said. "Computerss don't lie."

"Maybe they do," Cole said. "Maybe you just can't smell it on them the way you can on people."

The boy glanced up from his computer. "They're programss. They can only do what they're told." The elevator dinged, and the doors cracked open. Walter scrunched up his metallic face. "Unlesss they're *told* to lie," he mused aloud.

The elevator opened up on the lobby with the glass partitions. Cole strode out and saw another group standing nearby, waiting to enter a neighboring lift. It dinged open just as Walter strolled out. The Stanley with the group turned to survey the two boys.

Cole froze, speechless. He could see that they were about to get busted for walking around without an escort.

Walter didn't miss a beat. He turned and looked back into the empty elevator they'd just exited. "After we tour thiss level, can we get ssomething to eat?" he asked, as if there was someone in there.

Cole glanced from Walter to the empty lift, then over at the Stanley. The android gave him a fake smile and joined his potential clients in the neighboring elevator. The doors closed, meeting with a soft thud.

"We musst hurry," Walter said. Cole nodded. He watched the boy hold his computer level and stare down at it, swiveling in place as if he needed to line up the virtual with the real in order to get his bearings. He pointed to one of the glass partitions and then started walking in that direction; Cole followed.

The stolen passcard opened the glass door without a problem, and they hurried inside as an elevator dinged behind them. "Down here," Cole snapped, grabbing Walter and pulling him into the first hallway.

"No," Walter complained. "Third on the left!"

Cole put his hand on the Palan's mouth and tried not to recoil at the odd coolness of the boy's flesh. "In a second," he whispered. "We have to wait for the lobby to be empty."

Walter nodded and shoved himself away from Cole, shooting him a nasty look. They remained in the side hall, staring at each other, waiting for the muffled voices to leave. Cole finally looked away from Walter's sneer and up and down the hallway. The doors looked identical to the ones they'd been shown earlier. A meter square. Stacked four high.

The only difference: these had *names* on them.

○○○○

"I'm so happy to see the two of you getting along," Parsona chirped as she arranged a tray of snacks and tea on the coffee table. It suddenly struck Molly how *different* this Parsona seemed from the other one she'd been getting to know.

Could they really be the same person? she wondered. *Could years of different experiences alter someone this much, or does perpetual happiness do something weird to a person?*

"Oh, yes, we're getting along famously," Mr. Byrne answered. "And I think we're going to have a lot of time for catching up." He smiled at Molly. "More than enough time."

"I just wish Mortimor could be here. I can't tell you how lovely that would be."

"I would love that as well," Mr. Byrne said through a tight smile.

Molly gritted her simulated teeth. He was toying with her, and it drove her crazy. Then something occurred to her.

"Why am I doing this?" she asked out loud.

"Doing what, dear?" Parsona blew across her tea, poised for her first sip.

Molly stood up from her chair. "*This.*" She spread her arms out. "Pretending that any of this is real. Listening to this creep tell me—"

The room shivered. Molly looked at her feet as the floor waved. Her dress became a brighter shade of yellow, spotted with cheery flowers.

"Now, now," her mother chided her teasingly. "Let's not spoil the mood."

Molly leaned down close to her mom and pointed at Mr. Byrne. "Who in hyperspace is he?"

"Mollie! Language, please."

But Molly was in no mood for pleasantries. She had no idea how much time she had left, and she couldn't afford to leave these two together.

"It isn't a coincidence that we're here at the same time, Mom. I think this guy followed me here. I think he wants something from you. I—"

"Please," Parsona said, "let's settle down, dear."

Molly opened her mouth to continue, but Mr. Byrne interrupted. "She's right, Parsona," he said. "I did come here because of her."

"What?" Parsona asked.

"I told you," said Molly.

Mr. Byrne leaned over and put one hand on Parsona's arm. "I came as soon as the gentlemen here at LIFE called. They said your daughter had arrived to visit with you after sixteen years of neglect."

He looked up at Molly, an evil grin on his face.

"And I think she came here to kill you."

○ ○ ○ ○

Cole peeked around the corner and watched the elevator doors snap shut. They were alone again. He turned to tell Walter, but the boy had already rushed down the hall. Cole set off after him, voicing his doubts: "How could they have gotten her down here this fast? We were with her just half an hour ago."

"How long did it take *uss* to get down here?" Walter hissed over his shoulder.

"Maybe she talked them into showing her the body. That was always the prime objective here, anyway."

"Here sshe iss," Walter announced. He stopped in front of a column of square doors about thirty meters into the corridor. He glanced at his computer as if to confirm it, but he shouldn't have needed to. Her drawer was the third from the bottom, the handle a little over two meters off the ground. Beside it, the LCD readout showed, plain as day: "Mollie Fyde."

"Damn," Cole said.

"Ssee?"

"You think it's safe to open it? I mean, if she's in there?"

"Iss it ssafe not to?"

Cole frowned, then held out his hand. Walter reluctantly placed his stolen pass-card in it.

"I want that back," Walter told him.

Reaching up, Cole swiped the card through the reader, which made the LCD screen flash green, just as the demo unit had. A faint clicking noise followed. Cole grabbed the handle and gave it a tug; the door snapped open. A thick metal tray slid out slowly, like a robotic tongue.

Neither of them could see what lie on top. Walter hopped as high as he could, over and over. Cole grabbed the edge and put a foot on the lowest handle on the wall. He pulled himself up and peered inside.

The tongue mocked him. The mouth was empty.

○ ○ ○ ○

Molly felt her face flush after Byrne's accusation. She couldn't fib well, even in a simulated world. She thought it would be safe to drag the discussion out into the open: *What could possibly hurt me in this make-believe place?*

Parsona studied her face, eyes wide and searching. The scrutiny felt torturous, mostly because Byrne had spoken the truth.

"I'm not—" she began, but the world shivered, losing substance.

"I'll not hear any more of this," Parsona said flatly. The cabin disappeared. A dark room took its place. Light and noise from behind Molly made her spin around.

It was a play. Characters on a stage danced while a melodious voice carried through the room from some unseen singer.

"Sit down," someone hissed at her.

Molly spun around and searched for the source of the complaint. Around her, a shapeless crowd shifted and stirred in the darkness. She looked for an escape, but knees walled her off on either side. An empty seat, obviously meant for her, seemed to scoot forward. Her mother and Mr. Byrne glared at her from the next row back.

"Mother, please. Get us out of—"

"Shhhhhhh!" sang a chorus of leaking air.

"Stop it!" Molly yelled at her mother.

The theater descended into a deeper darkness, and then a bright light flashed in Molly's eyes. A stranger in a mask leaned over her. She tried to ask a question, but she couldn't speak. Molly fought with her arms and legs, but she was strapped down tight, her mouth forced open and tasting of metal.

In the back of her throat, a puddle of her own spit threatened to drown her. She tried to shake her head back and forth, but a padded headrest constrained even that movement. "Nnngh," she managed.

"Suction, please," the man said, his blue mask puffing out with the words.

Molly felt more metal in her mouth and heard the slurping sound of her saliva being pulled from under her tongue. Her eyes widened with fear, but relief from the drowning came as the puddle of spit was removed.

"We had such a good dentist on Earth when I was growing up," she heard her mother say. "I always worried about what we would do for you on Lok. We were going to be here for quite some time, I was sure. Luckily, we have Dr. Daniels in town now."

Her mother's voice emanated from beyond her peripheral. Molly couldn't move her head to see her, to plead with tear-streaked eyes for an end to the torture.

The doctor held his hand in front of her and bent his fingers in a small wave. "Just a routine cleaning, Mollie," he said. "Nothing to worry about. You girls *never* have cavities."

Molly struggled to form words but gargled and choked on her own spit instead. Somewhere in the back of her mouth, where only she could hear it, she begged them to let her up. The dentist just forced her jaw open wider and reached for something.

Molly could hear Mr. Byrne speaking just as a tooth-scrubber whirred to life, its high-pitched whine filling her ears as it pressed hard against her teeth. She tried to keep her moans of discomfort low. She strained to hear the conversation taking place just a few feet away. But as saliva pooled up beyond her tongue, her head filled with the scream of ground enamel and the dull roar of torturous agony.

Her mother, of course, was perfectly happy.

oooo

Cole lowered himself from the empty tray. "You idiot. I told you there was nothing down here."

"Then what about her name?" Walter asked.

"Maybe her father bought her a spot here for the future. Ever think about that? Look how it's spelled." Cole felt kinetic and knew Molly would be as well when she found out he'd let Walter drag him down here. They were probably looking for them right now while that Stanley reported his card stolen.

His stolen card.

Cole slapped his own forehead and turned to Walter. "Gods! *I'm* the idiot. We're sitting around waiting on Molly to try some miracle with her mom, and here we are in the very place we needed to get to!" He jerked around to scan nearby compartments. "Her mother must be here somewhere. We can pull the plug ourselves!"

Walter got busy with his computer while Cole went down each column, stooping to look at the bottom drawers and leaping up to check the ones high off the ground. "You find it?"

"Different hallway," Walter said. "And we have a problem."

"What's that?" Cole asked, pausing his search.

Walter held up his screen. It showed a camera feed, revealing the lobby down the hall. A dozen Stanleys could be seen fanning out, pulling out their passcards and swiping them in the various glass partitions.

"Is that live?"

"Yesss," Walter hissed. "*Idiot,*" he added under his breath.

Cole wanted to point a finger in his face and remind the boy just who had wanted to come down here and who'd been against it, but he could hear footsteps moving down the hallway. He used his accusatory digit to point upward instead.

Walter allowed him to give a boost. One of the boy's boots kicked at the air, grazing Cole's nose as he pulled himself up onto the slab. Cole grabbed the lip and hoisted himself after, his feet scrambling for any edge along the wall of doors. He could hear the footsteps squeaking down the hall as they turned to survey another corridor. Cole reached out to pull the door shut, activating the withdrawal of the metal tray.

He turned to Walter, who ducked away from the roof of the mouth as the tongue drew them inside. "Can I shut the door?" he asked.

He could see Walter's bright silvery eyes in the darkness as the slab pulled him in as well. Walter blinked once.

"I don't know," he whispered back.

Drenards, Cole thought. If he left it cracked, they might be spotted. If he closed it, they could be trapped.

A solitary set of footsteps drew near. Cole didn't know what to do; he felt paralyzed. Then, trusting Walter for some inexplicable reason—that he'd be able to open it from within—he snapped the hatch shut. Out of the darkness, a soft glow radiated from Walter's little computer, illuminating the boy's face and the walls around him.

Both seemed to be made of the same alloy.

The Palan looked down at the screen as he thumbed in some commands.

"That might have been a misstake," he told Cole.

○ ○ ○ ○

The wide doors on the service elevator split open, and Molly's body slid out, feet first. The bag of fluids hanging from the gurney swayed as the Stanleys wheeled her down the hallway. A wireless repeater plugged into Molly's headgear blinked rapidly with a strong signal. One of the Stanleys walking alongside spoke to the Stanley pushing the cart.

"Hangar six," he said.

"Of course," the other Stanley said. "And how long did Mr. Byrne say he would be? We can't have him tying up a hangar all day long, even if he is a valued client."

"Busy, busy," one of the other Stanleys chimed.

"I am to notify him as soon as the young lady is loaded into his ship, so it shouldn't be over an hour."

"Excellent," two of them said at the same time.

The same Stanley told them, "I will stay with her to collect our equipment; the rest of you can return to the rotation."

They all agreed that this was best.

Busy, busy.

The light by hangar six shone green. Molly's feet led the group through another set of opening doors and toward a loading ramp beyond.

○ ○ ○ ○

"What do you mean, that *might* have been a mistake?" Cole whispered.

Walter's eyes peered up from his screen. "The doorss aren't on the network," he said softly.

366

Cole held up a hand as the muffled sounds of footsteps went by outside. He felt torn. Part of him wanted to bang at the door and beg for it to be opened. It could be hours or days before another Stanley passed through. The other half of him urged caution, terrified of being discovered. His recent habit of touring the interior of every planet's prison was one he had hoped to break. While he struggled to decide, the sounds outside faded back the way they came, making his mind up for him.

"What do we do?" he asked Walter.

If Molly really was in danger, they were no longer in a position to help. If she wasn't, how long before they were found, and what kind of trouble would they get her in?

He could see Walter shrug in the glow of his display. Cole reached over and grabbed the computer, flashing it around the interior of their hiding spot. Walter hissed at him and tried to wrestle it back.

"Hold on," Cole demanded.

He shone the light on the cables and equipment at the far reaches of the space. It looked like life-support equipment and lots of other complex gizmos.

"Anything we can use?" he asked.

The Palan settled down at the sight of the gear. He took the computer and used it to study the head harness and electrical interfaces. "I'll try," he informed Cole, squirming back to fiddle with the gear.

"Could we join Molly's dream somehow?"

Walter's eyes flashed at the suggestion. He turned to his computer and started jabbing at it intently. He looked back up at Cole and then grabbed the headgear and worked it onto his head. "I need to download ssomething," he said with a sneer.

"Fine. Just hurry it up."

Walter scrunched down and rested his back against the wall of the small space, his hands adjusting the headgear. By the light of the computer, Cole could see his eyes moving below his lids, pushing side to side like orbs searching for a way through his metallic skin.

The boy's legs twitched several times, and at least two full minutes went by. The odd scene seemed to stretch out into forever. Cole considered breaking the connection, or shaking the boy, but then his eyes popped open on their own.

Wide open.

Cole turned around and tried the door, but it remained locked.

"Anything?" he asked Walter.

"Oh, yesss," the boy said. "*Everything*. And I found Molly." He removed the headgear and brought his computer back up; Cole crawled closer to view the screen. He expected a schematic that he wouldn't understand, or perhaps some computer code, but he recognized the feed as soon as he saw it. Video. And crystal clear. It

368

showed Molly's body strapped to a gurney. She looked asleep and was being pushed up a ramp and into a spaceship—but not *Parsona*.

"What in hyperspace?" he wondered aloud.

"Sstanley 8427," Walter said.

"Do what?"

"Thiss iss a vissual feed from a Sstanley."

"You can hack *them*?"

"Jusst the feedss."

"So you can't control them or anything."

"If I had their passscode, maybe."

Poised on his hands and knees, Cole had to fall to one side to free up an arm. He dug in his pocket and brought out the card that had opened their little cage.

"What about this guy?" he asked. "Where's he?"

Walter snatched the card and used the light from his computer to read it. He typed something into the small keyboard and sucked air through his teeth.

"Where is he?" Cole asked again.

Walter looked up from the screen. "I think he's looking for us."

27

The spinning pad whined madly, pushing grit between Molly's teeth and gums. The nerves at the base of her tooth ached; the chalky cleaning substance threatened to choke her. Every now and then, she received a welcome jet of water, but it just pushed the foul-tasting cleanser to the back of her mouth. She fought to not swallow, to form a barrier at the top of her throat using her tongue, and then the suction would come again and give her relief from one misery, only to start the process all over again.

Each of her teeth had been cleaned at least twice, but the dentist had begun a third round. Molly cursed the feedback loop operating between Parsona's pleasure circuits and the AI routines. The result was pure torture for her, as this "heaven" didn't seem to take any feelings into account other than its creator's. She felt certain that her three hours must be up by now; she should have already woken up in a padded chair, yelling at Stanley to get these restraints the hell off.

The dental tool was only halfway done with one of her molars when it spun to a stop. Molly could hear herself moaning and realized she'd probably been doing that for quite some time. The myriad bits of metal holding her jaw open were removed; she experimented with closing it.

Her jaw ached realistically.

The chair came up and her head moved free from the padding; she looked around for her mother and Mr. Byrne, but he was gone. It was just her mother, smiling.

"Let me see those pretty teeth," she said.

Molly wiped the saliva away from the corners of her mouth with the back of her hand.

"Where's Byrne?" she asked, her tongue and jaw aching from the effort.

"Now, dear, let's not get into any more unpleasantries. Mr. Byrne said he needed to go and that he would come and visit me soon. Why don't we finish our tea?"

Just like that, the dentist office vanished. Molly's spit-encrusted bib was replaced with a new dress. Only the pain in her jaw, something that didn't seem to affect her mom's happiness, remained.

Parsona sat down in the swing and patted the wood slats beside her. Molly remained standing. She worked her mouth open and closed a few times, then asked her mom: "What did you guys talk about?"

"No more talk of Mr. Byrne, Mollie. I mean it."

Fine, Molly thought. *This has been a waste of time, anyway.*

She started to say goodbye but no longer cared. There had been plenty of time to think about the horror of this place while the dentist did his work—and he had been wrong. She gave her mother one last, sad look and realized there were plenty of cavities here. All created by too much *sweetness*.

Without a word, she ran and leaped down the stairs leading from the porch. She ignored the laughter and chatter in the commons as she ran up to the door she'd entered. She heard her mother calling for her as she flung it open and jumped through, back to the real world—

But it was just a room. A room identical to the one in the other cabin, only with two chairs instead of three. Parsona sat in one and patted the other.

Molly felt absolutely certain that she'd been under for more than three hours.

O O O O

Stanley #8427 was walking down hallway 8C, looking for their missing guests, when his legs went goofy. His right foot slammed into the back of his left calf, sending him sprawling forward toward the floor. Automatic arm routines tried to compensate, but something went wrong with them as well. A hand flew out in front, fingers straight, and the weight of his gear-filled body crashed down.

Several metacarpal joints snapped back, and injury codes flashed red in his vision.

He flopped around on the ground for a few moments, one of his legs kicking a containment drawer noisily.

Gradually, some semblance of coordination returned. He used his undamaged hand to push himself to his knees; he looked purposefully at the handle of the nearest drawer and grabbed at it. His timing was off, but he managed to hook two fingers around the steel.

Stanley pulled himself to his feet.

He took a few experimental steps while he kept one hand on the wall beside him. Stanley #8427 turned around and stumbled back the way he had come.

He was on the wrong hall.

oooo

"You wrecked him!" Cole complained.
"Sshut up. I'm getting it."

374

"It looks like he's having a seizure."

The camera was sideways. On the ground, vibrating.

"Thiss sstupid computer only hass one analog sstick."

"I thought you were good at these things."

"You wanna try?"

Cole watched him work the controls and the small keyboard at the same time. The camera gradually made its way off the floor. He shook his head. "How long until he gets here?"

"I don't know. He'ss one hall over from here. Uh, oh. Another Sstanley."

o o o o

"Greetings, Stanley. Any luck?"

The other Stanley didn't say anything. It just waved a ruined hand awkwardly.

"You should have that looked at. Should I call maintenance?"

The mute Stanley staggered, its shoulder brushing the doors on its right side.

"Hold still. I'll call maintenance."

The helpful Stanley walked over, graceful as a cat. It reached out to steady the other android.

The hurt Stanley didn't have the dexterity of the approaching robot, but it also lacked its compassion.

The mangled hand spun around as fast as its servos could move it, brutal strength moving with no control.

It caught the nice Stanley on the temple, nearly taking its head off at the fragile neck-joint.

Both Stanleys went down from the blow.

One of them struggled to get up, getting the hang of it now.

○ ○ ○ ○

"If we get out of this," Cole told Walter, "I'm gonna make you practice your video games as part of your regular duties."

Walter hissed, ignoring him. His fingers tapped buttons in frustration. He had the Stanley in front of their door—they could even hear the damn thing banging against the wall outside—but swiping the card through the reader was infuriatingly difficult. The robot had already dropped the card once, and trying to pick it up off the floor gave Walter a new appreciation for everyday feats he took for granted. He had resorted to scooting the flat card across the floor with the robot's fingernails until it hit the wall, popping one edge off the ground. After that ordeal, he instructed the finger-grip servos to lock down and never loosen. The card would snap in half before he let it slide out again.

"I need the other hand," he moaned. He jammed Stanley's bad fingers behind the handle of a lower cabinet to steady the body, and then he pressed the edge of the card against the wall with the other hand, adjusting its angle of attack. Cole kept crawling back and forth between the screen and the door, egging both him and the robot on—it was driving him absolutely crazy.

One more swipe, and Walter heard a beeping noise. He yelped with delight, trying to get the Stanley to grab the handle before the green light on the LCD went off. Reluctantly, he instructed the robot to drop the card so he could use the good hand. He guided the digits up to grasp the door handle and ordered a yank.

There was a pop. Light came in through a crack. The metal floor of their tiny cell jolted forward, and both of them lost their balance, falling backward.

Walter laughed with relief and then remembered that last sight of Molly—her body being loaded into a ship.

Cole jumped down from the platform first. Walter could see the Stanley hanging casually from the door's handle, the body lifeless. His jacket had been torn, and his pants hung down around his thighs. Walter leaned over the edge and let Cole help him down.

"Can we use him?" Cole asked.

Walter shook his head. "I can't ssteer and walk at the ssame time." He watched as Cole picked up the dropped passcard from the ground.

"Which way to Parsona?"

"Through the hangarss," Walter said.

"Wrong Parsona," Cole told him, shaking his head. "We have something else to take care of down here."

Walter understood. He punched some keys and turned the screen so Cole could see it as well. Two hallways over, six side halls down on the left, compartment 3815.

"What about Molly?" he asked.

"We'll be quick," said Cole. "I promise. See if you can get our ship loaded in one of the hangars while we move."

o o o o

Molly sat quietly beside her mother. Ahead of them, a perpetual fire danced across logs that seemed to neither diminish nor budge.

As her mother's voice droned incessantly, Molly nodded to feign interest. The visit had been a complete waste of time. Worse than a waste, actually. She had failed to prevent Byrne from having contact with her mom. She had learned nothing of her father or what had taken place on Lok. And the dream of reuniting with her real mom had turned into a nightmare; dealing with her was like battling wills with a petulant child-god.

". . . the third heaven. Earth just couldn't do it for me in the long run, much like in real life, so that's when I visited Lok. It was children, always the idea of having lots of children that . . ."

Molly watched her mom's lips move, felt the words enter her ears and bounce around, but they weren't her mother's ideas. They were the thoughts of something who hadn't felt pain for almost seventeen years. Hadn't known suffering. How could that not change a person?

While Parsona talked about the miracle of a natural childbirth, Molly thought about the last few weeks of her life. She had endured much hardship, even some severe bouts of sadness, but overall, the time had seemed . . . exciting, if not quite happy. The time had been full of reminders that her life was temporary, and somehow that gave it extra meaning.

Hadn't Cole mentioned something similar on Drenard, during that long shuttle ride? He'd said something about not being scared of death while he was around her. Molly didn't understand what that meant at the time, except that he loved her.

Now she knew.

She surveyed her mother's face, saw again how *young* she looked. Her skin positively glowed in the light of the lambent flame. In fact, she was probably only ten years or so older than Molly—her body frozen in time, remaining as old as she remembered herself.

Emotionally, however, her mother seemed to be aging in reverse, the product of a hedonistic fantasy world of her own creation. It was the sort of existence only young children got away with, and one that only unknowing adults could crave.

If these visits were designed to sell her an eternal life, they'd failed. She would never want this. Would the program run for millions of years? Billions? What would this "heaven" look like by then? Would her mother even remember the real life she'd once lived? What would her father represent to her in a few billion years? Which Molly would she know and love? The real one, or the thousands and thousands she had given birth to virtually?

Molly pondered these things and felt an overwhelming sadness for her mom; she reached out a hand and placed it on her arm, squeezing it gently. Her mom broke off from her story and searched Molly's face.

"Sweetheart? You look sad. Do you need some more tea?"

Molly shook her head and fought back tears. She could reach out and touch her mother; it would feel very real, but her mother was long since dead.

"I want a hug, Mom."

Parsona beamed and reached out both hands. "Come sit on my lap, dear. Let me finish my story."

Molly got up and eased herself onto her mother's legs. She put an arm around her neck and rested her head on her shoulder.

Parsona continued her story, recounting the settling of a virtual Lok and how painless it had been to give birth there. One of her arms rubbed Molly's back while the other waved in the air, conducting the tale.

Molly settled in, smothered in sadness. One of her hands fell to her mother's round belly.

It was already larger than when she'd first arrived.

○ ○ ○ ○

Cole knelt beside Parsona Fyde's body, the metal slab fully extended from a bottom drawer. He could see why loved ones would never be allowed to visit in person. Dozens of wires and tubes snaked out of every natural orifice—and some that'd been created. Parsona's scalp had been removed completely and replaced with a clear plastic shell. The edges of something similar extended out of her armpits, and long, wispy hair on her thin legs suggested the purpose of these devices.

They made the quasi-living body easier to maintain.

A collar of metal ringed her forehead below the plastic shell, identical to the device Walter had used.

Pale flesh, laced with bright capillaries, hung from her bones except where it was pinched by the straps criss-crossing her body. They seemed ludicrous to Cole; he didn't see how those muscles were capable of strenuous movement. The gentle rise and fall of her chest, ridged with bony ribs, provided the only clue that this thing was alive.

Still, despite the dehumanizing nature of the apparatus, he couldn't do it.

Walter paced nervously behind him while Cole berated himself for his inability to act.

"How're you coming with the other *Parsona*?" he asked Walter, trying to stall.

"About like you're doing with thiss one," Walter said. "Sship docking iss on another network. I can open and sshut the bayss, but I can't control the loaderss to move the sship." He stopped pacing and pointed his computer toward Parsona. "We're wassting time."

"It's her *mom*."

Walter bent over the pale, naked form. "Sshe lookss dead."

"I don't think I can do it," Cole finally admitted.

Walter shoved the computer in its holster and knelt beside Cole. One of his hands rested on Cole's shoulder, a gesture of support that filled Cole with hope for the boy. He was about to lay his own hand on the Palan's, reciprocating the rare contact from him, when

Walter reached down with his other hand, grabbed a fistful of wires trailing off Parsona's torso, and yanked as hard as he could.

Cole reached for Walter's hand in shock, trying to stop him, but the boy moved fast—grabbing and tugging as calmly as if he were pulling weeds. Parsona made sucking noises when the tubes popped free of her nose and mouth; her chin came up; she gasped for air.

Fluids leaked out and puddled on the slab of metal; bony limbs jerked against the restraints; ribs heaved. All indications that this thing was *alive*.

Cole felt bile rise in his own throat, burning it. He swallowed it down and grabbed a hose, trying to remember where it went. He wanted to plug everything back in, to save her.

Parsona vibrated and gurgled.

Once again, he couldn't act.

Red lights descended from the ceiling and began flashing up and down the hallway as Cole felt overcome with shame and horror.

"Let'ss go!" Walter hissed, tugging on his shirt and pulling him backward. "They'll be coming to ssave her."

Cole fought to regain his balance, physically and emotionally—he needed to focus on Molly. And Walter was right: they needed to get out of there. He turned away from the open drawer and the dying woman, running back to the main hall. He caught up with Walter, who tugged him to a halt. A Stanley could be seen beyond the glass partition at the end of the corridor, talking to a human couple.

"Sservicse elevator," Walter said, looking at his computer.

"That's our way out? Which way?"

"No, that'ss what'ss heading thiss way. We need to go that way," he said, pointing through the partition.

Cole looked down the hallway at the glass door. "Can you stop the service elevator? No point in what you—what *we* did if they get here in time."

Walter nodded.

"While you're at it, call a single elevator to this floor and send the rest down to the center of the moon." Cole placed a hand on Walter's elbow. "And walk while you're doing it. We need to get close to that partition."

○ ○ ○ ○

Molly had her ear pressed to her mother's collarbone, listening to the distant thrum of her mom's voice as it resonated through her body. She spaced out again, not really hearing what her mom said, but rather marveling at how real her lap, their embrace, seemed.

And yet, the illusion remained incomplete.

It wasn't her real mother she embraced, but a nostalgic recollection of her. This felt more like the comfort

384

of a stranger, perhaps consoling a child for the loss of a parent.

Molly felt saddened by the irony of it all. A massive gulf had formed between her and her mom in such a short time. And while they were pressed close together—

And then the world went blank.

White light.

Everything was white light.

She had no eyes, and yet the searing brightness filled her vision. It was so intense, it made a sound, as if ocular neurons bled over to auditory ones. The result was something between a drone and a hiss. And her world smelled like an electrical fire, or rubber burning. Molly could taste it, but she had no mouth.

Her body floated, but not in some painful void—her body *was* the void.

She tried to scream or call out, but the agonizing hiss that filled her universe could not be modulated nor reduced. She was trapped in the center of a star, hot, white, burning, blinding, noisy.

And yet, her body was unwilling to melt away and end the torture.

It went on forever.

Unyielding.

28

Two elevator doors stood open on the other side of the glass partition. A Stanley, its back to Cole and Walter, faced the open doors, surveying the curious behavior from its less-evolved mechanical brethren. To one side, the human couple stood and conferred, going back and forth as if considering the purchase of a new spaceship.

"Now," Cole whispered.

Walter swiped his passcard, and the glass slid away. Cole pushed off the tiled floor like a sprinter. The sound of him coming made the Stanley turn around; its eyes locked onto the source of the squeaks just as Cole went airborne.

Slamming into the Stanley felt like tackling a refrigerator. Cole's air rushed out of him as the Stanley flew backward, skidding into the elevator he'd been peering into. Walter ran past, entering the other elevator door. Cole paused to regain his breath, but the Stanley had no such requirement. The android shoved off the floor of the elevator and rose with an unnatural power. Cole scrambled on all fours into the other elevator.

"Shut it!" he yelled, before his feet even crossed the threshold.

Walter swiped his stolen passcard and the doors began to move, the mechanical slabs closing with an agonizing slowness.

Nothing at all like the speed the Stanley used to dash between them just before they sealed tight.

"Hi," Cole said. "We've lost our tour guide, perhaps you've—"

It happened so quickly, it felt like teleportation. One moment, Cole was kneeling in the center of the elevator, trying to smooth talk the android. The next, he found himself pinned against the rear video wall, his feet off the ground, metal vises around his neck. The Stanley had both hands around his throat; the android began squeezing the life out of him.

Cole kicked his legs in the air, looking for something to support himself on, but unforgiving metal formed walls on both sides. He twisted his head to look for Walter, saw the boy frozen by the elevator controls. Cole tried to mouth a plea, but all he could manage was a grimace.

Walter sneered back at him.

○ ○ ○ ○

Time did not elapse in the buzzing, scorching, droning whiteness. It had gone on forever, or it had been a mere moment. There was no difference.

Then it stopped, replaced with the dentist chair scene once more. Molly found herself strapped down as someone hovered over her. She blinked him into focus. It wasn't the dentist—it was a Stanley.

She worked her jaw, trying to ignore the residual hiss in her head as she regained her senses. She could barely hear herself ask if her three hours were up. The Stanley nodded. Something else swayed in her vision. A clear bag of fluids. The IV.

She looked past it and the Stanley to the metal panels above her. *This isn't the visitation room,* she realized.

"Where am I?"

The Stanley ignored her. He tightened one of the straps across her chest before packing away various electrical gear. When he pulled the contraption from her head, he did it so roughly that it took clumps of her hair with it.

"Ow!" she complained. "Hey, loosen the straps, and I'll help you."

The Stanley said nothing. Molly heard him zip a bag below her and then watched him rise and stroll away.

"Help me take these straps off!" she begged.

Footsteps banged down a metal ramp—then she was alone.

Molly pressed her chin to her sternum to peer down her body. She was lying flat on a hard surface, dozens of strips of webbing pinning her down. She could see an IV needle taped to the crook of her left elbow.

She gasped and began crying out for help.

But the only person heading her way at that moment was a tall, thin man, who only needed to stop at the registration counter to thank his hosts for their call and hospitality.

○ ○ ○ ○

Cole felt his head lighten as blood struggled to reach his brain. He would pass out before the choking killed him, he realized. His eyes watered from the effort it took to breathe—and the odd sensation of not being able to manage a sound, even a grunt.

He pleaded with his eyes to Walter, who still hadn't moved from his corner of the elevator. With both hands, he pried at the fingers on his throat, but it was like trying to bend steel. He kicked and punched at the Stanley but only hurt himself. Grabbing the collar of the android's suit, he clenched the fabric in pain as his grip on consciousness slipped.

One of his hands came loose as he began blacking out. It slid down Stanley's coat, lifeless, and caught in the robot's pocket. He felt something there. A feeble signal tried to worm its way through Cole's dying brain:

Passcard.

Some still-conscious sliver of him heard the message. He fumbled for the plastic card with a numb hand, as uncoordinated as a poorly controlled robot. He felt it between his finger and thumb, yanked it free, and tossed it in Walter's direction.

Then his world went black.

○ ○ ○ ○

Walter watched the glint of red plastic fly through the air and settle on the elevator floor. Cole's body had stopped fighting, his legs and head completely limp, but the Stanley continued to hold him off the ground.

It hadn't noticed Walter yet.

This is working out pretty good, he thought.

Then he wondered what would come next. Would he have to fly a spaceship to rescue Molly? Would he have to fight a Stanley in the hangar hall? So many unknowns ahead, but one thing he felt sure of: he could get rid of Cole any time he wanted. The human thought he was stupid, which made *him* the dumb one.

He reached for the card, amazed at how easily his fingers could pry it off the floor. He studied it and then carefully punched the ID number into his computer. Taking control of these things had already become routine. He imagined the power he could wield if he lived here, or if he could just take a few of these androids with him.

I'd need better control inputs, he thought.

It wasn't obvious which direction on the analog stick would loosen the grip and which would tighten it. He tried one way and watched Cole's face turn a darker shade of purple. He chuckled to himself and moved the stick the other way.

The human boy fell free and collapsed in a heap.

Walter stepped around the motionless robot to try to rouse him.

He sure hoped he wouldn't regret saving this loser. *Again.*

○ ○ ○ ○

She was in a starship, but not hers. Human-built. A GU-class bird. Molly couldn't tell the exact model from her surroundings. The interior panels looked new—or possibly just incredibly well maintained. A medical station had been cobbled together and secured against a bulkhead. She could almost see across and into the cockpit, but the strap across her shoulders made it impossible to turn or sit up.

Outside, she heard footsteps; they stomped her way, clanging up the cargo ramp and near her feet. She didn't have time to scream for help, they arrived so fast.

One of the figures yelled her name.

"Cole?"

He bent over her, his face red, his hair matted down with sweat. "Hold on," he croaked, his voice hoarse. "We're getting you out of here."

"What's going on?" Molly asked. "Are you OK? Your neck looks—"

"I'm fine," he assured her.

"Thankss to me."

Molly looked down her body to see Walter fumbling with the straps across her thighs.

"What's going on?" she asked again.

Cole flipped back the strap across her shoulders and helped her sit up. "No idea and no time to discuss it. We need to get out of here."

"I ssaved Cole'ss life." Walter said. "Now I'm resscuing *you*."

Molly pried the tape off of her arm and slid the IV needle out with a gasp, mostly from the sight of the metal leaving her flesh. "What're you saving me *from?*"

Cole tore open a box of bandages, spilling them everywhere. She watched him pluck one and fumble with the paper. "Whose ship is this?" she asked. "Where's *Parsona?*"

Cole grabbed her arm and took her fingers off the wound so he could apply the adhesive strip.

"No idea and no idea," he whispered. "Our plan was just to get to you. We haven't had a lot of time to think past that."

"Company," Walter told them. He peered at the computer screen, but Molly could hear for herself: the sound of more feet approaching.

Cole reached over and hit the cargo ramp controls, bringing the door up. The stomping outside quickened into a run. Someone yelled, "Hey!" as the ramp came up too far to board.

Molly's head continued to spin, making her useless in whatever was going on, but she couldn't stand to be alone, either. She swung her feet off the gurney, steadied herself, and staggered over to join Walter and Cole by the door.

When an angry face flashed in front of the porthole, her wobbly legs nearly gave out.

"Byrne!" She pushed Walter to the side for a better view, holding onto him and Cole for stability. The tall, pale man stood outside, looking at the cargo ramp in a mixture of confusion and fury. When he saw Molly peering through the glass, his eyes narrowed, his lips clamping down into a flat line.

The line turned into an evil smile as he reached to the side of the porthole. Through the door, Molly could hear the hinges of an access panel open, and she knew he was about to manually lower the ramp.

"We have to do something," Cole said, looking around the bay.

"What?" Molly asked. "*He's* got the captain's codes."

Walter fumbled with his computer while Cole looked around in frustration. Molly remained frozen at the sight of the strange man in the flesh—just as he had appeared in her mother's fantasy.

Walter hissed. Molly turned to see him smiling—or sneering. The green environment and atmosphere lights above their heads flashed from green to red. Molly spun back to the porthole, confused. She could see wisps of white rushing up, swirling like a disturbed fog. The air in the hangar was rushing out through the ceiling; Byrne's jacket flapped up around his thin shoulders and vibrated there.

Molly watched him peer from the access panel to the opening hangar doors above. He looked back though the porthole at her as his suit settled in the new vacuum outside.

Byrne's nostrils flared despite the absence of air.

He appeared extremely annoyed.

○ ○ ○ ○

"What did you *do*?" Cole asked Walter.

"Killed him."

Molly shook her head, her eyes never leaving Byrne's. "He's not dead. I don't think he's human." She turned to her two friends. "How are we gonna get to *Parsona*?"

Cole pointed at the cockpit. "Can we fly?"

"I know where sshe iss parked," said Walter.

Molly nodded. "Cole, round up some space suits; we'll still be in a vacuum when we get there. Walter, come navigate."

Cole headed off to the rear of the ship while a giddy Walter followed her to the cockpit. The two of them settled into the flight seats. Byrne had a 500-series, Molly noticed. The seats were closer together in a narrower cockpit, and duplicate flight controls sat in front of each crew member.

"Don't touch anything," she commanded.

Walter nodded and pulled the harness over his shoulders, working it tight. Molly started the warm-up for the thrusters. She wasn't worried about Mr. Byrne getting inside—overriding the atmosphere sensors could only be done from within the airlock—but she did feel a sense of panic rubbing off from Walter and Cole. Yet again, they needed to get away in a hurry.

And the fancy thrusters were taking forever to check themselves out—too many mechanical systems in this model had given way to solid-state electronics.

"What's the danger here, Walter? Who's after us?"

"That guy outsside. And Sstanley."

"*Our* Stanley?"

Walter paused. "*All* of them," he said quietly.

Molly cursed under her breath. The thrusters finally went green, and she saw through the carboglass above that the hangar doors were open. The ceiling of the parking chamber, which held up the underside of the moon's crust, loomed beyond.

"Going up!" she yelled over her shoulder. She directed the rear thrusters down and routed some of their energy through maneuvering channels to the nose jets. The ship lifted slowly and evenly off the ground.

Walter pressed his head to the glass on his side. "That skinny guy issn't sso happy," he said, laughing.

"I bet not."

Cole ran up into the cockpit. "Bad news. Only one suit on the ship. I checked the staterooms *and* the airlock."

"Is it an extra-tall?"

"You got it."

"OK," Molly said. "You'll have to go over to *Parsona* through the airlock and bring our suits over."

The cockpit of the GU-500 rose up into the parking cavern, where a sea of gleaming hulls spread out in all directions. In the distance, a crane could be seen moving one of the ships farther away from them, a new arrival. Several other parking cranes stood idle, but one approached them with a ship in its clutches.

"I don't think we're gonna have time for that," Cole said, pointing toward the crane. It clutched a military hull, the words "LIFE SECURITY" emblazoned across the side. Missile pods could be seen under the wing as the crane lowered the ship into the hangar next to theirs.

Molly heard Cole swallow.

"I think that's meant for us," he said.

○ ○ ○ ○

The roof of the parking bay had several square openings in it from the lowered landing pads above. Molly spotted stars and the promise of open space through them—they should have more than enough time to fly out and make it to a safe jump point before the security ship warmed up. The Stanleys would have to pressurize the hangar in order to board. Just because

they were androids, that didn't mean they could vacuum the entire hallway beyond. Without airlocks, their
clients would be killed.

She considered the easy and quick escape, but
only for a moment. Whatever was inside her father's
old ship, it felt more like a mother than the one she'd
just spent time with. And the ship itself was the only
place that felt like home, where the nightmares of being
left behind never tormented her sleep. Then there was
the Wadi to consider, some sort of national treasure
that had become another companion, another part of
her family. She gave the stars another wistful glance
and then turned to follow Walter's directions, who was
pointing in the direction of *Parsona*.

Cole gripped the arm of her flight seat and turned
as the ship did, watching the menacing security ship
dip into the hangar bay.

"What's the plan?" he asked.

Molly estimated how long it would take to land near
Parsona, airlock Cole out of this ship, have him airlock
into *Parsona*, retrieve their flightsuits, and then repeat
the steps to get back. She and Walter would then need
to get suited up before all three of them airlocked over
one final time. There simply wasn't enough time for that
many depressurizations.

"How strong are airlock collars?" she asked Cole.

"I dunno. Why? What're you thinking?"

"You probably don't want to know." Regardless, Molly thought she knew the answer: most ships were designed to airlock with the old-fashioned stations that spun up for gravity rather than manufacture it with expensive grav plates. If ships could hang from their own weight at the outermost ring of those spinning stations, it meant her idea just might work.

"How far to our ship?" she asked Walter.

He checked his computer. "Half a mile."

"I'm not good with Imperial—"

"Less than a klick," Cole said.

"Alright. Cole, get in that suit. You might not need it, but just in case."

He plopped down in the cockpit hallway and started worming into the oversized suit. "What exactly am I gonna be doing?"

"Warming up *Parsona's* thrusters as fast as you can."

Molly slid the accelerator forward and moved off in the direction Walter indicated.

Below them, the hangar doors snapped shut on a furious Mr. Byrne.

○ ○ ○ ○

Cole stationed himself in the airlock as Molly began her crazy maneuver. He couldn't believe what she was trying. Through the small porthole, he watched the world slowly turn on its side as Molly rolled the ship over, the gravity panels keeping his boots firmly planted on the deck. Below, he could see *Parsona's* hull slide into view.

"Ten meters," he said into his mic.

"Copy."

They were nearly inverted now. The airlocks on both ships were arranged three quarters of the way up their hulls, out of the way of the wings. Molly was attempting to do something in the gravity of a large moon that most pilots have a hard time learning to do in zero Gs.

"Three meters," he said, calling out numbers as if this were an ordinary docking maneuver.

"Copy," she said.

"Go one meter aft." In the reflection of *Parsona's* hull, Cole could see the wash of the 500's thrusters licking out as Molly fought to hold them in an unnatural angle. "Two meters. Just a touch aft," he cautioned.

"Copy."

Damn. Her voice sounded so calm. As if she'd done this a million times. Cole had seen her work plenty of miracles in the simulators, but watching them in real life, like the rescue from the Palan canyons, it filled him with awe. And made him love her even more.

"You need to rotate a few degrees flatter, honey, and a few more centimeters aft. One meter." He already had the inner airlock door closed and the room vacuumed. One hand squeezed a grip by the porthole, the other hovered over the airlock controls.

"Copy. And don't call me 'honey.'"

The two hulls banged together, spot on. Cole engaged the collar locks and listened for them to snap into place.

"Secured," he said.

As the outer airlock doors slid open, he wondered if he'd *ever* be allowed to call her any pet names.

"Going up," Molly radioed. Cole felt the hull vibrate as the thrusters strained with the added weight. *Parsona* would get a few new burn marks to go with the old, but both birds lifted off the ground, struggling against the moon's gravity. Adding to the insanity: Molly's plan required Cole to transfer *in flight*, as *Parsona's* landing gear would never withstand the weight and imbalance of a ship attached to one side.

As she took them back toward one of the holes in the moon's crust, Cole considered his long jump from one airlock to the other. The two ship's ideas of "down" didn't match, which meant he'd be jumping through the side of one and into the roof of another. And his suit had a lot of extra material around the legs, making him feel clumsy. He held himself by the lip of the 500's hatch, swung out until the other grav plates grabbed him, dangled for a moment, and let himself fall to the metal plating inside *Parsona*. He rolled as he hit, trying to absorb the impact in all his joints instead of just a few.

Not bad, he thought, struggling to his feet. He looked up through the hatch into the 500, where the world that once seemed level now looked askew. Above *Parsona's* inner hatch, the atmosphere and pressure lights were green; Cole thumbed the doors open.

"I'm in," he radioed, stumbling toward the cockpit. Parsona said something through the speakers as he staggered through the cargo bay, the crotch of his outfit down around his knees. He couldn't hear her clearly through the helmet, so he popped it off and tossed it aside.

"Fire up the thrusters!" he told the ship as he made his way forward.

"I'm sorry, Cole. I can't do anything like that."

He waddled into the cockpit and reached over the flight controls to start the procedure himself.

"Is everything OK?" the ship asked. "Where's Mollie?"

"She's in the ship airlocked to you," Cole explained. "So, no. Everything is *not* OK."

○ ○ ○ ○

Molly turned both ships around and headed back for one of the openings created by the lowered landing lift. She didn't like the sight beyond the first hole: the security ship could be seen rising up through its hangar. She gave the 500 full thrust, filling the docking bay with a glow of harsh plasma and hoped Cole still had his suit on in case the locking collars broke loose, dispelling *Parsona's* air into the vacuum.

"Thrusters are coming up now," Cole radioed. "But they won't be ready for a full burn for a bit longer."

Molly thumbed the mic. "Roger. We've got company."

"Already?"

"Yeah. Change of plans. Get the thrusters up and get ready to hold us steady."

There was a pause. "Molly, I . . . I don't think I can do that—"

"You'll have plenty of room, just get ready."

She turned to Walter. "Go get in the other ship," she told him.

He holstered his computer and darted out of the cockpit.

"No looting!" Molly added.

Ahead, the security ship rose clear of the hangar, spun around slowly, and began accelerating their way. The radio was turned way down, but she could still hear nonstop threats being broadcast their way. She reached forward, flicked the unit off, and reduced thrust as she began rolling the two ships over. Gradually, she positioned *Parsona* on top, spinning her own view of the parking deck from the 500.

"Get ready!" she commed to Cole. She pulled under the first exit through the deck—nothing more than a large, square hole of trussed-up regolith left open by a lowered landing pad—and diverted the thrusters to boost them up. *Parsona* popped above the moon's crust, still attached to the 500, the security craft bearing down on them both. The armed ship would be on top of them as soon as they cleared the parking deck. The Stanleys inside were probably waiting to capture them where their clients' ships couldn't be harmed; they must have been thinking a clean escape was going to be impossible.

As the SADAR beeped with a missile-lock warning, Molly began to suspect the same thing. She tried to level her thoughts, even as the world outside turned sideways. It helped to imagine herself on the bottom of the moon, falling down through the crust, rather than half inverted and rising up. The whine of the overworked thrusters made the illusion hard to maintain, however, and she watched, powerless, as the parking deck fell away with agonizing slowness.

She waited until they were clear of the crust, counted to five, and keyed the mic.

"Now!" she barked into the radio.

She reversed the thruster controls but left the accelerator at full. Now, rather than forcing *Parsona* into the clear, the full power of the 500 was trying to drag them both back down into the opening in the moon. She jumped from her seat, sprinted down the center aisle of the ship, and grabbed the airlock jamb to swing herself through. She jumped up for the hatch, pulled herself over the lip, felt the switch in gravity fields, and crashed into a heap on the floor of her own airlock deck.

She groaned in pain and could feel the vibration in the deck as her ship did likewise, trying to counter the more massive thrust from the 500. She forced herself up through sheer will and jumped across the airlock to close the outer hatch. As soon as the indicator went green, she released the locking collars.

The GU-500 popped free, its thrusters and the moon's gravity, powering it back down through the landing pad shaft. Molly stood up and peered through the viewport, watching the ship race away as *Parsona* slowly rose. Just before it fell through the crust, she saw the blue hull of the security ship come into view.

The two crafts slammed together, the wings of the inverted 500 snapping in half and wrapping themselves around the small craft beneath it. It looked like a fierce bird of prey snatching a blue robin out of the air, driving its meal deep into its lair—

A massive explosion ended the illusion, the ball of fire spreading out among the gleaming hulls before rising through the regolith toward *Parsona's* belly. Molly turned away from the harsh scene and leaned out the airlock door, her hand on the jamb. She looked up the center of the ship and saw Cole gaping back at her from the pilot's seat.

"What in the world?" he yelled, his voice still raspy and weak.

Molly limped toward the cockpit, her ankle twisted from the fall through the airlock.

"Did you think we were keeping that ship?" she shouted back.

Cole shook his head, his shocked expression fading to a grim smile. He turned and increased thrust, leveled *Parsona* out, and headed away from the moon, careful to keep the Gs low and the vector straight.

None of them had flightsuits on, of course.

Which would pose all sorts of problems as a Navy fleet, led by Admiral Saunders, prepared for their jump into the Dakura system.

PART X

CAUGHT!

"Judge thyself."

~The Bern Seer~

29

Dani pulled the vehicle to a stop at the edge of the government district. Edison lumbered out of the back seat, and Anlyn followed. As she stepped to the sidewalk and approached the passenger door, the window slid open.

"Be careful in there," Dani said, leaning over from his seat to catch her eye.

"I will be," she said.

Dani glanced at Edison, then at his lance. "Don't use that unless you win the vote, and only outside. The spectacle will be just as important for our cause as the politics; otherwise, the vote won't stick."

Edison nodded.

"We need to go," Anlyn told them both. She pulled Edison toward the crowded walkway as Dani waved, then merged back into the traffic. The couple marched swiftly as the crowd parted to either side, the confused jumble of foot traffic becoming ordered and sedate ahead of them.

The crowd morphed into two walls of Drenards, all of whom gawked at the couple as they strode through the heart of the government district. Part of the treatment could be attributed to the royal regalia Anlyn wore, signifying herself as the next in line to the throne.

Her large companion explained the rest.

"Use English when you're conferring with me," she told Edison. "Few of the Circle members are fluent."

"Understood," Edison replied. "My Drenard vocabulary lacks finesse."

Anlyn reached up and put her hand in his. "Nonsense. I've never seen anyone pick up a language so fast. I just hope you don't overlearn it the way you have English."

"My understanding of that last is nonoptimal."

Anlyn squeezed one of his large fingers. "Exactly. Now, remember the rules. Most votes are controlled by kicking members out on technicalities. Any slipup and our voices won't be heard."

"My familiarity with such gatherings contains both accuracy and precision. Glemot Councils operated in parallel fashion."

"OK, here we go . . . "

They passed under the Clockwise Gate and into the Apex, the arbitrarily chosen "top" of the Drenard home planet. With all the important, habitable land arranged in a ring, locations were given by distance from the top, which was where the Circle met. One direction away from the Apex translated best as "clockwise" into English, but "spinward" would also work. The other direction was "counterclockwise."

Not only did land value plummet according to distance from the Apex, even elements of Drenard psychology could be accurately measured in the manner residents of the upper ring looked— metaphorically, of course—*down* on those who lived and worked throughout the lower half of the ring. Clockwise residents even argued with counterclockwise folk, as if the direction around the ring were somehow any less arbitrary than the chosen top and bottom of the planet.

Once one place had been chosen as special, of course, subsequent improvements surely made it so. While most of the great ringed city around Drenard stayed in perpetual twilight, a cone of reflected and filtered sunlight bathed the massive circle that made up the Apex.

It was one of the few places on Drenard where flora grew in the open, unshielded by glass. Acres of gardens spread here in a complex of labyrinths, all protected by a high exterior wall to shield out the persistent wind, but otherwise uncovered. The wall itself was webbed in colorful ivy that weaved around and up the barrier, popping with blooms that shivered up high where vortexes of wind dipped into the gardens.

Anlyn strolled through the gate, taking in the familiar sights, breathing the old smells. It took her a few nostalgia-filled moments to realize Edison was no longer beside her.

She turned and saw him back by the gate, his head turning from side to side as he absorbed the marvel of the Apex gardens, the small trees, the flowers, the patches of green grass. He had both arms raised, the light of the twin stars shimmering on his fur. Anlyn's chest heaved with pride for her home, but then she caught the movement along Edison's arms, the waving fur she recognized at once for sadness.

"Burn me," she cursed, hurrying back to him. "I should've warned you."

He looked at her, his eyes bright with moisture. "I'm within tolerances," he said. "Mere recollections of home."

She took his hand again. "I'm sorry, love. Just concentrate on the path."

"Negative. Observing remains important."

She nodded and guided him along. Together, they strolled over extravagant pathways of *real* wood, none of the less expensive marble used elsewhere. Anlyn tried to distract him by pointing to the Pinnacle, the building resting in the center of the large park.

"That's where the Circle meets," she said.

"Stupendously unassuming," Edison growled.

"To you, maybe. But this is one of the shortest buildings on Drenard, a rare luxury."

Edison swept a paw across the view, the top edge of the building just visible as it stretched across a good portion of the gardens. "Massive, nonetheless," he pointed out.

"It's wide, yeah. Another decadent waste. We could feed or house a lot of people here . . . don't get me started. Oh, and when we get to the top of the steps, let me do the talking. There'll be a lot of guards on the balcony and none of this crowd. Go ahead and hold your lance, just keep the tip like I showed you."

Edison unclipped the strap that held his modified lance to his back and moved it into his hand. He kept the weapon vertical, tip-down, and tucked next to his hip.

The modifications he'd made had been a romantic gesture, a gift for their looming wedding ceremony, but when Dani saw a demonstration, he insisted they bring it along. If everything went their way, they would use it to seal their victory, making the celebration legendary and less likely to be overturned.

As they wound their way toward the center of the Apex, Anlyn noticed most of the crowd was flowing in the same direction. Word of the meeting had already spread, as had the rumors of multiple deaths in the royal line. The entire planet buzzed with uncommon energy, a wild force that could be shunted toward war or peace, and it was up to Anlyn and Edison to make sure it went toward the latter.

The couple ignored the attention they got from the crowd and just followed the walkway as it snaked through the gardens. They went past small ponds full of floating flowers, through a fake canyon where manufactured Wadi holes leaked miniature waterfalls, and then through the dragonmoth plantings, where various colorful plants swarmed with the bright, silvery insects.

Eventually, the path wound back toward the Pinnacle, where a wide set of wooden steps awaited beyond the mingling and surging crowds. A sizable group of Drenard youth stood clustered near the bottom of the steps, listening to an adult speak. When the guide spotted Anlyn and her tunics, he directed the group's attention their way and launched into an excited spiel on royal finery.

"Ignore them," Anlyn told Edison. She pulled him through the crowd and up the steps, taking the first few too quickly before remembering her station—and trying to forget her youth. She bent forward slightly, grabbed her outer tunics with both hands, and concentrated on walking with perfect grace.

The tall steps leading up to the balcony made it difficult; they were designed by male workers for male strides. Beside her, Edison's problem continued to be walking *slow* enough to not get too far ahead. She marveled again at the irony: when she fled Drenard, she dreamed of falling for a more sensibly sized alien. A human, even, though that idea likely came from her desire to perturb her uncles.

No matter: whether by dumb luck or DNA, she'd ended up engaged to a man almost as big as her last fiancée.

The ruminations ended as she reached the top of the flight of worn steps and saw an entire battalion of the royal guard awaiting them.

The guards stood, neatly arranged in the sunlight, their number quadrupled exclusively for her and her partner. The commander stepped forward in his deep blue tunic; Anlyn didn't recognize him, but she could read everything in his layers and the way his heavily decorated lance nearly dragged on the ground. His posture communicated respect, but she knew better.

"Lady Hooo, the Circle is in session. Your distinguished presence really is not required." His hand rose, urging her to turn away.

"Step aside," Anlyn said, sweeping her arm to indicate the side she'd prefer. Her voice was cool, but her eyes were aflame.

The guard stood firm, possibly out of stark terror. His eyes had moved to Edison, darting up and down his tunics, obviously just now realizing they *both* outranked him. Edison moved forward, and Anlyn could see his fur rippling with the anticipation of danger.

"Step aside," Edison repeated in Drenard. "That's an order."

If the guard's legs were shaking, the tunic hid his embarrassment. He bowed and slid out of the way, waving his hand at the other guards. Anlyn wondered how long Bodi had hoped these clowns would delay her and whether the shock of hearing Edison speak fluent Drenard had done the trick.

As the guards shuffled aside, like a sea of blue parting down the middle, they revealed the Pinnacle beyond: squat, round, and wide. Anlyn moved toward the old building, glancing up at the twin shafts of light streaking down to the center of its low roof.

To either side, the Great Balcony stretched off, wrapping the entire Pinnacle with a wooden platform around which Circle members could walk and confer. Anlyn had been there several times with her father, but she never dreamed she'd return one day as a member, however temporary that status.

Ahead of her, the reflected sunlight from the orbital mirrors ended in a crisp line, and the perfect shade of the eclipsing disc began. The gardens were given the luxury of natural light, but it wouldn't do for the Circle to indulge. For that reason, the Pinnacle remained cloaked in darkness, a round slab of metal high up in orbit shielding it from the light. Anlyn sucked in a deep breath of warm Drenard atmosphere before stepping across the artificial terminator.

Edison followed, struggling to not overtake her as they moved toward the old Pinnacle doors, supposedly cut from the last living tree on old Drenard. When the two guards to either side moved to pull them open, Anlyn waved them off.

She needed to do this herself.

Reaching up, she grabbed the ornate handles on the old doors, each one standing not quite three meters tall. Male Drenards, to exaggerate their bulk, often made a show of bowing as they entered.

Especially those who had plenty of clearance.

Anlyn threw the wooden antiques open and took a step forward. She held her head high, remaining erect, despite how utterly small and insignificant she felt.

○ ○ ○ ○

"Contacts on SADAR," Parsona said.

419

Molly glanced up at the security cam as she limped through the cargo bay. *Mom.* The reminder of her failure on Dakura hit her hard. Nothing had been learned; her mother's old memories had not been taken care of. And now they'd never be allowed back.

"Navy!" Cole yelled. Molly hurried to the cockpit to find him leaning forward from her chair, Walter in his. She rested her hand on the back of the seat, the spot's emptiness reminding her of the Wadi locked in her stateroom. So many concerns swirled in her mind at once that she couldn't see any of them clearly.

"Let me have that seat, Walter."

He unbuckled himself and jumped out, his eyes fixed on the sight of the large ship that had jumped in-system.

Molly peered through the carboglass. "That's a StarCarrier," she murmured, awed. She'd never seen one in person. It lay out in the L1 between the moon and Dakura, but its blocky outline was instantly recognizable.

She took over control of the ship with her left hand and nosed around for the back of the moon. "They probably won't even notice we're here," she said. "We'll get on the other side and thrust out to clear space—"

"GN-290 *Parsona*, KML32, this is GN Naval Command Task Force Zebra KPR98. Maintain altitude and respond, over."

"Damn. Not good," Cole muttered.

Molly increased thrust. She'd developed a small habit of running whenever anyone said "freeze."

A second voice came through the radio: "Molly, this is Admiral Saunders from the Academy. We're prepping to jump Firehawks to the other side of the moon. Do *not* spin up your hyperdrive. If you do, I'm going to send every missile in our fleet down your tailpipes. Reduce thrust this instant or become a fireworks display. Your choice."

Molly took in the SADAR and nav charts. Several new contacts popped up in the free space she'd planned on escaping to. Her brain whirled, looking for an idea.

"This isn't good," Cole said again.

"Mollie . . . I don't think we have a choice." It was her mother's voice. In many ways, more familiar and real than the one she'd just spent hours with.

"We could jump blindly," Molly suggested.

Cole opened his mouth to protest, but it was Parsona who vetoed the idea first. "Absolutely *not*, Mollie Fyde. Don't you dare. It would jeopardize *everything*."

"As will being caught!" she countered.

"Who iss that talking?" Walter asked.

"The radio," Cole lied. "You might wanna go strap in, buddy."

Walter nodded and ran back to his seat.

"Molly, Admiral Saunders. We're firing missiles in five seconds. Reduce thrust and maintain altitude."

Molly thought about the last time she'd seen Saunders, just a few weeks ago. He'd been a captain then, and doubled over from a blow between the legs. Lucin, his boss, lay slumped over a desk, dead. She had a hunch the missiles weren't an empty threat.

She keyed the microphone. "Reducing thrust," she said, pulling back to hold her current altitude.

"What's the plan?" Cole asked.

"I don't have one," she admitted.

"You had better encrypt me if you guys are planning on getting caught," Parsona suggested. "If anyone searches the computer while I'm active, they'll see this isn't nav data, and your father went through a lot of effort to hide me from the Navy."

Molly looked at Cole. "I guess the plan is to be caught," she groaned.

"Thank you for complying, *Parsona*," the first voice said. "Hold position and prepare to enter hangar bay four."

"Roger. Hangar bay four," she radioed back to the Navy. She flipped off the mic and turned to Cole. "Get the Wadi plenty of food and water. Enough for a few weeks. Put it in the lazarrette under one of the thruster panels. Make sure the door's sealed to keep the atmosphere in there."

"It's in your quarters?"

"Yeah."

"You sure it won't bite me?"

"I'm sure. While you're in there, grab the two red bands in the top drawer of my dresser. Hide them with the Wadi."

"Gotcha."

"Oh, and tell Walter to go along with whatever happens and to keep his mouth shut."

"With pleasure."

Cole shook himself out of the tall spacesuit and headed back to lecture Walter. Molly pulled up the nav screen and sighed.

"Tell me what I need to do to encrypt you," she said to her ship.

To her *mother*.

○ ○ ○ ○

The balcony inside the Pinnacle stood thick with spectators, far more than Anlyn could remember in any of her childhood visits. She and Edison pushed through them, out onto the clockwise landing that overlooked the gathered Circle members below. A low murmur rippled through the crowded seats, and heads—even those around the Circle—turned to survey the source of the distraction.

Anlyn led Edison down the flight of steps between the rows of seated onlookers. Below lay the large circular table around which the council manipulated an entire empire. Anlyn noted grimly that several seats stood empty, draped with white mourning cloths. She forced herself to look straight ahead, ignoring the legion of onlookers filling the seats to either side of the aisle and stretching out through the darkness all the way around the Pinnacle.

The timing of their arrival, she saw, couldn't have been better. Bodi stood in the bright light that shone down within the circle, the table before his empty seat illuminated by a second shaft of harsh rays, signifying his turn to speak. She nodded to her former fiancé, baiting him, as she walked around the back of the Circle members and approached one of the empty seats.

"Anlyn," Bodi murmured, a hint of false surprise in his voice. He stood in full Royal regalia, some layers of which he hadn't actually earned, only *borrowed* thanks to their supposed engagement.

Several members turned to him before looking back to Anlyn, following her with curious gazes. She took her place behind Bedder's empty seat and waited while a council page hurried forward, confused, to remove the mourning cloths.

Anlyn rested her hands on the high back of the stone chair, the old petrified tree cool to the touch. Her eyes traveled up from the empty seat to meet Bodi's. "I am assuming Bedder Dooo's position within the

Circle." She turned slowly to sweep the words across the entire gathering. Edison took his place beside her at Muder Dooo's chair. The page hesitated, not sure what to do.

Bodi broke the tense silence from the Light of Speak: "Lady Hooo, you have been through much these past few months—"

"And I have learned *much* from these ordeals." The words contained a coo of sarcasm. Anlyn tilted her head slightly and used a wry smile to punctuate her bitterness. Everyone present knew full well Anlyn had fled Drenard to get away from Bodi. And his role in the recent ambush on her and her friends was assumed by all present.

Bodi smiled back at her, defusing the barb by pretending her warmness contained sincerity. "One of your high measure must also know that war planning is a lowly endeavor. Beneath your station and—"

Anlyn interrupted again, ignoring the Center of Speak and causing expensive tunics to shift uneasily. "Nonsense," she said. "The fate of our empire means more to me as a result of my position."

Bodi switched tactics. "Then perhaps I may appeal to your fairer sex and caution against getting dirt on—"

"Counselors." Anlyn looked at each of the dozen or more members. "I will—"

"You violate the Center of Speak!"

It was Tottor, the Navy Counselor, a distant cousin of Anlyn's. He'd won his high post over several other candidates whose Wadi were larger in every way—but *those* counselors did not have Royal blood within them.

Anlyn turned to address his outburst. "No, Counselor, it is *you* who violates the Center of Speak." Tunics fluttered at this. "When I entered the Circle, as is my *right*, I was addressed by Lord Thooo, who holds the Center. This conversation is *his* choosing, and it is over when *he* says it is over."

Anlyn turned back to Bodi while Totter seethed, his blue skin purpling with rage. Several members of the Circle who had won their posts due to merit attempted to cover their panting chuckles.

"Lord Thooo," Anlyn continued, "you call my gender to attention in an attempt to discredit me while pretending to honor me." All eyes turned to her again at this accusation. Anlyn once more addressed the entire room. "Many sun cycles ago—long before the threat we face today ever made itself known—female Drenards not only served on the War Circle, they served in the General Assembly and on every Planetary Board—"

"Enough," said Bodi, both palms held up to Anlyn.

Anlyn took this to mean that he had no further complaints. She stepped around and climbed up into her seat, kneeling on her shins to rest her arms comfortably on the male-sized table. She turned to Edison and gestured to the empty chair beside her. The pup nodded solemnly as the page hurriedly swiped away the mourning cloth. Edison held up his lance, as he'd been taught, and laid it lengthwise across the table.

Bodi complained immediately. "That is Lord Muder's chair. Your pet will not be allowed—"

"Lord Edison Campton is my *betrothed*. He is not my pet, and I am no longer *yours*," Anlyn laced her words with cold venom. "Lord Muder is the second uncle I have lost this week, and his widow has granted Lord Campton—"

"Lord?" snorted Bodi.

Anlyn smiled. "Ninth degree, Lord Thooo. And as you are an eighth-degree Lord, you will not be permitted to use his first name unless he permits it, a protocol I'm sure I need not remind you of again, lest you desire to leave these proceedings."

Bodi purpled at this. The entire Circle could surely see the hem of his tunics vibrating with frustration. "No alien, Lady Hooo, has ever—"

Anlyn cut him off again, each jab to her ex-fiancé's ego like a blow to a fighter's belly, sapping his endurance. "Lord Campton is a Drenard. If such a thing may be measured, he is more a Drenard than *you*. He will be my husband. He has been given this seat by Widow Muder. He will go before the election board during the next cycle to *retain* his seat."

"With all *respect*, Lady Hooo, his seat holds the Chair of Alien Relations, how will a nonlinguist—"

Anlyn smiled as Edison rose to respond. She spread her pale blue hands across the ancient table, its ten-meter diameter cut from a single petrified tree, the largest ever found on the cold side of Drenard. She rubbed the polished grain and watched each Counselor's reaction as Edison spoke.

"Distinguished Counselors," he said in a perfect Drenard coo, "the subject being discussed from the Center is my qualifications as Lord Muder's replacement." He swept his face across the circle, wide teeth flashing. "While my dialect has the lilt of upper Drenard, a result of my association with *Anlyn*," he stressed her common name as he met Bodi's gaze, a brilliant blow, "it might interest you to know that my race has a long history of rapid language acquisition. I am fluent in English, and I am already conversational in Bern."

Bodi seemed more stunned than the rest to see him speaking—with the accent of Drenard royalty, no less. The full implications of this creature's presence on the Circle appeared to finally settle through his thick skull. With Edison's status as Anlyn's betrothed and the recent death of two members of the royal family, Bodi was looking at a potential Drenard king!

Anlyn saw him sway forward as it sank in, ready to pass out, or perhaps he was considering a mad rush to kill his rival with bare hands.

Were he not so blasted timorous, Anlyn thought, *he'd surely attempt himself what others failed to do in cowardly ambush.*

Bodi glared at Edison. He opened his mouth to speak and then stopped, closing it. Anlyn hoped it wouldn't be the last time she tripped him up; one misstep on either side could result in expulsion.

"I call for a formal Vote of Protest—" Bodi began, his voice shaking.

"*Bodi—*," Edison began, cutting him off once more, but this time in a blatant breach of protocol. Anlyn spun in her seat to warn him, fearing all would be lost.

"—I would like to issue a citation for violating the Light of Turn."

The Circle grumbled, dozens of spectators in the packed house panting with laughter. All heads turned to the second shaft of light being reflected through the hole in the roof. Eight minutes ago, those photons had left Hori II, Drenard's smaller sun. They travelled through space—across millions of kilometers of vacuum—before reaching a series of occluding disks stationed in orbit. Those clockwork orbital machinations continually shifted, directing the narrow shafts of light down through the windy Drenard atmosphere, piercing the roof of the Pinnacle. One shaft remained stationary in the center, where all speeches of importance must be made. The other shaft slowly orbited the surface of the giant, petrified tree, indicating whose turn it was to speak.

Everyone in attendance—thousands of Drenards—focused on that spot of illuminated marble.

The Light of Turn no longer stood before Bodi's empty seat; it now rested before Lord Mede. He rose, purple with so many eyes turning his way, and nodded apologetically at Bodi.

"I forgive the transgression," he said meekly.

Anlyn let out her held breath and settled back against her seat. In the Center of Speak, on the symbolic highest point of the planet Drenard, Lord Bodi Yooo shivered with rage. Otherwise, he did not budge. His eyes focused on Edison.

His imagination concocted murder.

30

Molly surveyed her prison cell aboard the Navy StarCarrier. Due to a spate of recent events, she'd begun to consider herself somewhat a connoisseur of incarceration.

With its riveted metal plating, functioning sink with hot and cold water, flushable toilet, and padded double bunks, she gave it three stars. It couldn't match the filth and squalor on Palan, and it lacked the decadent touches of a Drenard prison. In a Navy known for operating along one extreme or the other, she'd discovered the one thing they did in moderation: lock people up.

In a strategy right out of the Navy manual of torture techniques, her captors had left her alone for an hour.

The idea was to marinate a prisoner's brain in guilt to prepare him or her for the grilling ahead. Molly knew all about the tactic, but that didn't prevent it from working. She had a lot to feel bad about: the Wadi locked up in the laz, just waiting to be discovered; the multiple failures on Dakura; the fact that she was no closer to discovering what her parents had been up to on Lok; and the utter lack of progress on helping rescue her father.

She felt positive that whatever Lucin thought could end the war was somehow connected to her parents, but she couldn't see it. And now she'd be court-martialed and airlocked for what had happened at the Academy, dead before she could unravel the mystery.

As the hour of guilt wrapped up, she half expected Saunders himself to arrive and begin the softening process, but her first visitor in Navy black didn't fit the profile. Too thin. The mysterious figure strode by the bars slowly, his fingers rapping against the cold steel.

Molly remained seated but leaned forward as the face centered itself between two bars.

"Riggs?"

"Hello, Fyde."

She couldn't believe it. Riggs had been one of her classmates at the Academy. He and Cole had taken turns flying as each other's wingman. He had graduated early during Lucin's cover-up of the Tchung Affair, and Molly had never found out where he'd been stationed. Now she knew: he'd been assigned to Saunders. She rose from her bunk and approached the bars.

Riggs took two steps back.

"Gods, Riggs. It *is* you!"

"Don't try anything." He looked at her warily. "I shouldn't even be down here; I . . . I just had to see for myself."

"See what? Riggs, this is just a misunderstanding."

"Misunderstanding?" His face contorted with rage. "You killed Lucin! You armed your spaceship, a spaceship you *stole* from the Navy, and I heard about your fight with Delta Patrol—"

"That wasn't a fight! We ran away!"

"So you don't deny the other stuff?"

Molly could see tears filming over Riggs's eyes.

"Lucin was about to kill *me*!" she said. "And I didn't steal that ship, it's *mine*!"

Riggs shook his head. He backed up and leaned on the wall across from her cell. "Not anymore," he said. "And they're getting everything from your little alien friend. You and Cole are gonna be tried as traitors."

"Who—?"

"The *Drenards*, Molly? Are you *serious*?"

Molly cursed under her breath. "Walter, you *flanker*." She saw Riggs's body stiffen and feared he might take her anger as a confession. "It's not like that, Riggs. We had a Drenard friend who needed—"

"You have Drenard *friends*?" He shook his head and crossed his arms. "I used to stick up for you. I treated you like a little sister. Me and Cole. I don't know what you did to him, but you aren't gonna sweet talk me into buying your bull. Ha! I guess I'm safe 'cause I always saw you as a *sister*."

"Riggs, I—"

"Save it for Saunders," he said. "We all know you killed Lucin, and we know how you left Saunders behind. You're just lucky the CO made sure the boarding party was full of the oldest marines, the people who don't understand what you did; otherwise, you probably wouldn't have made it to this cell alive." He leaned forward, the tears on his cheeks caught in the light overhead. "I can't promise you I wouldn't have joined in," he added.

With that, Riggs spun away from the wall and marched out of sight.

Molly clung to the bars, speechless.

○ ○ ○ ○

They gave her another hour to steep. Molly couldn't help but admire the plan. Even if the Navy had nothing on any of them, she knew they were all receiving the

434

same line from their grillers: your friends are flipping, and he who flips last gets burned worst.

She also knew the best course of action was to think about something else, but it was impossible not to focus on the very thing she concentrated on avoiding. And she knew Walter. She had little doubt the traitorous bastard was spilling his guts. It wouldn't be the first time he had turned them in to the Navy expecting some sort of reward.

Molly looked up through the bars and pictured Riggs leaning on the far wall, his arms folded, his eyes down. It was crazy how *young* he'd looked. He shouldn't even be out of the Academy. Neither should she nor Cole, for that matter. They were all little pawns staggering around a board that Lucin had set up and left unfinished.

She tried to mentally study that board, to determine which opening he'd used and which gambits to ignore. Once again, his tragic death at Cole's hands haunted her. The only person who could help her understand what was going on had been murdered—adding one more unpardonable deed to her growing list of sins.

She sat on the edge of her bunk, gazing down at the long, straight shadows the bars cast across the floor. It occurred to her once again that jail cells provided her with her only opportunities to calmly sit and ponder her mistakes.

How fitting.

A wide shadow slid over the lines at her feet, interrupting her thoughts. She didn't need to look up to know who it was.

"Admiral, huh?"

She meant it as small talk, a compliment, even. It came out snide and rude.

"Interrogation room B," he barked to someone else.

Molly looked over, but he was gone. Two guards in Navy black had taken his place. The bars of her cell descended into the floor, and the two men came at her with cruel smiles.

Rumors of her exploits had likely thinned the herd of people who could be trusted to handle her. They cinched the cuffs behind her back and wrenched them up high as they marched her down the hall. Molly walked on her toes, grunting from the pain in her shoulders, but that just brought sniffles of laughter—and the guy holding the cuffs responded by pulling them up higher.

Just like being back at the Academy, she thought, *only these are larger and stronger boys.*

Interrogation room B consisted of a metal-plated box broken up by a door on one wall and a mirror on an adjoining one. A metal table in the center had been welded to the floor, as had the wide benches on both sides. A precaution, Molly knew, in the event of gravity malfunctions. The guards cuffed Molly to one of the benches, nodded to the mirror, then walked out.

Saunders entered soon after with a reader and a glass of water. He slid his bulk between the table and the bench, took a sip of the water, and set it down with a clack of glass on metal. He stared at the reader for a moment before setting it aside.

Molly watched the condensation on the surface of the glass drip down, forming a ring of wetness around the base. The entire scene was so cliché, so much like every Navy drama on holovid, it was all she could do not to laugh. Just thinking about how awful and crazy she would seem if she did break out in a giggle-fit made it even harder to contain.

"You keep interesting company, Ms. Fyde." Saunders leaned forward, both his forearms resting on the table in front of him, his fingers interlocked into one meaty fist.

"I'm sorry," Molly told him. She looked him right in the eyes. "I'm sorry for attacking you that day."

Saunders smirked. "Oh? But not sorry for killing my friend, eh?" He grabbed the reader for a reference. "Are you sorry for Corporal Timothy Reed? Or Special Agent David Rowling? Or how about Staff Sergeant Jim McCleary? Aren't sorry about any of them?"

"Are those the guys from Palan?" Molly asked.

"The men you killed, yeah."

"I am very sorry for them. And I'm sorry for Lucin. But they were all in self-defense. You were the exception. You were the only person I attacked in anger, and I'm sorry—"

"I don't want your apology, Fyde. I'm actually glad you attacked me. I was going to spend the rest of my life at that Academy. I would have been happy, sure, but I turned down dozens of promotions out of love for that place. I *needed* a kick in the ass to get me out here fighting the good fight."

Molly was dying to point out that it wasn't a kick in the *ass* that she'd given him. Her desire to laugh returned—she swallowed it down, afraid she might be losing her senses.

"What about the fourth guy on Palan?" she asked. "Was he OK?"

Saunders looked at the reader again. "Agent Simmons? No, we know who killed him. Not that it's going to save your butt. We've got more than enough to jettison you into space. I'm just here to make sure we have it all."

That wasn't the person Molly was thinking about, but she ignored the discrepancy.

"I'll answer everything honestly, Captain—I'm sorry, Admiral. I've been hunting for answers for over a month, and you're welcome to the few I've found."

He smiled at this. "You sound as eager as your Palan friend. Boy had so much to say, we couldn't get it down fast enough. Horrible English with that kid. Turns out he is a fast typist, though. We put him in front of a computer, and the lad is writing a book on what you guys've been up to." Saunders set down the reader. "Now I want to hear it from you."

Been up to? Molly wondered how much Walter knew of the disaster on Glemot and just what kind of trouble he could really get them in.

As if they could airlock her *twice.*

"What do you want to hear?" she asked Saunders. She tensed up, afraid of his answer.

But, as it turned out, not quite afraid enough . . .

Saunders smiled at her and unclasped his hands.

"Why don't we start with who we're talking to on your ship's nav computer."

31

"I'm sorry?" Molly licked her lips and eyed the glass of water, but her hands were locked behind her back and fastened to the bench. She pictured a long straw extending from the vessel, ushering fluid into her dry mouth.

"Our computer guys found something in your nav computer. They think it might be an AI, or some sort of complex logic tree. It claims to be your mother, and of course, she thinks that our guys are *you*. Did you steal her off Dakura just now?"

"Yes," Molly lied.

"I thought you were going to tell me the truth, Fyde. I have to say, I'm disappointed. Lying to me on the very

441

first question. We've been talking to Dakura Security. They assure us that such a theft is not possible and that nothing in a standard ship could host one of their AIs. So. Who is she?"

"My mom."

"How's that possible?"

"I don't know. She said she was a copy from when they originally admitted her into Dakura years ago."

"You want to tell me why you killed your mother on Dakura?"

"What?" Molly furrowed her brow, confused.

"Your friend Walter confessed to doing it, but he said it was your plan. We just want to know why. Why kill your own mother? Or is there no reasoning behind your madness?"

"I didn't know she was dead," Molly said somberly. Her dry mouth suddenly felt full of saliva. She felt sure she'd vomit if she tried to swallow it, but had no choice. Her stomach twisted up in knots thinking about her mom, happily birthing and mothering little Mollies just a handful of hours ago—and now gone.

If any of it turned out to be true.

"Well, now," Saunders said, leaning away from the table. "I would expect you to be a bit more enthused to find out your attack was successful. Or are you just upset at getting caught?"

"I didn't want to kill her." Molly looked down at the desk as another layer of blackness heaped on top of her miseries. Each was like a smothering blanket, except they just made her more cold.

"Let's come back to that. I want to touch on a few things during this session to help steer the next one. We have several jumps before Earth, so you and I will have plenty of time to drill down to details." Molly glanced up, saw his chubby face break into a smile. She looked back down as he asked the next question:

"How did you get recruited into the Drenard Underground?"

"The what?"

"I'm getting sick of that as an answer, Fyde. The Drenard Underground. Your parents were members. Lucin's reports claim they infiltrated the group as double agents, but it's looking like they were actually taken in by these sympathizers. Now, you visit Drenard and take part in some kind of ceremony, get inducted as an honorary Drenard. Afterward, you set out to cover up any evidence left behind by your parents. I'm slowly piecing together what they were doing on Lok; I just want to know what sort of nasty business you're getting tied up in."

"I've never heard of the Drenard Underground," Molly said. She looked up at Saunders, a half-truth giving her a sense of dignity. But the other part of her knew she'd just sat in front of a simulated fire in one of their headquarters, chatting and having tea with her mother, one version of which spoke Drenard.

"Is your father still on Drenard? Is he working for them?"

"I don't know where my father is."

Saunders leaned forward. "Just so you know how this is working, Fyde, the cameras behind that mirror, and the microphones over your head, are all keeping track of your lies. We've already established that you're unwilling to be truthful with us, created a baseline. What we're looking for now are the things you withhold. The things you think are important." He spread his fat fingers, his hands folding out like an open book. "The things you don't tell us are worse than your lies." He lifted one arm and tapped his temple. "The egg-heads behind that mirror are telling me right now that the more you're aware of this inability to fool us, the more power we have."

He smiled with how clever he was, his cheeks folding down over the corners of his mouth. "Here's what I'm going to do: I'm going to let you return to your cell and think about what you're doing here. You're a traitor to the human race; you're aiding our enemy and leaving behind a long trail of dead and wounded, including the man who loved you and trusted you the most. You *will* be killed for these crimes, Fyde. I promise you that. It's a done deal. You and Cole both. It might help if you just consider yourself already dead.

"Imagine it for a second: imagine you're in whatever special hell they reserve for Drenard lovers. Now, someone gives you a chance to come clean. To give information that will help *our* cause. Help *your* race. Wouldn't you love to come back and give that information? Confess everything? Do a bit of *good* with your life?

"I know this underground business isn't you. I know you're just a hurt teenage girl, messed up because your mother and father abandoned you and you washed out of the Academy. You aren't brainwashed the way they were—you're just confused. I know this. *You* know this."

He stood up. "Go sit in your cell and think about what I've said. Think about where your lies and actions have gotten you so far. Think about the people you've hurt. And why have you done these things? For a dream of continuing something your parents started? What if what they were doing was *wrong*? Have you thought about that? Or do you just trust them because they birthed you on some backwoods planet and disappeared? How much do you know them? I think you should dwell on *that* as well."

Saunders left the room, waving at the mirror as he went by. The two guards entered soon after he disappeared; they undid her cuffs from the bench and hauled her back to her cell.

Molly tried to see herself through their eyes as they handled her roughly:

Traitor.

Whipped dog.

Beaten.

She could feel it in her own flat, shuffling steps, and the way her toes never left the decking. She knew how it looked, knew it made it easier for them to pull her hands up high behind her, inflicting as much pain as they could.

She couldn't really blame them.

o o o o

Not long after the guards left, having shoved her face into her bunk while they uncuffed her hands, Molly had another visitor. She had expected Riggs, or someone else from the Academy, but she was surprised to see Saunders's bulk looming through the bars.

"That's what you call giving me time to think?" she asked, still rubbing the circulation back into her wrists.

"Get over here, Fyde."

She pushed herself up and went to the bars.

"That was the speech they'll record and analyze. This is the one between just you and me. I've already established your propensity for lying, so good luck trying to get anyone to believe your side of what I'm about to say."

"Look, Admiral—"

"Can it, Fyde. Listen. I'm going to make a career off the mistakes you're making. I'm going to win medals for cleaning up the mess your parents made and that you're now smearing across the galaxy. But I meant every word of my speech back there. You can do some good with the little amount of life you have left, before you crash and burn in spectacular fashion. And before you start thinking on these things, I want you to know how I found out about your parents and their work on Lok. The official version is some miraculous sleuthing on my part—enough to skip a few ranks and get Zebra command—but I want *you* to know what really happened. Just so you realize what you're up against. How good my intel is."

"I don't understand—"

"Lucin told me everything."

"What?"

"Everything." His smile faded, jowls collapsing. "I held him as he died in his office. He was spitting up blood and spilling his guts, and not just those that you and Cole blasted out of him. He told me about the special assignment your parents were on. About the Drenard Underground. About what I would find on your ship if I looked hard enough. He told me *everything*."

"Saunders, listen. Whatever he said—"

"Let me guess, it was a lie? I think we've sorted out the liars from the heroes without your help. I'll take a dying man's word over a traitor trying to save her ass any day of the week."

Saunders stood as straight as he could, tugging down on his black jacket. "I'm telling you this so you can keep Lucin's last words on your mind as you think about what you need to do. The words he sputtered with his very last breath. He didn't ask me to tell his wife that he loved her. He didn't leave any inspiring words for the Academy or anything for him to be remembered by. He used them on *you*.

"'Save her,' he told me. 'Save her.' I think he meant for me to save your soul. Rescue you from yourself. It's going to be up to you whether or not you made that great man waste his final breath. Did a galactic hero perish worrying about a soul that couldn't be redeemed? Or was his hope for you justified?

"So, while you're in here scheming on how to fool me, think on that. You think on whether you want to keep secrets or if you should just tell me what you know."

He turned and stomped off down the hall, leaving her with her befuddled thoughts.

What *did* she know?

She knew Walter was a dead Palan if she ever got her hands on him. That was one thing she felt absolutely certain of. She now knew the Drenard Underground existed and that her parents had investigated them on Lok, maybe even gotten involved with them. There was a slim chance her father was a Drenard by rite, if her "mother" could be trusted. But what if Saunders and the Navy had it wrong about the Drenards? It was something she'd been dwelling on since meeting Anlyn. What if the war was some kind of massive misunderstanding? The Drenards had seemed no more prone to kill her or assist her than any other race had, humans included. What if they—meaning every race in the galaxy—were just terrified, confused, and lashing out?

What else did she know? She knew she could trust Cole. There was no point in questioning him. Even if she ended up wrong about him, she wouldn't mind if that mistake got her killed. She'd likely welcome it with open arms, as she nearly did the last time she doubted him.

What about Lucin? He had lied to her and used her. Would he really have lied to Saunders as he died? What would be the point? And what if Saunders had made up that entire scene?

Molly thought about the Navy men sitting in her pilot seat right then, chatting away on the nav keyboard and pretending to be her. What would her mother be telling them? Surely nothing more than she'd been willing to divulge already. And why wouldn't she see them on the camera? Or overhear their conversations? It didn't make sense, unless her mom was playing them for fools.

Then again, if it was something her mother *knew*, why would Navy cryptographers have to *ask* her? That knowledge would be stored as 1s and 0s on the nav computer. They could just *take* the info.

What about her *other* mom? Was she really dead? Would that explain the intense bout of white light and noise she'd endured on Dakura?

She lay back on her bunk and looked up at the underside of the sagging mattress above. What should she do? Carry these mistakes to her grave? Hope her father could rescue himself? Hope her mom would get whatever sensitive information she had to the right people?

And what about the Wadi? Molly rubbed her temples. The thing never even got a name. What would they do when they found an unknown species onboard her ship? Would they dissect her?

Then there was Cole. He would be killed, and for what? For helping her? For falling in love with her? He said on Drenard he wasn't afraid of his own death, but Molly was plenty afraid for him.

Maybe Saunders was right. Maybe all of this *was* her fault and she just needed to throw her chips in with the Navy. Every misadventure had been predicated on her absolute faith in two parents she hardly knew. Was it OK to love and trust people completely for no other reason than they birthed you?

And then there was Byrne. Molly had almost forgotten about him. Was he dead? She watched him stand there in a complete vacuum. Could you fit robotics that complicated in such a thin shell? Whether or not he survived, what did he have to do with all this? Why did he suggest he *owned* her?

Molly grabbed the rough pillow under her head and pressed it into her face. She used it to muffle a yell of frustration, her stomach clenching with the effort.

The screams gradually turned to sobs, her entire body giving in to the overwhelming sadness.

She pulled the pillow tighter to her face, smothering her despair and desperation.

32

Molly was wide awake when they came for her. Her brain had never stopped racing through the same loop of questions, so she was fully alert right when she should have been sleeping. As soon as she heard the footsteps approaching, she rolled from her bunk and moved to the shadows on the other side of her dimly lit cell. If this was an attempt on her life by zealous crew members, she would go out fighting.

Two silhouettes strode into view, the silver bars dividing their profiles into black slices.

"This the one?" It was barely a whisper, nearly inaudible. Molly shrank back into the corner, hid behind the pedestal sink, and pressed herself into the wall. One of the men seemed to fumble for something in his pocket; the other silhouette lurked behind. The figure closer to the bars murmured into a device, and the barrier slid into the floor.

The crew members were coming for her.

The larger man went straight for her bunk, putting his back to Molly. She flinched, thinking of rushing the man from behind, maybe trying to snap his neck. Then she thought of the bars, the man in the hallway, and the fact that she'd still be trapped inside. She rushed for him instead, pushing off the wall with her foot.

The dark figure by the bunk spun as she flew by, reaching for her. The one outside her cell had leaned against the far wall. He seemed shocked, unable to even raise his hands in defense as Molly hurled her entire body into his stomach, driving the air out of him in the form of a grunt. He crumpled in the dimly lit hall, his hands still clasped in front. Molly spun with clenched fists to fight the man coming out of her cell.

The dark figure hissed her name, walking toward her with his hands spread out. Molly stayed in a crouch, one hand holding down the man she'd already taken out. She tried to calm her breathing as she prepared to defend herself.

The tall figure emerged from her cell and called to his comrade. "Riggs? You OK?"

Molly looked down. A pale, familiar face glowered back up at hers. She recognized the rage as well as the man. Black tape covered his mouth, a detail Molly couldn't process properly. Her hand, pressing down on his shoulder, moved up to his neck. She looked to the standing figure and threw out her terms: "Another step and I crush his windpipe."

"Please don't," the other man whispered. "We need him if we're gonna get out of here."

Molly loosened her grip on Riggs's neck and looked down at him again. He was trying to reach up to fight her hands away, but his own were tied together and strapped to his belt.

She looked up once more as the other figure came forward another few steps, his hands still wide apart. She squinted into the simulated nighttime of the StarCarrier's hallway, his face coming forward into the pale light.

The first thing she recognized was the flash of his wary smile.

"Cole?"

He offered her a hand while pressing a finger to his lips. Molly reached out and grabbed his arm, squeezing it and fighting the urge to pull herself into him.

She looked back at Riggs, and at her empty cell. Somehow they'd gone from prisoners to captors. Her brain reeled as she attempted to rearrange her tactics.

"What's going on?" she asked him, halfway heeding his gesture of silence by keeping her voice at a whisper.

Cole knelt beside her and glanced at Riggs, making sure he was OK. "We're getting out of here. Let's lift him up."

They each grabbed one arm and hauled Riggs to his feet. As Riggs pulled his legs underneath him, Molly noticed the laces of his black Navy boots had been tied together. He could walk, but running would be hazardous.

"Is he helping us?" Molly asked. The disgusted and angry look on Riggs's face hadn't wavered from his visit the day before.

"Yeah," Cole whispered, "but not because he wants to. We need to get off this hall, and then we can talk about it."

Molly looked over her shoulder, back toward the guard station beyond a distant partition. Black security camera warts lined the ceiling, but Cole didn't seem concerned about them. After they passed through a series of open gates, Cole reached back into a pocket and withdrew a small shiny device. It looked like a Navy-issue communicator.

"Seal the hall," he said, and the gates behind them slid shut. Cole straightened as they did so, and several lines of worry disappeared from his forehead. Molly watched this with interest, frowning at the creases that remained.

"Can we talk now?" she whispered.

"Yeah, but we need to keep walking." He indicated a direction through the wide engineering space. "This way."

Molly helped pull Riggs along, glancing over her shoulder to assure herself that they weren't being pursued. "How'd you get out?"

"Walter."

"What? That little bastard—"

"Forget it. I thought the same thing when they questioned me and I heard what he was doing. I should've known when they said he needed to spill his guts on a computer. The sneaky little—"

"Oh, gods," Molly groaned. "They let him on a *computer*. I'm so stupid. I was ready to kill him—I felt like a *fool* for trusting him again."

Cole laughed at this. "We probably *are* fools for trusting him."

"How'd he do it?" Molly knew it wasn't important; they could go over the story later, but her curiosity gnawed at her.

"He's got access to almost everything. My old buddy Riggs here came by my cell to gloat earlier this evening. He was jawing at me through the bars when they receded into the floor. I had no idea it was coming.

I just wrestled him down and tied him up with his own laces. Meanwhile, Walter started hissing at me through his radio, giving me instructions and guiding me with the cameras." Cole looked up at one of the warts for emphasis.

"He opened a supply closet for me, got me these duds, guided me to you." Cole pointed to an open lift, and they led Riggs inside. The light shone brighter in the small space; Molly could see Riggs's nostrils flaring as he fought to breathe through his nose.

"How does Walter plan on getting us out of here?"

Cole laughed and shook his head. "He doesn't. He got *me* out, and I've been planning the rest. Hell, I'm not sure he woulda busted me out had he known how good a wrestler you are."

Cole flipped open the communicator again. "Down, please." The doors closed, and the lift vibrated into motion. He let Riggs lean against the far wall and turned to Molly. "Every guard between us and the cargo bay has been routed off-duty. Walter scheduled Riggs's Firehawk for a fleet patrol. He and I are gonna tow you and *Parsona* out of the hangar bay."

"Just like that?"

Cole smiled. "Just like that. You know, they pulled me off pilot training and taught me comms and navigation. It was supposed to be a demotion. You wanna know the truth?"

The elevator beeped its arrival and the doors hissed open, allowing the rhetorical question to float out into the vast hangar bay. Cole pushed Riggs ahead of them and winked at Molly.

"The person scheduling the guards is the one with *real* power."

33

Molly could see *Parsona's* profile standing above the sleeker Firehawks. She, Cole, and Riggs angled in the ship's direction, walking down the wide landing strip at the center of the hangar. The vast cavern bulged with metal shapes, but no crewmen. It appeared they'd be strolling out of here as casually as they liked.

Something about that filled Molly with unease. She had grown accustomed to nothing coming easily or without great cost. This felt like one of those gifts she'd pay dearly for later.

Riggs tried to make things interesting once by pulling away from Cole and stumbling for a few steps. His laces, however, made large strides impossible, and Cole caught up to him quickly, preventing Riggs from hurting himself in a fall to the metal decking.

"Stop that!" he told Riggs in a tone that suggested several earlier attempts.

Molly hurried to resume her spot by one of his arms. A dozen steps farther, Cole led them close to a Firehawk. Molly looked up and saw Riggs's name stenciled below the cockpit as the captain of the ship. "Marcelli" was listed as the navigator.

Walter sat on the decking by the Firehawk—leaning over a portable computer. Wires trailed from his screen up to an access hatch on the side of the ship. He beamed when he saw her.

"Molly!" He stood and ran over, throwing his small arms around her waist. She patted his back and thanked him—quite a departure from what she'd previously been planning if she ever saw him again.

He smiled up at her. "Almosst ready," he hissed.

"Did you disable the Firehawk's weapons systems?" Cole asked, indicating the wires tethering his computer to the craft.

Walter sneered. "Among other thingss," the boy said cryptically.

Cole shrugged. "Great. How long before we can go?"

"Almosst ready," he repeated.

"I'm gonna need help getting Riggs in the cockpit," Cole told Molly. Riggs shook his head at this and tried yelling inside of his own mouth, his cheeks puffing out.

"What're we gonna do with him? Why not leave him here?"

"Two reasons: I really don't wanna add Firehawk theft to my rapidly expanding criminal resume, so he'll be needed to fly the thing back. And unless you want to locate his auth chip and cut it out of him, we're gonna need his full presence in the Firehawk to tow *Parsona* out. Hold him for a sec."

Molly held Riggs's arm. Her old friend's eyes locked onto hers and flashed with raw malice. Cole grabbed a nearby boarding platform and rolled the steps over to line up with the cockpit.

"You don't think Walter could bypass the auth code?" Molly asked.

"I didn't ask. OK, here's the plan: once we get clear of the fleet, you'll power up *Parsona*. By the time she shows up on the Navy's SADAR, it'll be too late. We'll jump both ships to a rendezvous point where I'll shut the Firehawk down, pop the cockpit, and push off to you. You pick me up, and we'll jump out of there long before Riggs can reboot the ship or the Navy can trace the exit point of our jump signature. Easy as pie."

Molly shook her head. "I don't like it," she said, as she helped pull Riggs up to the cockpit. He tried to kick off the steps, so Cole reached down and grabbed the knot of his shoestrings, pulling both of his feet up. Molly held up half of him with both arms, and they literally carried him up the steps.

"What don't you like? We need the Firehawk's signature on SADAR to get out of here, and we need Riggs's auth code to get the signature." They pushed Riggs down in the navigator's seat and Cole fastened his harness, locking him in place. Riggs wiggled, testing them, and blew out his cheeks. Molly pulled Cole down the steps.

"I don't like bringing him along. I know what you're doing, and I love that about you, but Riggs is not going to come around, especially not bound and gagged. He's not our friend anymore, Cole. I mean, he thinks I'm working with the Drenards, for galaxy's sake. Walter can easily—"

Cole pulled her further down the steps. "Technically, you are a Drenard."

"You know what I mean."

"Yeah, and you know I need to try. I just need some more time with him."

"I get that, that's fine, but all this vacuum transfer nonsense—it just feels too risky." Molly glanced up at the cockpit. "Why don't we just meet at Lok? It's only a few jumps from here—"

"That's even riskier," Cole said. "The Navy will have two signatures to follow and more motivation to catch us. Plus, do you really want Riggs knowing where we go and what we do there?"

"Isn't that the reason you want him along?"

Cole shook his head. "Gods, I don't know. Maybe I'm being selfish; maybe I just want him to not hate us."

"Hey, if you need to do this for *you*, that's an even more compelling argument. Just say so. But no cowboy transfers in the vacuum. Let's meet on Lok and stagger our jump coordinates, give the Navy two trails to sniff. If we both double back at least once, or they're slow to mobilize, they'll never find us."

Cole sighed. "OK. The only logistical problem left is coordinating the tow without the fleet picking up our transmission over the radios. I haven't quite sorted out how we're gonna time that."

Molly smiled. "Let's go change into our flightsuits. I have *just* the thing."

○ ○ ○ ○

"Can you hear me?" Molly thought.

"Loud and clear," came Cole's words, but in Molly's voice. "The helmet makes the band ride down to my ears, though."

"Same here. What we need to do is sew these things into the liners. It'd be stellar to not have to thumb the mic to talk in the cockpit."

"Or worry that Walter's listening in," Cole added.

"Then again, it might not be too nebular to have Cole hearing everything," Molly thought to herself.

"Like what?"

"Huh? . . . That, uh, was a joke, silly. Um, my thrusters are warm if you wanna pull in the lock."

"Roger."

Molly watched the Firehawk rise off the hangar deck and fly down the center lane. She lifted up Parsona and pulled into his wash, following him toward the massive airlock at the end of the bay. During major engagements, the entire deck would be depressurized, pilots and navigators using the dozens of personnel locks to enter the StarCarrier's vacuum, allowing rapid take-offs and landings. For maintenance and patrol, the entire bay was kept pressurized to allow support personnel to work freely and without helmets.

With a little maneuvering, both ships fit in the airlock with room to spare.

Molly didn't have a prisoner to watch, so cable-duty fell to her. She typed a caution to her mother in the nav computer, moved the Wadi from her lap to the back of her seat, and gave Walter a pat on the shoulder.

"Don't touch anything," she told him for the third time.

He smiled through his visor and turned in the nav seat to watch her go. Molly grabbed the commercial nanotube towline and stomped down the cargo ramp.

Outside, she snapped one end to the eyebolt under Parsona's nose. The cockpit glass was too far above for her to check in on Walter, filling her with paranoia that he might be fiddling with instruments on the dash or discovering her mother. She had to force herself to not rush the job.

Double-checking the connection on her ship, she made sure the release mechanism wasn't stuck, then pulled the line to the back of Riggs's Firehawk, careful of the hot metal around the thrusters. She secured the other end of the line to a tow bolt outside the jet wash's cone of influence.

"All set," she thought to Cole.

"Great. Make sure you shut everything down—"

"I know."

"And after we disconnect the tow line, let me pull away before you jump out—"

"I know the plan, Cole."

"Come up to the nose for a sec."

Molly walked quickly to the front of the Firehawk, ducking under the stubby wings. She was surprised to see the hatch open, Cole's visor up.

"Problem?" she asked.

"No, I just felt like saying goodbye so you hear it in my voice."

"I appreciate you being romantic, but we don't have much—"

"I love you."

Molly snapped her visor closed and popped her helmet off. She brushed her hair back off her forehead and looked up at him.

"I love you, too. And stop worrying; this is gonna go smooth as milk." She watched the lines of worry in Cole's forehead deepen. "I'll see you on Lok," she said. "Walter's in your seat, and he'll have my back."

Cole laughed. "That's supposed to make me feel better?" He smiled down at her. "All right, see you in a bit."

With that, he snapped his head forward, throwing the visor of his helmet down without touching it. Molly laughed at the hotshot maneuver and watched the cockpit glass slide forward and seal tight. She ducked under the fuselage and looked up at Riggs, but only the side of his helmet was visible. She ran back to Parsona, pulling her own helmet back on.

Inside, she settled into her seat and nodded at Walter, giving him the OK to depressurize the airlock. He punched commands into his computer, and the atmosphere within the chamber became visible as it was sucked into the large side vents, condensing into moisture as the pressure changed.

Molly watched the thrusters ahead of her fire up, the Firehawk humming to life. She had to fight the urge to do the same with Parsona. It felt unnatural to watch the airlock empty of atmosphere while keeping her ship powered down.

As soon as the air had been completely evacuated, she gave Walter another thumbs-up. For Cole's benefit, she tried to keep her surface thoughts to a minimum; she didn't want to distract him while he sweet-talked the patrol watch.

In her own head, meanwhile, she could hear Cole read off Riggs's authorization numbers, sensing them on the surface of his mind as he spoke them, and then feeling the tension as he waited for the guard to acknowledge.

Beside the hangar bay's red atmosphere light, the integrity light went from green to red. The doors opened a crack, then slid apart and revealed the star field beyond. Cole eased forward, pulling the slack out of the towline. *Parsona* lurched, the landing gear scraped on the deck, and Cole angled up and brought both ships high in the lock before they exited into clear space.

As the two ships pulled out of the massive StarCarrier, the only eyes looking their way were electronic ones. Their signature on SADAR would appear a little larger than normal, but communications officers aren't taught to fear anything leaving the belly of their own ship, which meant the duo didn't merit a second glace. And besides, the ship ID blinking over the blip would perfectly match the newly revised patrol roster. Screen-watchers no doubt would sip their cold coffee and continue swapping lewd jokes and lewder lies.

It would be another hour before anyone was scheduled to check the hangar bay or deliver breakfast to the detention cells.

Should be more than enough time.

○ ○ ○ ○

"OK, we're well outside the fleet perimeter," Cole thought. "Any farther and they'll wonder what we're patrolling."

Molly laughed and glanced through the starboard porthole; the constellation of cruisers and destroyers flashed and twinkled like bright, nearby stars.

"This'll do," she agreed.

"What'ss sso funny?" Walter asked her. "I wanna wear a red band."

"They aren't toys. Now keep it down so I can concentrate."

Walter sank in the nav seat. "What a wasste, ssending one with him," he grumbled.

Molly ignored Walter and reached for the tow release. "Disengaging," she thought, as she pulled the handle. The taut cable ahead of her wavered with the release of tension, and they were free, drifting with their

470

forward momentum. Cole pulled the Firehawk far enough away to not throw her jump off with its small bit of gravity.

"Ladies first," he thought.

She smiled, but there were better reasons for her to jump before he did. It wouldn't look great if his ship ID disappeared from the fleet's SADAR, leaving hers exposed. Plus, if he jumped from the same general area, it might confuse both of their hyperspace signatures, confounding, or at least confusing, the pursuit efforts.

Her hyperdrive had been spinning up ever since they left the carrier. Molly brought the rest of *Parsona* online, her ship's identification moments from broadcasting to the fleet. She watched the nav screen, just waiting for the jump coordinates to register, her finger hovering over the hyperdrive switch.

"Be careful," she thought.

"You, too," Cole replied.

The ship came online. Half a second later, the nav indicator flashed green.

"I wanna pussh it!" Walter yelled.

But it was too late. The stars had already shifted.

○ ○ ○ ○

Cole watched his SADAR display intently. *Parsona's* ship ID flashed for a brief moment, then winked away.

Success.

His own hyperdrive was already spinning up; he checked the coordinates on his nav display one final time.

The radio on the dash cracked to life: "Flight three-two-seven, this is the Cruiser *Denali*. Riggs, we just had a glitch on our SADAR. Picked up a ship ID near you guys. Can you do us a favor and sweep that area? We might need to do a quick calibration with you."

Riggs writhed against his restraints and shouted into his cheeks, desperate to signal his allies.

Cole saw an opportunity to delay the pursuit. "Roger, *Denali*, we have an anomaly out here; we're gonna check it out for the science boys. Be right back."

After a pause, the radio cackled with more questions as Cole lifted the cover on the jump button. But something came through his consciousness besides the radio: Molly's words slicing through his own thoughts.

"Did you say something?"

"Molly?"

"Yeah? Where are you?"

"We haven't jumped yet. Uh, wow. I guess we'll be able to keep in touch on the way to Lok."

"Well, it might not be good for whatever kinda batteries these run on."

"Yeah. Hey, I gotta jump. One of the cruisers saw you leave."

"OK. Hey, Cole?"

"Yeah?"

"I love you."

"Me, too. See you soon."

But Cole was wrong. Dead wrong.

He pressed the red button with his gloved finger, and the instruction to jump coursed down a fiber optic wire, racing through the nav computer on its way to the hyperdrive. Normally, it would pick up the coordinates locked into the dash display and carry this location to the drive in the rear of the Firehawk.

Not this time. The program had been changed. No matter what numbers were computed in the nav display, only one set of coordinates were ever going to be sent to the hyperdrive ever again. Those numbers were picked up and sent back. If Cole could have seen them, looked at what they referenced on his nav chart, he would have been screaming right along with Riggs.

The Firehawk containing the two old friends winked out of space, departing the fleet forever.

The ship reappeared four light-years away, directly in the center of Delphi II.

The largest star within a single jump of the fleet.

34

The Light of Turn crept in front of Edison, signaling his chance to speak. Lord Rooo concluded his argument with a polite nod to the new member, gathered his tunics in both hands, and crossed to the wooden steps that led up and over the unbroken circle of the council table.

Edison rose, pushing back his stone chair with a loud squeak. "I defer my time to Lady Hooo," he said.

As he lowered himself back down, there were murmurs of disappointment in the crowd, likely from the xenophobes eager to see the hairy barbarian trounced by savvy, lifetime politicians.

Anlyn ignored them and rose from her seat. She walked clockwise around the circle, trailing Lord Rooo as he made his way back to his place. When she reached the legendary steps, she gathered her tunics and steeled her nerves for the walk over.

Looking down at the wooden treads, their centers worn concave with thousands of years of steady use, she took a slow first step, wondering when last a female had done so. She marched up and across the top of the bridge without pausing, not wanting any rumors of her lingering to spread among the spectators and leave the Pinnacle. If any action could be misread, she was certain it would be.

A spot of light stood in the center of the circle, an unmoving disc of photons from Hori I. Anlyn entered the shaft and felt the heat on her skin. She wondered if it had been a mistake to not coat herself in the new cosmetics used by wily politicians. She tried not to think about perspiring—knowing it would just hasten it—and surveyed those around her.

Large Drenard males, the most powerful figures in the race's empire, returned her gaze. Many of them had worn thin expressions of bemusement at Bodi's expense less than an hour ago. Those looks seemed to melt away as they absorbed the wisp of a female standing before them. Anlyn doubted the Chair on Drenard Cultural History could even remember how many cycles ago a woman had last served.

She bowed slightly to Edison—a Circle formality for deferred time—but also as a personal gesture. He flashed his teeth at her, wishing her well.

Anlyn thought back to a month ago, to watching him drill a small hole in one of her slave-chain links. Edison had worked the drill back and forth, hollowing out a thin channel and then had cleaned up the shavings. He had made sure she watched as he pantomimed snapping the link in half. Although both spoke English well enough, neither had said a word.

Edison explained later that it had been a favor for Molly, but that it had eventually liberated something within his own heart.

Two days after that scene, Anlyn had helped free Edison from a set of restraints aboard *Parsona*. The symbolism was not lost on them, and neither was the fact that both had felt alone in the universe: Edison by virtue of being one of the last of his kind, Anlyn due to her voluntary exile.

The week they'd spent together in the Darrin system, alone and working to repair *Parsona*, had blossomed into something more powerful than love. It was a connection that defied differences in species and their own internal barriers to *being* loved.

Anlyn shook the pleasant memories out of her head and cleared her throat to address the Circle, and then she worried that both gestures would be taken for weakness. She needed to appear strong, even though she felt weak. Brave, even though she felt scared. She concentrated on Edison's smile and began to recite the words her aunt had taught her:

"I am Anlyn of the Hooo." She swallowed and turned to take in more of the Circle. "I accept my Chair within this most esteemed Circle on behalf of Widow Dooo. I vow to put universe first, galaxy second, and myself last. I will serve, steadfast, on the thin border between Light and Dark. I will be guided by the fire of the passion in my heart and the cold calculation of my brain. Between these two extremes, I will find the truth of a good path and walk it straight."

Several of the older Circle members and seated spectators cooed softly at the fine acceptance speech; it was one of the more traditional, ancient ones. The younger members, some of those aligned with Bodi, frowned, expecting more. Edison bristled with pride.

Bodi rose from his seat and destroyed the moment for her: "With all due respect, *Lady* Hooo, you'll need to speak up to be heard."

It was one of the few exceptions to the Center of Speak, and revenge for Anlyn's handling of him an hour prior. Bodi's allies panted with soft laughter.

Anlyn felt the rage pushing its way from her heart to her head, her body flushing with heat, her center falling off its line. She took a deep breath before continuing, forcing her eyes away from the safety of Edison's and across the gathered males.

"The Circle has gathered to consider the eradication of the humans, a decision being made as inflamed anger burns from the events of the past days. From my Chair, I will be counseling *against* this distraction from the true Drenard purpose."

The laughter stopped immediately. Even the elders, proud to see Anlyn returned to her home in good health and taking a temporary seat on the Circle, seemed displeased.

"One cycle ago," Anlyn continued, "the first human to become a Drenard left our planet. There was much hope that the prophecy of the Light Seer would come true. When it didn't, this very Circle ringed to consider the fate of the humans. One of my uncles used to speak of that debate, of the constant swings from fire to ice. He was always glad that temperate heads prevailed.

"I am young, I know." Anlyn looked up into the audience, her hand on her chest. "I do not feel it, but I can see it on your faces: I am young, I am female, and I am royalty. Any side of this triangle is enough to cast doubt. All three will have each of you counting the radians to the next election. But know this: I have spent over a year of my life held captive by the worst sort of human. Despite this, I have seen what good can come of them. The one that you consider a threat? She is my friend. I have seen her Wadi Queen, and the rumors are true. I will do everything I can from my Chair to protect her people as she has promised to do everything she can to help ours."

She paused while the whispers grew, rumors of Molly and her Wadi crackling, spreading like a fire. Anlyn gave them a moment while she watched the Light of Turn move closer to her seat. She lifted her eyes from the Circle and swept them over the large crowd; her entire body followed, spinning in place, as if taking them all in, even as the light from Hori I made it impossible to see very far into the shadows.

"Our empire has moved to the darkness," she told them, and coos of discord swept the gathered. She raised her voice. "It moved to the darkness as we relied on the Seer's prophecy to light our way. It moved to the darkness when that light never came. And now we feel the urge to throw ourselves into the fire, eager to kill or be killed because we've grown frightened of the dark.

"I came here today to urge restraint." She placed one of her fists in the palm of her hand. "A few of our *true* enemy, posing as humans, have sown anger in your hearts. Some of you wish to eradicate them all, pushing throughout the galaxy and exterminating our neighbors. I come here to—"

"You come to urge *NOTHING!*" someone yelled from the audience. There were coos of surprise, the rumble of thousands turning in their seats. Blue tunics descended from the balcony as those seated near, moved away from the man, who continued to protest.

"We've tried nothing already!" he yelled. "We've tried restraint! We want *WAR!*"

The guards in blue seized the figure and pulled him up the aisle.

His tirade continued amid a growing chorus of nods and whispers.

Whispers growing to shouts.

○ ○ ○ ○

The conversation Molly was having with Cole stopped—his thoughts removed from her head and replaced with pain.

Molly shrieked and slapped at her helmet, fumbling for the clasps. Her brain wailed with the same white noise and painful light she'd felt on Dakura. She couldn't find the release clasps, so she shook her gloves free, feeling with her bare hands around the back of the smooth shell. As soon as she clicked them loose, she shoved her helmet up and tore the band off her head.

The noise went away immediately, leaving just a resonant hum in her skull. Remnants of the white light remained, however. She tried to blink the haze away, looking over at Walter to focus on something.

The Wadi flicked its tongue out from the back of the nav chair, scared clear across the cockpit.

"What'ss wrong?" Walter asked, recoiling.

"I—I don't know. I was talking to Cole, and then it went haywire."

"Lemme ssee."

Molly handed him the band. "Be careful. It hurts."

He lowered the band near his scalp hesitantly, like a cadet preparing to shoot himself with a stunner for laughs. Before it even made full contact with his buzzed head, Walter yelped and tossed the band to the side. The confused Wadi leaped from his seat and back to Molly's, claws digging into worn leather.

"It's OK," Molly told the Wadi.

"No, it hurt like hypersspacse!" Walter complained. "Ssoundss like the middle of a sstar or ssomething!"

"That's actually a pretty good analogy," Molly said. "I hope we didn't break them." She reached for her helmet, her vision nearly back to normal.

But in the pit of her stomach, something felt empty and raw, as if a hole had formed that her heart might drop down into. She stopped for a minute and concentrated on breathing, sucking in deep breaths, her chest constricted with . . . *something*.

The sensation was unique, but it stirred old feelings inside, as if she'd experienced this before. It felt like cold boredom, but deeper. The sensation of becoming lost, or just not knowing what to do next.

It reminded her of the day her dad went missing.

Molly shivered, her vision blurring again, but this time from natural causes. From tears. She grabbed the red band from Walter's armrest and rubbed it with one hand.

Meanwhile *Parsona* drifted idly in the vastness of the cosmos.

Silent and alone.

○ ○ ○ ○

"I'm sure it's nothing," Parsona said through her helmet.

Molly leaned back against the bulkhead, one of her pillows in her lap. The Wadi sat on her dresser, lapping at a saucer of juice, its eyes closed in contentment.

"I wanna jump back and check on him," she said.

"He's probably at his own jump-point thinking the same thing. What both of you need to do is keep heading to Lok, stick with the plan—" Parsona broke into laughter.

"What's so funny?"

"I'm sorry, it just reminds me of your father and myself. We spent a lot of time apart with our work on

Lok, and the comm towers on that planet were frightful. We were forever dropping calls and wrestling with ourselves over who should call back and who should wait. Gods, we were so in love . . . "

"So you think this is nothing? 'Cause it sounded just like getting disconnected from . . . the other you."

"I think we should continue to Lok, dear."

"Is there something you're not telling me, Mom?"

"Plenty. But it's for your own good."

"Stop saying that, seriously. I don't wanna hear how important our mission is without knowing what I'm doing. I mean, look at where that's gotten me. I have no home, almost no friends, no safe place to go, and barely enough to eat for a few weeks. Oh, and I'm being led around by my dead mom who I recently found out worked for the Drenard Underground."

"Sweetheart . . . "

Molly checked her watch. "Fifteen more minutes for the hyperdrive to cycle. I'm leanin' toward jumping back to the fleet's last position, seeing what happened."

"Your father and I did fall in with the Drenard Alliance. What the Navy calls the Underground."

"You've gotta be kidding. Why keep this from me? Anlyn's my friend; I would've listened."

"I know that now. I hate that you're caught in the middle of this, but it's so much bigger than you or me.

You just got interrogated by the Navy. Imagine if you'd known—"

"They interrogated you as well. What did you tell them?"

"I told them the same thing your father did ten years ago, just in case they'd listen. Of course, I repeated the same things over and over again, so they'd think it was a logic tree. I watched them board, let them think I thought it was you."

"What did you tell them? And you've got twelve minutes before I jump back to the fleet."

"That the Drenards are *not* their enemy."

"Ha. I'm sure that went over well. 'The race that's been blowing up your loved ones for almost a century really want to be your friends. Come hunt lizards in sunny paradise.' Was that it?"

"You're upset."

"Damn right. As much as I love Anlyn, I barely escaped that planet alive. People there tried to kill me—"

"A dispute between lovers was the way Anlyn explained it—"

"Yeah, but—"

"Have you ever wondered why the war never leaves the Drenard arm of the Milky Way? The Galactic Union and the Navy have both been told the war can end at any time; all they have to do is stop trying to enter that portion of the galaxy."

"Yeah, right."

"It's the same message your father came back to Earth to deliver in person. He had to flee after receiving the official reply."

"What a stupid thing to keep from me, if true!"

"Perhaps, but telling you the war is actually a block-ade action just leads to more questions. Difficult questions . . . "

She had a point, because the next one formed on Molly's lips, like a reflex: "What are they keeping us from?"

"Not keeping, Mollie. *Protecting*."

"Fine," she said. "What are they protecting?"

"Us."

○ ○ ○ ○

"My grandfather served on this Circle for two full cycles," Counselor Yur said from the Light of Speak. "He was adamant about the danger posed by the exist-ence of humans. Even when the first signs of the so-called prophecy came to light, he recognized this as mere coincidence. People finding what they sought. It's increasingly clear that my grandfather was correct. The existence of a race of people with such incredible resemblance to the Bern makes it impossible to perform our duty of policing this galaxy. We have allowed a dangerous forest to grow as we try to guard against individual trees.

"The decision is not an easy one, I agree. It never should be easy to wipe out an entire species. But when *not* doing so will lead to many thousands of races going extinct, the choice is much simpler. I will be voting, as I always have, for the extermination of the humans. The argument that we cannot guard the Great Rift while also launching an offensive against their fleets ignores our success at holding this arm of our galaxy while doing the same. Our Navy is more than up to the challenge of warring on both fronts.

"I defer the rest of my time and give up the Center to my good friend Counselor Bodi."

Yur bowed slightly, turned around, bowed again, and headed for the wooden bridge. He had not chosen to address any of the other Counselors and give them a chance to speak, a tactic that would not win him any favor. However, his arguments had been heard before and were unlikely to sway anyone on the Circle. Bodi, and others who planned to change their vote for war, represented the new wind. They were the ones etching away at canyon walls from unexpected directions—eroding new paths for Drenards to walk.

Anlyn watched her ex-fiancé take the Center of Speak for the second time. He refrained from looking at her, probably fearing she'd usurp him again. As much a bumbling fool as he could be, as thorough as he was at discovering and making mistakes, he rarely repeated them.

"Thank you, Counselor Yur, for the remainder of your time." Bodi bowed in his direction before turning to face the largest concentration of human sympathizers. "Fellow Counselors," he began, "as I was saying just a few hours ago, our duty to this galaxy is being *forgotten*."

Several Counselors stiffened at this accusation, the remembrance of duty being one of the five Great Virtues of any good Drenard citizen. Bodi let the insult hang in the air before continuing. He placed one of his pale blue hands on his own chest, fingers splayed out across the colorful regalia on his tunic.

"I am also to blame," he said. "And the lapse is easy to forgive once it is understood. There is an inherent tension between two of the Great Virtues: remembering our duty to protect the galaxy and remembering our duty to our neighbors. For too long, we have placed the latter virtue ahead of the former. We have tried to balance both, living on the fine line that exists between them, but I fear our grip on the scales is slipping. We have put the entire galaxy in danger in order to protect the humans."

Anlyn cringed from the mixture of metaphors. She couldn't understand what her father had seen in this man.

"And what have the humans done? Despite numerous envoys who have assured them complete freedom in the rest of the galaxy, they demand to know what lies in *our* corner. They attack, and their reason for attacking again is that we have defended ourselves. Upheld one of our Virtues.

"I respect our forgiving nature. I do not call for us to live in the full sunlight of war, but neither do I think we should move to the dark and allow ourselves to freeze due to the coldness of our compassion.

"We are a race born on the edge, squeezed on either side by two different dangers, and that is where we find ourselves today. Perhaps that is why we have grown too comfortable with the fire of humans on the one side and the black hole in space that we defend on the other.

"The vote has always been one of holding this line with the humans or of pushing out to extinguish them. I find this decision to be untenable. There is an alternative that has been discussed much in the past but soundly rejected—even by me."

He paused and scanned the crowd, lifting his arms and splaying his stolen tunics for effect. "We should tell the humans about the Bern threat," he said. "We should let them look among themselves for signs of infiltration. The vote I submit to the Circle today is this: either we tell the humans about the Great Rift, and the nature of the

Bern Empire, or we whittle their numbers down until the Bern can no longer hide among them."

"Second," cried Yur.

The Drenard beside him nodded. "Third," he said.

Anlyn froze, disbelieving. Five more Counselors cast their votes, putting the decision—if such a biased dichotomy could even be considered a "decision"—before the Circle.

Bodi had just succeeded in changing the nature of the vote. No longer would it be between war and peace; rather, it would be between a massacre they controlled or a rebellion they fomented.

Anlyn reached over and groped for Edison's hand, her plan unraveling before her eyes. The decision would now come before the end of the day.

And either way, it would spell the end of the humans.

○ ○ ○ ○

"They're killing us to protect us? That's crap, Mom. What are they really hiding?"

"Sweetheart, the universe is bigger than you know—"

"No more riddles, Mom. And you have seven minutes before I go look for Cole."

"No riddles, just facts."

It was eerie for Molly to hear an artificial voice fighting to remain calm, but that's what her mother seemed to be doing.

"Humans have had a hard time accepting changes in scope," Parsona said. "First, realizing the Earth was round, then that the stars are more suns, finally that the nebulae were entire galaxies. In many ways, being the dominant technological race in our galaxy has been a detriment to our growth, not the boon that we are—"

"Six minutes, Mom, and you still haven't told me anything."

"Our entire galaxy is at risk, Mollie. And other galaxies. All at risk of being invaded and completely taken over by a force of evil you can't comprehend. They are known to many other races, the Drenards included, as the Bern. They control most of the universe, perhaps all except the Local Group. For many years, they've been trying to invade and add us to their territory. The Drenards guard the hole in the Milky Way through which the Bern have been trying to enter—"

"Then why not just tell us this? Why keep it a secret?"

"Because the truth is—and this is something I shouldn't tell you: the Bern look a lot like humans. Or vice versa. We're almost identical to them. Now, can you imagine the witch hunt if this were common knowledge? It would tear us apart quicker than the Drenards could. Besides, there's a good chance the Navy is riddled with them, that the Navy is being *run* by people without our best interests—"

"*Mr. Byrne*," Molly muttered to herself, the pieces falling in place.

"Mollie. Where have you heard that name? Tell me this instant."

"He was on Dakura. He was in your—in the other Parsona's head. He came for *me*, Mom. Had me tied up in his ship . . . "

The Wadi flicked out her tongue, jumped from the dresser to the bunk, and ran up to Molly's chest.

"That's why we were fleeing Dakura, why we had that other ship airlocked to you. I'm sorry, but there wasn't any time to tell you—"

"Where is he now?" Parsona asked.

"Was he a Bern?" Molly thought about him standing in the hangar, smiling in the vacuum of space.

"Yes, one of the very worst kind. Do you know where he is? Did he talk to—did he get a chance to talk to the other Parsona?"

"Yeah. Oh, Mom, they had me strapped to a dentist chair, there was nothing I could—"

"It's OK. It's fine. We need to get to Lok, sweetheart."

"Yeah. Maybe you're right. Maybe I'm reading too much into those bands. Cole's probably gonna get there before me and start to worry."

Molly stopped petting the Wadi and glanced at the clock by her bed.

"Drenards," she said. "We shoulda jumped out of here two minutes ago."

She threw the pillow aside and ran toward the cockpit.

○ ○ ○ ○

Anlyn sank in her seat as Lord Vahi cast his vote for war. She and Edison hadn't voted yet, and it wouldn't even matter. Not that there had been a viable option, but her choice to abstain would have meant something different before the subject was already decided. Any formal complaint would now be registered as indecision.

The cooing in the crowd grew, nearly drowning out Lord Yesher's vote. Several Counselors slapped the table for order. The Counterclockwise door flung open, and several spectators from the balcony spilled out to relay the news. Others took this as a sign that the proceedings were over and began pushing their way to the aisles.

They were hoping to get out before a throng formed.

But they just *became* the throng.

Two more Counselors cast a vote for Bodi, becoming part of *another* mob, one protecting its political legacy by moving with the crowd. The member beside Edison voted the same and had the audacity to stand, preparing to race out after votes from the least senior members. The entire Pinnacle thrummed in anticipation. Males felt an urge to return home to families and prepare for the next step, the step the Circle had voted for:

War.

Edison growled "Abstain," but nobody heard. Only the Keeper of Time seemed to notice, moving the Light of Turn to Anlyn.

She stared at the circle of sunlight on the marble before her. Her peripheral vision vibrated with movement. The balcony doors opened and shut like organ valves, pumping hysteria into the streets and throughout the city. The noise had become a persistent roar, a growling fervor.

"Minority Position," Anlyn said to herself.

Louder: "Minority Position."

The Keeper of Time mistook her moving lips and ushered the Light of Turn onward, ending her chance to speak.

Anlyn watched the spot move away, a shock of resignation coursing through her. She rebelled against it. Wouldn't stand for it. She stood up in her chair, jumped to the top of the table, and grabbed Edison's lance. Fumbling with the switches, she wished she'd paid more attention to his demonstration. Several

Counselors scrambled for her, ready to pull her down. Edison pushed them back as several Drenards in blue scrambled down the aisles, wading through the frantic crowd.

"I invoke Minority Position!" Anlyn yelled, as loud as she could. She rested the butt of the large lance on the table, ducked her head, and pulled the trigger.

The tip of the lance erupted in a shower of light. Dozens of hues pulsed out in a spray of pyrotechnics, the charged plasma deflected by prismatic filters into harmless sparks of fire. The blossom radiated upward, arcing to the ceiling, bouncing off and exploding into even smaller slivers of flame.

Anlyn covered her head to protect it from the shower and squeezed the trigger all the way. The lance hummed, emitting Edison's favorite note at 349.229 hertz. It was F below middle C. The precise sound wave that creates supernovas, vibrating out from the core of collapsing stars and throwing entire solar systems apart.

It was the note of nebulas. The sound of destruction and creation.

Those who remained in the Pinnacle froze, including the Counselors and the guards. They shielded their eyes but couldn't turn away. Thousands of tiny bones, deep in hearing canals, resonated with the pure note, that lone chord of the cosmos.

Anlyn released the trigger and stood upright in the remnants of the plasma falling to the floor.

"I invoke Minority Position," she said, loud and confident. "I vote for telling the humans about the Bern threat, and I demand to give voice to the dissenters."

She looked down at Edison, needing another dissenter, an abstainer to change his vote.

"I second," he said.

The few who had not voted for war early on threw in their assent. The Keeper of Time, gathering his wits from the control booth, returned the Light of Turn to Anlyn.

The Light of Speak, meanwhile, stood empty in the center of the Circle. Throughout the beam, a shower of fine ash could be seen descending from the ceiling. The spectators who had not yet fled into the Apex stopped. They watched Anlyn.

And waited.

35

It was nighttime on the frontier side of Lok. Molly brought her ship down through the atmosphere, descending toward the darkness of her abandoned, childhood village. She leaned forward to get a better visual through the carboglass, disturbing the Wadi in her lap. It flicked its tail, claws skittering on the polished plate that moments ago had held Molly's leftover lasagna.

SEE?_ Her mother typed.

Molly checked the SADAR; a ship the size of a Firehawk sat right outside the commons. Cole had beaten her there. She didn't take her hands off the flight controls to respond to her mother, but she thought about the red band in her chest pocket, considered popping off her helmet to try it out, to see if she could contact him. Instead, she focused on a soft arrival, pointing her thrusters away from the other ship and using the old commons as a landing pad.

Parsona settled to the dew-covered grass. Her belly opened, and the cargo hatch lowered to the soft soil.

Molly popped her helmet off and set it on the rack. "Don't touch anything," she told Walter. "I'll be right back." She stroked the Wadi on the head and moved the creature from her lap to the back of the chair. She peered into her water bowl and made sure it was topped up, and then she headed through the bowels of her ship and out into the crisp night.

Byrne had his hands on her immediately.

Molly tried to scream, but cold, bony fingers covered her mouth. She struggled against his arms, but they were unnaturally strong; they pinned her against his body in a viselike grip, her feet dangling in the air. The flashlight fell from her hands and banged against the cargo ramp; it rolled into the grass, its beam snuffed out by the unkempt length of the dry blades.

Thin lips came down to her ear, brushing against them.

"You've been *expected*," Byrne whispered, his words close, yet no hint of breath puffed against her cheek. Molly reached back to claw at his face, but he just tucked her under one arm as he keyed the cargo door closed. When the ramp sealed, he struck the control panel with his bare fist, demolishing it completely and denting the hull around it.

Molly kicked her captor physically and herself mentally. She berated herself for not keeping her helmet on so she could warn her mom.

She struggled to take in a breath of air—the way she was being carried forced her to exert energy just to stabilize her body. Her legs hung awkwardly, her spine bent and jolted with pain from each of Byrne's steps. Even the red band added to her torment, the small lump jabbing into her ribs through her flightsuit pocket. She twisted around and grabbed Byrne's arm to support her weight—it was like clutching a solid-steel rod.

Just when she thought she'd pass out from the exertion and inability to breathe, Byrne threw her down in a patch of dirt. The area around her glowed in the soft light of a nearby work lamp, and something hummed softly in the distance.

Molly tried to launch herself up, but Byrne grabbed her again and pushed her back to the ground. His fingers dug between the muscles in her neck, squeezing nerves that shot numbness into her arms. The underlying pain made her mouth feel as if it were full of metal as her lungs continued to scream for air.

"You seem to have a problem keeping still, don't you, Mollie Fyde?"

Byrne's other hand went to her thigh, up near her hip. Fingers as hard and thin as screwdrivers dug deep at her hip socket, grinding against the bone. Molly had never felt such pain before. It wasn't something she could scream about—that would have required some degree of motor control. Instead, her jaw fell open in shock, her eyes wide with fear. Even the leg he *wasn't* gripping vibrated with pain, both flight boots thumping the packed soil. It was an agony on the verge of nothingness, a numbness that could be *felt*.

Her stomach lurched and bunched up in knots.

Molly turned her head to the side and threw up her lasagna. She spat, her eyes rolling up in the back of her head as she tried to will herself unconscious. She dreamed of the comforting blackness that usually overtook her in moments of raw shock.

But Byrne's iron grip held her just over the precipice of consciousness. Her legs continued to tremble uncontrollably from the pain.

When he finally let go, there was nothing Molly could do but relish the feeling of not being tortured. She tried to wipe her chin, but her arm flopped, limp and useless. Byrne remained crouched beside her, looking at her like a specimen of some sort.

"The next time you try to stand up, I'm going to do something very bad to you. Nod if you understand."

Molly nodded. Once. It was all she could muster. Just moving her eyeballs around to take in her surroundings felt like an accomplishment. She and Byrne were in a small plot of land; tall weeds grew up next to a low brick wall. There was a fireplace at the far edge of the pool of light, a chimney rising from it and up into the black Lokian night. It was the ruined foundation of an old building, all the wood long since ground to dust, carried off by the wind.

Byrne grinned. "Recognize the place?" he asked.

Molly tried to shake her head, but only her eyes moved, rolling back and forth.

"No? You should. We had tea in this very room back on Dakura. This is the little hell your mother chose for her eternity." He laughed. "Eternity! She didn't last another twenty years, thanks to you."

"Din't kill 'er," Molly slurred.

"Even worse. You had one of your cronies do it, didn't you? Just like Lucin. Tell me, where are you getting your information? I know it isn't from your father. And there's not an inch of that ship I haven't inspected. So I'm curious—how did you know to go to Dakura, and just what do you know about this place?"

A weak smile was all she could pull off. Byrne's hand came to her knee and started sliding up her thigh. Molly could feel the pain, like a memory, even though his fingers hadn't returned to the right spot yet. Her leg went numb in anticipation, and she tried to slide her pelvis out of the way—but it didn't budge.

o o o o

"WALTER?"

His name boomed through *Parsona,* scaring the hell out of him. He froze and then quickly slid Cole's things from the top of the human's dresser and back into the drawer. He pushed it closed as quietly as he could and peeked out the door—up, then down the hallway.

"Hello?"

It may have been his imagination, but he thought the camera in the corner of the cargo bay moved slightly. "Hello?" he asked again. "Where are you?"

The voice boomed down the length of the ship:

"COME TO THE COCKPIT."

Walter had the sudden urge to do the very opposite. He looked the other way, to the laz, then back up the shaft of the ship. The Wadi's head peeked around the corner from the back of Molly's seat.

Its tongue flicked out.

"What if I don't wanna?" he yelled to the Wadi.

The creature's head pulled back.

Walter crept up through the cargo bay; he glanced at the portholes, which showed nothing but pitch black outside. He wondered if he was about to get in trouble for looting Cole's room. He cautiously entered the cockpit, which hadn't changed since he left it. The Wadi flicked her tongue out at Walter, tasting the air.

"You have a very loud voicse," he told the Wadi.

The voice boomed in response, filling the cockpit: "HIT THE BUTTON MARKED 'MIC' ON THE RADIO. IT'S THE PANEL BESIDE THE LOUD HAILER, AND RIGHT NEXT TO—"

Walter flicked it before the voice could complete the sentence. "I know where the radio iss," he hissed.

"There you are," the lady said, in a more sensible volume. "I need your help."

"Sssure you do. But who are you?"

"Can you adjust the squelch?" the voice asked. "I'm getting quite a hiss from the cockpit mic."

Walter leaned across the controls between the two seats, his face just a foot from the radio. "That'ss jussst how I sspeak," he said, showering the dash with saliva.

"Oh, my apologies. Listen, I'm seeing a hyperdrive signature ahead of us—I mean ahead of you—that I don't like. I need you to run some tests for—"

"Who are you?" Walter interrupted. He shooed the Wadi from Molly's seat and plopped down in the captain's chair.

"I'm, uh . . . a friend of Mollie's. I—well, I was supposed to meet you guys here, but the door's stuck. The cargo ramp. Can you check it for me?"

"Are you outside?" Walter spun in his chair and peeked through the porthole. The planet was darker than space, but he could see a pale glow directly ahead of the ship.

"I was. I'm radioing from my ship. Can you check the door for me? I think something's wrong with it."

"Ssure," he said, working his way out of the seat.

"Just see if it'll open, but don't go outside. Oh, and I might need you to check something on SADAR when you get back. I'll tell you what buttons to press, and you can follow along."

"I'm not *sstupid*," Walter said, stomping out of the room.

This was so annoying. He hardly ever got time to himself on the ship, time to sniff around.

He walked past his crew area, and the sight of all the empty chairs washed away his frustrations. He could feel himself brighten. Literally—the sheen of his metallic skin taking a more silvery hue.

Then again, he thought, *our crew has gone from five to two in less than a week.*

He felt pretty proud of himself for that.

He strolled over to the ramp controls and lifted the glass. Tapped the buttons.

Nothing.

He hissed in frustration, his skin resuming its prior, duller sheen.

o o o o

Molly dripped with sweat, despite the cold. Byrne's question about her source of information hung in the air, his hands positioned to deliver more pain. She couldn't tell him about Parsona—so she fought to think of any other connection—anything he'd mentioned on Dakura. The fingers started to press in, and Molly remembered something. His reaction to hearing about her godfather.

"Lucin," she gasped, and then sucked in a lungful of air before it could be forced out of her with the attack.

But the attack didn't come. The fingers rested on the spots, little divots of torture burned into her body's long-term memory.

"I thought so," Byrne said, his hand not moving. "What else did he tell you?"

About Parsona, she thought. But protecting her was the only reason she'd lied in the first place. "He told me about my mom. About Dakura. The mission my parents were on."

"Which was?"

Molly took a deep breath. Even talking was exhausting. "Are you testing me? Or interrogating me?"

Mr. Byrne laughed at this, and his hand came away. He grabbed Molly by her armpits and carried her closer to the light, plopping her down in front of some odd contraption.

"Both," he told her. "Do you know what I'm doing here?"

Molly shook her head. "I don't even know what you are," she lied.

"Think of me as a scout," he said. "Behind me is an army of trillions. And I'm going to open a door and let them in." He turned to the side and waved at the silhouette of a device Molly found . . . *familiar*. It was a large cross of steel with wires leading to all four points. She traced the cables down to the ground, through the ruins, and off to the shadow of a ship outside the village square. She could see now that it wasn't a Firehawk.

She looked back to the contraption. "What is that?" she asked.

But she already knew. She'd built one just a month ago, on Palan. She'd used it to rescue Cole from that hellish prison.

"You know, don't you?" Byrne leaned in and studied her face. "Your mother knew more than she let on. Did she teach you how to use this?" The hand came to her thigh again. Without even looking, he seemed able to attach his fingers to just the right spot.

Molly shook her head. The bony digits pressed in, making the world flash around her and go silent. She moved her lips to say, "It was an accident," but couldn't even hear herself.

506

The fingers came away, the pain diminishing to a dull, lingering ache.

"What was an accident?"

She tried to force a long breath among the short and rapid ones.

"I built one," she whimpered. "On accident. To rescue a friend, I built one of those." She nodded her head toward the metal cross.

Byrne leaned in close. His eyes were wild, his face twitching with small muscles that bulged in odd places. "What did it do?" he asked. "Where did you build it?"

"I teleported some rock, moved a cell wall, to free a friend—"

"Bah! Then you didn't build what—"

"—on Palan," she finished.

Byrne reacted as if shocked by a bolt of electricity. Both hands, with uncommon speed and precision, flew to Molly's armpits. Fingers found nerves there between her ribs and under her shoulders. He didn't yet start squeezing, but Molly could tell this would be a level of agony beyond what had already transpired. Anticipatory pain tingled along tendons as if they knew what was coming; her shoulders crept up in fear.

"Where on Palan?" he spat.

"In the canyons." Molly forced out the answer as quickly as she could. She tensed her legs, stretching her spine, trying to levitate away from his grasp.

"Liar," he said. His fingers applied a little pressure. Molly felt dizzy, could smell something like ozone, could taste the pain. It was a new experience, and it hadn't really started. Her throat constricted; her eyes watered.

What is he looking for? she wondered in her haze. She would give it to him, whatever it was, she'd hand him everything for a quick death, that was how bad it felt.

"It was in space, wasn't it?" he yelled. "You did something in Palan's orbit. You opened a door!"

He no longer looked calm and in control. He looked *desperate.* In Molly's state, his thin face, spitting with rage, looked like the specter of death, come to take her away.

"I know it was in space," Byrne shouted, "because I came through it with *Parsona*. Tell me how you made it."

With Parsona? A door? From where?

"I'll help you," Molly hissed. "Just. Stop. Hurting. Me." She had to force each quiet word around a separate pant for air.

The hands relaxed. Byrne surveyed her face.

"There are two doors in this old house," he said. "Invisible doors. Both were opened by friends of your parents many years ago and then resealed. It was a daring, foolish invasion, and now *we* get to return the favor."

508

Byrne turned and nodded at the metal cross. "I can open old doors," he said, "but I can't create new ones. I'm thinking *you* can. You just don't know how you did it, do you?"

"And that's what you went to my mom, the one on Dakura, to find out about? How to make them?" Molly cherished the conversation, hoping it would continue. Her body tingled with the absence of pain.

"No. I went to her to determine *which* door to reopen."

The game show. Her mother's words came back to her, the innocuous analogy made deadly.

"One of these doors will open and end your galaxy, along with the threat it poses. My people will move in and systematically destroy this . . . *mutation.*" Byrne looked over Molly's head. "The other door *would* have led you to your damned father . . . " He peered down at her, his eyes narrowing as Molly felt her own widen. "But don't waste your time hoping; I've already sealed that one forever. And soon, the other door will open . . . "

His voice trailed off. "Wait," he said. "Your mother. What do you mean by *the one on Dakura?*"

Oh, crap, Molly thought, grimacing at the slip. She could see how tortured criminals were broken, how the pressure of layered lies smothered until desperation forced you to tear them off, exposing the truth underneath, forgetting the consequences.

In the glow of the work light, Byrne's face smoothed out, the bunched muscles disappearing. His grin grew into a menacing smile.

"Your father made a copy, didn't he?" The nasal laugh returned, which scared Molly more than his rage.

Byrne peered over Molly's shoulder, into the darkness of the commons. "How ironic," he chuckled. "To think that the answer was under my nose all these years!" His laughter swelled as his hands came away from Molly's armpits. One of them slid up her chest to her neck. She tried to pull away, but the other hand tangled itself in her hair, balling into a fist around a thick clump of her locks. The two sides of the vise worked together to squeeze off her air supply. She clawed at them, but they were made of steel. Indestructible.

"All these years, I had the hyperdrive under my feet! This galaxy and *more* could already be ours!" The hysterical laughter ceased as he looked away. Molly gurgled for air, arching her back and digging her heels into the dirt. She could feel her eyes bulging out; she looked up at Byrne with tears streaming down her face, wondering where Cole was, why he wasn't there to rescue her . . .

Byrne smiled down at her, as if calmly waiting for her to die.

When her esophagus closed completely, her ability to even gurgle was taken away. The world became silent, and the last of Molly's consciousness marveled at how quiet death could be. She teetered on the edge of life, peering over the other side, when—in the scary vacuum, the eerie silence that had ensued—a loud metallic *click* rang out. The release of something mechanical.

Byrne squinted into the darkness, his fingers relaxing. Molly wheezed a large gulp of crisp air past her burning neck, a temporary reprieve from the suffocation. Her captor leaned farther over her, peering toward the commons.

Molly turned her head as far as she could and looked back to her ship; Byrne grabbed the work light and shone it in *Parsona's* direction. A dark shape fell from one of the wings and into the tall grass.

"What was that?" Byrne asked.

Molly remained silent, save for her rapid pants for more air.

She had no idea.

Byrne scanned the commons with the work light, keeping a hand on Molly. "Who goes there?" he called out, playing the beam across the hull of the ship.

Another object fell from the wing, flashing briefly in the cone of light. It disappeared into the grass and clanged loudly against something else.

"Were those *missiles*?" Byrne asked Molly.

Molly clung to a fresh lungful of oxygen and pursed her lips. As the fingers dug back into her hair and neck, she asked her own silent question:

Walter—what in hyperspace are you doing?

o o o o

"Walter, what are you doing?" Parsona asked.

"Firing the missssilesss," he spat.

"You have to arm them first! I told you not to jump ahead, just follow my instructions."

"But—"

"Listen to me. We don't have much time, and it's very important. We need to stop a man from opening a door, and the readings on my sensors say he's already trying."

"But—"

"Those were our only two missiles, so you're going to need to get in one of the escape pods and eject into the grass. I don't care what you have to do to stop this, we're all going to be dead either way. Do you understand me?"

"But what about this wirelesss menu for the missssiless?"

"Do you hear what I'm saying? Very bad things are about to happen if you don't get out there and stop that man. Destroy his machine. Do something. Now leave those wireless settings alone, they're only for disarming missiles after they've been launched *properly*."

"I can arm them," Walter said flatly.

"No, you can't. Trust me, it doesn't work that way. It would take a quantum computer a dozen years to hack into—"

"I'm already in."

Silence.

"That's . . . that's impossible."

"No, it'ss the ssame key the Navy ussess on Palan for their mainframe. I ussed to log in and delete sstuff for fun."

Walter shook his silvery head as he armed the missiles. "It'ss a sstupid passsword," he added to himself.

oooo

Bright lights popped in Molly's vision as the choking resumed.

Flashes of pain. Explosions of misfiring, confused neurons. When another bright light erupted from the commons—the flash of a missile coming to life in the dewy grass—she could barely distinguish it from her own illusory fireworks. It wasn't until the object sailed overhead, trailed by a cone of plasma, that Molly could actually tease it apart from her misery.

The missile flew over the remains of the house and slammed into Byrne's ship, which exploded in a fury of twisted, glowing metal. The hyperdrive wasn't destroyed immediately, however. As the shockwave from the blast expanded out into Lok's atmosphere, the drive continued to hum on a low setting—still trying to unlock a gate through which armies were destined to spill.

The wave of compressed air hit the commons moments after the bright ball of fire. It slammed into the contraption behind Byrne, teetering it. The old agent almost had enough time to scream before the cross fell across his back and erupted in a glory of sparks.

The majority of him winked out of the universe, accompanied by a soft pop as air rushed in to fill the vacuum.

Beyond, in the engine room of Byrne's ship, the hyperdrive erupted, coating the wreckage with burning fusion fuel. The smell of something dead, billions of charred carcasses, wafted out over the commons.

The odor drifted down to Molly, coating her in its foul tartness . . .

. . . as she finally drifted off to black.

36

nlyn stepped over the wooden bridge, noting with horror the small flecks of charred ash her pyrotechnic display had created in the ancient wood.

She crossed the circle and entered the Light of Speak, which felt even warmer the second time around. There were fewer eyes upon her, but the intensity of each gaze had been multiplied.

Several of the Counselors had already left, the vote done and sealed. Only a few hundred spectators remained, likely those gossipers hoping some dollop of news would trump the Drenards who had escaped with the scoop. Anlyn saw that Bodi had remained, probably to gauge any potential threat.

She took a deep breath.

"I represent the Minority Position," Anlyn said, "and I wish to have my doubts recorded, that they be our doubts in the cycle to come." Several dissenters nodded, as well as a few who had voted "war" well after the issue had already been decided—swept up in the fury of the political mob.

Anlyn looked over the Circle and into the sparse crowd, directing her speech to them. "I am Anlyn Hooo of the Royal Tree. When I was born, my people believed in a great prophecy. In both song and rhyme, they celebrated the end of the Bern threat as foretold by the one we call the Light Seer but who our enemy refers to as the Bern Seer.

"There are many ways to read the Prophecy. Some have urged for peace with the humans because it seems our combined power alone can end this grave threat. But there are those who walk the way of the cold and see the Prophecy as a promise for doom. For them, the flood spoken of puts an end to our galaxy, to our entire universe.

"A cycle ago, a human couple came to this planet, first as prisoners under suspicion, then as guests. When one of these became a Drenard, a new interpretation of the Prophecy was seized upon. Soon, this new method of reading grew and became known as 'The One' reading. And yet—like all other readings before—the proclamation failed. The difference was, this time . . . "

Anlyn scanned the crowd through the glare of the cone of light. She took another deep breath and licked her dry lips. "The difference was that *this* time, so many of you *believed*. And your faith devastated you as it was pulled away. It had become attached, and it took something with it as it was discarded. I watched it happen as a youth, not affected as I had not yet learned to believe. I watched what transpired, and I promised myself it would never happen to me. I would never believe in anything."

Anlyn looked to Edison and then turned slowly, taking in the whole of the darkness beyond the circle.

"We are a people that thrive on the edge, balanced between the passion of our burning hearts and the rationality of our cold thoughts. When I ran from here, from my home . . . " she turned to Bodi. "When I ran from *you*, it was with a heart that had never been lit. It was with cold thought alone.

"Mortimor and Parsona Fyde came to Drenard a full cycle ago, and they were, neither of them, the One. But I believe . . . I *believe* they gave birth to the One. It's insane to hear it, I know. But it's not insane to *know* it. I have feared this burning in my heart, but not now. Now, I balance it with my cold, objective thoughts.

"Molly Fyde, the daughter of Mortimor and Parsona, rescued me from bondage. What are the chances of that? Born on Lok, and therefore more from that planet than either of her parents, she is human and Drenard alike. And the Wadi—I know the rumors don't agree, but take it from me, I've seen it! I've touched it! The Living Queen is real."

Anlyn met Edison's gaze, felt the tears streaking down her face. "The Prophecy is real. I don't know how, but I know that it is. You have been burned before by false hope and the passion of faith, and I watched from a distance. I will not ask anyone to go with me, but go I must.

"While the rest of the great Drenard Empire prepares for war with our neighbors, I will go to the great Bern Rift as the Prophecy decrees. I will await whatever comes through to harm us, alone if need be."

"You'll do no such thing," Bodi shouted. "The vote is *over*. You're reciting *superstition*, not a Minority Position. I demand that—"

Anlyn whirled on him. "My going will have nothing to do with your insane war or your false vote. I'll be going as an ambassador to the Bern people, as is my right as next in line to the throne." She nodded to Edison. "And if the Counselor on Alien Relations will accompany me, we'll take the full regiment of volunteers decreed for that purpose."

"Alien Relations? Ambassador?" Bodi scoffed. "For the *Bern*?"

"Ambassador, yes." She paused, turning in the Light of Speak to address Bodi once more. "For the Bern?

No." She lowered her voice as the wave of panic and confusion returned to the Pinnacle, spectators pushing their way to the exit to trump the other news bearers.

"Two can bend the rules, Bodi. For right as well as wrong. The Prophecy will not disappoint another generation, I know it."

"You're a fool," he spat at her.

Anlyn turned and walked back to the wooden bridge dotted with tiny burns.

"Aye, a fool," she murmured. "A happy, hopeful fool."

◦ ◦ ◦ ◦

When Molly came to, Walter stood over her, prying Byrne's fingers off her neck. She could feel the other severed hand still tangled in her hair; she reached back and touched it, a solid clutch of steel wrapped around a handful of her locks. It seemed the two arms were all that remained of Byrne in the galaxy.

Fighting for a breath, her throat burning, she croaked, "What happened?" as Walter pried the hand away.

"I ssaved you," he said through his helmet's open visor. He held Byrne's arm up with one hand and waved it in the air like a sword. The fallen work light illuminated the scene with a dramatic glow, flickering for added effect.

519

Molly fumbled with the hand knotted in her hair, wondering if she'd have to cut it out to free the thing. "How?" She turned to look back toward the commons.

"Your friend called on the radio," Walter said. He jabbed a finger against his helmet. "She taught me how to usse the SSADAR and fire the misssiless." He stopped swinging the sword and took his helmet off, dropping it into the dirt and leaning in close to Molly.

"Doess thiss make me your *navigator*?" he asked. He bent down, his metallic face flickering in the light of the burning ship. "Sshould we kisss?" He pursed his thin lips, his eyes wide and begging.

"Ew, no!" Molly turned her head and brought her hands up to his chest.

It came out harsher than she'd intended.

"Fine," Walter said, pouting. "The cargo door iss bussted, sso good luck getting back insside on your own." He marched off toward the wreckage of Byrne's ship, slicing the air with the severed arm and mumbling to himself.

Molly groaned and sat up, Byrne's arm tugging at her scalp. She yanked a clump of her hair through its grip, and it finally came loose, taking some hair with it. Grimacing, she scooted back to the low wall, dragging Walter's discarded helmet with her. Her entire body felt sore and on fire; she could still feel at least twenty fingers digging into various sensitive places.

She took a deep breath, rubbed her bruised neck, and then worked the helmet in place before keying the mic on its side.

"Mom?"

"Mollie? Thank the stars! Where are you? Are you outside? The door's stuck—"

"Mom, slow down." She swallowed painfully and flipped up the visor. Walter's silhouette stood out against the burning ship beyond the other wall, three arms waving.

Molly took a deep, painful breath, the putrid smell of death filling her lungs. "Byrne was here."

"Was? Where is he? I thought with the blast that you'd—"

"I'm fine," she whispered, her voice still hoarse. "And he's gone wherever his hyperdrive took him. It . . . it zapped him and left his arms."

"Oh, dear. He'll be very upset without them." Her mom paused. "I saw the device running. Nothing's happening there? Is there anything—"

"No—"

Molly coughed, her throat scratched and irritable. Tears welled up in her eyes from the pain, and then real tears followed as the rest came back to her.

"Dad," she sobbed. "He said Dad was here, but he locked him away—"

"Oh, Mollie . . . "

She looked toward the burning ship, forced herself up, and collapsed on the wall. She scanned the horizon.

"Cole . . . " More tears. "Mom, where's Cole? Something bad happened to him; I can feel it. It's just like when dad left—" She brought her hands up to the helmet, supporting her weary mind. "He's . . . Cole's dead, isn't he?"

"Mollie. Come back to the ship. You'll have to climb up through the pod bay—"

She shook her head. "I don't want to." Lying back along the length of the wall, she looked up at the bright stars in the moonless sky. "I'd be better off joining him," she said to herself.

Her mother was silent for a while.

"I might be able to help you," she said.

"Help me *what*?"

Parsona hesitated.

"*Join him,*" she said.

EPILOGUE
THE LAND OF LIGHT

"Of all the incredible places in the universe, none are so strange as what lies between."

~The Bern Seer~

Cole double-checked the jump coordinates and glanced at the gravity indicators. Everything looked great. Zebra command was scattered in the distance; it appeared they'd be making a clean getaway. Even better, the red bands worked across vast distances, allowing him and Molly to travel without losing touch.

"I love you." Molly thought, interrupting his own thoughts with some of hers.

"Me, too." He told her. *"See you soon."*

He lifted the carboglass shield and rested his finger on the red button. Beside him, he could hear Riggs grunting around the duct tape over his mouth, his helmet muffling his outrage.

Cole felt horrible for his old friend. He tried to think of something to say but figured it could wait until they were out of danger. Pressing down on the button, he engaged the hyperdrive and watched the field of stars before him disappear, expecting them to shift slightly in place.

Instead, the blackness of space shot full with a blinding light, accompanied by a torrent of deafening sounds.

The filters in the carboglass clamped down automatically, minimizing the passage of photons, but even so, he couldn't see a thing. His eyelids clinched tight of their own accord. He tried to crack them, but the light was too intense.

"What the hell?" he asked, as if Riggs could hear him over the noise. Unable to open his eyes, he attempted to make sense of the myriad warning beeps and alarms. It sounded as if all of them had been triggered at once.

Is someone there?

He tried to focus on what he could hear and feel, a wave of panic competing for control of his senses. There were too many sounds, too much stimuli, to distinguish any one.

Hello?

His hand went to the flight controls with habitual ease. He had to remember the simulators from the Academy, forgetting the past weeks on *Parsona,* where everything was laid out differently. He had hundreds of hours of flight time sitting in front of these Firehawk controls; he just needed to *think* about what to touch and allow his long-term muscle memory take over.

Pops, is that you?

As soon as he gave the flight controls a nudge, he felt his first problem: the stick gave him resistance. The haptic feedback system had kicked in, which meant they weren't in space anymore—they were in *atmosphere!* As soon as he processed this, Cole recognized one of the layers of beeping sounds: the stall alert. They were in free fall. He needed lift.

He flipped the switch that extended the wings fully and then shoved forward on the main thrusters while nosing the ship down. There was a sickening sensation as he gave *into* the plummet in order to create enough speed to fight it. The lift warning went away. Cole could now make out a gravitational proximity alarm. They were near something *huge.* If the frequency could be believed, it was bigger than a planet. Bigger than most stars.

His stomach flipped in fear.

Penny, silence your thoughts for a second.

Cole tried to open his eyes long enough to check his altimeter, but his lids had mutinied. He could only open them a crack before they snapped back shut. Tears streamed back from both eyes. He couldn't feel which way was up and couldn't see the dash to find out. He reached forward with his left hand and fumbled for the gravity panels. He needed to turn them off and get his flightsuit neutralized so he could feel with his body which way to fly.

Who is this?

There was very little change as he turned off what he hoped were the grav panels. He fumbled for the life support controls so he could shut down the anti-G system in his suit. His fingers rested on the button when a silent alarm in his head rang out above the din in the cockpit:

Riggs.

He was about to subject both of them to unknown forces. Riggs was already bound and gagged; he must be confused as hyperspace. No point in torturing him before they crashed and burned.

Pulling his hand away from the controls, he seized the breathing hose and wires attached to his suit instead. He yanked the umbilical cord loose.

His body sank instantly into the back of his seat, his ribs nearly crushed from the pressure.

They were going *fast*.

Penny, are you getting any of this?

Cole tried to shake his head clear; strange thoughts seemed to be leaking in with the myriad sounds and the blinding lights.

The lift problem had obviously been taken care of—they had plenty of velocity. Cole's arms felt heavy, maybe six to seven times their normal weight. The Firehawk had to be heading almost straight down to be pulling that many Gs—the amount of thrust he had given the ship couldn't account for a fraction of that acceleration.

Yeah. A lot of fear. A pilot?

He tried not to be scared. He was a trained pilot, after all. Pulling the throttle all the way back, he gave the flight controls a tug. Despite the heaviness of his arm helping out—sucked back with the force of acceleration—the stick provided too much resistance. The haptic feedback system was letting him know air flowed across the flight surfaces at dangerously high rates of speed. That meant atmosphere, or some other type of fluid.

Cole put all his weight into the controls. He couldn't remember the simulator ever getting this stiff, even when they practiced pulling out of full dives. He hoped that was a mechanical limitation of the simulator and not a testament to what he was up against.

Wearing a D-Band? That doesn't make any—wait . . .

A new alarm joined the chorus: a soprano performing some mad aria. Cole tried to navigate the sounds with his eyes clenched tight, his arm straining for lift. He found one voice he knew and reached over, closing the glass cover shielding the hyperdrive switch. The gravity alert went away. He concentrated and then recognized the high-pitched tune. It was the proximity alarm. They were on a collision course with something.

Something *big*.

What is it?

Cole wondered what it was. He pulled back into full neutral, gliding down with gravity. It was impossible to tell how much the nose had risen, but instead of just being pressed back into the seat, he could now feel the pain of his spine being compressed. Some of the Firehawk's directional energy was being deflected as the ship pulled up. The pain became a clue, sense becoming sensor. He just needed to increase this discomfort, or it'd be the last thing he ever felt.

I'm getting something . . .

He stopped fighting the urge to see now that he was getting something from his aching spine. It was clear his seared vision wasn't going to come back in time. He gave in to his lids, allowing them to clench as tight as they liked. More tears squeezed out, streaking back into his ears. With his left hand, Cole reached across his body and grabbed the docking controls. His torso screamed with the pain of holding himself against so many gravities. Still pulling back to lift the nose, Cole flipped the maneuvering thrusters on and used them to rotate the ship back. A continuous blast of waste air shot out of a nozzle in the nose of the Firehawk, attempting to spin the ship in space, assisting the flaps on the back of the wings.

Cole's legs went numb from the pain in his spine, which he took as an indicator that the maneuver was working.

What is it, Dad?

The collision alarm moved down to a tenor. They were still going to hit, but not as soon and not as fast. Cole needed to focus on that one sound, but another beeping fought for his attention: the navigational alarm.

The star charts had no idea where they were. *Too bright to triangulate star positions*, Cole decided. He locked the maneuvering thruster in place and reached out to the nav screen. Running his gloved hand down one side, he counted buttons until he reached the power. He shut it off, killing yet another blaring alarm.

Cole?

There were only three sounds left in the cockpit now: the soprano singing about the imminent collision, the sound of atmosphere rushing along the cockpit canopy, and a muffled voice—Riggs yelling through his helmet? Had the tape worked loose?

I felt the same name. You recognize it?

He felt horrible for what Riggs must be going through. Not the best start to winning him over. He considered keying the mic to talk with him, but there wasn't time. The warbling of the collision alarm was deepening, which meant the nose was actually rotating up. However, the rate at which it beeped had increased; whatever they were about to hit, it would happen soon. At least the majority of Cole's pain was straight in his back now. The Firehawk must be pretty level.

Penny, check with Joshua's men, see if they're moving.

532

Cole tried cracking his eyes, but the searing light was still coming from all directions. He was dying to know what they were about to hit. He could be about to crash into the surface of a star, or enter a black hole, for all he knew.

The location of the landing gear controls was fixed in his memory, but he knew better than to release them. In a crash landing, the smooth belly of a Firehawk was better than anything they could trip over. And if a sea of plasma awaited, it wouldn't matter either way.

Yeah, they're moving uphill. More jumpers?

He thought he heard Riggs shout something about jumping, but parachuting into the unknown would be foolish. Leaning back on the flight stick with both hands, he tried to imagine them pulling up in time, just like in the holos: they would dip precariously low, skim the surface of some deadly environment, and then fly away with pumping fists and a victory cry.

The thought forced a bit of a smile into his grimace. Then he remembered his flight suit was disconnected, that the Gs of impact would probably liquefy him. He fumbled for the umbilical cord, strained against the force of acceleration, pressed the hose to his suit, and rotated it, trying to line it up blindly.

There was a click, so soft he couldn't hear it.

Right about the time they made contact.

○ ○ ○ ○

The after portion of the belly hit first, the nose too high. The rear of the Firehawk bounced up, and the bow came down toward the ground. Only the maneuvering thrusters saved the ship from plowing in, catapulting into the air, or shattering into a billion pieces. For just an instant, the ship went level above the unknown surface, gliding in a sustained ground effect, a pocket of compressed air forming below the Firehawk's underbelly across which it slid, as if on rails.

The rear of the ship came down again, touching something soft. Instead of bouncing with the force of the last impact, it ploughed deep. When the nose settled again, the ship's speed was below a thousand kilometers an hour. If the wings had remained level as they made contact, it would have been a spectacular emergency landing.

Instead, it was a spectacle.

The leading edge of the starboard wing struck first. It was like digging a wide oar off one side of a canoe. Not only did it try to spin the Firehawk around, the change in momentum and the braking action of the wing sent the entire ship, all eighty thousand kilos of her, flipping upside down. The wrenching of Cole's already-battered body on his flight harness forced the air out of his lungs. Both of his arms went flying—there was nothing controlling the ship other than gravity and friction, anyway.

The smooth belly faced the air as the bumpy top of the Firehawk forced into the surface of their mystery companion. The vertical flight surfaces sheared off, but not before they drove the nose of the ship violently downward. He could hear the sound of cracking carboglass over all the other grinding and banging sounds.

Cole lurched forward against his harness, his ribs yelling over the pain in his spine. He imagined the dash and canopy being pressed back toward him at the same time. He tried to bring his arms up against his body to protect them, but the force was too strong, his muscles too fatigued.

The entire crash felt as if it took several minutes. But the Firehawk ground to a full stop only fifteen seconds after the first impact. Cole hung upside down in his flight harness, the grav panels knocked out along with the rest of the life-support systems.

The only positive was that they were still alive, for however much longer.

Cole cracked one eye open. The bright spot in his vision remained, but it was surrounded by something new: complete and utter darkness.

What's happening?

"Riggs?" Cole flipped his visor up and heard air rushing somewhere. It was hard to tell if it was rolling over the surface of the ship, or if their atmosphere was leaking into a vacuum beyond. He strained to listen, hoping it was the former. There was so much power behind it; if that was their air going out . . . they didn't have much time left.

Where are you? What's going on?

The only thing he could see in the darkness was the bright spot in his vision, which had turned a dull red. His head throbbed, making it hard to think. Pain pulsed out through his entire body as his weight hung on his harness, sore ribs and shoulders pressing into the straps.

"Riggs, I'm coming, man. We crashed into something. Gimme a minute."

He reached up and released the buckle on one side of his flight harness while he wrapped an arm in the other side. As his body came free, it twisted around the one arm, preventing him from falling face-first. Cole tried to hang on, but the pain in his ribs forced him to release his grip. He fell in a heap on the top of the canopy and slid down to the low spot of the inverted carboglass bubble.

Over the squealing of his flightsuit as it rubbed across the smooth surface, Cole heard a crunching sound coming from below the glass.

Crashed? Do you know where you are?

Cole pushed himself up and walked gingerly to Riggs's side of the cockpit. He pulled a glowstick out of his flightsuit and cracked it in half. "Cool your thrusters, man, I'm trying to help."

We can't help from here. You need to get out of there.

"What? Stop struggling." He lifted his own visor and reached up with one hand to grope for Riggs's helmet release. The radio speakers in his helmet sounded strange, altering Riggs's voice. Cole's eyes still hurt, his head ringing.

Cole? Can you hear me?

"Yeah, I can hear you. Hold still so I can work the release." The catch popped free, and Riggs's helmet fell through Cole's hands and smacked the carboglass by his feet.

In the dull, green glow of his emergency stick, he could see his old friend's eyes. They were wide with a mixture of fear and rage—his cheeks puffing in and out as he sucked, then expelled air through his nose.

The duct tape was still adhered to his mouth. "Riggs?"

Who is Riggs?

Cole reached up and released his own helmet. He pulled it off, his mind still dizzy from the crash. In the dim light of the glowstick, he could see the mic switched off on the side.

"Hello?"

Yes. Who is this?

Raising one hand, he touched the band around his head. It was soaked with sweat, but still in place. Above him, Riggs groaned in discomfort and then tried to force expletives through the tape.

Cole ignored him. He became lost in his own thoughts. His own, and those of others.

"My name is Cole Mendonça. I—we crashed in—where are we?"

"I'll tell you where you are: you're where bad navigators go, son. Now you need to get a move-on before Joshua's men get there."

"Where? I should be halfway to Lok; we should—"

"Listen to me, lad, you don't have much time. You need to destroy your fusion fuel and get out of there."

Pops?

Cole could feel it as another speaker, even though they were all in his voice. Each had a flavor, or a layer of emotions.

"Not right now, Penny."

They're almost there, Pops.

"You hear that, Cole? You don't have much time left."

Cole shook his head. Too many thoughts.

"Not much time for what? he thought. Who are you? Where am I?"

" . . . *My name is Mortimor Fyde, son. Welcome to hyperspace.*"